LYNSAY SANDS

IMMORTAL ANGEL

AN ARGENEAU NOVEL

AVONBOOKS

An Imprint of HarperCollinsPublishers

Untitled excerpt copyright © 2021 by Lynsay Sands.

IMMORTAL ANGEL. Copyright © 2020 by Lynsay Sands. All rights reserved. Printed in the United States of America. No part of this book may be used or reproduced in any manner whatsoever without written permission except in the case of brief quotations embodied in critical articles and reviews. For information, address HarperCollins Publishers, 195 Broadway, New York, NY 10007.

First Avon Books mass market printing: October 2020
First Avon Books hardcover printing: September 2020

Print Edition ISBN: 978-0-06-295630-9
Digital Edition ISBN: 978-0-06-295627-9

Cover design by Nadine Badalaty
Cover illustration by Tony Mauro
Cover images by ID 4046167 © Jeff Whyte / Dreamstime.com; ID 144253809 © Millafedotova | Dreamstime.com
Author photo by Dave Ramage

Avon, Avon & logo, and Avon Books & logo are registered trademarks of HarperCollins Publishers in the United States of America and other countries.

HarperCollins is a registered trademark of HarperCollins Publishers in the United States of America and other countries.

FIRST EDITION

20 21 22 23 24   QGM   10 9 8 7 6 5 4 3 2 1

'I'll get away from you, go back to England and—'

"No!" Ildaria protested with horror.

"Shh. You're just a dream. If you were real you'd be glad," he muttered and then made sure she didn't protest further by covering her mouth with his in a hard kiss.

Ildaria resisted for all of a heartbeat, and then gave in and kissed him back. She would tell him after. Immortals did not faint during dream sex. She would tell him afterward that this was a shared dream. She'd tell him that he wasn't losing his mind, or that if he was she was too, and it was only because they were possible life mates. And then she'd beg him to agree to be hers.

By Lynsay Sands

IMMORTAL ANGEL • IMMORTAL BORN
THE TROUBLE WITH VAMPIRES
VAMPIRES LIKE IT HOT
TWICE BITTEN • IMMORTALLY YOURS
IMMORTAL UNCHAINED • IMMORTAL NIGHTS
RUNAWAY VAMPIRE • ABOUT A VAMPIRE
THE IMMORTAL WHO LOVED ME
VAMPIRE MOST WANTED • ONE LUCKY VAMPIRE
IMMORTAL EVER AFTER
THE LADY IS A VAMP • UNDER A VAMPIRE MOON
THE RELUCTANT VAMPIRE
HUNGRY FOR YOU • BORN TO BITE
THE RENEGADE HUNTER • THE IMMORTAL HUNTER
THE ROGUE HUNTER
VAMPIRE, INTERRUPTED • VAMPIRES ARE FOREVER
THE ACCIDENTAL VAMPIRE • BITE ME IF YOU CAN
A BITE TO REMEMBER • TALL, DARK & HUNGRY
SINGLE WHITE VAMPIRE
LOVE BITES
A QUICK BITE

HUNTING FOR A HIGHLANDER
MY FAVORITE THINGS • A LADY IN DISGUISE
THE WRONG HIGHLANDER • THE HIGHLANDER'S PROMISE
SURRENDER TO THE HIGHLANDER
FALLING FOR THE HIGHLANDER
THE HIGHLANDER TAKES A BRIDE
TO MARRY A SCOTTISH LAIRD
AN ENGLISH BRIDE IN SCOTLAND
THE HUSBAND HUNT • THE HEIRESS • THE COUNTESS
THE HELLION AND THE HIGHLANDER
TAMING THE HIGHLAND BRIDE • DEVIL OF THE HIGHLANDS

THE LOVING DAYLIGHTS

IMMORTAL
ANGEL

Prologue

Pain dragged Jack back to consciousness, bone deep agony all over his body that made him grimace before he even opened his eyes. Unfortunately, grimacing just added to his suffering, so he flattened out his features again to avoid it and opened his eyes instead. That caused a new flare-up of pain, but he ignored it and peered out of sore swollen eyes at the dark open space he was in.

Glow-in-the-dark paint covered the walls in some imaginative graffiti. But he knew there was more that wasn't glow-in-the-dark. He'd seen it the last time he was conscious thanks to the light his captors had brought with them. He'd also seen the broken tile floor his chair sat on.

He was in an old abandoned building somewhere. Jack had decided that the last time he'd been awake. He had no idea where, though. He'd been unconscious when they brought him here, a result of a sucker punch he'd taken while distracted by Lacy having a gun to her head.

That thought was quickly followed by the sound of a whimper from across the room and Jack shifted his head until he could see Lacy. She lay curled up on the floor against the wall. The position and her whimpering cries had worried him the first time he'd regained consciousness. He'd feared their kidnappers had hurt her while he was unconscious. But it had turned out that wasn't the case. She was just frightened. Jack understood, this hadn't exactly turned out to be a dream date, but he could have done without her sobbing, weeping, and wailing as the men had beaten him. That had made him want to slap her. He was the one who'd gotten his ass kicked, but she'd carried on like it was her being beaten within an inch of her life.

Sighing, he closed his eyes briefly, thinking that his partner, Deedee, would have been untying him and fighting at his side to get them out of there, but not Lacy. She wasn't tied up, and hadn't been hurt, but wouldn't move from the spot they'd placed her in when they got here no matter what Jack had said to try to convince her when he'd first woken up to find them alone there. She was too scared to listen to him, too scared to save herself, let alone both of them.

It made him wish he'd kept fighting rather than stopping when the gun had been put to her head and he'd been told to stop or her brains would be blown out. At the time, Jack had thought, or hoped, he might find a way to get them both safely away later if he gave in then. A preference to seeing her killed. Now he knew that wasn't likely, and wondered if he shouldn't have risked her being shot and kept fighting. At least, one of them would have survived then, and really, if she wasn't even going to try, did she deserve to survive this?

Guilt drenched Jack's mind at these thoughts. Lacy was a teacher, not an FBI agent like himself. She had no training, or even any experience in dealing with high stress, dangerous situations. Unfortunately, she also apparently had no survival instinct at all.

Used to ball-busting female agents who could handle most any situation thrown at them, Jack had found her helplessness appealing when they met. She'd seemed delicate and ever so much a lady to him, like a fragile flower. He'd found that ridiculously attractive . . . until tonight. Christ, even roses had thorns, he thought as Lacy released another shuddering whimper.

Mouth tightening despite the pain it caused, Jack shifted his attention to the rest of the room, looking for something to help them out of this. His eyes had adjusted to the darkness, but it didn't help. Unfortunately, their captors hadn't thoughtfully left a weapon lying about, or anything that might be used to remove his ropes. It was just a large, empty room, the only furniture the chair he was tied to, and the only light came from the streetlights outside. Not much of it was making its way through the filthy windows. They were probably in an old abandoned government building, or one of the empty structures at or near the university, he thought and then let the thought drift away as unimportant. It didn't matter where they were if he couldn't get loose and get them out of there.

Jack's gaze slid back to Lacy as she whimpered again, and he was about to try one more time to convince her to at least flee for help and save herself if not him, when the sound of rusty hinges announced a door opening and the return of their captors.

"Awake, I see."

Jack considered closing his eyes and pretending he'd passed out again, but doubted it would work. So, instead, he raised his chin and glared defiantly at the speaker. Grizzly Adams, as he'd come to call him because he was huge with a lot of facial hair, was leading four men toward him while four more were spreading out around the room to keep an eye out the windows.

Just to be sure they weren't caught by surprise by someone hearing his screams of pain and approaching the building, Jack supposed.

"Your boss still not here?" he asked with more bravado than curiosity. Although, the attempt at bravado made a poor showing with his words coming out slurred and somewhat garbled by his swollen mouth and possibly broken jaw.

"Nope. He's been delayed," Grizzly Adams said with a grin. "Good news, right? Means we get to play a little longer."

Since getting to play meant Grizzly Adams could continue to pummel his face and chest with his big meaty fists while Jack sat there helplessly taking the blows and trying not to scream as he waited to pass out from the pain, he didn't really see that as a good thing. He'd almost prefer for "the boss," whoever that was, to show up and kill him or whatever the endgame was.

It seemed obvious he wasn't going to escape. Might as well get it over with. Although, it would be nice to know what this was all about. Grizzly Adams wasn't talking, however. All he'd say is the boss wanted to tell him himself. Obviously it had something to do with his work. The boss was probably someone he'd put away at some point in his career, or a relative of someone he'd put away and it would be nice to know why he was going to die.

Jack's thoughts were scattered by an explosion of pain in his chest as Grizzly Adams delivered his first blow and, he was sure, broke another one of his ribs. Christ, the man had fists like bowling balls. The impact and pain brought a broken woof of sound from him, but made Lacy shriek like they were connected and she felt the pain. He'd barely noted that when a second blow landed, this one to the already broken jaw. It sent his face turning sharply to the right.

Stars exploding in front of his eyes, Jack had to blink to clear his vision enough to see when a door burst open at the end of the room. It flew inward, crashing against the wall with the impact of an explosion, raising dust and dirt in a cloud that partially obscured the figure now standing in the doorway. At first, Jack assumed "the boss" had arrived, but as the dust storm settled and he took in the silhouette framed against the streetlight pouring into the room, he realized it was a woman and a very shapely one at that. Which didn't mean it couldn't be the boss, he supposed, but the reactions of his captors made it clear it wasn't.

For one second they were all tense and silent with

shock like himself, but then they each relaxed and even began to smile.

"Well, look what we have here, boys," Grizzly Adams said, a mean grin pulling at his lips. "Someone else to play with . . . The boss said no messing with the schoolteacher, but he didn't say anything about wild women who wander into our playing field."

Jack blinked at the wild woman comment. He couldn't see her well, but with the light surrounding her like a nimbus, she looked more like an angel to him than a wild woman. Until the men started toward her. The moment one got close his angel turned into a demon.

God in heaven, she moved fast, Jack thought with awe as she went from completely motionless to a Tasmanian-devil-speed spin from which her leg shot out and caught the nearest man in the head. It was a hard hit, lifting him off his feet before he flew backward and crashed to the floor. He didn't get up, Jack noted before shifting his attention back to the woman. The other men were converging on her much more swiftly now. No doubt they were angry at what she'd done to their cohort and eager to get some revenge.

Instead, what they got was pain and a close personal introduction to the same floor their unconscious friend now lay on. The woman took out all comers, one, two, and three at a time as they reached her. Jack could hardly track her, she moved so fast, and even he had to wince as he heard various bones snap and watched skulls bounce off the cracked tile floor. By the time his angel was done, nothing in the room was moving and there wasn't a sound to be heard. Even Lacy had stopped her whining whimper.

"Breathe." The word was a bare whisper of sound from where she stood halfway across the room, but Jack heard it and realized he'd been holding his breath. He sucked in a deep one now, and heard Lacy gasp in a shuddering breath of her own, but his gaze didn't leave the angel. Now that she was out of the beam of light coming through the open street door, he could see her better. Not well, but enough to note that she had long, dark hair pulled into a tight bun at the back of her head and every stitch of clothing she wore was black leather: high-heel black leather boots, skintight black leather pants, and a tight black leather jacket that was half-open over a black leather bustier. None of which hid the killer figure it covered.

The woman was walking sin, Jack thought faintly as he watched her slide a phone out of the black leather jacket and begin to punch in numbers. Just three of them. 911 was his guess as she murmured something into the phone and then pushed a button and put it away.

"Help will be here soon." The words were soft, almost a whisper, which made it hard for him to identify the trace of accent his ears caught. Without another word, she left the building the same way she'd entered, walking out the open door. But her exit seemed to leave a vacuum in the room that sucked the air out of it. At least, that was how it seemed to Jack as the darkness began to close in around him. His last thought before losing consciousness was that he had to find out who his angel was.

One

"Professor Straithe is late."

"*Si,* but he's always late," Ildaria pointed out as she pulled her notebook and a pen from her knapsack and then set the bag on the floor next to her seat.

"Yeah, but he's really late tonight," Lydia responded and then added eagerly, "Five more minutes and he'll be fifteen minutes late. Then we can leave. Class will be canceled and we can hit a bar or something."

Ildaria shrugged as she opened her notebook to a clean page and predicted, "He'll walk in one minute before the fifteen-minute point and we'll be stuck here. He's done it several times this semester."

"Yes, he has," Lydia agreed, sounding deflated now, and then her tone turning irritated she added, "It's a night class for cripes sake, not a morning class he has to drag his butt out of bed for, yet the man is always late." She scowled and then muttered bitterly, "And then he's a boring lecturer when he finally does get here. I swear if he weren't such a hunk, I'd hate him."

Ildaria chuckled at the claim. She doubted Lydia had it in her to hate anyone. The woman was just too kind. It was one of the things she liked about her.

"Oh myyyy. What have we here?"

Eyebrows rising, Ildaria glanced around and followed Lydia's gaze to the top of the tiered lecture hall where two men now stood just inside the door. Both were tall and muscular, dressed in black T-shirts, black jeans, and black leather boots. They were carbon copies of each other . . . from the neck down. Only their faces and hair coloring differed. The Nordic blond had sharp features and an aquiline nose, while the dark-haired man had blunter features. Both were gorgeous. Both also looked lean, mean, and dangerous as they surveyed the class, obviously looking for someone.

"No books, no bags . . . They can't be students," Lydia commented, ogling the pair, and then she suggested, "Ooooh, maybe they're new TAs."

She was probably already planning on requesting after hours help, Ildaria thought on a sigh and muttered, "Or bloodsucking *putas* here to execute someone."

"What?" Lydia turned on her with amusement, but Ildaria just shook her head and stared at the two men, her thoughts racing. She knew exactly who they were—Valerian and Tybo were Enforcers—or rogue hunters as her kind liked to call them. The immortal version of police, sent out by the Immortal Council to hunt down rogue immortals who had been misbehaving. Normal

people, or mortals, like Lydia, would have called them
vampire hunters if she had any idea that immortals ex-
isted. But Lydia didn't know that.

"What are you doing?" Lydia asked with amazement
as she watched her snatch up her bag from the floor and
unzip it. "You don't know those guys, do you?"

Mouth tightening, Ildaria didn't respond. Instead,
she quickly shoved her notebook and pen inside.

"You *do* know them," Lydia gasped with mounting
excitement. "Oh. You have to introduce me to them."

"Trust me. You don't want to meet them. They're
trouble," Ildaria said bitterly, wondering if she'd be
executed at once, or have to wait around for a Council
trial before the deed was done.

"The most interesting men are always trouble,"
Lydia assured her, gathering her own books with the
obvious intention of joining her to meet the men.

Ildaria didn't waste her breath trying to dissuade
her again. Instead, she simply said, "Stay here," and
slipped into the girl's mind to make her stay. When
Lydia immediately relaxed back in her seat and turned
to face the front of the class, Ildaria stood, slung her
bag over her shoulder and scooted sideways along the
row of occupied seats until she reached the stairs. She
ascended them quickly, keeping her expression blank
now that she was facing the men. She wouldn't give
them the satisfaction of showing her worry and fear.

Tybo and Valerian didn't say a word when she joined
them. They merely took up position on either side of
her to escort her from the lecture hall and then the
building.

It wasn't until they were outside, walking the dark path toward the parking lot that Tybo spoke.

"You couldn't resist, could you?"

Ildaria's shoulders hunched instinctively in a protective move, but she forced them straight again and said firmly, "I don't know what you're talking about. I haven't done anything wrong."

"You've been playing vigilante again," he accused.

"I haven't," Ildaria assured him.

"You were caught on video tossing around some big bastard twice your size," Valerian informed her, joining the conversation as they reached the parking lot. "It was uploaded onto Twitter or Instagram or something where Mortimer found it. He showed it to Lucian."

Ildaria sucked in an alarmed breath at that, but insisted, "I wasn't playing vigilante." Unsure which incident had been caught on film, she added, "I was walking to my car after class, heard a girl scream and tried to help. What was I supposed to do? Just ignore it?"

"Yes," Tybo said with exasperation.

Stopping, Ildaria turned on him with disbelief. "So you would have just ignored a woman screaming for help?"

Tybo's eyes shifted away, telling her that he wouldn't, but then his gaze returned to her, and he said, "Well, maybe I couldn't have ignored it, but I sure as hell would have made sure I didn't get caught on video if I did."

Ildaria opened her mouth to respond, but paused and glanced to the side instead, when a woman's scream sounded. Her eyes widened with dismay when she saw a struggling, young female being dragged toward the open door of a van at the far end of the parking lot. Ildaria had barely recognized that she was witnessing an abduction when Tybo and Valerian charged past her, racing for the other end of the parking lot at speed. Immortal speed. Inhuman speed.

Instinct almost had Ildaria charging after them, but Tybo's words were still ringing in her head: *Well, maybe I couldn't have ignored it, but I sure as hell would have made sure I didn't get caught on video if I did.*

Her gaze slid around the parking lot, noting a few other university students around. There were still more nearer the buildings. Some of them were alone, some in pairs, some in clusters. Several had started forward as if to help, but were now slowing as they saw Tybo and Valerian charging in. The rest were raising their cell phones. Some were probably just taking pictures, but others were undoubtedly videotaping and there were probably still others that she couldn't see who were doing both. Such was the world today. Camera phones had changed everything, she thought with a shake of the head, and then Tybo's words slid through her mind again.

I sure as hell would have made sure I didn't get caught on video if I did.

Snorting under her breath, Ildaria stayed where she was, pulled out her cell phone, and began to record too.

By the time the excitement was over, and Tybo and Valerian had handed the culprit over to the campus police and the young woman to the care of the EMTs, Ildaria's phone was back in her pocket and she was leaning against their black SUV, waiting. She knew it was theirs because the license plate was RogueH4.

When they reached her, she commented mildly, "So, you can't ignore a woman in trouble any more than I can."

"Yeah, yeah," Tybo muttered, exchanging a chagrined glance with Valerian as he pulled out his key fob and hit the button to unlock the SUV doors.

"Did you notice all the people videotaping?" she asked next.

Both men stopped dead at her words and turned to look around the parking lot. Many of the witnesses who had been filming were gone now, most leaving when the campus police had arrived. But there were still a few watching them with phones out, still recording.

"Damn," Tybo growled.

Valerian sighed and said, "You take the two on the right side of the parking lot, and I'll—"

"Don't bother," Ildaria interrupted as the pair started to move. "It's already been uploaded to the net at least once."

When both of their heads swiveled toward her with alarm, she smiled sweetly. "I tagged Lucian Argeneau on mine. He's probably looking at it right now."

"Ah, crap," Tybo muttered.

"Now you know how I feel," she said grimly and turned to get into the SUV, leaving them to follow at their leisure. When she finished doing up her seat belt and glanced out, she saw that the two men were still standing beside the vehicle, but with their phones out now. Looking for the video, she supposed with amusement and guessed they'd found at least one version of it when they both began to curse.

Releasing a satisfied little sigh, she leaned back in her seat to wait for them to get over their upset and take her to Lucian. Oddly enough, they didn't seem as eager to get her there as they had been when they'd pulled her from class. It was a very quiet ride to the Enforcer house, with a lot of angry and accusing glares cast her way.

"Ildaria! How nice to see you again."

Ildaria smiled crookedly at that greeting from Samantha Mortimer when Tybo and Valerian marched her into the Enforcer house. She stood stiff and still when the other woman hugged her . . . until Sam whispered, "It will be fine."

Relaxing a little then, Ildaria raised her hands to return the slender woman's hug and even managed a real smile when Sam pulled back enough to look at her face. Ildaria wasn't sure it really would be all right, but Sam's words at least gave her hope.

"Lucian and Garrett are waiting in the office," Sam said, finally releasing her. She then glanced to Tybo and Valerian and added, "For all three of you."

Ildaria bit her lip when both men groaned and cast her accusing glares, but Sam grinned with amusement and slid her arm through hers to lead her down the hall as she asked, "How are you settling in at Marguerite's?"

"Good," Ildaria murmured, forcing her worry aside for the moment. "Marguerite's very nice."

"Yes, she is, isn't she," Sam said with a smile that dimmed a bit as she added, "But I hope she's taking it easy. She and Julius were so crushed when she lost the last baby. I'd hate for it to happen again."

Ildaria halted and turned on her sharply. "Marguerite's pregnant?"

"Yes. But maybe don't mention it to her. She hasn't told everyone yet. I only know because I heard Lucian talking about it to Mortimer and warning him not to involve her in anything stressful until the baby is born," Sam said quietly and explained, "She was pregnant a year or two ago, but lost the baby and Lucian is sure it had something to do with stress so wants to be sure we keep her stress free this time."

"Oh," Ildaria murmured. She had been living with the woman for more than a month now and hadn't picked up on her delicate state. Although, Ildaria had noticed that Marguerite was consuming a lot of blood, which was a necessity for an immortal female to carry a child to term.

"In fact," Sam continued, "Lucian's so determined to keep Marguerite relaxed and stress free you almost had to stay with us when they dragged you here from Montana . . . which I would have loved by the way," she added sincerely. "But Marguerite had already got wind of your situation and insisted you should stay with her. She worried that your staying here would be uncomfortable. That the cells out back would feel like a constant threat to you of what could happen if you misbehaved."

Ildaria grimaced at that comment, because here she was, in trouble again and probably going to end up in those cells Sam had just mentioned.

"It will be fine," Sam murmured again, patting her arm. "And here we are."

Ildaria glanced around to see that they'd reached Garrett Mortimer's office—or Mortimer's office, since everyone seemed to address Sam's husband by his last name. Officially, Mortimer was the head of the Immortal Enforcers in North America, or rogue hunters, as they were often called. But Lucian Argeneau was the head of the North American Immortal Council and often stuck his nose in and usurped Mortimer's position.

As he was apparently doing in this case, Ildaria decided when she saw that the ice-blond Lucian was seated in Mortimer's chair behind the desk while Sam's dark-haired husband was perched on the corner of his own desk. The two men had apparently been discussing something, probably her, but stopped at their arrival.

"There are brownies and cocoa waiting in the kitchen when you're done," Sam said lightly as she released the hold she'd had on Ildaria's arm and urged her into the room. Ignoring the scowl Lucian gave her, the slender brunette then disappeared down the hall, leaving Tybo and Valerian to enter the room as well.

"Sit," Lucian said firmly when the three of them stood stiffly in front of the desk like naughty children in the principal's office.

Ildaria sat, taking the nearest chair, which happened to be the middle of three in front of the desk. It left Tybo and Valerian to take up chairs on either side of her.

Once the three of them were seated, Lucian turned the portable computer on the desk toward them. A frozen image of an obviously running Tybo and Valerian was on the screen.

Both of her escorts immediately began to speak, but Lucian held up a hand for silence. When they snapped their mouths shut, he hit the play button on the computer. They were all silent as they watched the action play out; Valerian and Tybo were as fast as cheetahs as they raced across the parking lot. Unfortunately, the parking lot was huge, and despite their inhuman speed, the attacker had dragged the woman into the van, slammed the door closed and somehow subdued her and got in the driver's seat before they arrived at the van.

Reaching the vehicle just as it started to pull away, Valerian leapt onto the roof like a monkey leaping into a tree and ran along the top of the van toward the front, probably intending to swing in through the front passenger window. It ended up being unnecessary, however, because instead of joining him on the roof, Tybo—just a couple of steps behind Valerian—caught the bumper and lifted the back of the vehicle off the ground in a beautiful display of superman strength that had the tires spinning in midair and brought the van to an abrupt halt.

Valerian then jumped off the van roof on the driver's side, reached through the window to turn off the vehicle and pulled the hulking driver out with one hand to let him dangle in the air. Meanwhile, Tybo set the van back on all four wheels and moved around to open the side door and retrieve the unconscious young woman inside. Valerian was still holding the would-be kidnapper by the neck and Tybo had just brought the girl back to consciousness when the campus police showed up on the scene.

"We didn't know she was filming," Tybo blurted when Lucian hit the button to end the recording. Turning a scowl on Ildaria, the dark-haired Enforcer added, "I still can't believe she did. She *knows* we aren't supposed to draw attention to ourselves."

"This is not Ildaria's footage," Mortimer said when Lucian remained silent. "It's by someone who goes by T.O.eyes, and their caption was *Holy shit! Superman times two in Toronto*."

"Shit," Tybo muttered, slumping back in his seat.

"Ildaria's video was from a different angle," Mortimer continued. "And hers was captioned, *Special project for Film class. Awesome job peeps! Looks so good even I almost believed it was real*."

When Tybo and Valerian both blinked in surprise and then turned to her, Ildaria shrugged irritably. She'd been rather enjoying their chagrin and anger, but the jig was up. "I thought I should do some damage control."

They were all silent for a minute, and then Valerian frowned and asked, "This will not affect the arrest of the bastard who tried to take the woman, will it?"

"We read his mind," Tybo put in with concern. "She wasn't his first victim. The bastard's a serial rapist. If the police think it was just a film class stunt—"

"No," Lucian interrupted firmly. "I will see to it that he is brought to justice."

The two men nodded, and then glanced from Ildaria

to Lucian, looking like they wanted to say something. Whether it was to stand up for her, or thank her for what she'd done with the video, she didn't know, and never would since Lucian turned to her then and said, "You have been naughty, Angelina."

Ildaria noted the startled expressions on the other men's faces at his use of her first name, but ignored them and said quickly, "I only did what Tybo and Valerian did on that tape. I just wasn't lucky enough to have someone with me to do damage control. I promise I wasn't playing the vigilante like in Montana. I wasn't wearing my leathers and didn't go looking for bad guys to beat up. I was just walking along minding my own business when . . ." She shrugged rather than say, *"the shit hit the fan."* Which was what had happened each of the three times she'd stopped to save a fellow student. The first time it had been a girl getting mugged. Ildaria had chased down the culprit, got the girl's purse back and returned it to her before walking them both to the campus police office so the man could be charged.

The second time it had been a drunken asshole beating up his less inebriated girlfriend. She'd taken them both to the campus police as well, having to control the girl to make her admit what had happened. Something Ildaria still had trouble fathoming. The minute she'd got involved, the girlfriend had sided with her boyfriend as if Ildaria was the bad guy.

The last incident had been a man who had attacked a student out for an evening jog and pulled her off the path into the woods intending to rape her. She suspected that was the one that had been videoed and got her in trouble. It was the only one where she'd been "tossing around" someone twice her size as Valerian had put it earlier.

Ildaria's mouth tightened at the memory. She'd known she shouldn't do it, but she'd been infuriated. She had a special hatred in her heart for rapists. She'd taken great pleasure in beating the man and wiping the path with his face before the campus police had arrived to take him into custody.

Unfortunately, while Ildaria had noticed that others had arrived at the scene, she hadn't even considered someone might record it and post it online until she'd spotted it this morning. She'd known then that she'd probably be in trouble once Mortimer or Lucian saw it. Ildaria just hadn't been sure when that would happen . . . until Valerian and Tybo had shown up at her class.

"Hmm," Lucian said finally. "There appears to be a lot of crime on campus at night."

Ildaria gave a small shrug. "It's a university with loads of beautiful young women. It's nirvana for perverts and draws them like flies to shit at night."

"At night," Lucian echoed thoughtfully.

"Si. Well, it's generally safer during the day. More people about and fewer dark places to hide," she pointed out.

"Yes." Lucian nodded. "That's the answer then."

Ildaria tilted her head to the side, positive her confusion was showing on her face. "The answer?"

"You will switch to day classes," Lucian announced.

"What?" she asked with disbelief.

Lucian considered her briefly and then said, "At Jess

and Raffaele's wedding your old captain, Vasco Villaverde, told me you were a trouble magnet, but had a good heart."

Ildaria sighed inwardly over the fact that the man had tattled on her about her tendency to get herself into scrapes. She'd been in trouble several times in Punta Cana. In fact, if it weren't for Vasco, she probably would have been executed long ago. He'd saved her hide repeatedly, and Ildaria would be forever grateful for that. She just wished he hadn't felt the need to mention it to Lucian.

"It seems obvious to me that Vasco was right," Lucian continued now. "If there is trouble around, you will find it. So, to ensure I do not have to execute you, it would behoove me to ensure you avoid situations where trouble might occur. That means no more night classes. You will switch to days. Immediately. You will never again be on campus at night," he ordered imperiously.

Ildaria stared at him nonplussed for a moment, anger building slowly inside her, and then she burst out, "Are you kidding me? First you pulled me out of school in Montana and dragged me up here to Canada, making me miss my finals there and have to take those classes over again, and now you're going to drag me out of my night courses and make me take day classes?" Scowling, she informed him, "I won't be able to get into day courses now. The summer term will be lost and I'll have to start again in the fall. Which means paying for them all over again, *again*. Do you know how expensive these courses are? Not to mention the extra blood I'll need to consume if I attend day classes. I'm trying

to save money to get my own place and stop being a
burden to Marguerite and Julius. I'll never be able to
swing that if I keep having to pay for courses I don't
get to finish and extra blood to attend day classes . . .
which with my luck, I again probably won't get to finish anyway. I need those courses to get my degree."

Lucian's eyes narrowed. "I pulled you from university in Montana because you were playing vigilante
down there," he reminded her icily. "You were uti-
lizing your abilities in front of mortals and drawing
attention to yourself, and by extension, our people.
Which is *against our laws*. My choice was to either
move you or execute you. Would you have preferred
execution?"

"Of course not, but . . ." Ildaria hesitated and then
slumped in her seat with defeat. She supposed the set-
back to her education was probably nothing more than
she deserved. She'd known she was playing with fire
when she'd donned her leathers and gone out to kick
some mortal bad-guy butt back in Montana. And she
knew she was lucky that Lucian Argeneau had given
her a second chance rather than have her executed. He
wasn't known for being soft on people who stepped out
of line, and she had stepped out of line. Her only excuse
was emotional distress, but she hadn't explained that to
Lucian when she'd been brought before him. She hadn't
had to, though. No doubt he'd read it from her mind and
it was the only reason she was still breathing.

Letting her breath out slowly now, she nodded in ac-
ceptance and simply said, "Thank you."

Lucian grunted at the soft words, his body relaxing.

"You may go. I believe Sam is waiting for you in the kitchen . . . with hot chocolate and brownies."

Ildaria couldn't tell if he was annoyed that Sam was waiting to give her treats to soothe her after she'd got herself in trouble again, or amused. His mouth was definitely twitching though.

Supposing it didn't matter, Ildaria stood and headed for the door, aware that Tybo and Valerian had also stood to follow her. They had to take her back to the university to fetch her car, she recalled then, and probably wouldn't want to wait for her to enjoy those treats. That or they'd gobble them all up on her. She'd seen Tybo eat. He'd inhale the brownies before she got her hand on one if she didn't run ahead of them.

But in the next moment, she realized that wouldn't be necessary because Lucian barked, "Not you two. I am not finished with you yet."

Ildaria glanced back to see Tybo and Valerian reluctantly returning to their chairs and had to smother the smile that wanted to claim her lips. Tybo had been so annoying with his nonsense about having the sense not to be caught on video that she didn't feel at all bad he was in trouble now.

Leaving the men to be raked over the coals by Lucian, she hurried out into the hall, headed for the kitchen and the promised brownies and cocoa awaiting her. There was nothing like chocolate to make you feel better after a stressful event. Between that and a chat with Sam, she hoped to be feeling at least a little better before the men rejoined her.

TWO

Ildaria pushed through the red door of the Night Club the next day and then paused, blinking rapidly. The early afternoon sunlight was bright still, but in this room there was only the one small window in the door to allow the sun's rays in. Most of the interior lights were off—only a set of five or six pot lights over the bar at the back of the room were on and they didn't illuminate much other than the bar itself. Her eyes needed a second to adjust to the darkness before she could properly see the rich dark wood and leather interior of the establishment she'd entered.

It was impressive, Ildaria decided as she finally started toward the bar. There were no clients in the place at the moment. The Night Club wouldn't officially be open until sunset. Without clients cluttering up the place and blocking her view, she could see everything quite clearly.

Her gaze slid with appreciation over the gleaming dark wood booths along the front and side walls, with their leather cushioned seats of a deep wine color, and then moved over the wooden tables and chairs taking up the center of the room, before shifting to the long dark wood bar along the back with high-backed bar stools lining it (again of rich dark wood and deep-wine leather seats). There was a set of swing doors in the back wall to the left of the bar, and then a huge mirror and the bar itself ran the rest of the length of that wall until it stopped at a hall leading to the back of the building. The mirror was probably forty feet long and reached to the ceiling. It was lined with shelves, but they didn't hold bottles of alcohol as they would in a mortal establishment. Here glasses of every size and description filled the shelves: cocktail glasses, highball glasses, wineglasses (both the smaller, more rounded glasses used for red wine, as well as the taller type for white), champagne glasses, brandy snifters. There were even cordial glasses, she noted and smiled wryly as she wondered what they used them for. Who would order a tiny cordial glass of blood mixed with flavor or mood enhancers?

Immortals who came to the club, she supposed and then paused halfway across the room when a man pushed through the swinging doors. He was mortal. He was also huge, a veritable giant at what she would guess was six and a half feet, and that didn't include the bright green Mohawk on his head that had to be a foot high. But it wasn't just his height that made him huge. He was also wide, with the shoulders of a linebacker and bulging arm muscles that made the tattoos revealed by his short-sleeved shirt move as he raised the plate he carried.

Ildaria's gaze shifted automatically to the plate piled high with food and she noted that it held two huge double stacked burgers and about a pound of french fries. Their delicious scent wafted to her and her stomach gurgled with interest.

"It's not for you."

Ildaria blinked at that growled announcement in a thick British accent and dragged her gaze from the delicious smelling food to the man's face to see that he wasn't looking at her. He was peering down toward . . . his groin? Confusion filled her at that realization. He couldn't be talking to his penis. She didn't think. Shaking her head, she said, "I didn't presume it was for me."

The big man stopped walking and jerked his head up at her words, his eyes widening when he saw her standing there. "Marguerite's Ildaria?"

"Si." She started forward again.

"Hi." He smiled and then added, "Sorry. I wasn't talking to you, I was addressing my . . . Arsehole!" he ended with irritation and did a little shuffling dance.

"You were addressing your arsehole?" she asked, amusement curving her lips as she reached the bar and stopped between two stools.

Looking flustered now, the man shook his head and then scowled down at something she obviously couldn't see below the bar. "No. I—" Pausing, he did another little shimmying dance and barked, "Dammit H.D.! Stop that! You aren't getting any food."

Curiosity rising within her, Ildaria stepped up on the brass rail that ran along the bottom of the bar and leaned over the dark stone top to peer at the floor on the other side.

"Oh, my," she murmured and then bit her lip to hold back a burst of laughter when she saw the tiny, cream-colored ball of fur that was presently humping the huge man's ankle. It looked like a fluffy teddy bear come to life, and he was really romancing the big guy's ankle.

"Your dog?" she asked mildly.

"Yeah," he grunted, giving his leg another shake in an effort to dislodge the determined little guy.

"What kind?" she asked with interest.

"Bichonpoo," the man said still glaring down at the dog, and explained, "Bichon Frise and toy poodle mix."

"Oh." Ildaria nodded, a grin pulling her lips wider as H.D. refused to be removed and continued to hump at the big man's lower leg. Lifting her gaze to the plate the man was holding, she snatched a french fry from the pile and tossed it to the dog. The pup was immediately off the man's leg and leaping to catch the treat. Really, it was an impressive catch. He got some serious height in his jump to snatch that fry out of midair. As the dog dropped to the floor to gobble up his prize, the man heaved a sigh, drawing her attention back to him.

Ildaria's gaze moved with interest over his muscular body before sliding up to his head. When Marguerite had asked her if she'd mind stopping to pick up some blood from the Night Club on the way back from the university, she'd said the man she would be getting it from was G.G. which stood for Green Giant. Ildaria had immediately asked why he was called that, but the other woman had merely smiled and said she'd understand when she met him. Her gaze moving over the green strands of hair standing up stiff on his head in a Mohawk, Ildaria understood.

"That's what he was working for and what I was trying to avoid," G.G. announced now, reclaiming her attention to the fact that he was scowling between her and the dog.

It took Ildaria a moment to return her mind to the conversation, and then she gave a disbelieving laugh and asked, "He was humping your leg for food?"

"It worked, didn't it?" G.G. pointed out dryly. "He humped my leg and you gave him food to get him off."

"Ah." She shifted her gaze down to the dog who had finished his fry and was now staring up from her to G.G., his tongue coming out repeatedly to lick his upper lip as if he was trying to tell them he wanted more. Shaking her head, she shrugged apologetically. "Sorry. But I couldn't resist. Damn that's one cute dog." Opening her eyes wide, she smiled at the pooch and added, "Aren't you, H.D.?"

When the dog focused his attention on her, she found herself using that cooing voice all humans resort to when faced with cute creatures like babies and puppies. "Aren't you a pretty puppy? Hmm? Yes you are. You look like a little teddy bear. I just want to cuddle you all up."

That elicited a high-pitched bark from the little fur ball, and then he turned and charged to the open end of the bar by the swinging doors and careened around it, his little nails clacking on the hardwood.

"H.D., no!" G.G. said with alarm, dropping his plate on the bar and chasing after the dog even as he warned, "Get on a stool. He doesn't like women and he's an ankle biter."

Ildaria ignored the warning, and turned to face the dog as he sprinted into view around the corner of the bar, still yipping as he came. Rather than climb up on a stool, she stepped down off the brass rail and crouched down to greet the little fluffy dog. When he reached her, she caught him under the front legs and lifted him fearlessly to her face so she could press kisses to his furry cheeks. He immediately began licking wildly at any part of her face he could reach.

"Well, damn."

Lowering the dog, Ildaria cuddled him to her chest and petted him soothingly as she glanced at his owner. The giant gave a huff of disbelief.

"That dog doesn't like anyone but me. Usually, anyway," G.G. added, his gaze shifting to the dog now licking her hands, neck, and chin.

Ildaria shrugged almost apologetically. "Dogs like me."

"So it would seem," he muttered, some of the tension sliding out of him now that the danger of the little fur ball attacking her had passed. His gaze slid from her to the dog and then to his plate of food before he heaved a sigh and headed for the swing doors. "I'll get Marguerite's order."

"No rush," Ildaria said, sliding onto one of the bar

stools and settling H.D. in her lap so she could continue to pet him. "Why don't you eat your food first so it doesn't go cold?"

The Giant paused with his hand on one of the swing doors and looked back with surprise. "Yeah?"

"Si. Marguerite expected me to be at the university for several hours so went to visit Lissianna. There's really no rush."

His lips quirked with amusement at this news and he asked, "Playing hooky?"

"You have to be enrolled in classes to play hooky from them," she pointed out unhappily.

That had his eyebrows rising and his feet carrying him back to stand on the other side of the bar from her. "I was told you were finishing your third year, taking accounting at the university."

"*Were* being the key word in that sentence," Ildaria said, her tone dry as dust. She pressed a kiss to H.D.'s head and then lifted her gaze back to G.G., surprised to find him eyeing her with concern.

"I'm sorry to hear that," he said in a deep, sympathetic rumble. "Were the courses here harder than—"

"Oh, God, no," Ildaria said quickly, dismayed at the idea that he might think she'd dropped out because she couldn't hack the courses here. "I was doing well. I didn't want to quit."

"Then what happened?" he asked with confusion.

"Lucian happened," Ildaria said bitterly, and then deciding that wasn't fair, added, "Or to be fair, the truth is I happened, and then life happened and Lucian was forced to intercede."

Now, the poor man looked thoroughly lost, she noted and smiled wryly, but merely reminded him, "You should really eat your dinner before it gets cold."

G.G.'s gaze moved back to the plate between them with surprise. Apparently he'd forgotten all about his meal. Reminded of it, he nodded, but didn't start eating at once. Instead, he raised his eyes back to her and said, "I need to get a drink. Do you want anything?"

Ildaria hesitated, but then asked, "Do you have any sodas without caffeine?"

His eyebrows rose slightly, but he asked, "Do you like Tahitian Treat?"

When Ildaria stared at him blankly, he grinned and said, "Hang on."

She watched him move along the counter, and then focused her attention on the pup in her arms when he shifted in her hold so that her hand could reach his belly. Grinning at the silent request, Ildaria rubbed his stomach and then chuckled softly when the dog released a little sound that was part grunt and part sigh and then rolled completely onto his back in her arms and let his legs flop open so she could cover more belly. It was a very trusting move. He was lucky she didn't drop him, but Ildaria managed to retain her hold and petted his belly as he appeared to want. Much to her amusement the dog closed his eyes then and seemed to fall asleep under her ministrations.

"Little gremlin. He's never like this with women."

Ildaria lifted her head to find that G.G. had collected two glasses of a clear, cherry-red liquid over ice and walked around to join her on the client side of the bar.

Settling on the chair next to hers, he placed one of the drinks on the bar in front of Ildaria and then took a sip of the other as he pulled his plate closer. After swallowing the drink, he set the glass down, looked at the dog again and shook his head. "Actually, he's not like that with anyone but me. You must be a dog whisperer."

Ildaria smiled faintly as she peered down at the sleeping dog. He was a tiny little thing. Hardly the breed she would have expected a big man like G.G. to have.

"Big dogs need room to run and in the UK I live in a flat four blocks from the club," he said, as if having read her mind, which as a mortal he couldn't do. She supposed most people commented on the size of his dog when he continued, "A walk to the Night Club there and back is enough exercise for this little guy."

He didn't have to say it wouldn't be enough for a larger dog. She got that, but asked, "And where do you live here?"

Her gaze slid from G.G. to H.D. as she awaited his answer, imagining the sight the pair must make walking down Toronto streets, a big, scary-looking guy with a Mohawk, tattoos, and piercings, leading the fluffy little fur ball on a leash. Probably a black leather leash with studs or something, she thought, taking note of the dog's black leather collar with spikes sticking out of it. If it was supposed to make the little fuzz ball look tough, it failed miserably. He was too damned cute to look scary. But she suspected the sight the pair made left most people gaping.

"Right now I'm living in one of the apartments over the club," G.G. told her. And then lowered his gaze to his plate and frowned before muttering, "If you drink soda, you probably eat too."

Ildaria raised her eyebrows at the comment. "Not as often as I used to, but si, I still eat."

G.G. nodded. "Would you like something? I can make you a burger."

Ildaria considered the offer briefly. She was hungry. It was a sensation she experienced less and less often lately, but which was presently gnawing at her stomach. She didn't want to make him cook for her though, so promising herself she'd hit a drive-through on her way back to Marguerite's, she murmured, "Maybe just a fry."

"Help yourself." G.G. pushed the plate to rest halfway between the two of them on the counter.

"Thanks," Ildaria breathed, and left off petting his dog to pluck a french fry from the mountain of greasy goodness.

The moment she bit into it, the dog in her arms sprang awake, his body jerking as if the slight sound were an alarm of some sort. The little mutt then squirmed to turn in her arm and climbed up her chest to sniff her mouth as she chewed. Chuckling, Ildaria caught the little beast and set him back in her lap.

"Ill mannered cretin," G.G. said with a scowl, scooping the dog out of her lap and setting him on the floor as he said firmly, "We're eating. Go lay down."

H.D. merely rose up on his back paws and laid his front paws on the man's lower legs, his eager gaze sliding from his face to Ildaria's, his eyes wide and tongue sliding in and out of his mouth eagerly.

Ildaria chuckled at the display, amazed at how human he looked with his big green eyes and lip smacking. Her laughter earned a scowl from G.G. and an exasperated, "Don't encourage him." He then turned his gaze back to the dog and repeated firmly, "We're eating, H.D. Get in your basket."

H.D. hesitated, the hope dying on his face, but then dropped back to all fours and began to walk slowly back along the bar to the end of it. He was walking as slow as molasses, head and tail down, looking back every couple of steps as if checking to be sure G.G. hadn't changed his stance on the issue, but G.G. just scowled and eyed him firmly until he disappeared out of sight around the bar.

"Where is he going?" Ildaria asked, raising herself up enough to see over the bar again.

"I put his bed behind the bar so he could stay with me until we open," G.G. said, picking up his burger.

"Oh." She settled back in her seat as he took a bite, and then commented, "Marguerite didn't mention that you brought your dog to the club. I'd have come in to check out the place sooner if I'd realized that."

G.G. shook his head as he chewed and swallowed, and then said, "I don't usually. But his sitter didn't come in today and I didn't want to leave him at home alone."

Ildaria's eyebrows rose. "You have a sitter for your dog?"

"Have to. The little monster eats things he shouldn't if he's left alone. And I don't mean human food."

"Like what?" she asked with interest.

"Shoes, rugs, clothing . . . my razor."

"Razor?" she squawked with alarm. "Was he all right?"

"It was a cordless electric razor," G.G. said on a sigh. "He chewed off those little round blade things. Didn't swallow any of the pieces, though, before I caught him."

"Oh." She relaxed a bit.

"He destroyed the razor though," G.G. added with irritation. "I was pretty pissed."

"I can imagine," Ildaria murmured.

"Not as pissed as I was when he ate my passport, though," he grumbled and bit viciously into his burger.

"Your passport?" she asked on a disbelieving laugh.

G.G. grimaced and nodded as he chewed, but once he'd swallowed, he added, "I was packing and it was lying on the bed next to my suitcase. I left the room, came back and he was chewing on it. He'd already managed to eat a corner of it, the one with the bar code." Shaking his head with disgust, he added, "This was ten o'clock at night, the evening before I was supposed to fly back to London. I had to cancel the flight and arrange for a new passport. I was not a happy camper."

"Oh, dear," Ildaria murmured and then bit her lip to keep from laughing at the gloomy irritation on his face.

G.G. took another bite of his burger, chewed, swallowed and then said, "The worst, though, was the cashier's check he demolished."

"Cashier's check?" she asked, her eyebrows rising.

❧

G.G. nodded glumly. "A hundred thousand dollar cashier's check. The down payment on this place when I bought it from Lucern. It was on the dresser in my hotel room. I had an hour before my meeting with Lucern and the lawyers, went to take a shower, came back out and he'd jumped on the chair next to the dresser, got a hold of the check and was curled up in the chair eating it like it was a dog bone."

"*Madre de Dios*," Ildaria breathed with horror.

"Yeah," he said unhappily and then added, "Fortunately, he hadn't eaten all of it and there was enough left of the destroyed check that the bank was willing to issue a new one. But I was sweating it until they agreed." His mouth tightened at the memory. "I started calling him the hundred-thousand-dollar dog after that."

"H.D.," Ildaria breathed with realization.

"H.D. for short," he agreed. "H.T.D.D. was a mouthful, and H.D. is close enough to his real name that he answers to it."

"What's his real name?" she asked with interest.

"Eddy."

"Eddy?" she echoed. Teddy would have fit better. He looked like a teddy bear after all.

"Edward Simpson Guiscard on his registration," G.G. announced. "Eddy."

"So you're G.G. Simpson Guiscard," she said with a faint smile.

"Joshua James Simpson Guiscard," he corrected quietly. "G.G. is a nickname. Joshua James Simpson was my birth name. My birth father was John Simpson, but he died when I was young and my mother remarried Robert Guiscard. Robert adopted me and Guiscard was legally added to the end of my name."

"Ah," Ildaria murmured, thinking Joshua was a nice name. It didn't really suit the Mohawked and tattooed man beside her though. G.G. did.

"And you?" G.G. asked with interest.

"Me?" she asked uncertainly.

"What's your full name?"

"Oh." She blinked, and then blurted, "Angelina Ildaria Sophia Lupita Garcia Pimienta." The moment the words left her mouth, she frowned and turned to stare blindly at the mirrored shelves behind the bar, wondering why she'd told him that. As a rule, she avoided telling it at all, or lied. The last two hundred years she hadn't used Angelina at all. She'd gone by Ildaria and used Garcia because it was as common as Smith in North America.

"Pretty name," G.G. said, and she turned back to him with surprise to see a faint smile tilting his lips before he popped the last of his first burger into his mouth and began to chew.

"I just go by Ildaria Garcia," she murmured, feeling her tension slowly subside as she watched him eat. Some part of her mind was assuring her that it didn't matter that he knew her name. It was fine. She was in North America now, far away from the Dominican Republic and the danger that revealing her name held there. Letting her breath out, she searched for something to say, and found herself asking, "So, how did a mortal end up owning and running not just one, but two nightclubs for immortals?"

G.G. shook his head, and swallowed the food in his mouth before pointing out, "You still haven't told me why you dropped out of uni."

Ildaria blew out a breath of irritation, but supposed it was only fair she answer his question if she wanted him to answer hers. Raising the drink he'd given her, she took a sip to give herself time to decide what to say. Her eyes widened with surprise when the taste hit her tongue. It was nice. Tasty. Sweet and fruity.

"Good huh?" he said with amusement, and she glanced over to see him grinning as he watched her face.

Ildaria nodded, and took another drink.

"So . . ." G.G. said as she swallowed and set the glass back on the bar. "You dropped out because . . ."

"I didn't drop out," she said at once. "Lucian insisted I should switch from night to day courses, but it's too far into the semester, so I had to withdraw so the classes won't show up as 'fail.' Worse yet, I can't get a refund on them."

"Ouch," G.G. said with sympathy.

"Si." Ildaria sighed the word and then shrugged. "It's my own fault, I guess."

"Why?" G.G. asked at once, and then added, "And why does Lucian want you in day classes?"

"Because he thinks it's safer," she muttered, answering the second question first.

"Safer?" G.G. asked on a bark of surprised laughter. "You're an immortal. Not much can harm you."

"Si, but—" She broke off with a grimace, and then took a deep breath and explained, "He's not worried about my safety that way. It's more that he doesn't want me to be put in a position . . ."

"He's worried about you going vigilante again," G.G. guessed solemnly when she fell silent.

Ildaria's mouth tightened. "You know about that, huh?"

He nodded almost apologetically. "This place is gossip central, and people seem to like to talk to me."

She rolled her eyes at that, and took another swallow of the drink he'd given her, enjoying the sweet treat.

"What made you go vigilante down in . . . some city in Montana, was it?" he asked with a frown.

Ildaria nodded, but didn't bother to say which city. That part of her life was over now. She was stuck in Canada for the foreseeable future. Setting her drink back on the bar, she ran her fingers up and down the condensation on the outside of her glass and muttered, "It doesn't matter."

"It does to me," he assured her quietly and Ildaria glanced his way, surprised to see the sincerity in his face. G.G.'s expression suggested that what she had to say was the most important thing in the world to him in that moment.

Three

Ildaria tore her gaze away from G.G.'s and swallowed thickly, trying to remove the sudden lump lodged in her throat. It didn't do much, and after another swallow she gave it up and shrugged. "Do you know Jess Stewart Notte?"

"Raffaele's life mate. Yes," he said, nodding. "I've met her a couple of times when she was up here with Raffaele visiting family. You lived with her in Montana, didn't you?"

"Si. Her and Raffaele," she added with a faint smile. Raffaele hadn't been able to stay away from Jess once he'd found her. Not surprising for life mates. But it had meant the three of them living in the house Jess had inherited from her parents, instead of just the two of them. Ildaria hadn't really minded after getting to know the man. She'd even ended up liking Raffaele as a person. Despite that though, she still wished Jess had chosen

Ildaria's old captain, Vasco, for her mate. She'd had the choice between the two, and Ildaria knew Vasco was a good man under all of his swagger. Besides, he'd saved her life more than once and was like family. Well, she supposed she hadn't let him close enough to be family, but he was important to her. Shrugging her thoughts away, Ildaria explained, "Well, as you say I was living with Jess and Raffaele, but as new life mates they were pretty wrapped up in each other."

G.G. nodded. "I've noticed that happens."

"Si." She sighed the word. She liked Jess. They had become good friends despite the little bit of time they'd actually spent together. "But that was okay. I made friends at the uni there. In my classes," she added.

"Mortal friends you mean," G.G. filled in for her, getting it.

Ildaria grimaced. "Si. I didn't want to specify and sound racist or something."

G.G. blinked. "By mentioning that your friends were mortal?"

"Well, you can't call anyone anything anymore without offending someone. Every time I learn the rules, they go and change them."

G.G.'s mouth twitched briefly with amusement, and then he pointed out, "So, you were explaining why you went vigilante?"

Ildaria grimaced, but nodded and said, "Well, as I said, I had mortal friends at uni. Three of them, like I have here."

"You have friends at university here?" he asked, eyes widening.

"You needn't sound so surprised. I'm a charming person," she informed him a bit testily.

That brought a laugh and he shook his head. "I'm just surprised because you haven't been here long."

"Almost two months," she told him and shrugged. "That's long enough to make friends."

"Yes, it is," he agreed soothingly.

"Hmm." She eyed him suspiciously for a moment, trying to figure out if he was patronizing her, and then let it go and said, "Anyway . . . So, one of those friends was a lovely girl named Alicia. She was beautiful, sweet, funny and super smart. And she never missed class. I mean, *never*. She could be hacking up a lung and sneezing up a storm, Kleenex in every pocket and trailing her like bread crumbs, and she'd show up for class."

When she paused briefly to take a sip of her drink, G.G. nodded to let her know he understood. Swallowing the sweet drink, Ildaria set down the glass and continued. "But then one Monday, she didn't show up for our Business Analytics course." Her mouth tightened at the memory. "I meant to call her that night to check on her, but . . ." Ildaria shrugged unhappily. "Between full-time classes and my full-time job waitressing, I forgot."

"Life gets busy," he said in an understanding rumble.

"Si, it does," she agreed on a sigh. "But when she didn't show up for the Thursday Mergers and Acquisitions class we had together, I headed straight for her dorm the minute class was done." She ran one finger over the condensation on her glass again. "Apparently her roommate came back to the room after class on

Monday to find Alicia's things gone, and was told she'd dropped her courses and moved home."

When she paused again, G.G. made a sound in his throat that was part growl and part hum. As if he suspected what was coming wasn't good and he was already angry at whoever was at fault for this unexpected occurrence.

"Alicia's family lived in a small town an hour outside the city," Ildaria continued quietly. "I waited until the next day because it was so late, and then I drove out to see her. Her mother answered the door, asked me to wait a moment and then went to find Alicia. She came back a few minutes later and said very apologetically, that Alicia didn't want to see anyone." Ildaria swallowed at the memory. "I could tell she was upset. That she wanted to tell me something to soften the blow of her daughter's rejection, but didn't feel it was her right."

"So you put the mind whammy on her," G.G. guessed.

Ildaria turned to him blinking. "Mind whammy?"

"You know, when you immortals read and control us mere mortals to get what you want," he explained, his voice a tad dry.

Ildaria grimaced at the description. Immortals could read the minds of mortals, as well as control them, although she did that as little as possible. For instance, she hadn't tried to read G.G.'s mind yet and wouldn't without a reason, and she was glad she hadn't, since the man obviously had some resentment about the practice. Probably, she thought, because he'd been the victim of it a time or two what with owning not one, but two nightclubs that serviced immortals. And since she hated it when older immortals read her, she could understand, so she let his attitude go for now, and nodded unrepentantly.

"I read her mother's mind to find out what was going on." She didn't leave time for him to comment on that and continued. "The Thursday before, after the last class we'd had together, Alicia had been attacked on her way back to her dorm. She was raped and beaten . . . badly. She'd fought back and earned a broken arm, cracked ribs, so much vaginal tearing they'd had to sew her up, and there was a question as to whether she'd see out of one eye again."

"Christ," G.G. breathed, sagging slightly next to her and setting his half-eaten second burger back on the plate. "Did they catch the bastard?"

Ildaria shook her head. "Not yet, and they probably won't. There were no witnesses, and Alicia's memory is messed up so she couldn't give much of a description . . . If she even got a good look at the guy before he half blinded her with his beating."

"Right," G.G. said unhappily. "So she won't feel safe on campus with him still out there."

"No," Ildaria agreed grimly, and then added, "Although I suspect she'll never feel safe again whether they find the guy or not."

"So she dropped out of her classes and retreated to her childhood home," G.G. murmured, sounding sad.

"No. Alicia had only gotten out of the hospital the morning I went to the house. It was her mother and father who had packed up her bags, moved her things out of her dorm room, and signed her out of her classes," Ildaria corrected him, and then added, "Although, probably at her request."

When he grunted at this, she continued, "Anyway, at that time she had a long road of recovery ahead of her and while her mother knew Alicia would heal physically, she was afraid that she wouldn't mend mentally and emotionally. Alicia was shutting down and shutting everyone out. Her mother was very scared for her."

Ildaria took another drink of her Tahitian Treat, recalling the worry and fear of Alicia's mother and her own rage and pain on learning what had happened.

"Did you fix her?" G.G. asked quietly.

She raised her head and eyed him warily. "What do you mean?"

He snorted at the question. "I know a lot of immortals. I know your abilities. Did you wipe the memory from Alicia? Help her get over it?"

Ildaria let her breath out on a gust of irritation and then shrugged. "I did what I could." When he raised his eyebrows at that, she admitted, "I'm not old enough, or maybe it's not practiced enough, that I was able to wipe her memory."

"Practiced enough?" he asked with interest.

"I don't read minds unless I have to," she explained. "It feels . . . intrusive. Besides, some of the things you hear when reading the minds of others can be . . ." She paused and shook her head with disgust, and then explained, "Mostly the only minds I've read are those of would-be donors."

"Donors?" G.G. asked, his eyes narrowing. "Immortals haven't been allowed to feed off of mortals since shortly after the advent of blood banks. Not in North America anyway." After a pause, he added thoughtfully, "And Punta Cana is in the Dominican Republic, part of the Carribean, which is also in North America."

"Si, but the South American Council covers the Carribean, Central America, and South America too. Basically anything below the United States. It's just called the South American Council to simplify matters," she explained, and when he merely raised his eyebrows, she added, "But it's not allowed there either . . . unless you take a boat out into international waters. Neither North American, nor South American rules apply if you're in international waters."

"Right," he said grimly. "And you did that? Took people out on boats and fed on them rather than using immortal blood banks?"

They weren't really questions, and he wasn't looking very pleased at the thought. In fact, he was starting to look at her like he found her distasteful now. Ildaria didn't know why that bothered her, but it did and she quickly explained, "Not by choice. The Dominican Republic has some pretty corrupt people, both mortal and immortal." She paused briefly, and then added, "I suppose they have corruption here too, but the difference is that Lucian Argeneau *isn't* corrupt. But down there, the head of the Council, Juan Villaverde, is very corrupt. And greedy. He owns a good portion of the beachfront property, but wants more, and inland property too if it's in a lucrative area. Of course, he's had no problem purchasing the property he wants from mortals. He just controls them and gets them to sell. But he can't do that with the immortals who have owned and had shacks or huts on the land for ages. The other immortals would protest. Besides, some are old enough to be able to resist him and have held the property for a hundred years or longer. Long before they became tourist traps. So Juan has resorted to using other tricks to get what he wants."

"Tricks huh?" G.G. said grimly.

"Yeah. Some work, some don't, but the latest trick is that he bought up all the blood banks down there and has jacked up the prices on blood to the point that less affluent immortals are having to choose between buying the blood they need, or paying their mortgages, or taxes, or rents, or hydro if they have it. He's forcing people out of their homes, taking them over and—" She broke off, shaking her head with disgust at the memory of what the man was doing to her neighbors and people she cared about.

Ildaria took in a deep breath, let it out, and then continued. "One of his sons, Vasco Villaverde, doesn't agree with what his father is doing and wanted to help those of us the most affected by his father's actions. So in an effort to get us the blood we needed, he geared up his old pirate ship, and—"

"Wait, wait, wait," G.G. interrupted. "His old pirate ship?"

"Vasco's five hundred years old or something and used to be a pirate back in the day," she told him with a crooked smile, and then added, "Well, a privateer . . . maybe."

G.G. was silent for a minute, his eyes dancing with

interest at this news, but then grunted and waved for her to continue.

"So, he geared up his old pirate ship, welcomed any immortal who had trouble affording their blood to join his crew, and . . ." She hesitated and then sighed and said, "It's kind of a tourist thing. There's a program where people go out to swim with the sharks and stingrays. When they return to the landing site, they watch a sort of pirate dance/fight routine and are encouraged to buy from stalls with local goods," she explained. "While they're watching the show, our crew, dressed like sexy pirates move—"

"Sexy pirates?" he interrupted. His voice was serious, but there was a definite twinkle in his eyes.

Ildaria grimaced. "I wore black leather thigh-high boots, a black leather bra and matching short shorts or skirt, and either a pirate hat or a head scarf . . . and a sword of course."

"Of course," he murmured, his gaze sliding over her as if he were imagining her in the costume she'd just described and liking what he was seeing in his mind's eye.

Ildaria wasn't one to blush, she was too old for that, but she was quite sure she was blushing now under his gaze. She also felt oddly warm and a little breathless. Clearing her throat, she tried to ignore his attention and quickly added, "The guys usually went topless, or with an open vest, or an open peasant top with long sleeves, tight leather pants, boots, a pirate hat or head scarf, and a sword."

"Right," he said slowly, but didn't sound all that interested in what the guys were wearing. She was quite sure he was still stuck on her costume.

Clearing her throat, she continued, "Anyway, the crew would move through the crowd, picking donors and inviting them on the pirate ship for a tour to feed the sharks."

A lot of the twinkle left his eyes then. In fact, he looked a bit grim when he said, "The sharks, huh?"

Ildaria sighed and shrugged unhappily. "We did take them out to see and feed sharks if we could find any. We also served them cheese trays and punch made with really watercd-down alcohol in it."

"Watered down because you didn't want to drink alcohol filled blood."

He sounded angry again, but she ignored that and nodded.

"When did you feed on them?" he asked grimly.

Ildaria shrugged uncomfortably. "We weren't supposed to feed on them until we reached international waters. That was the whole reason behind Vasco doing this. To get us thc blood we needed without leaving us homeless, or having to go without it until we were so desperate that we inadvertently attacked a mortal on land and were executed."

G.G. was silent for a minute, his gaze disapproving. "You weren't supposed to feed on them until you reached international waters," he murmured her words almost thoughtfully, and then said, "But you did, didn't you?"

Ildaria's mouth tightened. "What? Now you're a mind reader?"

He shook his head. "No. But you said you *'weren't supposed to,'* not *'we never fed on them until we reached international waters,'*" he pointed out in a low rumble.

Ildaria's mouth twisted at that and then she looked away and sighed. "I usually did wait. I always tried to. But there were three, maybe four times when one or the other of the idiot mortals managed to corner and try to rape either myself or one of the other women." Her mouth firmed with anger at the memory, and she confessed, "Those ones I fed on early and in the most unpleasant way I could think of."

G.G. didn't comment at once, and after a moment she huffed out a breath, letting go of her anger as she said, "Unfortunately, I couldn't leave the memory with them so it was really a stupid, useless thing to do that taught them nothing and endangered both myself, and Vasco, who didn't deserve that kind of trouble."

"Then why did you do it?" G.G. asked reasonably.

Ildaria hesitated and then shrugged unhappily. "I couldn't help myself. I just . . . I really hate men who think they can just take what they want and rape a woman."

Ildaria turned her gaze back to her drink then, staring at it grimly and refusing to meet his gaze after that admission. When he remained silent, seeming to be waiting, she added, "That's why I decided to leave Punta Cana. So I wouldn't make trouble for Vasco and the others anymore."

"And you moved to Montana," G.G. put in.

Ildaria nodded. "Jess invited me to stay with her

while I figured out what I wanted to do. She's the one who suggested I get a degree at college or university."

When she stopped talking again, G.G. said, "And you chose accounting at university, but then your friend was raped."

"Yeah." She breathed the word unhappily. "I didn't have enough experience to wipe her memories, but I did what I could to blur them for her. Soften them so she wasn't so terrified and traumatized."

"And then you went vigilante," G.G. suggested, bringing her gaze sharply to his. Smiling at her expression, he shrugged. "Like I said, the Night Club is gossip central. I did hear a little of why you are now in Canada and being watched like a hawk by Lucian and the boys."

Ildaria grimaced, and took a sip of her drink, but then nodded. "Yeah. Well, when I read her mother's mind, I saw that they'd learned that Alicia wasn't the first victim of this rapist. They suspected the same man was responsible for at least three other attacks. There was a serial rapist on campus, but they weren't advertising it because they didn't want the female students to panic, and risk female enrollment dropping," she said bitterly. Angry that the school would choose profit over concern for its female students. "So, I donned leathers and started going out at night looking for the bastard."

"Leathers?" G.G. asked, distracting her from her anger.

She blinked at him and then shrugged. "Injuries mean a need for more blood, and while I was working full time as a waitress, making great tips, and my rent with Jess was ridiculously low, university is expensive.

I couldn't afford a lot of extra blood," she explained. "Short of a Kevlar bodysuit or something, leather is the best thing you can wear to avoid or reduce injury. So I bought black leather pants, a black leather jacket and whatnot, put my hair in a ponytail or bun to prevent it being used against me and went out looking for him."

"Did you get him?" G.G. asked when she fell silent.

Ildaria shook her head slowly. "No. But I got a lot of other assholes up to no good." A small smile played around her lips as she recalled the people she'd helped and the criminals she'd dumped in the hands of local mortal law enforcement. But after a moment, she sighed, and added, "Unfortunately, there are a lot of fricking people out there with cell phones happy to film anything and everything everybody is doing. I got caught on film once or twice, which was bad enough. But then one of the people I rescued was an FBI agent . . . and didn't that just make them hot to catch me?" She rolled her eyes, thinking that was gratitude for you, and then said irritably, "Which, of course, caught the attention of the North American Council."

"Ah," G.G. murmured, picking up his own drink, but merely holding it as he said, "Which is how you ended up here in Toronto under Lucian's eagle eye."

"Yeah." She shrugged. "In truth, I was lucky. He could have had me executed. I was drawing attention that could have led to the discovery of our kind, and that's a no-no with every Council so . . ." She breathed out unhappily. "I just wish I'd caught the bastard who attacked Alicia before Lucian caught on and came to Montana to shut me down."

G.G. was silent for a minute, his expression thoughtful, and then he asked, "And what happened here?"

Ildaria turned to him in confusion. "What do you
mean?"

"Why did Lucian make you drop your night courses
and switch to days?" he asked almost gently in that
deep bass rumble of his. "Were you donning your
leathers and—"

"No," she assured him quickly. "Nothing like that. I
do learn from my mistakes."

He waited. Silent.

Ildaria could have refused to explain. It wasn't really
any of his business. But she found she wanted to. She
didn't want him to think she'd run off half-cocked and
repeated her error. "I didn't go looking for trouble this
time. But a lot of bad stuff happens at night on campus, and I can't just ignore someone's screams for help.
So . . ." She grimaced and admitted, "There have been
three instances since starting my night courses here in
Toronto where I've stumbled across someone in trouble
and tried to help."

She noted his wince at this news, and sighed inwardly, completely understanding it, but not sorry
she'd helped. Pushing his reaction away in her mind,
she continued, "One of those instances where I helped
was apparently caught on camera."

"Crap," G.G. breathed.

Ildaria nodded, completely agreeing with that as-
sessment of the situation. It was crap. "So, Lucian has
decided that Vasco was right and I'm a trouble magnet. That being the case, Lucian has decided the best

way to keep me out of trouble is to make me switch from night classes to day classes when there is less crime on campus for me to happen upon on my way to and from class."

They were both silent for a minute, and then G.G. pushed his plate away and turned to face her. Ildaria waited warily, unsure what to make of the thoughtful way he was eyeing her, but then he said, "Marguerite said you were taking accounting at uni."

Surprise sent her eyebrows upward, but she nodded. "I major in accounting, minor in business."

G.G. nodded slowly and then said thoughtfully, "And my dog likes you."

Ildaria tilted her head, trying to sort that one out. She wasn't at all certain what one thing had to do with the other.

And then he said, "Would you like a job?"

Ildaria stilled, startled by the question, but after considering his comment about his dog liking her, asked, "Dog sitting?"

G.G. nodded. "And doing the books for the Night Club." When her eyes widened in surprise, he added, "I'll pay you for both. An accountant's full wages, plus an extra twenty dollars an hour for looking after H.D. while you do."

Her mouth dropped open at that offer, excitement building within her at the thought of being paid for two jobs in one, but then she frowned and pointed out, "Wait. You already have a dog sitter. They just didn't come in today for some reason."

"I *had* a dog sitter," G.G. said dryly, and explained,

"She quit yesterday after H.D. bit her. Walked out in the middle of the night without telling me and left him alone to eat holes in my clothes and chew the hell out of one of my running shoes."

"Oh." Ildaria blinked, wondering what clothes the little fur ball had chewed holes in.

"And I've been looking for a bookkeeper since I bought this place . . ." G.G. shook his head with irritation. "The fact that I can't hire a mortal has made it impossible to find anyone."

Ildaria completely understood why he couldn't hire mortals. This club was for immortals. It served blood-based drinks, not alcohol. The accounts payable would be to various places but would include Argeneau blood banks. The drinks made were variations of blood, sometimes just different blood types: A+, A-, B+, B-, etc. Sometimes customers wanted specialized blood like that of people who were high on various drugs, or the sweet blood Marguerite had asked her to pick up on the way back from university. Sweet blood came from untreated diabetics and had a high sugar content. A rare blend to find since when the blood was tested on donation, the donor was advised that they were diabetic and should seek medical attention, reducing the donor base.

Sometimes, though, the blood was mixed with things to make it more interesting. Here a Bloody Mary was a true Bloody Mary, made with the standard Worcestershire sauce, hot sauce, lemon juice, lime juice, black pepper as well as celery and a lemon wedge for garnish. But there was no tomato juice or vodka in the Bloody Marys here. That was replaced with blood.

Actually, she thought now, G.G. would have trouble explaining having blood banks on the accounts payable list to the tax people too and she supposed he had to cover with switching names out from blood banks for alcohol distributors. He probably had to keep two sets of books, she decided. An immortal was really the only way he could go when it came to hiring a bookkeeper. She didn't know a lot of accountant immortals. Ildaria was sure there must be some out there, but considering the small pool to search from . . . well, finding a bookkeeper would be impossible.

"So?" G.G. prompted when she remained silent, lost in her thoughts. "Want a job? Or two jobs, I should say."

"Si," Ildaria said at once, feeling a lot of her stressors drop away like ashes crumbling in a fire. He was going to pay her for both watching H.D. and doing the books. It was like two full-time jobs in one. Her money troubles just went out the door. She'd be able to pay for the fall semester, get her own apartment, and maybe even buy furniture for it if she was careful. Damn. Things were looking up.

"Thank God," G.G. said, relaxing in his chair and smiling at her. Shaking his head, he added, "Actually, I suppose I should be thanking Marguerite. She's the one who suggested you might be able to help me."

"Marguerite did?" Ildaria asked with surprise.

"Yeah. When she called this morning about the blood, we got to talking and I was telling her about H.D.'s sitter quitting and needing a bookkeeper and she mentioned that you were taking accounting and looking for a job. And then she suggested sending you to pick up the blood instead of my having it delivered so that I could meet and talk to you. I thought that would take care of at least one of my problems, but instead, H.D. likes you and it handles both of my problems." He smiled widely at the realization that his troubles were over and then said, "I really need to send her flowers or something."

Ildaria smiled faintly in response, but asked, "So this was a job interview?"

He grinned and nodded, the expression making him look ridiculously adorable. The man was a big teddy bear . . . with tattoos, piercings, and a bright green Mohawk.

"So when can you start?" G.G. asked abruptly, his expression serious again.

"How about now?" she asked lightly, and then paused to frown. "No. I guess I need to take the blood home to Marguerite first. And then I should probably change into something more professional, but I could start after that. Maybe in two hours?" she asked and then explained, "It'll be rush hour traffic when I head back or I'd say sooner."

G.G. smiled faintly, but shook his head. "Take the blood to Marguerite and relax tonight, get anything done that you think will need doing and you can start tomorrow," he suggested, and then pointed out, "It's nearly sunset, and I wouldn't have time to show you the books and how they're done before opening anyway. Tomorrow you can come in at say . . . four? Then we can go over the books so you know what you're doing."

Ildaria nodded easily, happy to start whenever he wanted.

"Good. Then I'll go get that blood for Marguerite so you can be on your way."

"What about H.D.?" Ildaria asked with concern as he stood up. "What will you do with him tonight?"

G.G. hesitated and then shrugged unhappily. "One night in my office won't kill him. I'll just make sure there's nothing lying around for him to eat."

"Or I could take him home with me," Ildaria suggested quietly, and then added, "On the house."

G.G.'s eyes flew up in surprise, but then he shook his head with regret.

Before he could say no, though, she added, "I don't mind. Besides, I'd be upset thinking about him being stuck locked up in your office all night long . . . and I would bring him back with me tomorrow. That way he wouldn't be on his own and get into anything."

The large man hesitated briefly, but then considered aloud, "It's usually 7 or 8 A.M. or so before I finish cleanup and go up to my apartment. All I do is take H.D. out for a pee break, and then it's to bed. I sleep until three—" Pausing, he explained, "That's why I suggested you return at four. It would give me time for breakfast and a cup of coffee before you returned."

Ildaria nodded and then waited.

"So," G.G. said thoughtfully, "all he'd miss is sleeping time with me and watching me eat my breakfast.

That would work," he decided, but then paused and suggested, "Maybe you should check with Marguerite first, though. She might not want the little runt running around her house."

"I'm sure she won't mind," Ildaria said and was quite sure that was true. Marguerite loved dogs. Still, she pulled her phone out of her pocket, saying, "But I'll call her to be sure."

"Right." He nodded. "I'll get Marguerite's package while you do." Leaving her to her call, he picked up his plate and headed around the bar to pass through the swinging doors.

As she'd expected, Marguerite was more than happy to have H.D. come stay the night. The woman loved dogs almost as much as she did. Ildaria didn't tell her that she had a job now, she merely said that the dog sitter G.G. had hired to look after H.D. had let him down and she didn't want to leave the poor fur ball stuck in his office all night. Ildaria wanted to see Marguerite's face when she told her that she'd got the job she'd recommended her for, plus the dog sitting position as well. She also planned to stop and pick up some flowers on the way home to give the woman as a thank-you for recommending her to G.G. and she wanted them to be a surprise too.

Ildaria was smiling to herself at the thought as she put her phone away.

"It's all right with Marguerite then?"

A glance showed G.G. pushing through the swing doors, a medium-sized cooler in hand. Ildaria's smile widened. "More than all right. She's eager to give him cuddles. She thinks Julius will be grateful for the break."

G.G.'s mouth dropped open at this and Ildaria grinned with amusement and explained, "Julius the dog, not Julius her husband."

"Ah." He smiled wryly. "I always forget she names her dog after her husband."

"Do you know why?" she asked with interest. It did seem an odd habit to her, but she hadn't got around to asking Marguerite about it.

"Yes, I do," he said with a faint smile, and then carried the cooler around the bar, adding, "And I'll tell you another time. I need to set up for tonight right now."

"Oh. Of course." She hesitated, her gaze sliding from G.G. to the cooler he held and then toward the bar. H.D. was nowhere in sight.

"I'll grab H.D.'s leash, his favorite toy, and his food and treats," G.G. announced, setting the cold container of blood on the bar.

"Right," Ildaria said, relaxing and then she watched him slip back through the swinging doors. It didn't take long before he had returned with two bags.

Moving to the cooler, he opened the lid and set one of the bags inside, saying, "This is H.D.'s food and favorite treats. There are three separate meals, each in its own container. I make his dog food myself from fresh meat and vegetables, so it has to be kept refrigerated and then microwaved before serving. The containers are microwavable, and I usually put them in for twenty-two seconds, but each microwave is different, so check it before you give it to him to make sure it isn't too hot, because he'll gobble it up the minute you set it down without checking it himself," he warned.

"Okay. Check it first," she said aloud.

"Right," G.G. said as he closed the lid of the cooler. "He eats when he wakes up which is usually around 3 or 4 P.M., then again at 11 P.M. or midnight, and finally around 3 or 4 A.M. which is about four hours before bedtime, so three should do until you bring him back."

Ildaria nodded, silently repeating the times in her head so she'd remember.

"As for his treats . . ." G.G. continued, and waited for her to meet his gaze, before saying firmly, "He gets no more than three in twenty-four hours. Too many treats and he becomes a roly-poly little sausage on legs and can't jump up in his chair."

Ildaria's eyebrows rose at the "his chair" bit, but said solemnly, "No more than three."

Apparently satisfied that she wouldn't go wild and turn his dog into a roly-poly little sausage overnight, G.G. relaxed a bit and moved back around the bar, pulling a leash out of his back pocket. As she'd expected it was black leather interspersed with studs and miniature spikes, Ildaria noted before he bent, briefly disappearing from sight. He straightened again a moment later, H.D. in his arms, the leash already attached to his collar.

She watched the big giant of a man snuggle the small dog with a faint smile, and then picked up the cooler.

"I'll get that," G.G. protested, carrying H.D. around the bar.

"Nah." Ildaria shook her head and led the way to the door. "I get to snuggle him up all night. You should do it while you have the chance."

He didn't protest further, but followed her to the door, murmuring to the dog about behaving himself at Marguerite's, and telling him he'd miss him. It was really quite sweet, she decided as she shifted the cooler, balancing it on one hand to open the door and then holding it open with one foot for him to lead the way out.

Four

"Isn't that the most adorable thing you've ever seen?" Marguerite asked with a wide smile.

Following her gaze to the huge dog bed in the corner, Ildaria smiled faintly when she saw that H.D. and Julius were curled up on the bed. The little cream-colored fur ball was in front of the much bigger black dog, his back against Julius's curled feet.

"Maybe I should get Julius a brother or sister to cuddle with," Marguerite said with a small frown.

Ildaria chuckled at the suggestion, but didn't comment. She was busy pulling out her phone to snap a picture. She took three quick shots of the pair, checked them all to see which was best, and then stood staring at her phone with a small frown.

"Problem, dear?" Marguerite asked lightly.

"I was going to send this to G.G. so he can see H.D. is all right and won't worry about him, but I don't have his number," she explained and clucked with irritation. She'd have to get his number if she was going to work for him.

"Here." Marguerite stood and moved quickly around the table to her side to take the phone. She immediately began to tap on it and Ildaria saw that she was entering G.G.'s name and number in her contacts list.

The older woman had been pleased with her flowers, but almost ecstatic to learn Ildaria was now working for G.G. Over ecstatic really, she thought and worried that the lady, whom she liked a great deal, was finding her presence in her home a trial.

"Of course, I do not find your presence a trial," Marguerite said with exasperation, drawing her attention to the fact that she'd finished her chore and was now holding out the phone.

"Oh." Ildaria flushed as she took back the phone. She wasn't used to people reading her thoughts. Vasco, like herself, didn't read people unless it was absolutely necessary. No one on the ship had. Or at least, no one had made it obvious that they did if they were reading others. Neither had Raffaele if he had read her while she was living with him and Jess, and Jess herself was too new a turn to be able to read anyone. Not that she could have read Ildaria. Younger immortals couldn't read immortals that were older than them. As for Marguerite, as far as she knew her host hadn't read her much since her arrival in her home. At least, she hadn't said anything that gave away that she had read her. Until now, and Ildaria found her doing so a bit discomfiting.

"No, dear. I am not reading you. Not on purpose

anyway. Your thoughts are just a bit loud at the moment," Marguerite announced, moving back to her seat at the table.

"Loud?" Ildaria repeated uncertainly as she returned to her own seat.

"Hmmm." Marguerite focused her attention on pouring more tea into both their cups, and waited until Ildaria had finished sending G.G. the pic of H.D., before commenting, "You obviously didn't try to read G.G., did you?"

"I—No." Ildaria glanced up from her phone with a small frown. "There was no need. G.G. isn't a threat to me."

"No, I agree. G.G. is not a threat to our kind," Marguerite said at once as she pushed her teacup back to her.

"Right," Ildaria murmured, doctoring her fresh tea with sugar and cream.

"Do you know the symptoms that an immortal experiences on meeting a life mate?" Marguerite asked as she lifted her cup to her lips.

Ildaria peered at her blankly. A life mate was something every immortal hoped to find. That being the case, the symptoms of meeting one were well known to their kind from a young age if they were born immortal, and shortly after turning if they were not born immortal. Or usually before they were turned if a life mate turned them. Of course, she knew what the symptoms were. She just didn't understand why Marguerite was asking her that.

Clearing her throat, Ildaria finally said, "Si, of course.

A return of the desire for, and pleasure in, those things that often leave an immortal between the first and second century of their lives," she murmured, and then listed them off. "Food, drink, and sex topmost among them."

Marguerite nodded. "What else?"

"Shared sexual dreams if they sleep within a certain distance," she said now.

"And?"

"Experiencing each other's pleasure when indulging in sexual relations," she said a bit stiffly. "And then usually fainting or passing out at the end of a coupling. Although I've heard of cases where that doesn't happen."

Marguerite made a humming sound and nodded, but then waited expectantly.

Ildaria went through what she'd already said to see what she'd missed, and then added, "The inability to read or control the life mate."

They both fell silent briefly, and then Marguerite said gently, "There's one more symptom, dear."

Ildaria started to shake her head, but then blinked. "Oh, si. Both life mates' thoughts are easily read for the first year or two after finding their life mate, no matter their age."

"Actually, it isn't so much that they are easily read as the immortal's ability to keep their thoughts private is usually hampered after finding a life mate. It's almost as if they're screaming their thoughts. Other immortals can't help but hear them," Marguerite corrected gently and then added, "Like you are presently doing."

Ildaria stared at her blankly. "You think I've met my . . ."

When she fell silent, unable to finish the thought, Marguerite smiled faintly and lifted her cup before commenting, "G.G. is very handsome, is he not?"

Ildaria's eyes widened as she watched Marguerite sip her tea. "G.G.?"

Marguerite raised her eyebrows. "You do not find him handsome?"

"I—" Ildaria hesitated, images of the man rising up in her mind. Looking serious, looking amused, cuddling H.D. . . . Yes, she'd thought him attractive. Adorable even. Especially with the little fur ball in his arms. Dogs and babies always made men more attractive.

"I think you should try to read him tomorrow, dear," Marguerite said softly. "I suspect you will not be able to."

Ildaria started to nod, but then stopped and asked with alarm, "What do I do if I can't?"

"Ah." Marguerite frowned and set her cup down. She stared down at it briefly and then sat back with a sigh. "If you cannot, then I suggest you walk softly. G.G. . . ." She paused to grimace, and then said, "G.G.'s parents were both mortal. His father died in a car accident when he was just a toddler of three. Things were tough for him and his mother for the next two years and then she met Robert Guiscard. They were life mates, and he of course, turned her. Unfortunately, G.G. witnessed his mother's turn."

"Oh, no," Ildaria breathed. Going through the turn was not a pleasant experience. She remembered very little of her own. Most people didn't recall it afterward. But she'd witnessed others during the throes of theirs and it was a terrible, agonizing experience to watch. If the one being turned was tied down, chained down, or otherwise restrained, they screamed, shrieked, and thrashed, trying to break free. During two of the ones she'd witnessed, the turnees had thrashed so wildly they'd broken bones in their wrists, arms, ankles, and legs, just elongating the experience. But if they weren't restrained, they had been known to try to rip their own skin off or claw their eyes out in a desperate bid to end the agony.

Watching his mother go through that would have been more than traumatizing for a five-year-old child, Ildaria thought and shook her head with dismay. "How could they let him see that?"

"He was not supposed to. His mother, Mary, had asked her neighbor, who was also apparently a friend, to take him for the night. But Mary's turning took longer than a night. Sometimes, it does," she added gravely. "But Robert apparently did not realize that, or had not made it clear to Mary. She apparently told the neighbor that she would collect G.G. the next day. I gather her friend thought she meant in the morning, so when she hadn't shown up by noon, the neighbor brought G.G. home, and heard the muffled screaming coming from inside. Unfortunately, she was a good enough friend that she had a key, and she opened the door, in a panic to help her friend. She told G.G. to wait by the door, but he followed her upstairs, arriving at the most inopportune time possible. Mary had just snapped the ropes Robert had used to bind her and was clawing her stomach open in a desperate attempt to end the pain."

"Oh, God," Ildaria breathed with horror.

Marguerite nodded. "Unfortunately, Robert was so distracted between attempting to restrain Mary again and trying to control the hysterical neighbor, that he was completely unaware of G.G.'s presence." She sighed unhappily, and then said, "G.G. told me this some time ago. He said he wanted to run to his mother to comfort her, but she didn't look like herself. Her face seemed to be boiling."

Ildaria grimaced. She'd seen that on a turn a time or two. Usually on mortals who had acne or some other sort of scarring on their face. What young G.G. had thought was her face boiling, was the bioengineered nanos that made immortals what they were, working on removing the scarring and returning the skin to the perfect, unblemished complexion they'd been born with. It was their job. They'd been programmed with blueprints of both a mortal female and a mortal male at their peak condition, and their one directive was to return their host to that peak condition.

"Yes, but G.G. did not know that," Marguerite said on a sigh, obviously catching her thoughts. "So he ran before he was noticed, not stopping until he was outside. I gather the neighbor found him in the front garden, simply standing, staring at nothing when Robert sent her below with her memory erased and the thought that she'd talked to Mary and had agreed to keep G.G. another day."

Ildaria frowned. "Well, surely, once he was returned they read his mind, realized what had happened and erased . . ." Ildaria fell silent. If they'd erased the memory, he couldn't have told Marguerite about it.

"No. They did not realize. When Mary approached G.G. in the garden, he jerked as if just waking up, and then raced away when she tried to grab his hand to take him home. He ran right out into the street, in front of a lorry. It couldn't stop in time to avoid hitting him."

"Oh, sweet heavens above," Ildaria breathed.

Marguerite nodded. "I gather he barely survived the accident, and he woke up in the hospital several days later in terrible pain. Mary's turn had finished and she was at his bedside when he woke, but he had no memory of what had happened at all the day of the accident. He did not remember what he witnessed until years later, on his eighteenth birthday when Mary explained about immortals and offered to turn him. Then it came back to him in a rush of hellish memories." She shook her head unhappily. "Of course, he was hardly going to agree to the turn with that image in his mind."

"Of course not," Ildaria agreed with understanding, but asked, "Why didn't they wipe his memory when it came back to him?"

"It is not that easy," Marguerite said quietly. "You cannot reach in and remove something as old as that without the risk of damaging the mind."

"But—I mean, it may have been an old memory, but he only remembered it in that moment. It was gone before that."

"Not gone. Cloaked," Marguerite assured her. "It was always there in his mind, though, and while he didn't consciously recall it, some part of his mind was aware of it. Apparently, he had terrible nightmares for years after the accident. Mary thought they were because of the accident, but they were about her being an alien or pod person or some such thing."

"Invasion of the Body Snatchers," Ildaria murmured and when Marguerite raised an eyebrow in question, explained, "It was the first movie Jess and I watched when I moved to the States. I gather it was first made in nineteen fifty . . . something, remade in the seventies, and then renamed just *Body Snatchers* and remade again in the nineties. It's about these pods, from space I think, or maybe from the damage caused by pollution or something. I can't remember, but when near sleeping humans they grow perfect replicas of them that then kill them and take over that person's life." She noted Marguerite's wide-eyed expression and grimaced as she realized it didn't really matter what had influenced his dreams about his mother. "Never mind. Go on."

Marguerite nodded, took a moment to regather her thoughts, and then said, "At any rate, the memory was there all along, influencing him subconsciously, even if he couldn't consciously remember it. So, trying to remove it . . ." She shook her head. "It could have damaged him terribly." She paused briefly, and then added, "Besides, now that he knew about immortals, now that she'd explained them to him and he understood what he'd witnessed, it was a less horrifying memory."

"But he still refused to turn," she said, knowing that was the case, because the man was still mortal.

"Yes," Marguerite said unhappily. "He claims he just has no wish to be immortal. He's happy and fine being mortal, but I think what he witnessed is still affecting his choice. He does not wish to go through what he saw his mother suffer." She met her gaze. "Mary was terribly upset when he refused her offer to turn him. No mother wants to lose her child and his not turning meant she would have to watch him age and die. So Robert bought the Night Club in London as a birthday gift for G.G. His hope was that with so much exposure to a varied number of immortals, G.G. would meet one he would be a life mate to and change his mind about the turn. But I do not think it is going to be as easy as that."

Expression becoming grave, Marguerite warned, "I really think you need to take this slowly. If you cannot read him, keep it to yourself as long as you can. Hopefully, once he falls fully in love with you, which—as a life mate—he will not be able to resist doing . . . Hopefully then he will agree to the turn."

"And if not, I get to watch him age and die alongside his mother and have to go on without him," Ildaria said dryly, and then raised her head to the ceiling and growled loudly, "Argh! Why does everything in my life have to be so damned hard? Just once, couldn't you let something be easy?"

Marguerite cleared her throat, and when Ildaria dropped her gaze back to her, said, "I assume you are talking to God?"

"Who else?" she asked, flicking a glare toward the ceiling.

"Yes, well . . . perhaps you should consider that you are very young to find a life mate. Most immortals are not this lucky and have to wait millennia."

"Si, but—"

"And perhaps you should consider that all these difficulties, your troubles in Punta Cana, and then Montana, and now at university here . . . well, they did all work together to land you at the Night Club to meet G.G.," she pointed out gently.

A small smile tugged at the corner of Ildaria's mouth at Marguerite's pointing out the bright side to the hell that had been her life, but then she said, "Actually, *you* sent me to the Night Club to meet G.G., but I get your point. Quit my bitching. I'm lucky to have a problem like this."

"Basically," Marguerite agreed with a smile.

"Right," she breathed and then stood up. "Well, I guess I'll take H.D. upstairs to my room and ponder ways to make G.G. fall in love with me without revealing that we're possible life mates."

"It might help to consider the things he loves best in life," Marguerite suggested.

Ildaria had started to turn away from the table, but paused and swung back now, her eyebrows rising. "Do you know what that might be?"

Marguerite nodded. "His dog, food, and women."

Ildaria's jaw tightened. "Women? In the plural?"

Marguerite shrugged. "It's why women love him. He understands them, appreciates them, admires and loves them; all shapes and sizes and personality types. G.G. loves women."

"Great," Ildaria breathed and bent to scoop up H.D., muttering, "Come on, buddy. You're sleeping with me tonight. Or, at least, *you'll* get to sleep. I've got some thinking to do."

G.G. was on his third cup of coffee when he heard the knock at the Night Club's front door. Setting his cup down, he walked around the bar and headed for the door, moving at a quick clip.

Purely because he was eager to see H.D., G.G. told himself. It had nothing to do with the beautiful and charming Angelina Ildaria Sophia Lupita Garcia Pimienta. Even if just thinking her name made him smile.

Shaking his head at the thought, he quickly moved through the tables and chairs littering the center of this room of the club and unlocked the front door. The moment he opened it, H.D. started barking and launched himself at his legs.

Chuckling, G.G. bent to scoop up the little fur ball, crooning, "Hey buddy. How was your night? Did you miss me?"

"Of course he did." Ildaria's voice, soft and a little husky, brought his eyes to her and his smile widened as he took her in. She'd gone for a professional look for her first day on the job, donning a slim black pencil skirt and a white blouse. Her long, dark hair was up in a bun at the back of her neck, and while she wasn't wearing any foundation or blush on her face, she didn't need it. All immortals had a perfect complexion, but she seemed to have a soft glow to her skin as well. Maybe from years sailing the seas under the Caribbean sun with the wind in her hair, and salt spray peppering her body in the sexy pirate outfit she'd described to him.

All right, he acknowledged, she probably hadn't spent much time in the sun. She was immortal after all. But damn, did she glow. And while she wasn't wearing the face paint most mortal females depended on, she was wearing a bright red lipstick that drew the eye to her pouty lips, as well as a bit of eyeliner that accented her large, gorgeous deep brown and gold eyes. She looked beautiful, he acknowledged, and then realizing he was blocking her from entering the building while he stood gawping at her like a love-struck teenager, G.G. cleared his throat, muttered a gruff, "Morning," and turned away to head back to the bar, leaving her to follow.

"How was traffic?" he asked as he claimed one of the high-back bar stools, settled H.D. in his lap, and reached for his coffee.

"It started to pick up at the end of the drive, but was good most of the way," Ildaria said lightly, taking the seat next to his.

It put her close enough that he could smell her perfume, a mix of vanilla and spice. It made him think of muffins, which made him hungry. And then he became aware of the heat coming off her body, and realized that if he shifted just the tiniest bit to his left, his arm would rub against hers. It made G.G. think perhaps they had too many bar stools along the bar. Maybe a few should be removed and the remaining stools spaced out farther to give customers more personal space.

"How was your night?" she asked.

Fighting the urge to shift a bit to his left to better feel her heat and perhaps even rub up against her, G.G. took a sip of coffee before answering. "Good. Busy as usual. Thanks for the pictures," he added, recalling the photos she'd sent him during the course of the night and morning. The first had been of H.D. cuddled up with Julius on a dog bed, the pair both sleeping. The next had been of H.D. curled up against Ildaria's legs on a bed. The picture had focused mainly on H.D. and had only shown her legs from mid-thigh down, but they'd been bare, and he'd found himself staring at them and wondering what she wore to bed, if anything. The next two pictures had been waiting for him when he'd woken up this morning, one of H.D. and Julius playing in Marguerite's large backyard. The other of H.D. and Julius, side by side, gobbling up their breakfast. The last picture she'd sent had been just a little more than half an hour ago and had been of H.D. standing on the front passenger seat of the car, looking out the half-open window, his fur blowing in the breeze. Which reminded him—

"You shouldn't be taking pictures while you're driving. You could have got in an accident."

"We were stopped at the end of Marguerite's driveway, waiting to turn onto the road when I took that picture," she assured him with a faint smile, and then explained away the windblown effect by adding, "It's windy today."

"Oh." He nodded, but the tension in him didn't ease much. He just couldn't seem to relax for some reason. G.G. had no idea why. He wasn't usually tense around women.

"Have you had breakfast yet?" she asked suddenly, and he glanced her way in surprise, and almost wished he hadn't looked. Damn, she was smiling at him so sweetly, her luscious lips curved up, red and wet, as if she'd just licked them, and he had the sudden urge to lick them too.

"No," he said finally, forcing his gaze away from her lips. "I slept in. I've only been up half an hour or so. Took a shower, made coffee . . ." He shrugged.

"And fixed your hair," she teased lightly, her gaze sliding up to the Mohawk he'd tended to and formed after stepping out of the shower. He'd had the Mohawk so long, that fixing it every morning was second nature, and now took only a couple of minutes to do. G.G. was used to the looks he drew with it, and hardly noticed them anymore. Usually. But right now, with Ildaria examining the tall straight strands, he found himself shifting uncomfortably and wondering—not for the first time—if he wasn't getting too old for the style. But when he felt his face heat up a bit and realized he was actually blushing like a kid, he slid off the bar stool and started away from her, heading for the swinging doors, muttering, "I should grab some toast or something."

"Toast?" Ildaria exclaimed with dismay and he heard the *tap tap tap* of high heels behind him. With H.D. tucked under his arm like a football, G.G. couldn't resist glancing back and down to see her shoes. He'd missed them on first greeting her, but now saw they were shiny, black, high-heeled pumps. Damn. She looked like a sexy secretary.

"A big guy like you needs protein not just toast for breakfast," Ildaria said now, drawing his gaze back up to her smiling face. "I'll make you an omelet."

Grunting, G.G. turned and led the way into the Night Club's tidy kitchen. It wasn't as large as one would

find in a mortal club, but it wasn't tiny either. Most of
the room was taken up with industrial refrigerators to
store the blood, but there was also a grill, oven, microwave, and pots and pans dangling from a center rack.

G.G. had renovated the kitchen when he'd taken it
over. He worked from well before dusk, to long after
dawn in the Night Club, and as a mortal, he had to
eat. He hadn't wanted to be running out to fast food
joints for every meal, so a kitchen had been a necessity. Now, he paused and swung back toward Ildaria,
absently petting the still snuggling H.D. as he took in
her reaction to the kitchen.

"Nice," she pronounced, but her eyes were wide and
glowing as she peered around the gleaming stainless
steel surfaces. Returning her gaze to him, she raised
her eyebrows. "So? An omelet. Si?"

"I don't want you to go to any trouble," G.G. said
mildly, but the mention of an omelet had made his
mouth start watering, and he was glad when she went
to check out the refrigerators, quickly finding the
smaller one with food inside of it.

"No trouble," she assured him. "And look. You have
the ingredients."

G.G. looked, but not at the eggs, cheese, onions,
and peppers she was retrieving. Instead, his gaze
landed and stayed on her bottom where her skirt had
pulled tight over her generous curves as she bent to
check the shelves.

"How can I help?" G.G. asked, forcing his gaze
away from her behind when she straightened.

"Make toast," Ildaria instructed, carrying what she'd

found to the stainless steel prep table before returning to the refrigerator for milk.

He watched her set the milk by the other ingredients, but when she grabbed a knife and began to clean and dice the vegetables, he set H.D. down and moved to fetch bread, butter, a plate, and a knife, before pausing to ask, "Have you had breakfast? Shall I get you a plate too?"

"No. I'm good," she assured him. "Marguerite makes big breakfasts every morning and I ate before we left."

Nodding, he carried the items to the counter where the toaster waited, and set everything down.

They worked in silence for a minute, and then Ildaria asked, "So . . . you never did answer my question yesterday. How did a mortal end up owning and running an immortal Night Club?"

G.G. looked around at that question, his gaze sliding over her figure as she worked. He would have expected her to ask Marguerite, or for Marguerite to volunteer the answer, but apparently not. Or perhaps she wanted to hear it from his point of view, so he divulged, "My mother and father bought it for me for my eighteenth birthday."

"Wow." She kept her gaze on the knife as she quickly chopped the peppers, both red and green, he noticed. "I've heard of watches, bracelets, and even cars being given on special birthdays. But this is the first time I've heard of someone being given a business."

"Yeah." G.G. made a face she didn't see and quickly opened the bread. "It was a bit over the top. I paid them back for it as quickly as I could out of the profits."

"Really?" She turned to eye him with surprise.

G.G. nodded, but didn't comment further and turned his back to her to set four pieces of bread in the double toaster.

Ildaria was silent for a moment, the only sound in the room the *clack, clack, clack* of the knife hitting the stainless steel surface, and then she commented. "You call Robert your father."

G.G. shrugged. "He's the only father I know. I don't remember my birth father. And Robert has been my dad in every way that's important since I was five. That's thirty-two years. He's earned the title."

G.G. glanced over in time to see her nod and curiosity made him ask, "What about you?"

"What about me?" she asked easily.

"What about your parents?" he clarified. "Are they—?"

"Dead," she said, her voice flat. "Long dead."

G.G. considered that, but then asked, "They weren't immortal?"

"No." Ildaria's voice was almost hollow.

"So you were turned at some point," he said, frowning now as the memory of his mother's screams of agony rang in his ears, and the vision of the skin on her face jumping and rippling as if it were boiling came to mind along with the way she'd clawed at her stomach, as if trying to tear it open. Robert had been trying to stop her, but she had been unstoppable and G.G. had fled at the first sight of blood appearing under her clawing fingers.

"I was turned in a back alley in Punta Cana when I was fourteen."

The words drew G.G.'s mind from his memories and he peered at her sharply. Her voice sounded empty, emotionless on the subject. He frowned briefly, and then said, almost with disbelief, "Your life mate turned you in a back alley?"

"He was not my life mate," she said grimly.

"A rogue turned you?" he asked, his brow furrowing with concern.

"No. Si. I don't know," she said finally. "He was an asshole who attacked me, but I do not know if that makes him rogue." After a pause, she admitted, "I turned myself, by accident, while fighting him off." Sweeping the peppers up in her hands, she dumped them into a frying pan with butter and then plucked up the onion only to pause and purse her lips. "You like onions and peppers, don't you?"

"Yes," he said at once, and watched her relax and start to work at dicing the onion now. He wanted to ask about the attack and how she'd accidentally turned herself, but she suddenly seemed . . . removed. As if she had shut down her emotions. It seemed better to wait. Besides, it had probably been something like how Jackie Argeneau had been turned. Jackie was a private detective and the wife of Vincent Argeneau, one of Marguerite's nephews. Jackie had bit into an immortal's arm during an attack, and then had held on, inadvertently swallowing the nano-filled blood as she struggled with her attacker. She'd got enough to start the change. An accidental turn you could say.

The sound of the toast popping caught his ear, and G.G. turned to snatch the hot pieces of crusty bread out of the toaster. He dropped them on the plate and began to slather them with butter.

"Do you have any brothers or sisters?"

G.G. shook his head in answer, but then realizing she was watching what she was doing and not looking up to see the small movement, he said, "No. Only child."

"Your mother and Robert haven't had a child of their own yet?" she asked with surprise.

"Not yet," he said easily, and then smiled faintly and added, "But I'm sure they will. I think my mother just wanted to wait until I was grown up. Or maybe they just wanted to enjoy each other for a while before getting into diapers and teething." Finished buttering the toast, he set the knife aside and carried the plate to where she was working, adding, "I can't imagine teething is fun with fangs."

Ildaria chuckled at the suggestion. "No. I don't suppose it is."

He watched her finish with the onions and gather those up to throw in with the peppers and then commented, "Come to that, I doubt breastfeeding is fun with fangs either." After a brief pause he added thoughtfully, "Or maybe not. Like mortal babies, immortal ones probably don't have teeth when they're born."

Ildaria seemed to consider his words seriously for a moment, and then confessed, "I don't know. But the job of the nanos is to see to our well-being. That means getting blood. Immortal babies need blood too, so they might be born with fangs already in place."

G.G. grimaced at the thought of a cute little cuddly baby with fangs. Except . . . "Your fangs don't show though. I mean, unless you're using them. They just look like normal canines until they shift and drop or whatever it is they do."

"True." She grabbed a spatula from the metal canister full of cooking utensils and used it to move the diced peppers and onions around in the pan. "So maybe they're born with their fangs looking like canines as ours do."

"I'm guessing from your words that you've never seen an immortal baby either?" G.G. asked now, curious.

"No," Ildaria said quietly. "I lived in the poorer areas of the Dominican Republic. The immortals I knew couldn't afford to buy enough blood to feed themselves properly, let alone a baby. And unlike mortals, they don't expect the government or others to pay for them or their offspring. They simply do not have children."

"And lure tourists out to international waters to feed themselves," he suggested dryly.

Her gaze slid to meet his, unrepentant and a little cold. "Do not expect me to apologize for doing what I had to, to survive. A lion doesn't feel guilty for eating a zebra, and I don't feel guilty for what I've done. At least, my donors survived, and I made sure they always left with the memory that they had fun and were happy. Which is more than you can say for the poor zebra."

"Even the ones who attacked you?" he asked.

Ildaria's mouth firmed, anger flashing briefly across her face before she had it under control. "Even they left feeling happy and believing they had a good time." Turning back to the pan, she muttered, "Though they didn't deserve it."

G.G. immediately felt bad, but when he opened his mouth to apologize, she suggested, "You should put your toast in the oven on low so it doesn't get cold. This will be another minute."

Sighing, he carried the plate to the oven, set it inside and turned the knob to warm. Feeling something rub against his leg then, he glanced down and spotted H.D. pawing at him.

"Hey, buddy," he murmured, scooping him up again. Rubbing the little beast affectionately between the ears, he carried him back to where Ildaria was working. She'd turned the heat down under the peppers and onions, and was now grating cheddar cheese.

"I can do that for you," G.G. offered.

Ildaria hesitated, but then set the grater and cheese in the bowl, and pushed the whole thing toward him before reaching for another bowl and the eggs.

Setting H.D. down again, G.G. began to grate cheese, but his mind was chasing itself in circles in search of something to say to get them back to the relaxed and happier state they'd been in before he'd said something stupid. In the end, sticking to business seemed the safest bet and he began to explain the accounting methods he used in England and what would have to be done to satisfy the Canadian government when it came to taxes. She listened, occasionally commenting, or asking a question as she continued to cook, and it seemed like no time at all had passed before she was sliding a beautiful, perfectly formed omelet stuffed with cheese, peppers, and onions onto a plate and topping it with a dollop of salsa.

"Grab your toast, and sit down wherever you're going to eat. I'll fetch you a coffee," Ildaria said as she pushed the plate toward him.

G.G. didn't argue. The aroma coming off the omelet was heavenly and he couldn't wait to try it. Carrying the plate to the oven, he opened the door and started to reach in, but paused when a dish towel appeared in front of his face.

"It will probably be hot," Ildaria pointed out, placing the folded dish towel in his hand.

"Thanks," he mumbled, and used the cloth to grab the plate. Since he could feel the heat through the layered material, it seemed obvious the cloth had been a good idea. Shaking his head at his own thoughtlessness, he pushed the oven door closed with his elbow and then paused to stare at the knobs, debating how to turn the oven off with his hands full. Perhaps if he set the toast plate on—

"I'll get it. You go on and start eating before your breakfast gets cold," Ildaria called from her position by the coffeepot.

G.G. didn't have to be told twice. He turned and carried his plates out to the bar, pausing with the swing door open long enough for H.D. to scoot through. He chose one of the booths rather than the bar. That way, H.D. could curl up on the seat next to him. He'd barely settled himself and the dog when he realized he didn't have any silverware.

Before he could scoot out, Ildaria came through the swing doors with two coffees, the cup handles caught through the fingers of one hand, and silverware clutched in the other. She also had a jar of marmalade and a jar of raspberry jam caught between her arm and one breast. The woman thought of everything. She was also showing her waitressing expertise.

The omelet was amazing, and G.G. gobbled it up pretty quickly, grateful that she'd not only suggested it, but had made it for him. They then talked more about what the job entailed over their coffees, until Ildaria nodded and slid out from her side of the booth, taking his dirty plates and both their cups with her.

"All right, then. I think I've got it. I'll take H.D. into your office and get started, so you can prep for tonight's opening."

G.G. wanted to protest that she didn't have to go yet, that there was plenty of time. He was enjoying talking to her. But then his gaze slid to his watch and his eyes widened. They'd been talking for a lot longer than he'd realized. Three hours had passed since she'd walked in with H.D. The clientele would start arriving soon.

"I gave H.D. the last container of food for breakfast," Ildaria announced as G.G. picked up the jam and marmalade. "Where will I find the food for his lunch and dinner?"

"It's in the refrigerator in my apartment," G.G. said, giving H.D. a nudge to get him to hop off the end of the seat so he could slide out of the booth. "I'll run up and grab a couple now."

"Okay." She smiled and then turned away saying lightly, "Come on H.D., we're going to the kitchen."

The words were enough to make H.D. follow her. He even pranced happily at her side, his tail and ears flopping as he looked up at her and then ahead, before looking up at her eagerly again. The dog might not be able to talk, but he certainly understood a lot, and *kitchen* was one of those words he liked best since it usually meant food or a treat coming.

G.G. shook his head with amusement at the dog's behavior, and then his attention slid to Ildaria, landing briefly on her sexy high-heeled shoes before moving up to her legs. The woman had killer legs with delicate little ankles and strong, slender calves. She was also wearing stockings with seams down the back, which was just sexy as hell, he decided before following those seams up to her black skirt. Now he noticed there was a slit up the back, just enough to make walking in the pencil skirt possible. It reached halfway up the back of her legs, showing a hint of the top of her stockings so that he could tell she was wearing thigh highs and a garter belt of some sort . . . which was sexy as hell to him. Damn. Who knew accountants/dog sitters could be so hot?

Down boy, he thought grimly. Lusting after Ildaria was wrong on so many levels. Not only was she an employee, which made her off-limits, but she was an immortal. Not for him.

Suspecting he'd have to remind himself of that often, G.G. set the jam and marmalade he was carrying on the bar and took the hall to the back of the building. He'd go up and get H.D.'s food . . . and maybe take a very fast, very cold shower.

Five

"Who's a pretty puppy? Hmmm?"

G.G. paused in the doorway to his apartment at those words. Blinking, he glanced inside but all he could see was the end of the dining room table on the right at the far end of the room, and the back of his couch across from it on the left.

"Who's a pretty puppy?"

Letting the door ease silently closed, he locked it and then started up the hall, passing the open door to the bathroom on the right and the closet on the left before the hall opened up to a large open space with the kitchen and dining area on his right and the living room on the left, both ending at a large wall of windows. What the building lacked in windows on the main floor, it made up for on the third and fourth floors. His apartment was one of two on the fourth floor. High, plate glass windows made up the outer wall here and in all the other apartments in the building. It made for a light, airy atmosphere that he usually enjoyed. But at the moment, he paid the view and the lighting little attention. Instead, his gaze found and fixed on the woman and dog in the open area between the gas fireplace and the coffee table in front of the couch.

H.D. was lying on his back on the large three-foot round dog bed. Ildaria was on her elbows and knees, her arm backs flat on the dog bed, cocooning H.D. between them, as she cooed, "Who's a pretty puppy?" She then leaned down to nuzzle the happy dog around the cheeks and neck, then gave him a smacking kiss on his chest between his front legs before raising up to coo again, "Who's a pretty puppy?"

H.D. was wriggling ecstatically, rolling his head from side to side with delight, and Ildaria's bottom was waving about as she moved, her skirt pulled tight over her gorgeous butt.

G.G. had the mad urge to rush over, drop onto the floor before her and say, "I am, I'm a pretty puppy." And beg her to hold and nuzzle him that way. Instead, he simply stood, watching her repeat the routine one final time, and then she ducked her head to nuzzle and kiss H.D. before scooping him up and suddenly rolling onto her back, taking H.D. with her so that he landed with his body on her chest and his face above hers. H.D. immediately set to licking her face with eager excitement, and Ildaria laughed and twisted her neck from side to side to keep him from getting her nose or mouth with his little, wet tongue. Her body was rolling back and forth during this exercise, her legs shifting and her pencil skirt sliding up her legs a bit more with each movement.

G.G. was watching its slow ride upward with breathless anticipation when H.D. suddenly stilled, his head jerking in his direction like a heat-seeking missile finding its target. In the next moment, the dog abandoned Ildaria with one leaping bound and raced toward G.G., ears flopping and fluffy tail wagging.

Disappointment pinched G.G. at the end to the game he'd been watching, but he forced it back and managed a smile as he knelt to greet his dog.

"Hey, buddy. Did you have a good night with Ildaria? Hmm?" he asked lightly, scooping up the little fur ball and cuddling and petting him as he straightened. His gaze slid back to Ildaria to find that she was on her feet, her skirt dropping to cover her shapely legs as she tugged her blouse back into place and then reached up to check her hair.

The neat bun she'd arrived in and managed to keep for the first eight hours that she'd worked in his office, had loosened and fallen. Most of her hair was a long black wave, ending at the part still caught in the knot. Grimacing, she tugged the fastener loose and let her hair fall free. She then moved toward him in a relaxed walk, a smile claiming her lips.

"All done for the night?"

"Yeah." Hearing the husky sound to his voice, G.G. cleared his throat and nodded. "All done."

"Great." She beamed at him brightly and moved past him, giving H.D. a pat on the head. "I guess I'll head back to Marguerite's then. He was good, by the way.

Didn't eat a single thing he shouldn't, or get into any trouble. What time do you want me back tomorrow?"

G.G. turned, watching as she scooped up her shoes, and bent to slip on one then the other. They were damned sexy shoes with a little black bow on each heel that he hadn't noticed earlier.

"G.G.?"

He liked the way the nickname sounded on her lips, kind of husky and sweet. Then he realized she was waiting for an answer, and cleared his throat again. "The club doesn't open until sunset. Half an hour before that is fine. I only had you come in early today so I could give you some pointers on the bookkeeping. But I can keep H.D. with me until the club opens."

"Awesome." She gave him a brilliant smile. "That means I have time for a nap before I go apartment hunting."

"Apartment hunting?" His gaze had dropped to her legs and feet in the pretty little shoes again, but he lifted it back to her face with interest.

"Well, I can't stay with Marguerite and Julius forever," she pointed out with a wry smile. "I've felt guilty staying with them at all. And that's on me, not because they've acted like I'm a burden," she assured him, as if he might believe Marguerite had made her feel unwelcome. "They've been really kind, but I'm not used to depending on others. Fortunately, now that I have not one, but two full-time jobs, I don't have to. I can use the money I've saved up for first and last months' rent and save the money for my tuition out of my wages." She shrugged. "So I'll take a nap and then get up and start searching the internet for apartments."

"Or you could stay here." The words were out of his mouth before his brain could filter them. But when she stood with her mouth open, her eyes blinking in surprise, he mentally reviewed what he'd said and quickly added, "I mean in the building. This is one of four apartments above the club. There are two on the third floor and two on this floor. Sofia—she works the bar," he paused to explain before continuing, "She has one of the apartments on the third floor, and I'm the only one on this floor. There are still two apartments available, one on each floor. I expected one of them would go to the bookkeeper and the other to the dog sitter if they didn't already have a place in the city. But—" He shrugged wryly and pointed out, "You're both the dog sitter and the bookkeeper so get your choice of apartments."

When she didn't respond right away, he added, "H.D.'s last sitter was mortal. I couldn't find an immortal to do it, and had to make do with a mortal. Fortunately, she already lived in the city because I wouldn't have been comfortable with offering her an apartment here. It was risky even having her around the building, but I was desperate. I did make it clear she was never to step foot in the Night Club though."

He paused briefly, but her continued silence made him add, "Living here would solve your apartment problem, and the rent is cheap. Also, you wouldn't need to commute to work, just head downstairs, and if an emergency crops up you'll be nearby, and . . ." He let his voice trail away, not for lack of excuses to move her into the building, but because he realized he was yapping. G.G. wasn't a yapper. Usually. He was a listener. Women loved to talk and he was always happy to listen. They revealed so much about themselves when talking and he'd always found women fascinating.

"Si, it would be handy," Ildaria agreed finally, a small smile playing on her lips, and he could feel the wide, probably goofy smile, stretching his own lips. Damn, this woman affected him oddly.

"Well, can I see them?" she asked finally when a full minute had passed in silence.

"Oh, yes, of course," he muttered, realizing while he'd stood there gaping at her, she'd been waiting for him to make the offer. Turning, he hurried into the kitchen to grab the keys to the empty apartments.

Rejoining her in the hall, he shifted H.D. under one arm and unlocked his apartment door, then held it for her to precede him into the corridor.

"As you know the Night Club takes up the first two floors of the building, but there are also a storage room and laundry room for the club on the third floor. So the two apartments there are smaller with just one bedroom each. The apartments on this floor are much larger and nicer and have two bedrooms each. Sofia was already in one of the third floor apartments when I took over the place. I offered her the chance to move up to the other larger apartment on this floor, but she didn't want the hassle of moving," he explained and then added, "Sofia usually works behind the bar. I think you met her tonight. Well, last night now," he corrected, remembering that it was now morning. Working the hours that he did, it was hard to keep the days straight at times. To him, this was still yesterday and would be until he went to bed. For the rest of the world, it was already a new day.

"Si," Ildaria said, distracting him from his thoughts. He could hear the smile in her voice as she added, "Sofia introduced herself to me. So did the other servers in the club; Char, Ruby, Ryia, Rowan, and Elijah. They all seemed nice."

"Yeah. They are, and good at their jobs too," G.G. said as he led her across the hall to the second apartment. As he unlocked that door, he added, "Lucern was good at choosing employees. Sofia is the only one who lives in the building though. She's basically the manager. Runs the place when I'm not here and so on. The rest of the servers all share a house nearby. And, here we are," he said as the door swung open.

Stepping aside, he let her enter and then followed, absently rubbing H.D. under the chin as he glanced around the large open space, trying to see what she was seeing and hoping she liked it.

"It's huge. As big as your place," Ildaria said with amazement as she looked around the living room area and the kitchen.

"Yeah. It's the same size, the mirror image of my apartment," he murmured, absently setting H.D. down when the dog kicked his feet, making it known he wanted to explore.

"Oh, G.G., it's beautiful," she breathed, staring at the wall of windows, before turning to move up the short hall to inspect the bedrooms.

He smiled wryly at the claim. It was a huge empty

room really. Although there were appliances in the kitchen, a long island separating it from the living room, a fireplace in the living room, and a stacked washer and drier in a closet in the hall to the bedrooms. But other than that, it was an empty space waiting to be filled. Not what he would call beautiful.

"I couldn't possibly afford this," Ildaria said a moment later as she came back into the living room. She was shaking her head, her expression full of regret. "I mean, this place must cost an arm and a leg, and while you're going to be paying me well . . ." She sighed unhappily. "If I didn't need to finish my degree, I could afford it. But I have to—"

"I give employees a cut rate," he said quickly, and it wasn't a lie. He'd left Sofia's rent at the same low rate it had been before he'd taken over the Night Club. And the house the others lived in was part of the Night Club sale. He'd left that rent alone too even though the rental rates for both the apartments and the house were probably a quarter of what he could get if he rented to mortals. But having mortals coming and going from the building that housed the Night Club was not a smart idea. Besides, happy employees were good employees to his mind, and giving them a safe, low priced place to live went a long way toward making them happy. So, G.G. told her the amount Sofia paid, added fifty bucks to it for the extra bedroom, and then held his breath, waiting for her decision. For some reason, he really, really wanted her to live in this apartment.

"You're kidding?" she asked with disbelief. "That's all?"

"That's it," he assured her.

Ildaria bit her lip and peered around the apartment silently, but then murmured, "I suppose I should at least look at the one-bedroom too."

"Of course," he said at once, and then on inspiration added, "I just thought this way you'd have a spare room for Vasco, or Jess and Raffaele to stay in if you wanted them to visit."

That made her pause and her eyes widen, as she no doubt considered being able to invite people to visit. He was pretty sure she was struggling between fiscal responsibility—i.e. taking the less expensive one-bedroom apartment—and the freedom to have people over which was only fifty dollars more a month. Feeling oddly desperate to have her on this floor with him, he reminded her, "And I of course, will pay your university tuition now that you're working for me."

Ildaria had started to turn to survey the apartment again, but swung back at that, eyes wide and mouth agape. "What?"

"I pay half the tuition for the courses any of my employees want whether at college or university or just Dale Carnegie or something," he informed her. "Both here and in the UK. In fact, Elijah's taking courses at the university right now and I paid half his tuition."

Ildaria frowned. "So you'd pay half mine too?"

"All of it," he corrected. "I'd pay your full tuition."

Ildaria had started to shake her head before he finished speaking. "Half is one thing if you do that with all your employees, but why would you offer to pay the full ride for me?"

"It's a smart business move," he assured her. "I was desperate for an accountant. I've been looking for one since the day I bought this place. Now that I've found you, I want you to keep working for me after you get your degree, not run off to work somewhere else," he said, and that was the truth, but only part of it. He *was* desperate for an accountant, but he was also oddly desperate to have her live here, close to him, where he could see her every day, even on days she wasn't working, and G.G. wasn't sure why. At least . . . well, obviously he liked her. He liked that she cared enough about her friends that one of them being attacked had made her go vigilante. He liked that after being pulled from Montana and dragged down here, she'd risked getting in further trouble to help strangers in peril. And he respected her like hell for taking responsibility for her own actions and accepting the punishment for them rather than trying to blame someone else.

G.G. also liked her determination to get the education she wanted. A lot of people would have given up after being pulled from the same classes for the second time and losing the money they'd worked hard for and invested in those classes, but she was already signed up for the next semester. Angelina Ildaria Sophia Lupita Garcia Pimienta was smart, and brave and determined and he liked her. In fact, he already liked and respected her more than every one of the women he'd dated over the years.

Which was scary as hell when he thought about it. Ildaria was an immortal, and G.G. was a mortal who had no intention of turning. This could not end well.

Pushing that worry aside, he finished what he'd been saying by pointing out, "Many companies pay for upgrading skills or degrees of their employees. I'm happy to pay your full tuition."

Ildaria bit her lip briefly, obviously considering the offer. But in the end she said, "Thank you, but no. I probably will continue to work for you after I get my degree. So far, it seems like a great working environment, but no. I'll pay for my own education. All of it." She hesitated and then added almost apologetically, "It's something I have to do myself. A pride thing. I hope you understand."

G.G. nodded slowly, getting it. It had been important to him to pay his parents back for the Night Club in England. He'd wanted to succeed on his own and suspected she felt much the same way. "Yeah. I understand."

She relaxed and smiled as she added, "But I will take this apartment and not the one-bedroom. With what you're paying me, I can afford it. In fact, it is much less than I expected to have to pay for an apartment. Less even than I thought I'd have to pay to share an apartment with someone. And it would be nice to be able to invite Jess and Raffaele here to visit."

He noticed that she didn't mention Vasco, and wondered about it, but before he could ponder it too hard, Ildaria said, "Well then, it looks like I don't have to search for an apartment after all." Grinning, she asked, "When can I move in?"

"Whenever you want. Here are the keys," he said, unhooking this apartment's key ring from the larger ring and offering them to her. "Bring some stuff back with you tonight, or hire a truck when you can to bring it all."

"Thank you," she said sincerely as she took the keys. "I'll bring a cashier's check for first and last months' rent when I return tonight."

G.G. shook his head. "Use that to buy furniture or anything else you might need. I'll take first and last out of your first paycheck. Payday is every two weeks, by the way."

"Oh." She beamed and then frowned by turn, and headed for the door, muttering, "I need to go shopping."

G.G. smiled to himself and then glanced to where H.D. was nosing his way around the room. He whistled for the dog to come, and then followed Ildaria out of the apartment, the little fur ball chasing after him.

"You cannot sleep on a sleeping bag," Marguerite said with exasperation. "Take your bed. It can be my housewarming gift to you."

"That's so sweet, Marguerite. But I bought a new bed on my way home," Ildaria assured her. After hitting the furniture store for a new bed . . . well, really just a mattress and box spring, Ildaria had hit the dollar store as well as JYSK and Walmart to pick up a set of dishes, silverware, glasses, and cooking utensils. Everything she'd bought was on sale or pretty cheap to begin with and it would all do her just fine. Ildaria had also purchased towels, sheets, pillows, and a comforter, as well as toilet paper, and various kitchen items. Cheap as each item had been, in the end she'd spent a lot of money. It was amazing how quickly you went through money when having to furnish an apartment. She'd had nothing of her own to take except for her clothes and the small thirty-two-inch television she'd bought while in Montana. She'd purchased it for her bedroom there so that Jess and Raffaele could have the living room to themselves some nights. She'd brought it with her when she'd moved to Canada.

Ildaria still needed a couch, chairs, a dining room set, etc. But she'd get all that as she could. Sleep was the most important thing. She needed to be well rested for working with numbers. And really, she could sit and relax in bed until she had everything else, Ildaria thought and then noticed the concentration on Marguerite's face, and realized the older woman was reading her mind. Marguerite obviously didn't believe she'd bought a bed. Probably because she'd asked to borrow the sleeping bag, foolishly mentioning she planned to sleep on it.

"I did buy a bed," she assured her, deciding to save her the trouble of reading her. "But it won't be delivered until next week. The sleeping bag is just a temporary solution until it arrives."

"Or you could stay here until it arrives," Marguerite suggested at once. "We are more than happy to have you stay, Ildaria. In fact, I have enjoyed your company and will be sorry to see you go."

Ildaria had spent her life on the run, keeping barriers between herself and others by necessity. Both to keep herself safe, and to keep others safe as well. But her situation had changed, and at those sweet words from Marguerite, a woman she liked and respected, Ildaria felt some of those shields collapse and her heart go a little mushy. It made her smile, and she instinctively hugged the woman as she said, "And I've enjoyed being here. You and Julius and furry Julius are wonderful." Releasing Marguerite, she stepped back and added, "But I'll feel better in my own place. I—I'm not used to leaning on others."

"I understand." Marguerite patted her shoulder gently. "But that is what family is for, Ildaria, and I now consider you family. Please remember that in the future, especially if you need anything. Anything at all," she added firmly.

Ildaria swallowed a sudden lump in her throat, and nodded before managing to get out a husky "I will."

"Good." Marguerite nodded. "Then I shall go search for the sleeping bag and—"

"You don't have to do that," Ildaria interrupted, not wanting to put her out. "Just tell me where to look and I'll—"

"You," Marguerite interrupted firmly, "will go ahead and drive over to the Night Club. You have a lot of stuff to unpack and put away before work. I'll find the sleeping bag and follow. I should like to see this apartment anyway. We can have tea."

"Oh. Si, of course." Ildaria smiled crookedly and nodded, but she was thinking she would have to stop at the grocery store on the way. Food was something she'd neglected during her shopping spree. Fortunately, she still had a little money left, certainly enough to buy tea, sugar, and milk. Maybe some cookies too. Maybe, she'd even have enough left over for bread and peanut butter to eat until her first paycheck, Ildaria thought as she gave Marguerite a distracted parting wave and headed out to her car.

Thinking of her first paycheck from the Night Club had her recalling that it was almost Friday, which was payday at the part-time waitressing job she'd managed to get and the only reason she had the money she'd just spent. Which, in turn, made her realize that she hadn't yet given her notice there and she was scheduled for an afternoon shift the next day.

That wasn't so bad, Ildaria decided. She could manage the shift and still make it to her job at the Night Club on time. But she'd have to give them notice . . . and spend her break switching any evening shifts they'd scheduled her for with someone who had day shifts so that she could finish out the standard two weeks. The manager there was a good person, she didn't want to just leave her high and dry with no time to hire a replacement. Unfortunately, that would mean a lot of hours working between the two places for the next two weeks, but she could handle it. Besides, it would give her more money for food. Something she was much more interested in now that she'd met G.G. Her flagging appetite had returned. If she was lucky, she might even make enough in tips to buy a chair or something to sit on besides the bed.

That had her smiling faintly as she got in her old silver Ford Fusion. It had belonged to Jess's deceased parents. Jess had let her use it to get to school and her job and such when she'd first moved in with her, and then had sold it to her cheap when Ildaria had scraped enough money together to buy it.

Ildaria loved her car.

It was old, at least ten years, but it was in great shape, and worked well. Judging by the mileage on it, Jess's parents hadn't had it long before they'd died. She suspected it had been left to sit in the garage between then and when Jess had given it to her to use. Whatever the case, it hadn't given her a lick of trouble since she'd bought it, and it gave her the freedom to go where she needed to go.

Right now her car was stuffed with her television and the shopping bags holding all the things she'd bought today. The front passenger seat was the only available space for the groceries she planned to get on the way to her new apartment.

Her new apartment.

Just thinking the words made Ildaria smile. She knew she was rushing it moving in this quickly and with absolutely no furniture. Certainly, continuing to stay with Marguerite and Julius would have been more comfortable.

But she was desperate for a home of her own. A place where she wasn't beholden to others. Ildaria hated that feeling. It was probably her worst flaw. She'd rather go hungry and sleep on a cold, hard floor than accept charity, and kind and sweet as Marguerite and Julius had been to her, she was still very conscious of the fact that she was residing in their home, a charity case. At least to her mind.

Pulling on her seat belt, Ildaria started the engine, and headed off, mentally working out how much money she had left and what she could afford to buy with it. In the end, she was able to buy tea, cream, sugar, bread, peanut butter, and even some bakery cookies to serve with the tea. She still had no idea where she and Marguerite would sit while they had it, but was hoping G.G. would let her borrow a couple of the high-backed bar stools from the Night Club if she promised to bring them back down before the club opened at sunset. If so, they could sit at her island to enjoy their tea and cookies.

Before seeing her off that morning, G.G. had shown her the back door to the Night Club and apartments, and told her how to access it through an alley of sorts behind the building. He'd also given her a spot in the small parking lot behind the building. Ildaria parked, gathered several bags and headed for the door to the back of the building. She didn't have any problem with the lock, and didn't run into anyone on her first two trips up to her apartment. Ildaria wasn't surprised. G.G. was mortal. Unlike immortals he couldn't make up for a short sleep by taking in extra blood. He'd need the full eight hours and since it was after eight by the time he'd seen her off that morning, and it was only 2:30 in the afternoon now, she suspected he'd sleep a couple more hours.

However, on her third trip into the building, she encountered Sofia obviously on her way out.

"You're up early," Ildaria said lightly, moving to the side to allow the other woman to pass.

"G.G. only makes two of us stay to help with cleanup each night. Last night was my night off cleaning duty.

I was in bed by 6 A.M. I've had plenty of sleep," she said with a smile and then glanced at the bags Ildaria was carrying. "Moving in?"

"G.G. told you?" Ildaria asked with surprise, but knew at once that such couldn't be the case. Sofia had just told her that she'd been in bed since 6 A.M. and G.G. hadn't offered her the apartment until after that.

"No. But you're working here now, and it's early to start work so . . ." She shrugged and then nodded toward the bags in her hands, and asked, "Is there more? Can I help?"

"Oh, you don't have to . . ." Ildaria's voice trailed away when Sofia took half her bags and turned to lead her inside and up the stairs. It seemed she was getting help whether she liked it or not, Ildaria thought and followed with a wry, "All righty then."

"Oh, get over it," Sofia said with amusement. "You work at the Night Club now. You're part of the family. And we help each other. Get used to it."

Ildaria didn't comment. It was the second time today she'd been informed she was now part of a family. And then there was Jess, who called her sister. After more than a hundred years on her own, she appeared to have "family" springing up everywhere. Weird.

Ildaria had expected to have to make four more trips up and down the stairs, but with Sofia's help they managed it in two. Even better, while traipsing back and forth to the car, Sofia had asked about furniture and when Ildaria said she only had the television and a bed coming for the moment, Sofia had dragged her to the storeroom G.G. had mentioned. It was crammed full of furniture as it turned out. Most of it was stuff from the rooms G.G. had renovated. The furniture was all perfectly good. It just hadn't suited the esthetic G.G. wanted. But it was all expensive, so he'd stored it until he decided what to do with it.

Sofia had insisted that she take what she needed, that G.G. wouldn't mind. When Ildaria had still balked at doing so, she'd said to think of it as borrowing. She could return each item to the storeroom when she'd managed to find replacements she could afford. That had made her feel better, so she'd borrowed three high-backed bar stools for the island, and a table with six chairs. It was all very modern-looking. The high-backed bar stools were metal with black leather seats and backs, as were the chairs that went with the table. But the table itself was the most contemporary thing she'd ever seen, featuring a sleek glass table surface tinged black and big enough to seat six more than comfortably, as well as a chrome finished pedestal that looked like mirrored horns coming out of the glossy white base beneath. Ildaria had never seen anything like it and couldn't decide if she loved or hated it. She did know that she certainly wouldn't have picked it herself. It was interesting, but cold. Like G.G., she preferred the warmth of real wood.

"There," Sofia said as they set the table down. "All done."

"Si. Thank you." Ildaria sighed. Grabbing the backs of two of the chairs they'd brought up first, she slid them up to the table.

"No problem," Sofia said lightly, starting to move chairs around the table as well. "So you and G.G. . . . ."

Ildaria froze briefly and then lifted her head to stare at the woman uncertainly. "What?"

"You can't read him," she said as if that was all she had to say.

Ildaria supposed it was all that needed to be said. It was also true. She'd finally tried to read him last night. He was a very solicitous boss, bringing her blood, coffee, food when checking on her, and then sending her upstairs at midnight, pointing out that she'd arrived at four, had been working for eight hours and that was all the accounting he expected her to do. The rest of the time she should "relax with H.D." She'd argued that she hadn't started working on the accounting at once, but had been out in the main room of the club with him. And he'd pointed out that while that was true, he'd spent that time talking to her about the books and instructing her on how they were kept at the Night Club, so she'd been working for eight hours and that was enough. Besides, he'd argued, H.D. was surely growing bored being stuck in the office.

Once G.G. had brought H.D. into the argument, Ildaria hadn't protested further. Feeling guilty for keeping the poor pup there for so long, she'd nodded, scooped up H.D. and taken him upstairs to G.G.'s apartment where she'd worked off her guilt by cuddling, playing fetch with, and spoiling the little fur ball. Which had also worked nicely to keep her from thinking too much about her attempt, and failure, to read G.G.

Marguerite was right. G.G. was a possible life mate for her, one of those rare people that an immortal could not read or control. Sometimes they were immortal, sometimes mortal. But that was one of the main signs of a life mate and she definitely could not read or control G.G. As for the other signs, Ildaria hadn't yet reached the age where she grew tired of eating, so that wasn't a tell with her. And she'd have to wait to see if they had shared sex dreams, or shared pleasure during lovemaking. But none of that mattered. Not being able to read or control him was enough.

"He's going to be a hard sell on agreeing to the turn," Sofia said softly, her gaze troubled.

"Si. Marguerite warned me of that." Ildaria pushed the last two chairs up to the table and then walked into the kitchen to start going through the bags and boxes they'd set in there. "Can I get you something to drink? Ice water or tea? I'm afraid I don't have anything else yet."

"Tea would be lovely," Sofia said, following her. "I'll give you a hand."

Ildaria was soon grateful for the help, since they ended up having to unpack more than half the kitchen items to find the electric kettle, teapot, spoons, cups, and teabags. With Sofia helping, it was done much more quickly than she could have done it alone. They unpacked the other half of the items and started cleaning and putting things away while they waited for the kettle to boil.

"What time are you starting tonight?" Sofia asked as Ildaria returned to the kitchen from throwing a load of her new towels in the washing machine.

"Not until sunset from now on. I only came in so early yesterday so G.G. could familiarize me with the books before the club opened," she explained and then added, "Although, I'm not sure what nights I'll be working. I know the club is open on the weekends. Do we close Monday and Tuesday to make up for it?"

Sofia shook her head. "We're open every day, but everyone gets two nights off a week except G.G. He works every night." Scowling, she added, "I've tried to tell him he should take two nights off too, and have one of us man the door, but so far, no go."

"Hmm," Ildaria murmured, wondering what days he'd want her to take off. And then worrying about what he'd do with H.D. during those two days. The thought was a troubling one. She didn't like the idea of the little guy having to be stuck alone in G.G.'s apartment two nights a week.

"G.G.'s planning on giving you whichever two nights off a week you want. But he's debating on asking you to keep an eye on H.D. those nights if you wouldn't mind. He won't be upset if you can't, or say you don't want to, but he'll pay double time if you do. Otherwise, he'll just keep H.D. in his office," Sofia announced, and when Ildaria glanced at her, eyebrows raised, she shrugged mildly. "Unlike you, I can read him."

"Right," she said wryly and returned to emptying the bags around them. They'd actually done a pretty good job at the task. She had towels in the washing machine, her new glasses, pots and pans, and dishes were all out of their boxes and stacked in the dishwasher. Or at least, most of them were. Everything hadn't fit in one load. Pots and pans took up a lot of room. But those that hadn't fit in the first load were waiting on the counter for their turn. Except for three cups and the teapot that were all drip-drying on the rack she'd purchased along with the other kitchen gadgets.

"Tea," she muttered suddenly and moved to the kettle. It had come to a boil a good half an hour ago, but they'd both been busy and it had automatically shut off, so they'd forgotten about it. At least, she had. Ildaria couldn't say for sure if Sofia had. She couldn't read her mind. But then she had the sense that the woman was older than her, and younger immortals could never read older ones.

"Yes. I'm older. By a good three hundred years," Sofia announced, obviously catching her thoughts. "And no, I didn't forget about the tea, but we were doing such a good job of getting rid of boxes and bags I decided the tea could wait a bit. I'm almost ready for one now though."

"Me too. This shouldn't take long though," Ildaria said, moving to the electric kettle to get it going again. Once that was taken care of, she moved to sort through the few remaining bags for the sugar. It was easy to find. There were only two grocery bags in the half a dozen bags remaining.

"What's in the rest of these?" Sofia asked with interest, bending to peer into the bag nearest her.

"Hand soap, shampoo, a cheese grater, colander, whisk, spatula, measuring spoons . . . Basically odds and ends." Ildaria carried the sugar to the counter and then moved to fetch the sugar bowl and cream holder set she'd unthinkingly put in the dishwasher just moments ago. Realizing she'd have to wash and dry them by hand as well if she wanted to use them, Ildaria set the items in the sink, and then returned to the dishwasher to retrieve a couple of spoons too.

"Plates for the cookies," Sofia reminded her, and Ildaria snatched several of those too.

"You start washing these and I'll run down to my apartment to grab a clean dish towel."

Ildaria glanced up with surprise. "Oh, you don't have to do that. I can use—"

"You are not wasting half your paper towel drying dishes," Sofia said firmly, reading her thoughts. "I'll be right back."

"Thanks." Ildaria sighed the word as she watched the other woman slip around the kitchen counter to head for the door. Shaking her head then, she squirted dish soap into the sink and turned on the hot water as she contemplated how uncomfortable she was at having to accept help from others. Even after three years of living with Jess, something as little as Sofia letting her use a dish towel left her feeling extremely . . . well, uncertain and awkward. Like she owed her for it.

Although, to be fair, Ildaria thought now, while she'd known Jess was there if she needed anything, in truth, she had helped Jess as much if not more than Jess had helped her. Her friend had been trying to balance school, wedding plans, and constant, exhausting life mate sex with Raff during the better part of those three years, and had leaned heavily on Ildaria during that time. But that had been fine. In fact, it had made her feel needed and useful rather than like a charity case. They'd become really good friends. Almost like sisters as Jess liked to claim.

Marguerite had been different, of course, Ildaria acknowledged as she turned off the water and began to wash the dishes she needed for tea and cookies. There was very little Marguerite and Julius needed in the way of help. And she and Marguerite had spent a lot of time together these last almost two months. Ildaria had come to look up to the woman, respect and like her a great deal. Still, it was hard to accept help from her. Maybe that was something she should work on, Ildaria thought pensively, and then glanced around expectantly when she heard the apartment door open.

"Okay. Walk straight backward, G.G."

Blinking at those words in Sofia's voice, Ildaria gave up on the dishes and wiped her hands on her jeans as she hurried around the kitchen island, only to stop and gape at the men carrying in—"Is that a couch?"

G.G. was backing into her apartment carrying one end of a large faux suede sofa that looked very familiar. He was moving slowly to avoid hitting the doors or wall with the feet, but risked a glance over his shoulder at her voice, and smiled, his mouth opening to say something.

Before he could speak though, she gasped, "That's the couch from Marguerite's rec room!"

"Yes, it is dear. I've decided to redecorate and was going to throw it out, but then I thought, why not give it to Ildaria? She can use it until she finds something she likes better."

Marguerite's happy trill was coming from the hallway, but Ildaria couldn't see the woman past G.G., the couch, and Julius, who was carrying the other end.

"Isn't that brilliant?"

Ildaria turned at Sofia's cheerful comment to see her over by the windows, setting down the chair that matched the couch. It was a large, overstuffed recliner in the same faux suede as the couch. Mortals wouldn't have been able to carry it by themselves, but Sofia set it down like it weighed next to nothing. That was one of the benefits of being an immortal. Increased strength, speed, and night vision came with it.

Straightening, Sofia grabbed the dish towel that had been slung over her shoulder and walked over to hand it to her.

"I saw them out my apartment window when I went to get the dish towel and ran down to offer a hand," she explained with a shrug.

Ildaria just stared at her blankly, not sure what to say or do.

"There," G.G. breathed with relief, drawing Ildaria's attention to the fact that they had made it to the center of her living room and had set the large sofa down. Straightening now, the big man smiled, and then headed for the door, saying, "Now let's go get that bed."

"Bed?" Ildaria echoed with disbelief.

"It's the bed from your room, dear," Marguerite said, moving past her and toward the kitchen with half a dozen grocery bags dangling from each hand. "It's my housewarming gift to you. I figured since I was re-decorating the living room, I might as well redecorate the guest room too. I'm growing rather tired of the rose color scheme in there. I'm thinking all in pale cream."

"Marguerite," Ildaria said with dismay, her gaze

sliding from the groceries the woman was carrying to the furniture now filling her living room.

"It's a gift," Marguerite said firmly.

"But—" She shook her head helplessly, her thoughts a complete jumble. People just did not do these things in her experience. And she couldn't accept such a generous gift.

"It's not generous, dear," Marguerite insisted. She'd set the grocery bags on the island. "It's all used furniture that would have ended up being given to charity or sent to the dump if they didn't deem it acceptable."

"Acceptable?" Ildaria asked with disbelief. "Of course they'd deem it acceptable. It's in perfect condition." Her gaze slid to the groceries Marguerite was now unpacking and putting away. Her refrigerator and cupboards were going to be full by the time the woman finished. There was everything from fresh fruit and vegetables, eggs, milk, meat, and a multitude of boxed and canned goods, including large sacks of sugar and flour. Shaking her head, she said pointedly, "And the groceries? I suppose they're a housewarming gift too?"

"No. They are to aid you in your efforts to make G.G. fall in love with you," Marguerite said easily, and then reminded her, "G.G. loves food. Greeting him at the door in the mornings with sweet baked goods or meals will no doubt help make him fall in love with you."

"Marguerite," Ildaria said with exasperation, grateful G.G. was not there to hear this.

Marguerite paused in her unpacking and met Ildaria's gaze before saying, "I'm very fond of G.G., my dear. And I have hoped for a very long time to find him an immortal he could be a life mate to. I was very pleased when I recognized it was you. You deserve a life mate, and he . . ." Marguerite sighed and confessed, "I no more wish to watch him age and die than his mother does. It would break my heart, and I intend to do everything I can to prevent that and help you claim him. So"—she pulled a package of steaks out of one of the bags and moved to place them in the refrigerator—"these groceries are really for me, not you."

Ildaria didn't know how to respond to that and glanced to Sofia for help, but the other woman raised her hands in a "leave me out of it" attitude and headed for the door, saying, "I'll go bring up the other chair."

"Thank you, dear," Marguerite called after the tow-headed woman, and then waited until she was gone before moving around the island to Ildaria's side and taking her hands. "Breathe," she instructed gently.

Ildaria took a deep breath, and then used it to blurt, "I can't accept all of this."

Marguerite nodded as if she'd expected that reaction, but then said, "Well, I have to say, I think that is very selfish of you."

The words made her blink in disbelief. "What?"

"I have already mentioned that G.G. means a great deal to me and I would hate to lose him to mortal death."

"Si, well, that's the groceries," Ildaria said uncomfortably. "But the furniture—"

"That's necessary for his seduction too. Besides . . ." She squeezed her hands gently. "Dear girl, do you not realize how unhappy I would be imagining you here in this apartment without any furniture? It would prey on my mind," she assured her. "So it would please me if you accepted these gifts in the spirit in which they were intended and saved me that suffering."

"I—You—" Ildaria stared at her helplessly, even more unsure how to respond, and then Marguerite glanced past her and smiled brightly.

"Oh, look. You have a dining room set too," she said, releasing her hands and leaving the kitchen to examine the table and chairs. Running one hand over the glass surface of the table, she grinned and said, "Julius will be relieved. I was considering renovating the dining room and giving you that furniture as well, but now I will not bother."

"Marguerite!" Ildaria gasped and then shook her head. "This is too much."

"It is *used* furniture, Ildaria," Marguerite said gently. "An excuse for me to get new things for myself. Although, I admit I really wanted to buy you new furniture for your new apartment, but Julius was positive you would not accept new furniture and in the end I agreed he was probably right."

"He *was* right. I wouldn't have accepted new furniture," Ildaria assured her grimly.

"But you will accept this, will you not?" she said now. "Aside from my concern for G.G., you cannot make the men carry it all back down. Besides, it will ease my mind to know that you are not sleeping in a sleeping bag, or sitting on the floor while taking your leisure." Expression becoming sad, she added, "It really would cause me a great deal of distress to both lose G.G. and to imagine you in an empty apartment, and right now I am trying to avoid stress. I am with child, you know."

"I know," Ildaria said with a frown, and then blinked and asked with disbelief, "Marguerite Argeneau, are you trying to guilt me into accepting this furniture?"

"Not at all," Marguerite assured her, and then gave a sniff and added, "Really, Ildaria, you have to get over the idea that everything is about you. This is about me. I am merely explaining the consequences of your actions should you refuse this gift I wish to give you," she said with a shrug. "You do not want me to lose my baby, do you?"

Ildaria stared at her blankly, feeling guilty at the suggestion that she was being selfish and threatening Marguerite's unborn child. None of that was true, of course. Was it?

"Give it up, Ildaria," Julius said, reentering the apartment carrying a mattress as if it weighed no more than a sheet of paper. Passing through the living room, headed for the short hall to the bedrooms, he added, "You cannot win in an argument with my wife. I know this from experience."

Ildaria let out a slow breath, her gaze sliding distractedly to G.G. as he entered the apartment, carrying part of her bed frame from her room at Marguerite's. When he beamed at her, she smiled weakly back, and watched until he disappeared down the hall before turning back to Marguerite. She opened her mouth and then closed it as she struggled with herself, but finally she gave in and simply said, "Thank you."

Marguerite beamed at her. "There! See? That was not so hard, was it?"

"Saying thank you?" she asked uncertainly.

"No, dear." Reaching out, Marguerite squeezed her hands again. "Letting others in."

Marguerite turned and walked back into the kitchen then, leaving Ildaria standing alone between the dining room table and her no longer empty living room. In that moment, it occurred to her that this apartment was like her life. She'd lived more than a century without anyone in her life. It had been as empty as this apartment had been when she'd led Sofia in two hours ago. But then she'd met Vasco and Cristo, and Jess and Raff . . . Now her life was filling with people, just as her apartment was filling with furniture. The problem was, she was more comfortable with the open, empty space. While the couch and bed offered more comfort than the floor, they could break, become damaged or have to be removed. They also presented opportunities to stub her toes and trip over things.

Letting people in meant giving them the opportunity to hurt you. It was a lesson Ildaria had learned young and she had learned it well. She had always thought of herself as fearless and brave. But that was easy when you had nothing to care about and nothing to lose. Now . . . Ildaria was scared.

Six

Ildaria pushed through the dark oak door of the front room on the second floor of the Night Club and paused with surprise to take it in. There were four rooms in the club, the main bar and dance club on the main floor, and two alternate rooms on this floor. She knew the back room was a game room with pool tables and arcade games, but this was the first time she'd seen the front room. It was impressive in an old English manor kind of way. She could see it appealing to some of the older immortals. In fact, each room seemed to have been created to appeal to a different age group of immortal. The dance club was for the younger immortals. The bar catered to the mid to old immortals who came for company. She supposed the game room would appeal to different age groups, but this room seemed most suited to old, old immortals who were probably coupled.

The clink of glasses drew her attention to the man

presently cleaning the room and a small smile curved her lips as she watched him work. The high green Mohawk didn't really fit with the black dress pants and dress shirt he was wearing. Jeans or leather would have suited him more, Ildaria thought as she watched him carry a half-full tray of glasses to the next table, one of many small side tables that accompanied the groupings of sofas and chairs in the room. G.G. bent, set the tray on the table and began gathering the used glasses and adding them to his growing collection.

"I don't know why you don't have Sofia and the others help with cleanup," she said to announce her presence. "It would be done in no time with the three or four of you working."

G.G. stilled and then glanced over his shoulder at her for a moment, his gaze moving over her slowly before he turned back to continue gathering glasses. "They work long hours as it is. The shortest night in the summer is nine hours, but it can be as long as fifteen hours in the winter that they have to work. And they do it without complaint," he pointed out. "Letting them go at closing is the least I can do."

"You work longer," she pointed out. "You start early to prep, and clean up after. Surely—"

"The Night Club is my business. I get the profits. As such, I should work longer hours. Most business owners do. No employee is paid well enough to have to work as long as I do."

Ildaria raised her eyebrows at the words and reminded him, "I do your books. I know how well you pay your employees, and you pay us all ridiculously well. On top of that, you're charging us a pittance in rent for the apartments and house. It barely covers the cost of electricity and water. Not to mention that your prices in the club are very reasonable. Your profits are a lot smaller than they could be."

G.G. shrugged and moved to the next table to gather the glasses there. "How much money does a person need? You can't take it with you. Besides, I pay well so that my employees are happy. Happy employees make good employees, and good employees stay."

"You're a good boss," she said, meaning it. He cared about people more than money. Few businessmen were like that.

G.G. snorted with disbelief, and shook his head. "I used to be. Now I'm turning into an aging pervert who spends all his waking hours fantasizing about one of his employees, and his nights dreaming of her." Straightening, he turned to wave his hand toward her with exasperation. "I mean look, I've put you in glasses, for heaven's sake."

Ildaria reached up to feel her face, surprised to note the eyeglasses resting on her nose. She hadn't even realized they were there until he mentioned them. She'd never in her life even imagined wearing them. She was immortal. Immortals didn't need glasses. The nanos saw to that. But she was wearing glasses . . . which meant this was a dream.

Ildaria let her gaze skate over the rest of her outfit now, wondering if anything else was unusual. But she was wearing a black skirt and white blouse, one set of several she'd purchased to work at the fancy restaurant in Montana where she'd sometimes acted as hostess and sometimes as server. She'd been fortunate that they were just as suitable for her job in the office here and she hadn't had to buy new clothes.

Her shoes were different though, Ildaria noted. They were still black high heels, but open-toed, and the black bow had been moved to rest on the band across the top of her foot rather than the heel. A quick swipe of her hair told her that it was up in the customary bun she wore to work, though. So he'd only changed the shoes and added glasses. Not much of a change to her mind, and she turned her thoughts to wondering how she'd been so slow to realize this was another shared dream.

The answer was obvious. Despite the fact that she was asleep, it seemed so real, and so natural. It wasn't like she'd pushed through a door into an upside-down circus or something. She'd walked into one of the rooms of the club and had assumed she was awake and this was reality. But in reality she hadn't seen much of G.G. for the last two weeks since she'd moved into the apartment and the dreams had started. He'd been avoiding her. It hadn't started right away. The night she'd moved in, he'd checked on her in the office often, and had his breaks there with her and H.D., sharing meals and chatting comfortably, laughing a lot. An hour before closing, he'd shown up to tell her that her eight hours were up and she and H.D. should go up to her new apartment and relax. He'd pick up H.D. once he'd cleaned up after closing.

Ildaria had taken H.D. upstairs and played with the pooch. When G.G. finished cleanup and showed up to collect his pup, she'd greeted him at the door with the offer of hot chocolate and they'd sat on her couch talking for several hours before he'd left for his own apartment. Ildaria had dragged herself off to bed then and fallen into the first of their shared dreams.

The next day had followed the same pattern, with G.G. checking on her often, sharing his meals with her, and enjoying hot chocolate and laughter together as they unwound afterward. Again it had been followed by a restless sleep full of shared dreams. Those dreams had continued every day for the last two weeks, but her waking hours had slowly changed. G.G. had started sending Sofia to check on her rather than doing it himself, and then he'd stopped having meals with her, and finally he'd stopped having hot chocolate at the end of the night too, claiming he was too tired for it. Now, the only time she saw him was in dreams. She supposed that alone should have told her this was a dream, because in reality, she would be upstairs with H.D., not searching him out in the club after closing.

"The damned glasses were supposed to make you less attractive," G.G. said with irritation, drawing her attention to him again. "They were supposed to slow me down a little so I wouldn't jump you the minute you walked into the room. Instead, you look hot as hell. Like some sexy librarian or something." He clucked his tongue with self-disgust. "I'm dressing you up in my dreams like a bloody sex doll, Ildaria. If you had any idea—"

Pausing abruptly, he scowled and turned back to his task, his movements abrupt and angry now as he swiped up glasses and slammed them onto the tray.

"G.G.," she said with a small frown and crossed the room quickly to his side. But the moment she touched his arm, he jerked upright and stepped back.

"No. Don't touch me," he snapped, and then closed his eyes on a sigh when she retrieved her hand and stared at him with embarrassment and confusion.

"I'm sorry," he breathed wearily. "I'm just tired. I spend my days having all these dreams that leave me feeling like I haven't slept at all, and then I spend my nights working the door of the Night Club, but fantasizing about you the whole time." Irritation flickered over his face, and then he burst out, "And I know the customers are reading every dirty little thought in my head. They give me these knowing looks and grins as I let them in. They know that I'm stripping you naked in my mind and—"

He closed his eyes on a short laugh, and muttered, "And now I'm talking to myself in my dreams."

"Talking to yourself?" she asked with confusion.

His eyes opened, a wry half smile twisting his lips. "Well, dreams are supposed to be your subconscious trying to work out things, right? So, really you're me."

Ildaria stilled, realizing that he didn't know that these were shared dreams. G.G. knew about immortals, and she'd assumed that he'd recognize that these were the shared dreams that immortals and their life mates experience. In fact, she'd been waiting for him to comment on them. But apparently he hadn't yet realized that was what was happening. He thought he was just having sexual dreams about her.

"G.G.," she began, but paused when he suddenly took her hands in his.

"I'm sorry," he said glumly. "I know I have to do something about this. I'm becoming obsessed with you to the point that I'm afraid of what I'll do. Every night when I pick up H.D. I'm fighting the urge to drag you into my arms, strip you naked, and explore every inch of your beautiful body with my tongue."

Ildaria swallowed, her body responding to the image.

"The only thing stopping me is that you're my employee, an immortal, obviously not interested, and could easily kick my ass for even trying to kiss you. Never mind the sexual harassment suit," he added with a wry grimace. "It's gotten so bad that last night I spent most of my time at work fantasizing about how I could do that for real. Seriously," he insisted when she blinked in surprise. Then he squeezed her hands almost painfully before dropping them and whirling to stride several steps away. His voice thick with shame, he confessed, "I was actually fantasizing on a way to do it. I thought maybe if I got my hands on blood from someone with Rohypnol in their system, I could knock you out, drag you to my apartment, and chain you to my bed and—" He bowed his head in shame. "I'm losing my mind, Ildaria. I can't stop thinking about you, and the more I think about you, the more I want to—"

G.G.'s words stopped abruptly as he turned to look at her.

Ildaria stared back, slowly realizing that her view of him had changed. She'd been standing just moments ago, but now was flat on her back. Glancing down, she saw that she was lying on a bed in the middle of the club room, naked and chained. Judging by the slack-jawed expression on G.G.'s face now, he hadn't put her there. But his admission had. It had turned her on when he'd talked about having her naked and chained to his bed, and her subconscious had changed the dream situation to suit.

"God, I'm turning into a sick bastard," G.G. breathed, moving toward the bed.

"No. You're not," Ildaria whispered. Her heart was thundering in her chest. Her subconscious might have put her there, but that didn't mean she was comfortable being naked and staked out. In reality, she was equal parts excited, anxious, and embarrassed to be in such a position. But mostly she was uncomfortable. Ildaria wasn't used to being powerless. Not anymore. She hadn't felt this helpless since—

The brush of his fingers on her calf sent tingles of sensation up her leg and made her thoughts scatter.

"Goddamn, you're beautiful," he breathed, his gaze sliding over her with awe.

She found herself holding her breath as he examined her, and then it left in a sigh as he continued along the side of the bed, trailing his fingers up her leg, hip, and stomach. A moan slid from her lips, though, when they crested her breast and brushed over the nipple. It immediately went hard, need pushing her anxiety and discomfort away.

"G.G.," she breathed, wanting to tell him they were sharing this dream. Wanting to tell him that she wanted him too, but her voice deserted her when he suddenly dropped to sit on the side of the bed and bent to claim her nipple with his mouth.

Pressing her head back into the pillow, Ildaria moaned, her body arching upward invitingly, her wrists pulling at the chains restricting them as she tried to reach for his head. He sucked her nipple into his mouth and lashed it with his tongue before grazing it with his teeth as he let it slip from his mouth.

"Mm," he murmured, his lips trailing down her breast to the valley between them. "You smell like muffins."

Ildaria's eyes popped open, surprise pushing some of her desire aside. Muffins?

"Vanilla and spice. Delicious," he announced and then his tongue swiped up her second breast and lashed the nipple there. "I love muffins," he growled before claiming that nipple and suckling it into his mouth now.

Ildaria groaned, promising herself she'd make him muffins as he began to nip and lash at the hard bud, sending bolts of excitement through her body. But then he released that as well and breathed, "You'd hate me if you knew I did this to you in my dreams."

"No," she gasped, shaking her head on the pillow as his lips moved over her stomach, sending it rippling.

"Yes, you would," he said, sounding sad, one hand shifting up to cover her breast and squeeze lightly, the other fanning out over her hip before sliding to her upper leg. "But I swear I wouldn't drug you or chain you up in real life. I'm losing my mind over you and I know it, but I haven't completely lost it yet. I'll do what I have to, to keep you safe. I'll get away from you, go back to England and—"

"No!" Ildaria protested with horror.

"Shh. You're just a dream. If you were real you'd be glad," he muttered and then made sure she didn't protest further by covering her mouth with his in a hard kiss.

Ildaria resisted for all of a heartbeat, and then gave in and kissed him back. She would tell him after. Immortals did not faint during dream sex. She would tell him afterward that this was a shared dream. She'd tell him that he wasn't losing his mind, or that if he was she was too, and it was only because they were possible life mates. And then she'd beg him to agree to be hers. She wouldn't even ask him to turn. She just needed him to be hers. She just—

Her thoughts died as his hand slid between her legs and her body responded, pushing everything but the feel, taste, and need for him from her thoughts. God, she wanted to touch him, Ildaria thought and then the chains melted away, freeing her to touch him.

G.G. moaned into her mouth when her hands slid around him and ran over what she could reach of his back, but he didn't stop kissing and caressing her until she began to tug at his shirt. Breaking their kiss, he nipped at her lower lip and then retrieved his hand from between her legs and stood to quickly undo the buttons of his dress shirt.

Ildaria watched him, panting, her body aching. A small sigh slid from her lips when the shirt was open and he began to shrug out of it, his tattoos shifting with the movement. He was so beautiful, his chest wide and rippling with muscle. Ildaria had never thought much of tattoos in the past, but had to admit G.G.'s were beautiful, a pattern of black whorls and curved thorns that ran around his upper arms to his shoulder, leaving his chest un-inked. She knew from past dreams that the same pattern ran down his muscled back, following the length of his spine. They looked beautiful on him, and she thought it would be a shame if he were turned and lost them.

Movement distracted her from her thoughts, and she focused in on G.G. as he walked to the foot of the bed. He was watching her as he went, his gaze intense, and she stared back, suddenly holding her breath when he paused between her spread, still chained feet.

"Beautiful," he murmured and then knelt and placed a kiss on the instep of first one foot and then the other. He began to move up her legs then, licking and nipping at each ankle, and then her calf, crawling onto and up the bed as he went. When he licked and nipped at her inner knees and she gasped, shifted and gave a startled sound almost but not quite a giggle, a smile claimed his lips and he raised his head to look up her body to her raised head.

"Ticklish." The word was a soft rumble in the silence, but he moved on, kissing and nibbling up her inner thighs, moving so slowly Ildaria thought she'd die from the anticipation of his reaching her core. But he surprised her there, bypassing the aching spot altogether and letting his lips travel to her hips and her stomach instead.

Ildaria moaned in disappointment and then gasped

and arched as his lips found her breasts and feasted on first one and then the other. Rasping each nipple, nipping, and then suckling, before lifting to claim her mouth. Groaning, Ildaria kissed him back, her suddenly free feet sliding up the bed so that her knees rose to frame his legs and then she used them to lift her hips against his as he ground into her.

G.G. murmured something she didn't catch as he broke their kiss, and then raised his upper body as if doing push-ups, and watched her face as he ground his lower body against hers. Ildaria tried to meet his gaze, but her eyes kept closing and her head was starting to twist on the pillow as the pressure inside her built.

"So goddamn beautiful," he breathed and then suddenly slithered back down her body, pressed her thighs open and buried his face between them to taste her.

Ildaria cried out at the first rasp of his tongue, her body jerking in response, and then tangled her hands in the sheets on either side of her and held on for dear life as he went to work driving her crazy. He did things with his mouth and tongue that had her eyes rolling back in her head, and brought a long ululating sound of need chorusing from her mouth.

It wasn't the first time he'd done this in their shared dreams, but every time was both a revelation and a struggle. While her hips were thrusting up into the caress, her legs were trying to press closed but being held open by his big hands, and her head was thrashing, shaking back and forth in what might have been taken for denial even as her whole body fought toward the release she knew was coming.

When it hit, she screamed, her whole body convulsing, and her mind briefly insensate with the power of it so that she wasn't sure she would have been able to give her name if anyone had asked what it was. When she finally regained some of her senses, G.G. was over her, completely nude though she had no idea if he'd stripped or just wished or imagined the clothes away in this shared dream, and then she didn't care as he was thrusting into her.

Ildaria cried out, her arms and legs wrapping instinctively around him as he filled her. Her body beginning to quiver again as he withdrew and thrust forward over and over. This time when she found her pleasure, he was right there with her, roaring in triumph as he found his own. He collapsed on top of her, and just as quickly tried to roll away, but she held him in place, enjoying his weight on her, holding him as they regained their breath.

Ildaria hadn't forgotten that she had to talk to him, explain about the shared dreams and tell him that they were life mates. But she waited a few moments for their breathing to slow, and then just as she opened her mouth to speak, the phone rang.

Ildaria stiffened, her arms instinctively tightening around G.G. as if to protect him from the intrusion, but it rang again and she turned her head to peer at the bedside table in the bright sunlight pouring through her bedroom window. The ringing had woken her and the dream had slipped away with consciousness, breaking her connection to G.G.

Cursing, Ildaria glanced at the digital display of the

alarm clock next to the phone to see that it was only noon. She'd slept a little more than three hours and was not in the mood for dealing with telemarketers or wrong numbers. She just wanted to go back to sleep and back to her shared dream with G.G., so ignored her phone and closed her eyes. Much to her relief, after two more rings the sound stopped, the call switching to voice mail, she supposed.

Ildaria turned on her side and snuggled under the blankets, eager to return to sleep, but stiffened when the phone began ringing again. Obviously, whoever it was wasn't going to be put off.

Muttering under her breath with irritation, Ildaria dragged her arm out from under the blankets and snatched the phone off her bedside table. She didn't even check to see who was calling; she simply hit the green icon to accept the call and brought the phone to her ear.

"Si?" Her voice was groggy with the sleep she wished she was still enjoying and she let her eyes close yet again, hoping it was a quick call and she could get back to sleep.

"I have tea and a sausage breakfast sandwich with your name on it."

Ildaria's eyes blinked open at once. It wasn't just the fact that it was Sofia's voice speaking to her, but the mention of a sausage breakfast sandwich. Ildaria loved sausage breakfast sandwiches. She'd tried her first one just a week earlier, compliments of Sofia, but they had become her favorite food. She was addicted to them. They were one of the few foods she was willing to miss out on sleep for. On the other hand, she'd planned to talk to G.G. . . . .

"Ildaria?"

Heaving a sigh, she shook her head. "I was about to talk to G.G. about . . . stuff."

"G.G.'s there?" Sofia asked with surprise.

"No. In our dream. I was going to explain that we're life mates and—"

"What the hell?" Sofia interrupted. "You were going to tell him in a dream that he's your life mate? Ildaria," she said with exasperation. "He'd just think that was wishful thinking, and part of his dream. Or maybe his nightmare," she muttered with disgust, and then grouched, "Get out of bed and open the door right now or I'm giving this sausage breakfast sandwich to Elijah."

"Fine," Ildaria snapped irritably. Sitting up in bed, she asked, "Why am I opening the door?"

"Because I'm standing on the other side of it with your tea and sandwich. Why else?"

"Well, why didn't you just knock then?" Ildaria asked, some of her irritation giving way to exasperated amusement. Sofia couldn't do anything the normal way. Rather than call, she'd text you to call her, and rather than knock, she apparently called and told you to open the door. The woman was whacked, she thought as she pushed the sheet and blanket aside and climbed out of bed.

"Because I would have had to pound pretty loud for you to hear all the way from the bedroom and I didn't want to wake G.G. He needs his sleep."

"And I don't?" she asked sounding just a bit pissy. She padded out of the bedroom and down the hall.

"You might," Sofia allowed. "But you aren't the one who's been acting like a grumpy bear for the last week and a half . . . which is what I wanted to talk about."

Ildaria grunted in response to that as she crossed the living room, knowing she was acting a bit like that grumpy bear right now. But it was nothing compared to how G.G. had been acting the last week. At least, when he was awake. So as she turned into the short hall to the door, she said, "G.G. has been a bit short the last week or so. Is that not normal for him?"

"Definitely not," Sofia assured her, and then lowered the phone when Ildaria unlocked and pulled the door open. Ending the call and sliding the phone into her pocket, she added, "Which is why I wanted to talk to you when G.G. wouldn't interrupt, and perhaps give him a chance to get some proper sleep since you won't be sleeping so . . ." She arched her eyebrows meaningfully. ". . . no shared dreams."

"Right," Ildaria breathed wearily as she watched Sofia bend to pick up a takeout cup and two bags from the floor—one a small paper bag with a coffee shop logo, and the other a cloth bag.

Straightening, Sofia held them up with a smile. "But I come bearing gifts to make up for it."

Toning down her scowl, Ildaria managed not to snatch the paper bag no doubt holding the sausage breakfast sandwich from her, and stepped back, gesturing for the platinum blonde to enter. Once Sofia moved past her, she closed the door and locked it before following her to the kitchen island.

Sofia settled herself on one of the chairs at the island and waited until Ildaria claimed the chair next to her before pushing the takeout cup and the paper bag in front of her. She then pulled blood out of the other sack. Four bags of blood, in fact.

"To make up for waking you," Sofia explained, sliding the bags in front of her as well. "We can get by without sleep. A little blood and it's like we slept soundly all night. G.G. doesn't have that advantage."

"No, he doesn't," Ildaria agreed. She wasn't at all sure if she'd accept the blood, but wasn't awake enough to argue yet.

"Speaking of lack of sleep," Sofia said brightly. "How is it?"

"How is lack of sleep?" Ildaria asked with disbelief as she opened the drinking tab on her cup of tea. But she was thinking here was the proof that she wasn't awake yet because Sofia's words made no sense to her at all.

"Not the lack of sleep itself," Sofia said with a faint smile. "The reason for it."

When Ildaria stared at her blankly, Sofia shifted impatiently and said, "You've lived here for two weeks now, right across the hall from G.G. Close enough for shared sex dreams and I know that's the dream you were talking about earlier. You're having them. So . . . how are they?" Sofia asked, her eyebrows wiggling up and down on her forehead. "Are they super hot? They are, aren't they? Tell me they are."

When Ildaria started to shake her head, Sofia gave a "bah" of exasperation, her hand waving away what she obviously thought was a denial. "Don't even try that. If you'll remember, I can read G.G.'s mind and what I'm reading there is straight-up Mimi porn."

"Mimi porn?" Ildaria echoed uncertainly.

"Mortal/Immortal making it," she said helpfully, and then added, "If you went out with myself and our coworkers once in a while like we've asked you the last couple of weeks since you started, you'd already know these things."

"You're right, of course," Ildaria said apologetically. "I'm just still trying to adjust to my working hours and living alone."

"No, you're not. You're exhausted from all the shared sex dreams messing with your sleep," Sofia countered easily, and then announced, "So is G.G. Half the time he looks like an exhausted zombie, and the other half he's a grumpy bear. As are you," she added, mouth pursing with displeasure and eyebrows arching on her forehead. "You really need to jump the poor man's bones or something. Then he'll pass out and maybe get some real sleep."

When Ildaria didn't respond, Sofia added, "We'd all appreciate it. We are not used to a grumpy G.G. The guy is usually a teddy bear, not a grizzly."

Ildaria shook her head wearily. "I can't believe you're asking me to sleep with G.G. for your sake."

"And yours," Sofia assured her quickly. "I mean, you're suffering the frustrations of hell at the moment, so . . ." Turning in her seat to face her, Sofia leaned her elbow on the island and raised her eyebrows. "Tell Mama all about it. What are shared sex dreams really like?"

Ildaria bit her lip, her thoughts turning to the dream she'd been having before Sofia had woken her. It was one of many she'd enjoyed the last two weeks. She'd had the first one her first night. She'd gone to bed in the lovely, comfortable bed from Marguerite's home that they'd brought for her, and—exhausted from all the setup she'd done in the apartment that day, and then the hours she'd spent working before continuing with laundry and cleanup after taking H.D. up to her apartment until G.G. came to get him—Well, between all of that, she was nearly asleep before her eyes were fully closed.

G.G. had obviously been asleep already by then, because she'd fallen right into a dream. She'd found herself in the Night Club office, H.D. curled up in his basket, and her working in the tight pencil skirt and blouse she'd worn for her first night of work, and G.G. had come in to check on her. Only instead of just popping his head in and speaking for a few moments, he'd entered and crossed the room to come around the desk, his eyes smoldering as they slid over her body.

He hadn't said a word. He'd simply reached out, caught her by the upper arms to lift her to her feet and then had clasped her face in his hands and claimed her lips.

G.G. was an amazing kisser. At least, he was in dreams, and Ildaria had hardly noticed when his hands had slid into her hair, delving through the strands until the neat bun she wore it in for work was gone and her hair was sliding down to curl around her face, neck, and shoulders.

He'd lifted his head then, saying in that deep sexy rumble of his, "I want you. You're immortal and I know I shouldn't. But I want you so damn bad."

The next thing Ildaria knew, she was climbing him like a palm tree. While his mouth claimed hers again, and she responded, she was also tearing at his clothes, desperate to touch his skin. Ildaria wasn't the only one. He was tugging her blouse out of her skirt, sliding his big hands under to span her waist before they began to rise. Ildaria had pushed his shirt up his stomach, and was eagerly running her hands over the wide expanse of his chest when he suddenly scooped her up and turned to set her on the desk.

G.G. nudged her knees apart, and moved forward to fill the space he'd created. He didn't stop until he was pressing against her core, and then his kiss turned deep and voracious. His hands moved to the buttons of her blouse and suddenly it was undone, allowing him to tug it open to reveal a lacy black bra beneath that Ildaria had never seen before. Obviously, it was his input to the dream, which she didn't mind at all. It looked much nicer than the white cotton bra and panty sets she always wore in reality. At least, that's what she'd always worn up to now. Though, she had gone out and used some of her tip money from her waitressing job to buy a black lace set similar to the one he'd dreamed up. It was pretty and sexy and she only had one set, so couldn't wear it every day in the hopes that something would happen. So, she hadn't put it on at all yet. She was saving it for a "special" occasion.

"Oh my, sex in the office," Sofia breathed, drawing her from the memory. "That *is* steamy. The whole secretary-boss thing, love on the desk, the risk of one of us entering unexpectedly and catching you. My, my, my."

"Accountant-boss," Ildaria muttered, feeling her face burn with embarrassment at Sofia's reading her thoughts.

"Yeah. That might be a problem."

Ildaria glanced up in question. "What?"

"His being the boss," Sofia explained with a frown. "G.G. might look like a rebel, but he has a lot of honor. I suspect he would never hit on an employee. It would be too much like taking advantage of his position."

Ildaria was frowning now too, sure G.G. had said something about her being his employee in the dream and sexual harassment or something. But until now, it hadn't occurred to her that her working for him might be a problem.

"Which means you'll have to do the hitting," Sofia concluded with satisfaction. "He wouldn't feel he was taking advantage if you jumped him. And it can't be sexual harassment either, since you're the underling."

"Right." Ildaria sighed the word unhappily, rather doubting she could do that. She didn't have a lot of experience in such things . . . unless you counted the dreams she'd been sharing with G.G.

"Never say you're a virgin?" Sofia whispered with

amazement, obviously having caught her thoughts about her lack of experience.

Ildaria shook her head stiffly. "No. I'm not a virgin."

Recognizing the way Sofia's eyes were concentrating on her forehead, Ildaria began to recite a nursery rhyme, but either she wasn't quick enough or it just didn't work now that she'd met a possible life mate. She realized that when Sofia's expression turned sympathetic.

Ildaria stiffened. If she showed her the least bit of pity—

"Right," Sofia said firmly. "Well, maybe we could work on it."

Ildaria blinked, her grim expression turning to bewilderment. "Work on what exactly?"

"On your lack of experience. We could have you practice."

"Practice?" Ildaria roared, outraged at the very thought. What was she thinking? That Ildaria should go pick up some man and—

"Not the sex," Sofia said with exasperation, obviously picking up her thoughts. "The showing that you're interested part, flirting and how to hit on him and make your interest known. Or maybe we can come up with ways for you to show your interest in other ways. Like wearing a sexy negligee when G.G. arrives to pick up H.D. one morning after the club closes."

She paused and pursed her lips briefly, and then said, "Although, you'd probably still have to make a move on him. I suspect other than your ripping his clothes off and tackling him to the floor, nothing short of a

Fuck me sign hanging from around your neck when you answer the door is going to move him past his honorable disposition. If that even worked. It might make him worry there's something wrong with you. Mentally."

"The very fact that I'm sitting here listening to this nonsense proves there is something wrong with me mentally," Ildaria said dryly.

"That and many other things," Sofia agreed easily, but then softened the words by adding, "But then most of us have our issues. You can't live life without gaining an issue or two along the way."

Ildaria nodded at those words of wisdom, believing them wholeheartedly. She'd met a lot of people in her life, especially while sailing with Vasco. They'd lured a lot of people onto the ship, and almost all of them had had something in their minds that was distressing when she read them. Body issues, anger issues, memories of childhood abuse haunting their thoughts and actions. The few that had seemed well balanced and pretty much okay had been through some kind of counseling, easily read in their thoughts.

"Have you considered counseling?" Sofia asked softly.

Ildaria's gaze shot to her and then away, but she just shook her head. She'd never been in a position to be able to afford counseling. Besides which, who could she go to? She couldn't tell a mortal counselor or psychologist about being immortal.

"Marguerite's son-in-law, Greg, is an immortal and some kind of psychologist or psychiatrist," Sofia announced, obviously still picking up her thoughts. "Maybe he'd be willing to work out some kind of payment plan you could handle," she suggested, and then added, "Failing that, Elijah says the university offers free counseling services to students. He's taking medicine at the uni. Plans to be a doctor."

"Si, he mentioned that," Ildaria said. "But I can't talk to a mortal counselor, Sofia."

"Not about being an immortal, no," she agreed, but then pointed out, "But a lot of your issues around sex seem to come from your childhood, when you were mortal. So if you stuck to that, the free counseling at university could work. Just avoid mentioning that your childhood was nearly two hundred years ago and you should be fine."

Ildaria frowned at the suggestion, not at all comfortable with the thought of getting counseling.

"It's up to you, of course," Sofia said lightly, and then asked, "But would you really rather continue to carry around the trauma of your childhood for the hundreds or even thousands of years you might live?"

She let Ildaria think about that for a minute, and then said, "Hurry up and eat. Then get dressed. We're going shopping."

"Shopping?" Ildaria jerked her gaze back to the woman.

"For a nice little negligee or something. And romance novels."

"Romance novels?" Ildaria asked with disbelief.

"They have lots of sex in them," she said, as if that should explain the matter. It didn't, and when Ildaria's expression showed as much, she patiently explained, "For pointers. Maybe ideas on how to seduce him, or at least what to do with him. We need to move this train along before it goes off the tracks."

Ildaria started to shake her head. "I can't afford—"

"It'll be my housewarming gift to you. I haven't given you one yet."

"No. You—"

"Ildaria, you're running out of time," Sofia said, her tone serious. "G.G. has been avoiding you as much as possible since the dreams started."

Ildaria dropped her eyes, a frown tugging at her lips. She had noticed that she saw less and less of G.G. during their waking hours. It was only in dreams that they spent time together and while they did some talking and sharing, most of the dreams were taken up with sex. Constant, heart-stopping, wake up sweaty and exhausted sex.

"He's really struggling with his attraction for you, I mean seriously struggling. He's starting to fantasize about kidnapping you and having his way with you and it's scaring the crap out of him. He's afraid he's becoming an obsessive stalker type guy. Which he kind of is. I mean, all life mates go through it, but he doesn't understand that's what's happening, and just thinks he's turning into a freak," Sofia told her unhappily, just reaffirming what Ildaria had picked up on in the latest dream. "You need to get him into bed soon, or he'll fly off to England to avoid you, or to save you from him. I'm not sure which it is. He's pretty messed up right now."

Ildaria bit her lip and admitted, "He mentioned something about England in the dream, but—" But her memories from the dream were already getting fuzzy. They always did. The only thing that remained long was the memory of the sex. What they talked about before or after, always faded quickly.

"He's thinking about heading back home to London, England," Sofia said quietly. "The original plan was for him to stay through the summer and spend the winter in England at the other club, before returning for the summer here again. But he's started making noises about flying back early and leaving me fully in charge all the time now that *everything seems to be working smoothly here.*"

"Oh no," Ildaria breathed. "You don't think he'll really do that, do you?" That would certainly make it hard for her to convince him to be her life mate.

"Yes, I do. He was putting out feelers last night, mentioning to everyone who entered the club that he has a nice apartment and good pay for anyone who wishes to take over his job as doorman," she told her sadly. "It's why I came to see you today."

"Damn," Ildaria breathed, dropping back in her seat.

"Yeah." Sofia eyed her sympathetically. "You need to step up your game, Ildaria, or you might lose the chance. I suspect he's uncomfortable enough with his feelings for you that he might not return at all. He'll just leave me to run the place and stay in England."

Ildaria sat still for a moment, her mind racing. The last two weeks had been wonderful in a way. She had her own place, and she loved her job. It was true she and G.G. hadn't spent a lot of time together when not dreaming, but the truth was she'd been too tired to really worry about it too much. And it wasn't just the shared dreams that had been making her tired. Aside from her double duty at the Night Club, Ildaria had been working at the restaurant as well. She'd given her notice two weeks ago and had rearranged her shifts so they wouldn't interfere with her work hours here, but that still meant she had been missing a lot of sleep, and what sleep she had got was not very restful thanks to the shared dreams. Dreams G.G. didn't even realize he was sharing with her.

"He knows about immortals. Why doesn't he realize we're having shared dreams?" she asked with bewilderment.

"From what I've read from his mind, while he does know about shared dreams, and did wonder at one point if that was what he was experiencing, in the end he decided not."

"Why?" Ildaria asked with surprise.

"Because he doesn't feel like you are really there," Sofia said gently, and when Ildaria's confusion showed in her expression, she explained, "You're letting him have his way in the dreams. The settings come from his thoughts, as does what happens. You never take control yourself, you just kind of go along for the ride. That's probably because you're not all that experienced," she added quickly. "But whatever the case, it's convinced him that he's just having these dream fantasies about you on his own, and they're so powerful and incessant that he's beginning to feel like a perv."

She let that sink in and then said, "While Marguerite was concerned about how he might react to finding out he's a possible life mate to you, and I did too, I think at this point he'd be relieved that he isn't just gaining an unhealthy obsession with you."

They were both silent for a moment as Ildaria considered that and then Sofia said, "Come on then, go throw on some clothes and we'll head out to find you sexy outfits and books to help you seduce G.G. You can eat your sandwich in the car."

Even Ildaria was surprised when she slid docilely off her chair and headed for the bedroom without argument. But she had to do something or G.G. would fly off to England. If he did, she could lose him altogether. Ildaria couldn't afford to follow him right away, and he was mortal. Accidents happened. She needed to step up her game, and she had no idea how to do that. She needed help.

Seven

Ildaria glanced at the dashboard clock as she pulled into her parking spot, surprised to see that it was only 2 P.M. She and Sofia hadn't been shopping long. Well, actually, Sofia was still at the mall. She said she had some things to get and would Uber it home. Ildaria had offered to wait, but Sofia had insisted she head home. She wanted her to get to work reading "the instructive books" she'd chosen and "get an idea" of what she needed to do to seduce G.G.

"Instructive books," Ildaria muttered, reaching over to grab the two bags on the passenger's seat. One held half a dozen romance novels and the other, a see-through nightie, all of which Sofia had picked and purchased for her. Getting seduction advice from romance novels was ridiculous enough, but the nightie . . . ? It wasn't her style, but Sofia had guaranteed it would drive G.G. mad. Ildaria wasn't so sure herself. She might as well stand around naked as wear the sheer white nightgown. It looked like it had been made from a bride's veil, and to her mind was as obvious as that *Fuck me* sign Sofia had mentioned.

In fact, maybe wearing a sign would be good, Ildaria thought as she opened her door and slid out, dragging the bags with her. At least, with a sign, he couldn't misunderstand what she—

"Ms. Pimienta?"

Ildaria paused to eye the approaching man who had spoken. He was coming from a dark sedan parked next to G.G.'s pickup. Which she would have noticed if she hadn't been distracted checking the time and thinking about the seduction paraphernalia she'd brought home with her. Honestly, she'd spent nearly two centuries in a hyper state of awareness, always double and triple checking any area she entered or moved through. Now, suddenly she was flouncing about like an idiot, not looking around at all. This was how a girl got dead . . . or harassed by the FBI, she thought as she recognized the man.

His name was Jack Barr. He was the FBI agent she'd saved from a pack of gang members in Montana. Which had put the FBI on her tail there.

But as far as she knew the FBI hadn't got anywhere close to figuring out who she was or tracking her down in Montana. How the devil had the man found her here?

She didn't ask. Instead, while she normally avoided it, Ildaria read his mind . . . and nearly blushed at his thoughts. The man was terribly excited. He was sure he'd found his "angel" at last. Fortunately, he didn't think of her that way because he knew her real first name, he just thought of her as "his angel." It seemed he'd been obsessed with finding her since she'd saved him some months ago. He was also the impetus behind the FBI's hunt for her in Montana which had caught Lucian's attention.

Ildaria wasn't sure whether to thank him for that or not. On the one hand, it appeared he was the reason she'd been dragged out of Montana and lost a term's worth of courses. On the other hand, he was the reason she'd been dragged out of Montana and brought here to meet her life mate. Which was another problem in itself. But the kind of problem every immortal wished for. Although, most would rather have an easy go of claiming their life mate than she appeared to have before her.

"Ms. Pimienta, my name is Agent Jack Barr. I'm—"

Ildaria cut him off right there, and continued to read his mind. Irritation flickered through her as she realized he'd found her through the video of her saving the student who had nearly been raped. Unfortunately, Lucian wasn't the only one to spot that video. It seemed when she'd disappeared from the scene in Montana, Jack Barr hadn't believed she'd simply stopped helping people. He'd thought perhaps she'd moved because things had got hot there. He'd started looking for similar incidents elsewhere and Toronto had popped up on his radar. He'd seen the video of her tossing around that would-be rapist who had been twice her size, and had been positive she was his "angel."

Her name, however, had not been on the video that

was now floating around the networks. But since that incident had happened on campus, as had most of the incidents in Montana, he'd looked for a student, professor, or employee who had moved from one university to the other.

Much to her surprise, her name wasn't the only one to pop up; two others had transferred up from Montana this summer. Jack had got the contact numbers and addresses for each of them from the university, and was going through the admittedly short list, interviewing them one after the other. He'd interviewed the first two yesterday. Ildaria was last because he'd had trouble finding an address for her until he'd approached the university today and flirted shamelessly with a student helping out in the registrar's office to get her to look up the address.

Luckily for him, Ildaria had made sure to give the university her new address the day she'd moved into her new apartment. She hadn't wanted to miss any notices, or the information packets about her courses. And so here he was, about to try to get her to confess she was the vigilante he'd become so obsessed with.

Ildaria had no idea how he planned to do it, mainly because he had no idea either. He had no jurisdiction in Canada, but was hoping she didn't know that and that the very name FBI would be enough to scare her into confessing. Worse yet, while he was supposed to track her down for the FBI, he was really doing it for himself and had no intention of turning her over to his bosses . . . unless she rejected him. Then he'd give his boss the information he had on her and leave it to him to get her charged and extradited for her vigilante activities back in Montana.

More than a little irritated that her assistance, and actually saving the man's life, was being paid back this way, Ildaria had no qualms about sliding into his mind and taking control of him. She quickly rearranged his memories of this meeting, put it into his mind that he was positive she couldn't be his "angel," eased his desire to find said "angel" and then sent him back to his car with the mindset to let go of his fruitless hunt, return to the head office, and move on to his next case.

She watched him drive out of the parking lot, worrying about any other possible repercussions from that video. Lucian had seen it and dragged her here. Jack Barr had found her because of it. What if Juan or one of his people saw it? Would she have to go on the run again?

Mouth tightening, Ildaria closed and locked her car door then headed inside, quite sure she wouldn't be reading her "homework" now.

Ildaria was wrong. After pacing and fretting uselessly for half an hour, she actually snatched up one of the books Sofia had insisted on getting just to escape her worries for a bit. It had actually worked. The stories were engrossing and worked beautifully at taking her away from her own life for a bit. Ildaria managed to read all of one, and half of a second book before she had to stop to get ready for work.

She was actually looking forward to continuing with the stories after work. But not for any seduction advice they offered. There wasn't really much help regarding that. It seemed to her that the sex in the books was situational, rather than a matter of seduction. The women didn't wear risqué outfits, or spout suggestive lines to lure the men. It just kind of happened. But, she still wanted to finish reading the one she was halfway through, and then move on to the other books. Because, much to her surprise, she was actually enjoying them. The one she'd finished and the one she'd started weren't at all the bodice rippers she'd expected. The stories were full of adventure and action, with heroines that were strong and intelligent, not helpless creatures needing rescuing. They fought alongside the men in the stories, saving themselves and occasionally even saving their male counterparts. She was enjoying them, and anything that took her mind off Juan and the possibility of his finding her was a welcome diversion.

Of course, her worries about G.G. leaving and Juan finding her returned the moment she put the second book down and began to get ready for work. And it continued to weigh on her mind as she worked, but Ildaria was no closer to coming up with a solution to either problem by the time her eight hours of office work were done.

Since keeping G.G. from leaving was the larger concern in her mind, she continued to ponder the problem as she took H.D. up to her apartment to wait for G.G. to collect him.

Maybe if she quit working for him, she thought.

Then G.G. would have no reason to flee and she could come to the club as a customer and . . . what? The *what* was the problem. She still had no idea how to handle the situation. Could she even afford to come here without a job? Not to mention, she'd be homeless. The apartments were for employees; if she quit she'd have to find somewhere else to live.

Things would be a lot easier if she could just tell him the truth and work things out from there. G.G. might have a thing about turning, but that didn't mean he would refuse to be her life mate . . . necessarily. She wasn't sure. Besides, if she succeeded at seducing him, as Sofia wanted her to do, he'd realize he was her life mate the moment they did. Life mates felt each other's pleasure and then passed out at the end. Although the passing out part wasn't guaranteed. There *were* instances where it didn't happen. But the shared pleasure part definitely happened every time and would give away that they were life mates.

She wasn't sure what to do now. Tell him, not tell him. Seduce him, not seduce him.

H.D. shifted beside her on the couch. When she glanced down, he craned his head around, and licked her hand where it rested on his shoulder.

"Hey, sweetie. Feeling neglected? Sorry, I'm just trying to sort out what to do about your daddy," she murmured, rubbing him between the ears, and then smiling faintly, she asked, "Any advice?"

H.D. tilted his head and then got to his feet, rested his paws on her chest, and licked her chin.

Chuckling, Ildaria scooped him up and got up from

the couch. "How about a treat to make up for neglecting you?" she asked, carrying him to the kitchen.

Recognizing the word *treat*, H.D. panted excitedly, and went wild in her arms, desperate to lick any bit of flesh he could reach: hands, neck, chin.

Laughing, Ildaria set him on the floor in the kitchen and moved to the refrigerator. She retrieved a container of cherry yogurt as well as the homemade dog treats G.G. had given her, and set both on the counter, then retrieved a bowl and spoon. She quickly scooped out some yogurt, and then retrieved a treat from the second container before returning both to the fridge.

"Come on," she said lightly to H.D., heading out of the kitchen. Sitting on the couch, she set the bowl of yogurt on the coffee table, and then offered the homemade bone-shaped cookie to H.D. The pup nearly took her finger off snatching it from her.

"Keep that up and I'll stop giving you treats, buddy," she warned. Not that he listened. He was too busy devouring his cookie. Shaking her head, Ildaria grabbed her bowl, and started to sit back, only to pause when she realized she'd forgotten a spoon. Setting the bowl down, she hurried to the kitchen for one. It only took her a moment, but she returned to find H.D. with his front paws up on the coffee table and his face buried in her yogurt.

"H.D.!" she barked.

The Bichonpoo startled, jerking back before his chin was out of the bowl and bringing it down on top of himself.

"Oh damn!" Ildaria gasped, hurrying forward to snatch up the pup before he could spread the mess around. She started to bring him to her chest, but then realized she was still wearing her work clothes, and held him away from her body instead.

"Well, it's your own fault," Ildaria said firmly when H.D. yipped in protest at the way he was being carried. But she also moved a little more quickly, rushing up the hall to the bathroom to set him in the tub. She expected H.D. to try to scramble out right away, but he surprised her and instead dropped to sit and set about trying to lick the yogurt off himself.

Ildaria didn't risk leaving him alone though. She quickly undid the buttons of her blouse, removed it and hung it from the hook on the bathroom door, then knelt beside the tub in just her skirt and bra.

H.D. was still trying to lick himself clean. An impossible task. There was no way he could reach the yogurt on his head and back. Which meant bath time for H.D. The only problem was Ildaria didn't have any dog shampoo for him. But she didn't want to leave H.D. on his own for the length of time it would take to fetch it. At least, not until she'd rinsed the worst of the yogurt off him.

Grabbing the handheld showerhead from its holder, she pointed it away from H.D. and turned on the water, waiting and repeatedly checking the water sprinkling out of it until it felt warm enough. Then she pushed the button on the handle until the sprinkle turned into a light spray. She used that to rinse H.D. off.

H.D. did not like baths. That became apparent rather quickly. The minute the first splash of water hit him, the pup began trying to climb out of the tub and up her chest, soaking her through. Ildaria tried to urge him back into the tub, but it was impossible with one hand. Deciding she couldn't get much wetter, Ildaria left him pressed to her chest, held him in place there with her free hand and simply leaned forward over the tub so that most of the water would land in it as she rinsed him down.

Once she had the worst of the yogurt removed, and the water ran clear, Ildaria turned off the showerhead. She tried to set him back in the tub then but he still wasn't having that. Pressing closer, he rubbed his face against the cloth of her bra, and then pretty much tried to bury his head inside it between her breasts.

"Come on," she said with amusement, getting back to her feet. "Let's get you dry."

H.D. didn't respond except to press his snout deeper into her bra until she snatched the towel off the rack next to the tub and wrapped it over him. Then he lifted his head out and tried to bury himself in what he could reach of that.

"Si. Enjoy it while you can," Ildaria murmured, rubbing the towel over his back as she carried him back out of the bathroom. "But your bath isn't done. We still have to find your shampoos and give you a proper bath or you'll be sticky."

She didn't know if H.D. would have understood her words, but it didn't matter. She was pretty sure he couldn't hear them what with the way he was twisting his head back and forth against the towel.

Wrapping him more firmly in the cloth, Ildaria carried him out to the kitchen to fetch the keys G.G. had given her to his apartment in case of emergencies. She then took him across the hall to fetch the dog shampoo and conditioner.

Ildaria found them under the kitchen sink where G.G. had told her they would be the first night she'd watched H.D. after moving into her apartment. Then she carried him and the items back to her apartment and straight to the bathroom to set him in the tub again.

Ignoring the betrayed expression he was now giving her, Ildaria gave him a proper bath this time, soaping him up with the dog shampoo and rinsing him, then soaping him up again and repeating the rinsing process, before moving on to the conditioner.

Ildaria had never realized they had such a thing as dog conditioner, but H.D. had small tight curls that G.G. swore became a frizzy tangled mess if the conditioner wasn't used, so she applied it liberally, and let it sit for a couple of minutes, before rinsing that off him as well.

The first towel was a sopping mess and a new one was needed for drying him this time, but Ildaria slicked her hands over H.D. first, removing as much of the liquid as she could. It helped that H.D. gave a shake as she grabbed a fresh towel for him. Well, it helped him, but just managed to soak her even further, sending water spraying everywhere. Her bra was already soaked through so it made little difference there, but now her face and hair were soaking too.

Ignoring that, Ildaria wrapped H.D. up in the towel and scooped him out of the tub. She then knelt to set him on the floor, intending to rub him dry, but the moment she set him down, H.D. scampered out of the bathroom. The towel was dragged along the first few feet, but fell off as he skittered out the door and turned right.

"H.D.!" Leaping back to her feet, Ildaria hurried after him, catching up to him just at the entry to the living room. She noticed G.G.'s black Doc Martens only a couple feet away as she scooped up the pup. Straightening abruptly, she clutched H.D. to her chest and took a startled step back, as she took in G.G.'s stunned expression. Blushing, she muttered, "Sorry. I was bathing H.D. and didn't know you were here."

"I knocked," he said quickly as if she might think he hadn't. "When you didn't answer I got worried and used my key."

Ildaria had enough wit to realize the sound of the shower must have kept her from hearing the knock, but that was all the wit she had at the moment. G.G. hadn't been this close to her in quite a while, not since shortly after the shared dreams had started. That was when real contact between them had stopped. She didn't remember being affected by his nearness like this before the dreams, but right now she was experiencing a strange . . . awareness. That was the only way she could think to describe it. It was like the very cells in her body were all suddenly wide awake and hopping about inside her with a strange excitement that turned to horrible disappointment when he suddenly began to back away and then turned toward the door saying, "I should go. Good night."

Ildaria was so stunned by the abruptness of his retreat that she might have let him go, except she was still holding H.D. G.G. was leaving without his dog. He was also muttering something under his breath. Even with her superior hearing, all she caught was what sounded like "turning into a bloody pervert."

"They're shared dreams," she blurted.

G.G. paused at the mouth of the short hall to the door, but didn't turn or say anything. He just stood as if frozen.

Ildaria hesitated briefly, and then licked her lips and said to his back, "You're a possible life mate for me, G.G., and you've been experiencing shared dreams. I've been with you for every one."

That did make him turn, but his eyes were doubting. "You weren't—it didn't feel like you were there."

"I know. Sofia said you were sure you were alone," she said quietly.

"She knows I hate it when she reads my mind," G.G. complained with irritation.

"She probably wasn't trying to read your mind," Ildaria said quickly, not wanting him to be angry with Sofia when she had only been trying to help. "Marguerite says new life mates tend to have an issue keeping their thoughts to themselves. She says it's like we are screaming our thoughts, that no reading is needed at all."

He grunted at that, and then said with uncertainty, "Were you really sharing the dreams?"

"Si," she assured him. "But I was—I just—I let you take the lead because . . ." She swallowed, surprised to feel little prickles of heat ride up the back of her neck and head and sweat start under her arms. She hadn't expected this to be so hard. Finally, she simply said, "I don't have the experience to take the lead when it comes to sex, so I just let you control the dreams. But I was there." She paused briefly and then added, "The first dream took place in your office. On the desk."

When he just stared at her, she added, "I can't remember which dream came next but last night's involved chains." When he continued to stare blankly, she added, "But they've taken place everywhere. There were others in the office, some here in my apartment, some in yours, some in every room of the Night Club, at the beach, in the dressing room of a clothing store, and some in England I think. At least, it was somewhere I've never been before and there were people there with English accents."

G.G.'s shoulders sagged and Ildaria knew he believed her even before he said, "It was the Night Club in England."

"Oh," she said softly, but was recalling the rooms she'd seen in the dreams there and thinking the man had good taste. The Night Club in England was as impressive as this one, if not more. The rooms were more . . . posh, she supposed was the best description. More sedate, old-fashioned class, fit for Lords and Ladies, similar to the room the dream had taken place in last night. But the other rooms here were more relaxed. It made her wonder if there were more relaxed rooms in the Night Club in England as well that she just hadn't yet seen.

"So . . ."

Ildaria shifted her attention back to G.G. to see the frown on his face.

"You were sharing the dreams but not really contributing to them because you lack experience," he murmured. "You're over two hundred years old and still a . . . ?"

"I'm not a virgin," Ildaria said stiffly. "I'm just inexperienced."

She wasn't surprised to see the confusion on his expression, but it wasn't something she could clear up quickly. Straightening her shoulders, she said, "We need to talk. Why don't you sit down and I'll make us some hot chocolate."

G.G. hesitated, his gaze flickering downward briefly before returning to her face. "Better yet, I will make the hot chocolate while you change into something . . ." Grimacing, he said, "Just go put some clothes on or talking won't be what we do."

Ildaria glanced down. H.D. was cuddled between her breasts, leaving her bra on display. It was a very old bra, embarrassingly old, and it was so thin that— wet as it was—it was as see-through as that veil nightie would have been. Ildaria felt her face flush with heat, but refused to let her embarrassment show otherwise and lifted her chin defiantly as she muttered, "Fine. I'll be right back."

Turning on her heel then, she headed for her room. Ildaria had the brief concern that he might flee once she was out of sight, but H.D.'s squirming to a more comfortable position in her arms had her relaxing. The man might want to flee now that he knew they were possible life mates, but he wouldn't go without H.D. This was an instance where "man's best friend," was true. Because that man loved his dog.

The minute Ildaria set H.D. on the bed, the fur ball dove headfirst into the pillows and then dragged himself across her blankets, doing his best to dry himself.

Shaking her head at his antics, Ildaria spared a moment to rub the little beast down, and then straightened to strip off her clothes. She was soaked through, not just her bra, but her skirt and panties had also taken a soaking from the water dripping down from the dog against her chest. She donned a fresh pair of white cotton panties, and an equally boring white cotton bra. This set was as worn and threadbare as the ones she'd just taken off, but they were clean. She didn't even consider the black lace lingerie set she'd purchased after the first shared dreams. What they had to talk about was not going to lead to anything that would call for black lace.

Mouth tightening, at the thought of the unpleasant task to come, Ildaria pulled out a pair of baggy jogging pants, and an oversized sweatshirt and tugged those on as well. Fully dressed now in the most unattractive clothes she owned, Ildaria stopped to drag a brush through her damp hair, put it up in a ponytail, and then take several deep breaths.

It didn't help much, but then she doubted anything would, except getting this over with. Turning away from her reflection in the mirror, she patted her leg and said, "Come on, buddy, let's go see your dad."

H.D. leapt off the bed and scampered out the door the moment Ildaria opened it. She followed more slowly, half hoping G.G. would snatch up H.D. and leave before she could get to the living room, and half afraid he would.

He didn't. G.G. was standing by the island with H.D. in his big, brawny arms, petting him when she reached the kitchen. But he stopped to give her the once-over, a wry smile tugging at his lips.

"Only you could make sweats look sexy," he said with weary amusement as his gaze slid back up to her eyes.

Ildaria frowned. There wasn't anything the least sexy in what she was wearing. But perhaps it was the effect of the dreams, she thought. With the memories of those dreams crowding the mind, she could probably wear a potato sack and look sexy to him. Just as he would appear sexy to her in whatever he chose to wear. But he wasn't dressed in unattractive clothes. He was wearing his usual Night Club outfit of black dress pants and black dress shirt with the top two buttons undone. Sort of casual dressy, but still very sexy.

"Your cocoa," G.G. said quietly, nodding toward the two cups on the island. "I had a sip of mine. It doesn't taste as good as yours, but I just followed the directions on the can. I suspect you do something different."

"I add a little cream," Ildaria explained, moving past him into the kitchen to fetch the cream Marguerite had brought with the groceries two weeks ago. It was nearly gone now. She'd have to buy more soon, she thought as she carried it back to add a little to both their cups.

"Thank you," G.G. murmured, setting H.D. down and taking one of the cups as she replaced the cream.

When she returned, he was standing to the side of the table, waiting for her to take a seat. Ildaria picked up her own cup, and then chose the nearest end chair. She wasn't surprised when he chose the opposite one, as far from her as he could get. Now that he knew they were life mates, he would avoid touching her at all unless he decided to agree to be her life mate. She had no doubt he knew enough about life mates to realize how highly combustible they were. One touch could be enough to set them off and have them tearing at each other's clothes.

They were both silent at first. Ildaria had no idea what G.G. was thinking, but she was fretting over where to begin her explanation for her lack of experience. In the end, she just admitted, "I don't know where to start."

"Just start at the beginning," G.G. suggested.

Ildaria nodded. "I guess it starts with my mother then. She was apparently something of a wild child. My *abuela*—my grandmother—said my grandfather was very strict, and my mother was always rebelling against his strictness. At sixteen, my mother decided she'd had enough and ran off with her boyfriend, telling my grandparents they'd never see her again."

When G.G.'s eyebrows rose dubiously at that, she smiled wryly and said, "Yeah. Famous last words. She popped up a year later with me in tow. I was six months old. She'd been three months pregnant when she left, but too ashamed to tell them."

"Ah," G.G. murmured with understanding.

Ildaria nodded. "Anyway, had my grandfather still been alive, my abuela thinks things might have turned out differently, but he'd suffered a massive heart attack and died six months before. The same day I was born as it turns out. My abuela always thought that was important for some reason." She shrugged. "Anyway, Abuela took us in, and agreed to help raise me, but only if my mother stopped drinking and partying and got a job."

"But she didn't," G.G. guessed.

Ildaria shook her head. "I gather she was there for less than a month before she found a new boyfriend to move in with. My abuela begged her to leave me with her, but she refused and dragged me along. It was the first of many such moves. I guess it was the same pattern over and over. New boyfriend, she'd move in, taking me with her. They'd drink and party and fight and fall apart, and then she'd land back at Abuela's with me three to six months later. I don't remember any of that, but Abuela says the first couple of men were mean drunks and verbally abusive, which was bad enough, but then my mother moved on to men who were physically abusive.

"Same pattern," she added with a shrug. "She just came crawling back to Abuela with bruises and whatnot rather than in a high dander about whatever the latest boyfriend had done. My abuela tried to talk to her, worried about her but also about me. I hadn't been hit yet by any of the boyfriends, but she felt it was just a matter of time. She begged her to not move in with these men. Just live with her and date them. But my mother was headstrong."

Sighing, Ildaria turned her cup slowly on the island before continuing, "And then one day, when I was four, she didn't crawl back to Abuela's. Instead, one early morning, one of my mother's neighbors brought me to my abuela, explaining that my mother was very sick and asked that she please look after me for a couple of days. Once she felt better, she would come fetch me back.

"Abuela wanted to go speak to my mother, but had to leave for work and the neighbor assured her my mother was fine, just under the weather and unable to look after me properly. So, in the end, my abuela decided she would check on my mother after work and since she didn't have time to find someone to babysit me, she took me to her job with her."

G.G.'s eyebrows rose at this news and he asked, "Where did she work?"

"She was the head cook on a large plantation owned by Ana Villaverde," Ildaria explained.

"And this Ana didn't mind her bringing you to work with her?" G.G. asked.

Ildaria smiled at the suggestion. "My abuela was an amazing cook and sought after by rival plantations. I think her boss pretty much let her do what she wanted."

"Ah," G.G. murmured with understanding. "Good employees are hard to find."

"Si, so anyway, she took me with her and kept me in the kitchen while she cooked. Apparently, everything was fine until late afternoon when her boss, Señorita Ana, came into the kitchen to meet me. It came out then that my mother wasn't sick, she'd been beaten very badly."

"You told them?" G.G. guessed.

"No." Ildaria shook her head, but she didn't explain

how they learned it then. Instead, she blurted, "They also learned that while my mother's latest boyfriend wasn't beating me, he *was* sexually molesting me." Ildaria lifted her chin defiantly as she said that, her teeth grinding together as she waited for his response.

G.G. breathed out as if he'd been afraid this was coming, but was still disappointed that it had. His expression compassionate, he said gently, "I'm sorry."

That was all, no gasping horror, no outrage and vows of vengeance or justice. But it had more effect than those other things would have. Ildaria's mouth wobbled with the bottled-up emotion that wanted to escape, and then firmed again. It had happened two hundred years ago. She didn't even remember it. She'd be damned if she was going to get all emotional now.

Clearing her throat, she nodded in acknowledgment of his words, and then said, "My abuela was apparently very upset to learn this, so Señorita Ana very kindly suggested she take me home, telling her not to worry about my mother or her boyfriend. She would send men to take care of the boyfriend, as well as to fetch my mother back to my abuela's along with a doctor to see to both she and myself."

Ildaria paused to take a sip of her cocoa. She didn't usually talk this much and her mouth was growing dry. The hot chocolate didn't really help much, but it was still warm and tasted good, so she took another sip before continuing. "When my abuela took me home, my mother and her boyfriend were there waiting. My mother was apparently a mess, but insisted she was well enough to look after me, and wanted to take me home.

But the way she kept a wary eye on her boyfriend and flinched whenever he moved made my abuela suspect it was he who wanted me back and not to look after me. She had no intention of letting me be taken back to be abused, so sent me to my room and then told my mother about the abuse."

Ildaria grimaced. "As you can imagine, that didn't go over well. The boyfriend at first tried to deny he was abusing me, but my mother came to my room and asked me about it. I don't remember it, don't know what I said, but apparently it was enough that she went storming back out." Ildaria blew out a breath and shook her head. "All hell broke out then. I gather my mother grabbed a knife and went after her boyfriend. He got the knife away and used it on her, and then went after my abuela when she tried to help my mother. I have no doubt he would have killed them both, and maybe even me. Fortunately, Señorita Ana had sent men to deal with the boyfriend as promised. When they arrived at his shack to learn he and my mother had come to get me, they followed and arrived in time to save my abuela. Unfortunately, my mother wasn't as lucky. She died in hospital several days later from her wounds."

Ildaria stopped to sip at her cocoa again, hardly hearing his murmured condolences. Talking about it brought back the dark feelings that always accompanied discussing this subject. Were she to analyze those feelings, Ildaria would probably have to say they were a combination of shame and anger, but she didn't bother analyzing them. It was her past. Best forgotten, as her abuela used to say.

She did feel sad, though, that she never felt much loss when she thought about the death of her mother. But she'd been too young to have much in the way of memories of her. To Ildaria, she was just a photo that her abuela used to show her. Just as the fact that she had been abused was just a story she'd been told. She didn't recall much of either.

Even so, Ildaria knew it affected her to this day. She suspected it was why she'd never been interested in sexual intimacy, and the reason she had so little experience with the opposite sex. Sexual situations brought those dark feelings rising within her and morphed into all-out rage. Or they had before G.G. She hadn't had any of those feelings with him, not in their shared dreams anyway. He'd never so much as touched her in passing when they were awake, though. She had no idea how she'd react if he touched or tried to kiss her . . . which was rather concerning now that she thought about it.

"So your abuela raised you after that?"

Glancing up at that question, Ildaria realized she'd broken off the story. She gave her head a shake to clear out her other worries and nodded. "Si. There was no more bouncing from boyfriends to my abuela's. It was just Abuela and I." Her mouth curved into a soft smile. "The next ten years were wonderful. She was an amazing woman and I was nothing like my mother. Probably by choice. I didn't want to be like her."

"Understandable," G.G. murmured.

"So I was a dutiful granddaughter, always doing what I was told, and spending a lot of time with Abuela, rather than with children my own age. She used to walk me to school on the way to work, and then I would go to her employer's after school and do my homework in the kitchen until she was done and then walk home with her."

"What about friends?" G.G. asked when she paused to take a breath.

"Oh, I had school friends," she said with a shrug. "But I never saw them after school. Abuela worked late enough that my friends were inside when we got home." Ildaria smiled faintly. "I know most people would consider that abnormal or unhealthy, but I didn't really miss not having friends my own age. I had my abuela and she was always doing things with me. Teaching me to cook and clean, helping with my homework. We played board games and cards and laughed a lot. I loved my abuela. She was wonderful."

G.G. nodded, but pointed out, "You said the next ten years were wonderful. What happened after that?"

Ildaria was silent for a minute, her mind going back to that time. "My abuela usually finished work around dinnertime when the night staff took over, and then we'd walk home to make our own meal. But if her employer was having a party, she'd stay late to help and send me home alone. It only happened perhaps once or twice a year over those first ten years, but then Señorita Ana got engaged. She was rich and from an important family, so the engagement meant a lot more parties, two or three a week. My abuela was getting older, and I knew she found these parties exhausting after working all day. I wanted to stay and help, but she refused to even consider it. She wanted me nowhere near these parties. She'd send me home every time.

"It was as I left before one of these parties that a man approached me at the end of the driveway. He introduced himself as Juan, a friend of my abuela's employer, assured me I was safe with him, and insisted on walking me home. I wasn't completely comfortable with him, but I didn't want to offend my abuela's employer by offending him. So, not knowing how to make him go away, I let him walk me home, thinking it would be a one-off. But a couple days later there was another party, and again my abuela sent me home alone, and there he was, appearing at the end of the drive to accompany me.

"As I say, I wasn't comfortable with him, but couldn't have told you why at the time," she said unhappily. "Juan never did anything wrong, never touched me or said anything untoward. He was very polite and even charming, but I — " she hesitated and then tried to explain, "I was very naïve, but even so I think I sensed that he wanted . . . something," she said helplessly, unable to better describe the creeping sense of discomfort he'd caused her when he hadn't done anything that she could point to as being threatening. Grimacing, she gave it up and said, "I began to loathe the nights my abuela had to stay late for parties."

Her gaze slid to G.G. and she paused briefly as she noted the grim expression on his face. He knew something was coming and was mentally preparing himself. It was part of the reason he didn't gasp in horror or outrage at things he was told. Which, she suspected, was also part of the reason women liked to talk to him. He was a good listener, really listening . . . with interest and caring and calm. G.G. was a good listener in the way that a good driver kept an eye on the traffic ahead, not just on the car ahead. The driver who watched only the car ahead didn't know there was trouble until the brake lights of the car in front of them came on, often too late to keep from hitting them. The good driver watching the traffic ahead, saw the brake lights of distant cars coming on and automatically slowed down, preparing for the coming trouble and usually avoiding hitting the car in front when it suddenly braked. G.G. listened that way, sensing something coming and preparing himself mentally for it so that he could remain calm and sympathetic, rather than making it about himself and his reaction to what he was hearing.

A nudge at her ankle drew her attention away from G.G. and down to see H.D. curling up against her. She smiled faintly, and reached down to pet him briefly before straightening and continuing, "Anyway, I think my desire to avoid the man was why I committed my first act of rebellion."

"And what did you do?" G.G. asked.

"My girlfriends from school were always asking me to go places and do things. Not wanting to worry or upset my abuela I always said no. But Emilita, one of those school friends, was having a birthday party on the Friday night and invited me. I knew Señorita Ana was having another party that night. I didn't want to have to walk home again with Juan, so I asked if I could go to the birthday party. It was directly after school, and we would all walk there together where her family would be in attendance. I was fourteen, certainly old enough to go to a birthday party, but I was still surprised when my abuela gave me permission."

"Why wouldn't she? You were always a good girl," G.G. pointed out softly.

"Si," Ildaria breathed unhappily. "I meant to be that night as well, and everything was fine at first. A group of us went to Emilita's house after school. There was food, non-alcoholic drinks, and a piñata. I had fun, so when the party started to wind down and some of the girls talked about going to a cantina where Emilita's brother worked, and invited me . . ."

"You agreed," G.G. guessed.

Ildaria grimaced, but nodded. "Emilita's brother did work there. He served us alcoholic drinks we shouldn't have had, but he did try to keep an eye on us too. Unfortunately, he couldn't watch all of us at once. The other girls had apparently drunk before. They handled it better than me, who after one drink was drunk. After two I was stumbling drunk. I stopped counting drinks at four," she admitted and shook her head with disgust at the stupidity of youth.

"What happened?" G.G. asked softly.

"Good question," she muttered, and then said, "One minute I was with my friends, and then—I don't even know how it happened, but suddenly these men moved in and I got separated from the group. In the next moment, I was outside in the alley behind the cantina and these two men in uniform were pushing me to the ground and tearing at my clothes."

Ildaria crossed her arms protectively at the memory, and took a few deep breaths before continuing, "I was crying and saying, 'No! Stop!' and trying to get away, but there were two of them, and they were so strong. And then suddenly the one on top of me was gone, and then the other one was too. At first I was too stunned by the suddenness of their absence to react, but then I struggled to my feet. I staggered the moment I was upright, my head spinning. I grabbed the wall to balance myself and then I looked around and saw one of the men on the ground near me, unconscious. The other was struggling with a man in a suit, my savior. It almost looked like they were hugging, but then the one in uniform suddenly sagged and after a minute my savior dropped him and whirled toward me. It was Juan. There was blood on his mouth and I thought he'd been injured. I wanted to ask if he was all right, but his eyes were glowing, and he looked so enraged. I just stared at him stupidly and shrank against the wall as he stormed over to me."

She felt the skin tighten on her face as if shrinking away from what was coming, but said, "He was bellowing at me furiously, and I started babbling I'm sorry and thank you, I was so grateful. But that just seemed to incense him more. He slapped me hard and I stumbled to the side, lost my footing and fell to my knees, and then I just cowered there while he screamed at me about how he'd controlled himself, wanting to wait for me to be ready, and I'd nearly given it away like some cheap *puta*. Was that what I wanted? To be taken in some back alley like a prostitute? And then he snarled, 'If that is what you want, I can give you it!' and I glanced up to see him undoing his pants.

"I just gaped at him. I didn't understand. He'd saved me and now he was—" She shook her head with remembered bewilderment. "I didn't understand what was happening. Why he was acting like that. Or maybe part of me did. There was a reason I'd been so uncomfortable with him. I'd known he wanted something from me, I just didn't want to know. But while I was sobering quickly, I still wasn't thinking clearly and I didn't really understand what was happening . . . I still don't to a certain degree."

"What do you mean?" G.G. asked slowly.

"He was an immortal," she explained. "I didn't know about them at the time, but he was. He could have controlled me, made me do what he wanted, go to him willingly, but he didn't and he was almost insane with rage. I think the whole exercise was just to humiliate and hurt me at that point. He was so angry and frustrated with me. But he stopped with his pants open, and grabbed me by the hair, yanking my head back and shouting 'Look at me when I'm talking to you!'

"I cried out in pain, but I doubt he heard me, he'd moved on to bellowing again about my behavior and what could have happened to me. Then he bent and grabbed me by the shoulders and shook me and I just—I lost it," she said, remembering the mad rage that had welled up in her the moment he'd touched her in that dark alley. It had filled her, pushing her fear and confusion aside and consuming her.

"What did you do?" G.G. asked.

Ildaria closed her eyes briefly as she recalled the moment. "He'd opened his pants, but not all the way, and he hadn't taken himself out, but his movements had dislodged his cock. It was dangling in front of my face and—" Opening her eyes, she tried to explain how she'd felt. "I wanted to hurt him for threatening and frightening me, for even thinking of raping me in that alley, and I pushed forward in his hold and bit the weapon he'd threatened me with."

G.G. blinked, and then asked carefully, "You mean his penis? You bit his penis?"

Ildaria grimaced. "I didn't just bite it, G.G. I clamped down on it and started sawing my teeth back and forth, determined to bite through. I wanted to unman him," she confessed, almost ashamed of herself and still a little bewildered by the insane rage that had claimed her. It had come on so hard and fast. Shaking her head at the memory, she continued. "Blood was squirting into my mouth, but I was so furious that I didn't care. I just swallowed and kept gnawing away at his cock, determined to remove it from him so he could never hurt or humiliate another girl again."

G.G. had released something like a grunt, his legs instinctively closing protectively as she spoke. Now, he asked, "If he was immortal, why didn't he take control at that point and stop you?"

"I don't know," Ildaria said helplessly. "Maybe the alcohol was making me hard to control. Or maybe he was just so shocked and horrified that he didn't think to take control of me then. But he didn't," she said with a shrug, and then added, "Instead, he pushed me away rather violently . . . which had the unfortunate effect of finishing what I was trying to do . . . I fell back on my butt with the amputated bottom half of his cock in my mouth."

G.G. made a pained sound, but she ignored it and continued, "He dropped to his knees clutching himself and screaming in agony, then fell over and lay writhing on the filthy ground. I just watched him with a kind of horror at first. The rage was gone as suddenly as it had struck, leaving me confused and shocked by what I'd done. But when his agonized screams turned to moaning, I regained enough sense to know I should probably get out of there. I lurched to my feet and staggered away . . . I didn't even realize I still had his member, or part of it anyway, in my mouth until I reached the end of the alley. I took it out there and threw it across the road, and then I ran home.

"Or tried to," she said after a moment, and then explained, "I hadn't sobered enough to be steady on my feet, and then the pain struck and hampered me. I didn't understand what was happening, but I'd taken in enough blood that the turning was starting. I did make it to the house, but not inside. My abuela found me on the doorstep when she came home. Apparently I was convulsing and moaning in pain."

"You didn't hurt her?" G.G. asked with concern.

"No," Ildaria said at once. "No. Thank the saints. I couldn't have lived with myself if I'd hurt her." She sighed. "Fortunately, she recognized what was happening. I guess the blood on my face and the metallic glint growing in my eyes gave it away. She dragged me inside, and then ran to her employer. Señorita Ana came back with her, took one look and carried me back to her home. She was immortal, and why my abuela had recognized what was happening. Abuela was one of those servants who is trusted with the knowledge of immortals."

"Which explains how Señorita Ana knew you were being abused when you were four. She read your mind back then," G.G. said with realization.

Ildaria nodded. "She read my mind and saw the beating of my mother that I had witnessed, as well as the abuse I'd suffered."

"But your abuela worked days, not nights usually?" G.G. asked with a small frown. "If Ana was immortal why would she need a cook during the day? Most immortals sleep during the day."

"The Villaverdes are a very wealthy and powerful immortal family. Ana had a huge sugar plantation with security and a large household staff. She had both daytime and nighttime security and household staff as well as workers in the fields. Most of them lived on the plantation, either in barracks if they were single, or if they had family, in one of the *bohios*— huts," she explained, "on the property. Almost all of them took meals there too. My abuela cooked for the daytime staff and security and Ana's first daily meal. She only worked nights when there were large parties and more help was needed."

"So you lived on the plantation in a *bohio*?" G.G. asked.

Ildaria shook her head. "No. My abuela had her

own home on the edge of Santo Domingo. She and my grandfather inherited it from his father who was a wealthy merchant. It wasn't far from the plantation, an easy walk."

G.G. nodded, and then said, "I'm sorry. I interrupted. Please continue. Your abuela brought Señorita Ana to you and she took you . . . ?"

"She took both myself and my abuela back to the plantation," she finished, and told him, "Señorita Ana was very kind. She saw me through the turn, bringing me donors to feed on, making sure that I didn't take too much blood from each donor, and ensuring they didn't feel the pain of my feeding."

"This was before blood banks," G.G. murmured.

"Si," Ildaria agreed.

"What happened to the immortal who turned you?" G.G. asked when Ildaria fell silent.

She shrugged unhappily and pointed out, "He didn't really turn me so much as I accidentally turned myself."

When G.G. didn't comment and waited patiently, she sighed and continued, "I didn't remember what had happened when I first woke. The shock of the turn on top of the attack left me somewhat scrambled. Señorita Ana assured me that was normal and it would come to me eventually once the nanos had finished their business.

"Anyway," she continued when he merely nodded again. "Once I was through the turn, Señorita Ana explained the basics. That I was an immortal now. That I'd somehow ingested blood filled with nanos that had been programmed to keep me healthy and repair any wounds I sustained. She explained that because the nanos used blood to both do their work as well as to propel themselves, they used more blood than a mortal body could supply, so during the turn the nanos had provided me with fangs, added strength, night vision, mind control and mind reading to be able to get the blood I need. She also told me the origin story of the nanos, that they'd been created in Atlantis eons ago. That the mythological Atlantis *was* advanced technologically as some stories suggested. That scientists there had created the nanos as a noninvasive way to cure disease and repair injuries. But that it went wrong. The nanos didn't self-destruct and flush from the body once they returned it to what was considered a peak condition as intended, but continued to keep their host at their peak, making us basically immortal.

"She also told me about the South American Council, explained that they were our governing body, and then she told me about the Enforcers the Council sent out to make sure we followed the laws the Council made. She followed that up with our laws; that we are allowed to turn only one, which is usually saved to change a life mate. That we are only allowed one child every hundred years. That we are never ever to draw attention to ourselves, and—at that time before the existence of blood banks—that we must always be careful not to take too much blood and harm mortals. After making me repeat those laws to her to be sure I understood, she left me to rest.

"The next time I woke up Señorita Ana was there

again and she started right into my training. First she taught me to bring on my fangs and make them retract, then she concentrated on teaching me to read mortals, and then on controlling them. Once I'd mastered all of that, she took me out to teach me to hunt for safe donors and so on." Ildaria paused to take another sip of her cocoa, and then set the mug down with a small sigh before admitting, "But when three weeks of training passed and I still had no memory of how I had been turned or who had done it, Señorita Ana decided my inability to remember was psychological rather than physical. She felt sure the turn should be far enough along by that point that the memories must be there. I was simply refusing to face them for some reason. She wanted to involve the Council. Her father was the head of the South American Council and would surely help if she asked. She felt sure they would be able to get into my thoughts and find the memories I was refusing. She was also sure they would want to know who had turned me.

"The idea of meeting the Council was frightening to a fourteen-year-old girl. The Council passed life and death sentences, but I wanted to know what had happened, so didn't protest and Señorita Ana said she would send a message to the Council that night. She warned me, though, that it might be several days before they could convene to meet with me. Which, to be honest, felt like a reprieve in my mind.

"It was nearing dawn when she left me. I had been up all night training, and was exhausted, so fell asleep the minute I was alone. But I didn't sleep well or long.

I guess the idea of meeting with the Council was more troubling to me than even I had realized."

Ildaria shrugged. "Whatever the case, I was awake well before noon and went down to the kitchens to visit with my abuela." She smiled softly at the memory. "I had seen her every day, but not for long. Usually just for a few minutes before she left at night. But that day we spent all afternoon together. I helped her with the cooking, and we chatted and laughed, and then before she left, she told me that she was glad that I had become immortal. That she would never need worry about me again. No *chico malo* could take me away from her like my mother had been taken away. And she told me that she loved me, and saw only good things for me in my future."

Ildaria paused for a minute, recalling her grandmother's shining eyes filled with happiness and hope that last afternoon. "To her mind, my being turned had lifted me up. I was now one of the *immortals,* above the rabble to her mind. She was sure only good things could come to me now." Ildaria sighed at the memory. "Neither of us could know how wrong she was. I certainly didn't, and I didn't know when I hugged her goodbye that it would be the last time I saw her."

Eight

"Tell me."

Ildaria glanced up with surprise at those quiet words. They weren't an order or a plea, just a request. And they made her realize that she'd been silent for a long time, lost in the memories of the last afternoon she'd spent with the woman who had raised her and been more a mother than her own could ever have been. Those ten years with her abuela had been the happiest of her life.

Sighing, Ildaria gave herself a mental shake and straightened in her seat. "Señorita Ana always came down to the kitchens when she woke up, usually shortly before my abuela left, but sometimes earlier. That day she hadn't come, though, so after Abuela left I went looking for her, expecting my training to continue. Her fiancé, who I now understood was her life mate, was coming downstairs as I came out of the kitchen, so I knew she was probably awake. I headed upstairs, intending to go to her room to see what she wished me to do," she explained. "But as I approached her door, one of the maids said Señorita Ana was in the salon, expecting company, and wished for me to join her there now that my abuela had left. So I headed back to the stairs.

"I heard one of the servants opening the front door and greeting someone as I approached the landing. I arrived at the top of the stairs just in time to see a man enter. I recognized him at once. It was Juan. And recognizing him brought everything back to me. It was like being punched in the stomach. I think I actually moaned and half bent under the impact. Fortunately, he didn't notice me or my reaction and walked into the salon, saying, *"Saludos hija."* Meeting G.G.'s gaze she translated, "Greetings, daughter."

"Bloody hell," G.G. breathed.

"Si. The man who attacked me was Juan Villaverde, Señorita Ana's father as well as the head of the South American Council. And I had bit off his cock."

G.G. closed his eyes briefly.

Leaving him to digest that, Ildaria stood and moved into the kitchen. All this talk was drying out her mouth and making her thirsty. The hot chocolate hadn't really helped. Water would, she thought, and found a glass, then grabbed a second one as well and moved to use the ice cube maker on the refrigerator door. She smiled faintly as she did. Ildaria loved this refrigerator. She loved not having to mess with ice cube trays as she'd had to do at Jess's place. Here, she simply pressed the glass against the pedal and ice dropped into it with a rattle. Of course, Marguerite's refrigerator had had an icemaker too, but this one was hers. Well, it was hers as long as she lived here . . . which might not be long if G.G. completely rejected her and sent her on her way.

Mouth tightening, Ildaria moved to the sink to run water into each glass of ice and then carried one over to set down in front of G.G. before returning to the kitchen. As she opened cupboard doors and retrieved a bowl and ingredients, she reminded herself that she would be fine. She had survived much worse in her life, she could survive his rejection. She would just get a job somewhere else.

Ildaria was even beginning to think that might be easier than she'd previously thought. She'd taken wait-ressing jobs since moving to the United States and Canada, not even considering trying for accounting work. But now she realized G.G.'s couldn't be the only business in need of an immortal to work the books. Immortal accountants were not thick on the ground. She might not have her degree yet, but with three years under her belt, she could get another job in her field. She would work, rent a room somewhere and fin-ish her degree. She would survive this.

"What are you doing?"

Ildaria glanced around to see that G.G. had moved to stand by the island, the glass of water in hand.

"Making muffins," she answered automatically, and then paused as his expression changed, and she real-ized she was *making muffins*. They blinked at each other briefly, the memories of last night's dream rising between them.

His lips trailing down her breast to the valley between them as he said, *"You smell like muffins."*

She'd been startled by the announcement, but then he'd added, *"Vanilla and spice. Delicious."* The words had been followed by his tongue swiping up her second breast and lashing the nipple there, and he'd growled, *"I love muffins,"* before claiming that nipple to suckle it. Ildaria had promised herself she'd make him muffins as he began to nip and lash at the hard bud, sending bolts of excitement through her body.

"Muffins sound good," he said, his voice deeper even than usual.

Ildaria noted the heat in his eyes and swallowed, her body suddenly vibrating just a bit. Turning away abruptly, she returned to what she was doing, measuring ingredients and putting them in the bowl as she said, "I was thinking blueberry muffins. Do you like blueberries?"

The silence was long, but finally he said, "Yes," in his normal voice and she relaxed with relief. Like her, he'd pushed down whatever that memory had made rise between them. Now was not the time for it.

A quick glance in his direction showed her that he'd settled at the island with his water, and now held H.D. in his arms. He was petting the dog soothingly as he watched her. She turned back to what she was doing.

A moment passed and then G.G. asked, "What happened when Señorita Ana realized it was her father who had attacked and turned you?"

Ildaria shrugged. "I don't know if she ever found out."

"Explain," he requested gently.

She nodded, but grabbed eggs from the fridge before admitting, "I didn't go down to the salon. At first I didn't even move. I just stood there at the top of the stairs awash in horror." She shrugged. "I don't know how long I stood there, but finally the maid who had told me Señorita Ana wished me to join her approached. She asked if I was all right, and was I not going down? Señorita Ana was waiting. When I nodded and started down, she moved away. I heard her walk back up the hall, and I just—" She grimaced, cracked an egg's shell on the side of the bowl, and let the egg drop out on top of the dry ingredients as she finished. "I just walked calmly down those stairs and straight out the front door. I even managed to stay at a walk until I'd reached the end of the drive. Only then did I break into a run." She met his gaze again. "I have been running ever since."

G.G. frowned. "Your abuela?"

Ildaria turned away to set down the now empty shell and pick up another egg before admitting, "I never saw her again."

"What?" There was such horror in his voice that she winced. It was the same horror she felt when she thought of it. Her abuela had been everything to her. She had given her a home and unconditional love. Her abuela had supported and fought for her. She'd deserved better.

Sighing, Ildaria cracked and added three more eggs to the batter, then gathered all four of the broken shells and tossed them in the garbage under the sink. She then washed her hands quickly, before grabbing a large spoon to stir the batter and said, "I wanted to go directly to her, tell her what I had remembered, and ask what to do. But I needed to feed."

She glanced over to see G.G. nod, but knew he didn't really understand. She needed to explain. Picking the bowl up off the counter, she cradled it in one arm and turned to lean against the counter so that she could watch him as she stirred the batter and spoke. "The start of the turn, what you saw when your mother was turned," she added, pinning him with her gaze and noting the way his expression tightened before she continued, "I'm sure it's painful, but all I remember of it is terrible nightmares. I gather that's what most turns recall afterward, horrifying nightmares."

He looked so startled by this news that a small smile tugged at her mouth.

"It's true," she assured him.

"Not my mother," he said with certainty. "She was in agony."

"Si. I'm sure I was too," she told him. "But the mind . . ." She shrugged. "It doesn't hold onto the memory of it. Perhaps it is the nanos, or perhaps the brain just cannot process such sustained and powerful sensation and short-circuits. I do not know, but I do not really remember the pain. Just the nightmares, and I have been told it is the same for all turns."

G.G. shook his head stubbornly, refusing to believe.

"Have you ever asked her?" Ildaria queried.

G.G. frowned now, but reluctantly shook his head.

"Perhaps you should," she suggested gently. "Because from what I can tell, that part of the turn is harder on those overseeing it than the person turning."

The stubbornness on his face told her that he wasn't prepared to entertain this idea yet, so she let it go. The suggestion was in his mind now and he would wonder about it, and hopefully, someday ask his mother. It might not convince him to turn. His repulsion was ingrained from a young age, subconsciously affecting his decisions just as her abuse as a child had worked under the surface all these years to make her avoid sexual situations.

"At any rate," she said, dropping her gaze to the batter as she returned to the subject, "the hell for me was once the worst of the turn was over and I'd regained consciousness. The hunger was constant. I didn't recognize it as hunger though. To me it was just pain. Sometimes it was just a mild discomfort, what I experienced as a mortal when I was hungry. But sometimes it felt like my stomach was eating itself. If I didn't feed then, it would spread out and change, feeling as if my blood had turned to acid and was boiling all my organs.

"Those first weeks I always woke up hungry, usually just with the mild discomfort type of hunger, but sometimes with the stomach gnawing kind. Fortunately, Señorita Ana was always there with a donor, waiting to help me feed. At least, for the first two weeks. But the third week, she started coming later and wasn't there waiting. I had to remain in my room and suffer until she came. I was never to leave my room without her. I was actually breaking the rules by going to visit my abuela."

"What?" he asked with surprise. "Why weren't you allowed to leave your room?"

"For the safety of the mortal staff," she said simply,

and deciding the batter was stirred enough, set the bowl on the counter, turned the oven to bake at 400 degrees and then retrieved the muffin pan and muffin cups.

"She didn't think it was safe for you to be around mortals?" G.G. asked as he watched her drop the paper muffin cups into the muffin pan one after another.

Ildaria shrugged. "I was a new turn. No new turn is safe for a mortal to be around."

"Why?" he asked at once.

"We don't always recognize the sign that we're hungry as a need for blood," she explained, moving on to dripping batter into the paper cups. "We automatically reach for food, because the first hunger pangs are similar to the hunger for food and we haven't adjusted to our new needs and their signals. Even the sensation of the stomach eating itself is similar to that of the hunger for food when a mortal is really hungry. But the acid attacking your organs feeling isn't. Unfortunately, by the time you get to that point, you can be extremely dangerous."

Frowning, she added, "But you're dangerous before that too. Your stomach might just be a little uncomfortable, you think you're hungry, and then a mortal moves close and smells lovely. You might think, what a pretty perfume. I just have to get a better whiff, and move closer. Maybe you hug them and press your nose to their throat and . . . your lizard brain takes over. The next thing you know you're licking the vein pulsing there, or biting into it."

"Your lizard brain?" G.G. asked with disbelief as

she set the batter aside and popped the muffin tin in the oven.

Straightening, Ildaria turned toward him and shrugged helplessly. "I don't know what else to call it. You aren't really thinking clearly at that point. Some basic survival part of your brain takes over and goes after what you need. You don't realize what's happening and that you're biting someone until the screaming starts."

"Screaming?" he asked with alarm. "I thought you could control mortals and ensure they don't feel pain when you feed."

"We can. If we're in control. But a new turn has to be taught that control, and that was why Señorita Ana was making me wait longer before taking me to feed. She needed me to learn to control myself even when the hunger had reached the critical point."

G.G. considered that briefly, and then nodded that he understood. But then he asked, "That last afternoon with your grandmother—abuela," he corrected himself. "You weren't hungry?"

"Si. I was, but not critically hungry yet so I was able to control myself. However, when I went to hug her goodbye it got iffy," she conceded. "I found myself nuzzling her neck, and then realized what I was doing and ended the hug, told her I loved her and walked her out. Then I went in search of Señorita Ana. I was hoping she wouldn't make me wait long to take me out to feed. Actually, I was surprised that she didn't have someone keeping an eye on me. Or maybe she did," she added thoughtfully. "There was security all over the place that day."

"And yet they didn't stop you from running," he murmured thoughtfully.

Ildaria nodded slowly as she thought about that now too. "I didn't see anyone in the hall when I walked out, and I was walking not running. They may have thought I was just . . ." She shrugged. "Going for a walk."

"Until you ran," G.G. said.

"Si." Ildaria picked up her own water and took a long gulp, but it didn't really quench her thirst any better than the hot chocolate had. Realization striking, she rolled her eyes at her own stupidity and moved to the refrigerator to retrieve a bag of blood.

G.G. smiled faintly as he watched her pop it to her fangs. He was used to immortals feeding in front of him. Clients might drink it from glasses at the Night Club, but his mother and father were both immortal and would drink from bags at home as she was doing, so she wasn't surprised he seemed more amused than anything.

"All this talk of blood made you hungry, did it?" he teased.

Unable to talk with the bag at her mouth, Ildaria just shrugged. But the truth was she'd been so distracted with their talk that she'd made the rookie mistake of missing the signs that she needed blood. Seriously, how stupid was that? She could have accidentally bit G.G.

"So you didn't go see your abuela right away because you needed to feed," G.G. said when the bag had emptied and she tore it from her fangs.

Nodding, Ildaria tossed the bag in the garbage and then leaned against the counter. "Unfortunately, when I ran from the plantation, I used immortal speed, which means using blood that was already low," she explained. "By the time I stopped I was well into the stomach eating itself phase and verging on the acid in the organs stage."

She grimaced at the memory. "That meant I couldn't risk going anywhere there were a lot of people. The smell of their blood would have been overwhelming and I might have just attacked someone. I needed to find someone on their own. So, I went down to the waterside, hoping to find a fisherman on their own, or someone walking the beach in the moonlight. Tourism wasn't a thing in the area back then," she added. "This was 1826. We were under Haitian occupation, which had caused a lot of upheaval, but it was still safer to walk around at night than it would be now. Well, mostly," she added to be honest, because the soldiers had been a problem. Haiti hadn't been able to provision their soldiers properly, so the men were stealing the food and supplies they needed locally. They had called it commandeering or confiscating, but it was stealing.

Food and supplies weren't all that the soldiers had taken without permission. A lot of half-Haitian babies had been born during that period. Though Ildaria had been relatively ignorant of all that at the time. She and her grandmother had been left alone. She supposed that had something to do with Señorita Ana. She had always protected her people.

Ildaria turned to glance at the stove's clock and then opened the door to check the muffins. Deciding they needed another couple of minutes, she closed the door and continued. "I did eventually find someone on their own, but it took a while, and really I needed more blood than one donor could safely supply. Fortunately, that first man eased my need enough that I thought I could safely be around crowds again, so I decided to head back toward my abuela's and look for someone to feed from on the way. Still, by the time I neared my abuela's home, it was more than an hour since I'd left Señorita Ana's."

She paused briefly, as she remembered the moment her abuela's home had come into view. "Juan and Ana were there. They were arguing in front of my abuela's house. I couldn't hear it all, but caught enough to gather that Señorita Ana wanted to question me. Juan wanted her to go home and leave me to him. I was his 'problem now,' he said."

She grimaced. "Eventually, Señorita Ana was persuaded to leave and let him deal with me and Juan went into my abuela's home."

Ildaria bit her lip as she recalled her fear in that moment. She'd been terrified for her abuela, afraid Juan would take out his rage over her having unmanned him on the dear old woman. But he hadn't stayed very long. "Juan was only inside for twenty, maybe thirty minutes. When he came out, my abuela accompanied him. They walked to his horse chatting like they were old friends. And she was smiling happily, as if he had gifted her with something wonderful. She was also promising Juan she would contact him the moment I returned home."

"Mind control?" G.G. asked at once.

"I don't know," Ildaria breathed unhappily. "Maybe, or maybe he just lied and said he was concerned for my well-being and wished to help. She had no idea he was the immortal who had attacked and caused my turn," she pointed out. "But it didn't matter. Juan left four men to watch my abuela's home in case I returned. They were immortals, Enforcers, I suspect. Come morning, six more immortals came, four to replace the men guarding the house, and two who followed at a distance when my abuela walked to work and back. I couldn't approach her," she said with remembered helplessness and frustration.

"In the end, I had to give up. I wrote a note to tell her that I remembered what had happened and who my attacker was. That I hurt my attacker while defending myself and accidentally turned myself in the process. I told her I loved her so very much, but feared retribution and had to flee, both to keep her safe as well as for my own safety. I then gave the note to an old friend of my abuela's to give to her."

"And never saw her again," G.G. said, sadness in his tone.

Feeling tears prick the backs of her eyes, Ildaria turned away to grab the tea towel she'd left folded neatly on the counter. Using it as a makeshift oven mitt, she opened the oven and pulled out the muffins. They were golden brown and smelled delicious, but she'd lost her appetite. Still, she set them on the stovetop to cool a bit, and then fetched plates, knives, and butter.

"I'm sorry, Ildaria. You lost everything. It must have felt like the end of the world," G.G. said softly.

Ildaria shrugged as she set the items she'd collected on the island in front of him. She was not going to feel sorry for herself. She never did that, and muttered, "I did it to myself. Obviously, I didn't learn from my mother's mistakes. I just had to rebel and go to the bar."

"Bloody hell, do not tell me you have been blaming yourself for all of this for the last two hundred years?" he exclaimed with dismay.

"If I hadn't gone to the bar and drank—"

"If your mother hadn't been an alcoholic slut jumping from one bed to the other," he interrupted, shocking her into silence so that he continued. "Or if her last boyfriend hadn't molested you and killed her. Or if Juan had just saved you and walked you home rather than sexually assault you himself . . ." He paused, glaring at her. "That's what you should be saying. You didn't bring any of those things on yourself, and the small part you played by accompanying your friends to the bar where an older brother was going to look out for you was something every kid does at some point, and you *were* the kid," he reminded her firmly. "You were a fourteen-year-old girl. A child, and you were only four when you were first molested. Do you blame yourself for that too?"

"No, of course not," she said at once. "Mostly I don't even think about that part of my history."

"But it and the attack ten years later are the reason you lack experience with sex," he said quietly.

Ildaria blinked several times, and then sighed with defeat as she recalled that had been the point of this talk. Explaining her lack of experience while not being a virgin. "Si."

"And why you haven't really been . . . assertive in the shared dreams, but have left me to lead," he suggested.

She nodded, and then smiled crookedly and pointed out, "Although I'm pretty sure I am the one who put myself naked in a bed and chained to it in the English room of the Night Club. You looked pretty shocked when you turned and saw me like that."

"Yes. I was," he said, a smile tugging at the corner of his mouth. "I was also surprised when your wrists were suddenly loose later."

"I wanted to touch you," she admitted simply.

G.G. nodded, but then asked wearily, "What are we going to do about this?"

Ildaria stiffened warily. "About the dreams?"

"About my being a possible life mate for you," he corrected.

She stared at him briefly, and then turned and grabbed a large plate and started to move the still warm muffins from the muffin pan to the plate before she said, "That is up to you."

"But what do you want?"

"I would like you to agree to be my life mate," she said stiffly.

"Even if I refuse to turn?" he asked.

Ildaria let out a slow breath. At least, he hadn't refused outright to be her life mate, or gone running screaming from the room at the idea, as Marguerite had feared. Turning, she carried the plate of muffins to the island and set it in front of him before meeting his gaze. "Si."

G.G. considered her briefly, and she could almost see the cogs turning in his head. She had no idea what he was thinking though.

"Okay," he said finally.

Ildaria stared at him uncertainly. "Okay?"

"Okay, I would like to be your life mate," he explained gently.

Ildaria beamed at him, feeling like she'd just won the lottery. She had a life mate.

"But," he added, and her smile faltered. "You need to accept that I won't agree to the turn. Ever. I'm happy having one life, Ildaria. I don't want to drink blood to survive."

Ildaria merely nodded. It was no more than she'd expected, and she could deal with that. It would be hard to watch him age and die, of course, but she wasn't the first immortal with a life mate who refused to turn and she could deal with it. She'd have him at least for a while, Ildaria told herself and simply said, "I suspected that would be the case. I accept."

G.G.'s eyebrows rose. "That easily? No trying to convince me? No argument?"

She shrugged. "One piece of cake in your life is better than never having any."

That surprised a short laugh out of him. "Did you just call me cake?"

"Maybe," she said with a small smile. "Although it probably should have been beefcake."

They shared a smile and then he grabbed a muffin off the plate and moved it to his own. As he cut and buttered the muffin, he said, "I think we should go slow for now."

"Slow?" she asked, moving back to begin putting fresh paper muffin cups in the now empty muffin pan.

"I think we should go on dates, get to know each other better . . . but stick to dream sex for now," he suggested.

Ildaria continued what she was doing, finishing off with the paper muffin cups and then switching to filling them, but her mind was working. If he thought they could do that, he didn't know as much about immortals as she'd thought. At least, not about life mates. Resisting each other would be damned near impossible.

"I know it will be hard," G.G. added, when she didn't comment. "We'll have to be careful, but I think if we avoid touching each other—"

"Why?" she interrupted, finally turning to look at him.

He paused with his muffin halfway to his mouth, and lowered it slightly before admitting, "Because I don't think you're ready for the real thing yet."

"But—"

"And I'm mortal. My parts don't grow back if you have a flashback, panic and bite anything off me."

G.G. had spoken in a teasing tone, but she didn't think he was really joking. He was worried about how she would react during real sex. She supposed she shouldn't be surprised since she'd just told him she'd bit off Juan's penis.

A sigh from G.G. drew her attention as he set his uneaten muffin back on the plate. Meeting her gaze then, he said, "I dated a mortal girl once who had been sexually abused as a child. I didn't know and she didn't tell me. We dated for several months and it was nice. We fooled around a lot, but never had sex. She always shied away before getting to that point, and I didn't push it. I was fine waiting until she was ready. Then Valentine's Day rolled around. I got her a card, flowers, and chocolates. She gave me a card, and inside were condoms. When I glanced at her with surprise, she nodded and whispered, 'I want you to be my first.'

"I should have realized then that there were issues. We were both twenty-one. There aren't a lot of beautiful, hot twenty-one-year-old virgins out there," he said with a shake of the head. "Anyway, I didn't jump her bones on the spot like I wanted. I'd booked a fancy restaurant for dinner. I took her there, wined and dined her, talked and laughed, but I noticed she was drinking a lot. I figured she was just nervous and looking for a little Dutch courage. But I didn't want her first time to be a drunken blur, so even though I hadn't planned it, I took her dancing. Once at the dance club I stopped buying alcohol, switching to water for both of us instead, telling her we had to stay hydrated. She didn't protest and we danced like crazy for the next few hours. When I thought we'd worked off the worst of the alcohol, I took her back to her place."

G.G. smiled with wry amusement. "I half expected her to be too exhausted from the dancing to go ahead with her plans, but when I asked if she was tired and wanted me to go, she took my hand and led me inside."

He was silent for a minute and then cleared his throat. It actually looked like he was blushing when he said, "I wanted her first time to be special for her, and so I really worked the foreplay. I gave her three orgasms before getting to the main event." Pausing, he met her gaze and said, "I know it's crass to kiss and tell, but I want you to understand that it wasn't just a 'rip her clothes off and stick it in' deal. I did everything I could think to make it good for her. But when it came to the big moment— " He blew his breath out slowly at the memory. "The minute I started to enter her, and I mean the very moment—hell, I wasn't more than millimeters in and she just freaked; kicking, screaming, thrashing, scratching and punching me. And all the while she was screaming, 'No, Daddy! Please don't hurt me, Daddy!'"

Ildaria swallowed and sat back, her emotions a confused mix of pity, concern, fear, and anxiety.

"Well, my first reaction was to jump back and give her space, but that didn't seem to help and the way she was thrashing around I was afraid she'd hurt herself, so I pulled my pants up quick and then I just pulled her into my arms, held her and rubbed her back soothingly. All the while, saying over and over, 'It's okay, it's me. It's G.G. You're safe,' until she calmed. She was as silent and still as a stone for a minute and then pulled back and looked at me with confusion. And it *was* real confusion.

"*'I don't—What happened?'* she asked, and I really don't think she knew what had set her off and why she'd panicked. When I told her what she'd been shouting, she just kind of closed down. Emotionally. She didn't seem to believe it, and she couldn't get me out of there quickly enough. I left, but as I dressed I tried to suggest as gently as I could that there might be something in her past that she needed to look at and maybe counseling would help. That I'd be there for her in whatever capacity she needed. She just kept nodding and waiting for me to leave."

He took a drink of his water, and then said, "I was shocked to see myself when I got home. I looked like I'd been in a fight; black eye, fat lip, scratches and bruises down my cheek, neck, chest, and arms." He turned his water glass on the island and said, "I wasn't surprised when she called and broke it off with me the next day. I knew when I left that she wasn't ready to deal with whatever had happened in her past."

Releasing his glass, he shifted his glance to her. "It took weeks to heal from all the physical damage she did, and she was mortal. If you freaked like that, you could kill me," he pointed out.

Ildaria wanted to protest that she'd never attack him, but the truth was she couldn't guarantee she wouldn't. She'd attacked three men on the pirate ship. Each man had attacked her first, but she could still remember her rage and determination to hurt those men in response. She couldn't swear the same thing might not happen with G.G. at that most important moment, and that being the case, she said, "So, we'll take it slow."

G.G. nodded, but said, "And I'd like you to go to Marguerite's son-in-law for counseling."

Ildaria's head jerked back under the emotional blow, but she managed to hold on to the temper that exploded inside her at the demand. Swallowing her anger, she merely said, "Fine. If you go to him for counseling too."

Now it was G.G.'s turn to rock back in shock. "I don't need counseling."

"Really? So seeing your mother mid-turn didn't affect you at all? Make you resistant to the turn?"

G.G. stared at her silently and then warned, "Counseling might not make a difference about that."

Ildaria shrugged. "It might not make a difference for me either, but we can both give it a try, can't we?"

After a short pause, G.G. nodded. "All right. We'll both go for counseling."

"All right." Ildaria turned and plucked a muffin off the large plate, set it on her own smaller one, and picked up her knife to cut and butter it as if everything was fine. But she was already worrying about this counseling thing. She wasn't used to talking to people about her past. In fact, G.G. was the first person she'd told it to, and she'd only done that because she'd felt he should know if they were life mates . . . and despite not knowing him long, she trusted him. Opening up to someone else . . . Yeah, this was going to be hard.

Nine

"Yo."

Ildaria glanced up from the computer and smiled faintly as Sofia pushed the office door closed and crossed the room.

"Yo," she greeted back. "What's up?"

"That's what I was wondering," Sofia said dryly as she dropped into the chair in front of the desk. "What *is* going on? G.G. only stuck around for a few minutes tonight and then he left that new guy, Jarin, to man the door and went *to take a nap*." She widened her eyes incredulously. "What the hell? I never thought I'd see the day. The man is always working."

Ildaria shrugged mildly, but her mouth was twitching with amusement. "I guess he's tired."

"You think?" Sofia asked sarcastically, and then asked. "So what has him so tired? And what's going on with you two? This last week he's still exhausted, but in a much better mood. And where did you guys go today? I saw you pull up together in his pickup just before we opened. Where were you coming from? Why is he smiling all the time when he's still exhausted and there's been no Mimi yet? Or has there been Mimi and I'm just misreading things? Because what I'm getting from his head feels like shared dreams rather than the real deal."

Ildaria stared at her with eyebrows arched for a moment, torn between annoyance at the intrusive questions, and an eagerness to spill her guts and tell Sofia about her and G.G. When Sofia simply waited, apparently impervious to the look she was receiving, Ildaria finally gave in to her urge to talk about the man. "We talked last week. The day you took me shopping. Well, the morning after when he came to collect H.D.," she corrected. "I told him that the dreams he's having are shared dreams and that he's a possible life mate. He agreed to be my life mate."

"Yeah?" Sofia asked with a smile, and then smirked. "Yeah, you look and sound all stoic and calm on the surface about this, but your inner voice is doing the squealy girl thing."

Ildaria sneered at the suggestion. "I don't do squealy girl."

"Oh, yeah, you do," she said on a laugh. "You're practically singing 'Sweet Mystery of Life' in your head."

"I am not," Ildaria denied quickly, but she and G.G. had watched *Young Frankenstein* the day before, and the song Madeline Kahn sang when Frankenstein

made love to her had been running through her head
ever since.

When Sofia just laughed at her, Ildaria scowled and
turned her attention back to the spreadsheet on her
computer.

The room was silent as she pretended to concentrate
on work, but Ildaria was very aware of the woman
seated across from her. She knew Sofia was trying to
read her thoughts and tried to block her, but couldn't
think of anything to recite at the moment except
"Sweet mystery of life at last I've found you."

"Wow."

Ildaria looked up sharply at the word to see Sofia
frowning now.

"So, he's agreed to be your life mate, but not to the
turn and you aren't having real sex either?" she almost
whispered with dismay. "Oh, man, Angel."

Flinching at the pity in her voice, Ildaria scowled.
"Don't call me that."

"Sorry," Sofia said unapologetically. "G.G. has
started calling you that and it's kind of stuck in my
head."

Ildaria didn't comment. G.G. had started calling her
Angel since agreeing to be her life mate. He said it
was her real first name, and suited her better anyway.
But when she'd instinctively protested at his using the
short form of the first name she'd forsaken for safety's
sake centuries ago, he'd offered to pick a different endearment if she wanted and suggested a couple. But
when faced with either Petal, Flower, or Angel, she'd
said Angel was fine. She was in North America now,

far from Juan Villaverde, and at least Angel was the short form of her real name. The other two endearments made her sound like some weak, delicate—

"And counseling," Sofia murmured suddenly, and then blinked and said, "And you went *bowling*?"

Ildaria's thoughts scattered and she scowled at her coworker sharply. "Will you stay out of my head?"

"Nope," Sofia said without guilt. "I like G.G. I like you too. I'm rooting for you both, so I'm going to be all up in your business until you two sort things out. Now tell me how your first session with Marguerite's son-in-law went, and explain why you went bowling of all things?"

"It's called dating," Ildaria snapped with irritation, answering the second part first. "We are dating. Getting to know each other."

"Building trust," Sofia said with a nod. "At Marguerite's son-in-law's suggestion."

"His name is Greg," Ildaria snapped. "Dr. Greg Hewitt."

"Right. Dr. Greg," Sofia said with disinterest. "So . . . how was your first date?"

"It wasn't our first date. We went out for breakfast and then watched *Young Frankenstein* the afternoon before that," Ildaria told her reluctantly.

"Ah, that's where 'Sweet Mystery of Life' comes from," Sofia said knowingly.

Ildaria rolled her eyes. "Is there a reason you came in here other than to annoy me?"

"No," Sofia said with a grin. "Mostly I wanted to hear about the bowling thing because I picked up something weird from G.G.'s mind about his never having been kicked out of anyplace . . . before you.''

"We didn't get kicked out," Ildaria said at once, but felt her face heat up.

"Only because you controlled the bowling alley owner's mind, calmed him down and made him let you stay," Sofia argued.

Ildaria huffed irritably. Really this having her mind read all the time was becoming tiresome, she thought, but admitted, "Yeah, well, he thought we were deliberately breaking those white thingies."

"You mean the pins?" Sofia asked, amusement claiming her expression.

"Whatever," Ildaria said with a shrug, and then added, "He mistakenly thought G.G. was the one who had done it and was sure it was on purpose just because of his Mohawk. But it was me, and I didn't do it on purpose." She grimaced. "I just couldn't seem to knock all the pins down at once like G.G. did, so thought if I hit them harder I might. But I used a little more strength than I meant to."

Sofia was laughing now, and Ildaria found herself smiling at the memory of G.G.'s expression when the pins had exploded in all directions with her strike. It had been like a bomb going off. Pin pieces had spread over at least two lanes on either side of the one they were using. It had been quite the show. But they'd had fun. This whole last week had been fun. Ildaria had never dated before, so hadn't realized what she'd been missing.

They'd started slow, grocery shopping together

one day, and then washing their vehicles the next.
Grocery shopping had been interesting in that it had
shown her what G.G. liked when it came to food and
such. As for washing the car, that had ended in a water
fight that had left them both soaked and laughing.
The day after that they'd taken H.D. to a dog park,
and chatted as they walked along together. The next
day had been Ildaria's first appointment with Greg
Hewitt, and G.G.'s had been the day after that. Those
days they'd had breakfast together before the appointments and grabbed lunch after, but neither of them
had talked about the appointments. Not that Ildaria
had had much to talk about. All she'd done was give
Dr. Greg a brief, emotionless rundown of her history
and the reason she was there. By the time she'd finished, her time was up, but Greg had suggested dating and getting to know each other was good as he
walked her out.

In truth, Ildaria wasn't sure how this counseling
business would go. Dr. Greg seemed nice enough,
but . . . She supposed she just didn't understand how
talking about something she'd avoided even thinking
about for a couple of centuries was going to help her.
But she'd continue to go and see. She didn't want to
get intimate with G.G., have a freak-out, and hurt him.
She hadn't worried about that before he'd brought it
up, and she hadn't panicked so far in the dreams. But
Ildaria could remember her reaction to Juan as clearly
as if it had been yesterday. It had been so sudden and
shocking. One minute she'd been weeping, confused,
and frightened, and the next she'd been enraged and

determined to hurt him. She was willing to go slow and get counseling to avoid something like that happening with G.G.

"Wow, Ildaria," Sofia breathed. "Biting off an immortal's dick? You are one fierce bitch. Even I wouldn't have the balls to do that."

"He deserved it," Ildaria snarled.

"Yeah," she agreed easily.

"And I didn't know he was immortal at the time," she pointed out. "I didn't know about immortals at all."

"No," Sofia said, and then tilted her head. "So that's how you got turned, huh?"

"Si." She sighed the word.

Sofia nodded and then said, "Weird, huh?"

"What is?" Ildaria asked with uncertainty.

"Well, when you think about it, you were really kind of lucky that an immortal attacked you," Sofia said slowly.

"What?" Ildaria gasped the word with disbelief.

"Well, you never would have become immortal if he hadn't, and then you never would have met me or any of the other awesome peeps who work here," she pointed out. "Not to mention G.G." Standing now, Sofia headed for the door, saying, "Time for you to knock off and take H.D. upstairs. See you tomorrow."

Ildaria stared after her blankly, her mind whirling. She would never be able to think of that attack as being even a "kind of lucky" event in her life. But as she considered Sofia's words she realized that if Juan hadn't attacked her, she never would have been turned.

One hundred, fifty, or even ten years ago she might not have thought that was a bad thing. But now . . .

Ildaria glanced around the office and then down to where H.D. was curled up by her feet. She liked her life. She was not only studying, but working, in the field she wanted. She loved school, loved her apartment, loved her job, both jobs actually. She had G.G. who was kind and considerate and funny, and she had great friends like Jess in Montana, and Sofia and the others who worked here, not to mention Marguerite, who was quickly becoming more of a surrogate mother or aunt. The woman called twice a week to check on her, and had had her out to dinner at the house at least twice since she'd moved out.

True, her life wasn't perfect. She was making good money, but tuition and books would eat up a lot of that when the fall semester started. And no doubt working the hours she did and attending full-time classes would be hard. Then too while G.G. had agreed to be her life mate, he hadn't agreed to turn and they hadn't consummated their relationship yet. But still, she liked her life. She was happy and hopeful and . . . and she liked herself too, Ildaria realized. All of her experiences had shown her that she was strong and smart and a good person who risked herself to help others . . .

In that moment Ildaria could see how the events in her life—even being molested at four, and being attacked at fourteen—had led to her being who and where she now was.

So . . . while she would never use the word *lucky* to describe the attack, she could at least accept that without it, she wouldn't be who and where she was today.

The idea was new, and one it would take her a while to get used to, but she kind of liked it. She remembered hearing the saying once that every cloud had a silver lining. She'd snorted at it at the time, but Sofia had just helped her see the silver lining in the cloud that had hung over her life for ages. If she hadn't been attacked, first by those soldiers from the bar, and then by Juan, she wouldn't have everything she did today, and she had a lot.

Smiling faintly at the idea, Ildaria closed up the program and the computer, and then scooped up a sleepy H.D., murmuring, "Time to go upstairs, buddy. Do you need to potty?"

Twisting his head, H.D. gave her cheek a swipe with his tongue and Ildaria smiled. "I'll take that as a yes."

H.D. could have walked, but she had to take him out into the hall leading to the bathrooms and bar. She didn't trust the little guy not to take off on her and rush into the bar so she always carried him out when she finished up for the night. It was that or a leash, and leashing him in what was basically his home seemed cruel.

The noise from the bar when she stepped out into the hall made her glance toward the tables. Someone had the jukebox on and there was the general rumble of conversation, but it was loud enough to suggest it was busier than usual for a Wednesday.

Shrugging, Ildaria turned left and pushed through

the door leading to the outer door and the stairs to the apartments, then continued through the outer door into the parking area.

Once he had possession of the Night Club, G.G. had brought in landscapers to break up the pavement in the parking space nearest the door and put in a green space for H.D. to do his business. Ildaria set the fur ball down there and leaned against the wall as she waited for him to be done. It could be a time-consuming event, since H.D. tended to sniff almost every inch of the grass twice before deciding on the spot he wanted to use this time. She didn't know if he was sniffing to be sure his turf hadn't been invaded, or looking for the freshest spot, but she didn't mind usually. She suspected she'd be less patient when winter came with its biting cold, but was hoping H.D. would be less picky then.

H.D. had just finished and was kicking at the grass with his back feet when the door beside her opened. Ildaria didn't glance around to see who had exited the building. Regular customers sometimes parked in the small lot back here, and she was more concerned with grabbing H.D. before he launched into barking and ankle biting mode and went after the exiting patrons.

"Angelina Pimienta?"

Ildaria froze just steps from H.D., a shaft of ice sliding up the back of her neck at the use of her birth name spoken with a deep Spanish accent. This hadn't happened for a very long time. Not for over a century and not since she'd left South America. Still, it brought about the same response as it had the last time it had happened. Her body surged with adrenaline and she crouched and spun, attacking before she could be attacked.

Ildaria didn't exactly look like a kick-ass fighter. But she was. Two hundred years of training in everything from Capoeira to Vale Tudo had made her a finely honed weapon, and while the Enforcers she'd gone up against had always been surprisingly careful not to hurt her, trying to restrain rather than maim, she didn't pull punches or hold back on kicks in return, at least not with immortals. She struck with purpose, not satisfied unless she heard the crunch or snap of bones breaking. Ildaria did the same now, her leg coming up as she spun, aiming for the general direction the voice had come from. She was right on the mark, connecting with the speaker's face. Ildaria had forgotten that she was wearing high heels, but didn't feel the least guilty when her stiletto pierced the man's cheek. It was just inconvenient because she had to leave her shoe behind or be slowed down trying to drag it out again, and there was no time for that. The man wasn't alone. A curse, and movement to her side alerted her to that and she turned abruptly to see a large brute with dark hair charging, arms open to try to grab her.

Ildaria almost dropped and swept his feet, but then spotted H.D. attached to the man's ankle. The little dog had joined the fray. Not that the attacker seemed to notice the little teeth that were sunk into his boot. Afraid of H.D. getting hurt, Ildaria backed up, trying to think of what to do. She'd never had to worry about anyone else while she was fighting, and it took her brain a second to change strategy. She had to hit higher, and in a way that wouldn't have the big behemoth falling on the tiny dog, Ildaria decided, and struck out with her still shod foot, aiming for the man's groin. That, she thought, should bring him to his knees as it had Juan, and give her the chance to scoop up H.D. and run inside.

Her aim was again good and she put enough force into the strike that her heel was buried in the front of the man's black jeans. As she'd hoped, it brought him to his knees, and as he screeched in agony, she ran around behind him, snatched up H.D., pulling him off the man's ankle, and then turned to head to the door, only to slam into Tybo.

"Whoa," the dark-haired Enforcer said as he caught her arms to keep her from stumbling back. Glancing down at H.D., he frowned. "Is the gremlin okay?"

Ildaria glanced down with concern, but relaxed when H.D. immediately began to bark at Tybo.

"Yeah, I would say so," Valerian said dryly, drawing her attention to the second man. Once he had her attention, he explained, "We saw them follow you outside, and came to see if you needed assistance." His gaze slid to the two men, the first still trying to remove her shoe from his face, and the second now rolling on the ground, clutching himself around her shoe. "I guess you did not need our help though."

Ildaria shifted slightly, her gaze sliding between the two sets of men, and then muttered, "No. I handled it."

"Yeah. Good job," Tybo said. "Ever consider becoming an Enforcer? We could use you."

Ildaria started to shake her head, but then paused. "Would becoming an Enforcer mean they couldn't drag me back to the Dominican?"

"You do not need to be an Enforcer for that," Valerian assured her firmly. "Lucian already told them they were not allowed to force you out of the country."

"Lucian knew they were here and didn't tell me?" Ildaria squawked with a combination of shock and anger.

"He called to warn you, but you didn't answer the phone so he left a message and then had us follow these guys to make sure they didn't cause trouble," Tybo explained patiently.

Ildaria scowled at this news. She hadn't answered her phone because it was presently up in her apartment in a Ziploc bag full of rice. She'd stuck it in her back pocket while she and G.G. were bowling, and forgot about it . . . until she went to use the public washroom and it had tumbled out of her pocket into the toilet. She'd been having such a good time on her date that she'd laughed at it at the time. She wasn't laughing now, and made a mental note to herself to keep her phone safe and on her person at all times. It was an important lifeline now that her past had caught up to her.

"Sadly, it appears they decided to ignore Lucian and come after you anyway," Valerian commented, drawing her attention back to the men as the one with the shoe in his mouth tried to talk. The shoe made his speech too garbled to understand.

"Can you read him?" Tybo asked Valerian, obviously curious about what the South American was trying to say.

The blond shook his head. "With the pain he is in I am not even going to try."

Tybo grunted, looking disappointed, but then shrugged. "Well, I guess we'll find out once we get him back to the Enforcer house and heal him up."

Nodding, Valerian glanced at Ildaria. "Are you all right?"

"Si," she murmured, but didn't mention that the two men hadn't got the chance to lay a hand on her.

Valerian hesitated and then asked, "Are you done out here?" When she nodded, he suggested, "Then perhaps you should take H.D. inside. We do not know how many of them are in the city and will not be here to watch you until we deliver these two to Mortimer."

Ildaria stiffened at that. She hadn't even considered that there might be others. Now her arms tightened around H.D. and her wary gaze slid over the dark parking lot. She didn't see anything, but that didn't mean there wasn't someone there, hiding behind a vehicle or something.

"There could be others inside," Tybo pointed out.

Valerian clucked with irritation at the suggestion and then turned back to Ildaria. "On second thought, wait until we knock these two out and truss them up, then one of us will walk you up to your apartment and check it out before we go."

Ildaria considered refusing the offer. She'd been alone a long time with no one to turn to for help before Vasco and Cristo had entered her life ten years ago. And she hadn't turned to them so much as they'd looked out for her, whether she liked it or not. Jess and then Marguerite had followed, both insisting on helping despite her best efforts to avoid it. But that didn't mean she was used to accepting aid.

On the other hand, she didn't really feel like having to fight again if a compatriot of one of these two was waiting inside. Besides, she was out of shoes.

A hissing *pfffft* of sound caught her ear, and she glanced around to see that Tybo had just shot the man who presently had her shoe heel buried in the side of his face. Once he fell, she saw that the heel had entered through his maxilla—the bone that forms the upper jaw. It had entered at a slanted upward angle too, going in just below and to the side of his nose and she suspected hitting and piercing his nasal bone at the top between the eyes. At least, there was a lump there that could be the end of the shoe heel.

Ildaria eyed the shoe now stuck to his face and felt her shoulders droop unhappily. They'd been super expensive because of the metal heels, but she hadn't been able to resist buying them. She'd really liked the little black bows on the back. So had G.G. At least he'd had her wearing them, or a version of them in every dream they'd shared. Sometimes, they were all he had her wearing.

"We'll get the shoes back to you," Valerian said beside her.

Ildaria watched Tybo move on to shoot the man with her other heel in his groin and grimaced. She didn't really think she wanted them back now, but she didn't say that. Valerian was already moving to pick up the shoe-faced man while Tybo bent to the other one and heaved him over his shoulder.

"Fortunately, we parked back here," Tybo told her as he and Valerian carried the men to a black SUV parked next to G.G.'s pickup.

"Convenient," Ildaria murmured, petting H.D. soothingly as she watched the Enforcers dump both men in the back of the SUV.

The two men didn't debate who would do what, Valerian simply told Tybo to wait with the vehicle and shoot the men again if they stirred, then returned to Ildaria.

He took her elbow to lead her to the door, but pulled her behind his back and took the lead when they reached it, so that he could check inside first and be sure the way was clear. He then led her up to her floor and did the same there.

"Which one?" he asked glancing toward the two doors in this hall.

"The left," Ildaria answered and shifted H.D. to one arm so that she could retrieve her keys from her pocket and hand them to him. She waited patiently as he unlocked the door and slid inside to check the apartment, but her gaze kept sliding to the door to the stairway as she waited, half afraid another South American Enforcer would come rushing out and try to grab her. But nothing like that happened before Valerian returned to tell her the place was fine.

"Keep your door locked and call if you have any problems. Lucian will probably order Tybo and I to watch the building for any more trouble, but it could take us an hour to get back here. Of course, Tybo is probably calling to report in right now, and Lucian might send another team rather than risk leaving you alone. I will have Tybo text you either way so you know what is happening," he promised as he handed her the keys and ushered her into her apartment.

"Thanks," Ildaria called as he closed the door. The minute it was shut she locked it, and heard Valerian's satisfied grunt on the other side. She suspected he'd waited purely to be sure she locked it, but he needn't have worried. Damn right she was locking that door, Ildaria thought as she set H.D. down. Her problem now was deciding if she shouldn't pack a bag and run. Juan had found her.

Ten

G.G. rolled over in bed and opened his eyes, feeling just wonderful. Well rested, and well sated from the dreams he'd shared with Ildaria. Damn, if life mate sex was ten times better than that as he'd once heard an immortal claim, it might kill him. But what a way to go, he thought with a grin and closed his eyes to savor the memories still swimming in his head.

The dreams had changed since Ildaria had told him they were shared and told him he was a possible life mate. She no longer just came along for the ride. She was starting to instigate things and really get involved. Last night she'd taken their dream to a beach he suspected was in Punta Cana. They had been alone, the sand soft as silk beneath them, the moon and stars bright overhead and a balmy breeze caressing their bodies as they'd kissed. She'd been wearing the pirate costume she'd described to him, explaining with a grin that it was just for him. However, his costume, she'd added, was just for her and he'd looked down to see that he was in boots and tight black pants, a blousy, white cotton pirate shirt open to show off his chest.

"Will you ravish me, El Capitan?" she'd asked, her eyes glowing golden brown as they always did when she got excited. "Or should I stake you out in the sand and ravish you?"

G.G. had to admit the idea of being ravished had been an exciting one. It must have shown on his face, because the next thing he knew he was flat on his back on a blanket on the sand, his arms and legs tied to stakes in the ground. He'd been a little surprised to see his clothes still on, until he noticed Ildaria standing over him twirling a wickedly sharp knife in her hands.

"I will, of course, unwrap my gift," she said with a grin and then knelt and began to do just that, slicing through the cloth of his clothes with deft movements that quickly left him in nothing but the boots. But while the cutting away of his clothes was quick, her attention afterward was painfully slow as she'd licked and nibbled and kissed her way up and down and around his body, exploring every inch of him except the part that wanted her attention most. G.G. had been hard pressed not to take over control of the dream, free himself of his bindings, grab her, roll her in the sand, and make love to her. But he'd held back, interested to see where this would go, and most interested to see if she would find her way to his very hard cock, and lick it or freak out and bite it off.

Ildaria didn't bite it off, and by the time she finally

closed her mouth over him, G.G. was crazy close to spilling himself. It had taken mad concentration to keep from doing that, and he'd only managed it for half a dozen strokes of her beautiful mouth before losing it. Fortunately, he recovered quickly in dreams, and within moments he had turned the tables on her, and she was suddenly staked out on the ground while he stripped and loved every inch of her until she was crying out with her release too.

After that, they'd gone for a swim and ended up making love in the surf. Then Ildaria had dragged him to his feet and pulled him behind her as she raced up the sand and into the palm trees. They were naked when they started out, but by the time they stepped out of the forest and into a crowded street, he was in his pirate gear again and she was in a lovely white dress with red and blue stripes running around it in ruffles. The top was what G.G. thought they called a peasant top. He wasn't sure, he was no fashionista, but she wore the short sleeves off the shoulders and her hair was piled on top of her head, and falling away down one side in large curls that were interwoven with white, red, and blue flowers. She looked magnificent . . . and G.G. wanted her all over again, but a sudden shout drew his gaze around to see a man in the crowd clutching his behind and howling in pain.

G.G. had barely taken that in when his attention was drawn to another man, this one dressed in a red cloak, shiny shirt, and broad trousers covered in tiny bells, ribbons, and what looked to be bits of broken mirror. This character was also wearing a horned mask with bulging eyes and large teeth that included fangs. The teeth were stained red as if with blood.

"That is Diablo Cojuelo," Ildaria shouted into his ear to be heard over the merengue music a small band of costumed men were playing.

"A vampire?" G.G. turned to ask in a shout. Even in dreams he wouldn't shout the word *immortal* out loud.

"No." She laughed and explained in a yell, "This is Carnaval. He is the Limping Devil. He was banished to earth because of the childish pranks he pulled. But his leg was injured when he landed, so he limps. At least, that is the official story. My grandmother used to say that he really represented the Spanish who invaded the island and enslaved the native people."

"What is that he's carrying?" G.G. asked, eyeing the balloon-like thing the Limping Devil was carrying. It really did look like a pale sort of pinkish skin-colored balloon, but G.G. was pretty sure that was what the howling man had been hit with. A balloon wouldn't make a man shriek in pain like that.

"His *vejiga*. A dried and inflated cow bladder, cured with ashes, lemon, and salt. It is very hard. Come, he is getting too close. If he hits you with his *vejiga* it hurts and you will be bruised for a week," she warned, and began to pull him away.

G.G. nodded, but glanced back over his shoulder as she pulled him along and thought he caught a glimpse of a naked woman with long black hair, or maybe wearing a dress of long black hair. Only there was something wrong with her feet. Turning back to Ildaria, he yelled, "What—?"

"La Ciguapa. Like a succubus. She walks naked, her long hair her only cover. Her feet are backward to confuse anyone who follows her footprints. She comes out at night and enchants men," Ildaria explained, as they made their way through the crowd.

"Is this where you grew up?" he asked, catching glimpses of other costumed figures. A man in a woman's dress carrying a chicken, a woman shrieking hysterically, a large group dressed in attire that looked almost native American but with much more intricate and colorful beading than he'd ever seen.

"Si. It is my village during Carnaval," she yelled, and then paused and took a quick look around. Seeming satisfied that they weren't near the Limping Devil and his *vejiga*, she turned her attention to the street scene and smiled faintly. "This was how the Carnaval was when I was young. Now it is as commercialized as Christmas, with sponsors and concerts and . . ." She shrugged unhappily. "It is not the same anymore."

"You sound like an old woman," he teased lightly.

Ildaria turned to him with a crooked smile. "I *am* an old woman," she pointed out, and then grinned at his stunned expression as he realized she was right.

She had said she was born in 1812. That meant she was over two hundred years old, older than any mortal alive. She should be a shriveled old prune. But the nanos kept her young and beautiful. G.G. knew about immortals, and intellectually he knew that most if not all of them that he met were older than him, but for some reason he didn't think of them that way.

"Oh, G.G., you are dating an older woman," Ildaria said suddenly, with wide eyes. "A cougar."

G.G. snorted at the claim. "You're no cougar."

"Si. Lydia, my friend from university, said an older woman with a younger man is a cougar. I am a cougar," she assured him. "And you are *mi perrito*."

"What is that?" he asked suspiciously.

"My puppy."

"My puppy?" he gasped with disbelief.

"Well, it's better than my kitty. That just sounds wrong. I could call you Osito."

"Which means?"

"Cuddly teddy bear." When he scowled, she said, "*Semental?* It means stallion."

"Yeah, well that's not what it sounds like," he said dryly.

"Or *polla grande*," she offered, and then smiled wickedly and explained, "It means big cock."

G.G. felt the grin spread over his face. Yeah, he was a guy. He liked that name.

Ildaria burst out laughing at his expression, sidled closer, and he felt her hand slide up his leg, toward his groin. "I like you in this outfit, *polla grande*."

"Naughty," he said softly, catching her hand. It might be a dream, but it still felt like there were hundreds of people around them. Unfortunately, as usual, one touch and he was ready to go. Hell, one look and he was usually ready to go. Ildaria was like a drug and he was addicted. Still holding her hand in his, he slid his free hand to her hip. "And I like you in this dress, Angel. It makes me want to slip my hand under your skirt to see what you're wearing under it." He let his hand glide down over her bottom and urged her closer as he squeezed gently. "But I really think you look even better out of it."

Ildaria smiled slowly, and then pulled away and tugged him along behind her, leading him through the crowd, moving toward the edge of it until they broke away and escaped into an alley. It was narrow and dark, and felt isolated from the celebrating villagers behind them, the music, laughter, and chatter muted a great deal. G.G. was just wondering where they were going when she stopped and turned to face him. Before he could ask what they were doing, she leaned back against the wall, and tugged her top down, revealing her breasts.

G.G. stared for a moment, awed by the sight, and then moved forward, reaching for the perfect round globes even as his lips found hers. She greeted him warmly, her mouth opening at once to welcome him, and her body arching into his touch. G.G.'s tongue thrust and hips surged as he cupped and squeezed the breasts on offer. Her skin was so soft and warm, and she felt so damned good in his hands. He toyed with her nipples as he kissed her, plucking and tweaking them until she moaned, and then one hand fell away and dropped to tug up her skirt. Catching the cloth between them with the pressure of his body, he reached under it to skim his hand up her leg, smiling against her mouth when she shivered and shifted restlessly, little mewls of sound slipping from her mouth to his. He loved those sounds. He wanted more of them, and slid his hand between her legs to find no panties to bar his way.

The woman thought of everything, he marveled as

he pressed against her heat. He felt her fingers tighten on his shoulders, and her legs spread a bit to make it easier, and then he let his fingers glide over her warm wet skin, and she was so wet for him. He wanted more.

Ildaria gasped and shuddered, her hips shifting as his fingers slid between her folds and caressed her. Moving gently but firmly around the nub he felt there, he just brushed the edges of the delicate spot and swallowed her gasps and moans as she began to ride his hand, chasing his touch as her excitement mounted. When she broke their kiss and gasped, "Please!" in that needy voice he loved, G.G. moved his mouth to her ear and nipped lightly before asking, "What do you want, Angel?"

"You," she moaned.

"You want me inside you?" he asked.

"Si. Oh!" she cried out as he slid a finger inside her, shifting to continue caressing her bud with his thumb now, and doing so more firmly as he eased in and out of her.

"You like that?" he growled, nipping her ear again.

"More," she gasped, nearly sobbing now. "Please, *mi amor*. Please."

Turning his head, he caught her mouth with his in a brief hard kiss, even as his free hand reached for the front of his pants. He had them undone before he recalled it was a dream and he could have wished them undone or even gone. Pushing the thought away, he left off caressing her briefly, and retrieved his hand to catch her upper legs. When Ildaria immediately clutched at his shoulders and wrapped her legs around his hips, he guided himself into her, hissing between his teeth as she closed around him warm, and wet and—

"So damn tight," he breathed as the head of his erection was swallowed and squeezed and drawn farther in. Then he surged upward, burying himself in her, a groan slipping from his mouth even as he heard hers. Pinning her body to the wall with his, G.G. turned his head and kissed her again. This time he continued to kiss her, his tongue thrusting in time to his body pushing into hers, slowly at first, and then with increased speed when she began clawing at his shoulders, her nails biting into the skin. It was a mistake. He almost came before she was ready, and had to fight the urge, mentally shouting at himself. "No. Wait. Christ, you can't—" and then Ildaria broke their kiss on a cry and strained against him, her inner muscles tightening and pulsing around him as she found her release. Nothing could have stopped G.G. then, and he followed her into that pleasure with a shout of his own, before sagging against her, his forehead resting on hers.

They were both silent for a moment as they caught their breath. But when he slipped from inside her, Ildaria stretched lazily and ran her hands over his back before sliding them up to clasp his face and urge his head up. G.G. opened his eyes to see her smiling at him softly.

Letting her legs drop, she stood on her own and then leaned up to press a soft kiss to his lips. "Thank you, *mi amor*. I am sure you have banished the nightmares. I will never think of this spot again without remembering this."

G.G. blinked as his mind absorbed her words, and
then he turned to peer around the small alley. It was
dark and narrow and somewhat smelly, and he was
suddenly quite sure it was the alley where she'd been
assaulted by the soldiers and then attacked and turned
by Juan Villaverde. When he turned back to her in
question, she nodded and then kissed him again.

It started out a soft brushing of lips like the first.
She was the one to deepen it, her tongue skimming
his lips and urging them apart to allow her to slip in.
G.G. started kissing her back then, but was careful to
let her lead the way. She led them deep, her kisses returning to the passion of moments ago, and when her
hand found him and slid his length, he groaned into
her mouth as he felt himself grow.

He didn't resist when she turned them so that he
was the one against the wall, but his eyes popped open
when she suddenly broke their kiss and he sensed her
shifting. She had dropped to her knees before him,
and concern nudged aside some of his passion then.

His worry must have shown on his face, because
a small smirk tilted Ildaria's lips and she whispered,
"Coward," against the head of his semi-erect cock as
she took him in hand.

"I'm kind of attached to my parts," he said for explanation.

"So am I, *semental*," she assured him and then took
him in her mouth.

G.G. wanted to close his eyes and enjoy the sensation as she ran her lips and tongue his length, but was
nervous enough that he couldn't. However even here,

in this spot, she wasn't moved to bite him, and bloody
hell, watching her mouth moving on him was about
the most erotic damned thing he'd ever seen. Despite
having just loved her, it didn't take long for her to
push him over the edge. In fact it was fast enough
he would have been embarrassed if it hadn't felt so
damned good and she didn't look so bloody pleased.

Shaking his head on a helpless laugh, he sagged
against the wall and then closed his arms around her
when she straightened and leaned against him.

"You're incredible," he murmured, pressing her
close and dropping a kiss on her forehead.

"Si. And so are you. It is why we are life mates," she
whispered, kissing his chin softly.

G.G. peered down at her silently for a minute and
then suddenly spun her to the wall, and knelt before
her, his hands pushing her skirt up her legs and his
mouth following in their wake, trailing kisses.

"G.G.?" she whispered, already sounding breathless.

"I'm going to give you one more good memory to
replace the old ones here," he said, drawing one of her
legs over his shoulder and finding her with his lips and
tongue. And he was pretty sure it was the best damned
memory ever. G.G. used his mouth and hands, and went
at her until she came, screaming in that alley with her
pleasure, and then he started all over again. G.G. helped
her find her pleasure half a dozen times that way. When
he finally stopped, her legs were shaking so badly she
couldn't stand and her hands were clumsy as she tried
to straighten her clothes. G.G. helped her, tugging her
top back up into place. Then he straightened his own

clothes, before sweeping her off her feet. He then carried her out of the alley, murmuring, "Time for bed."

Ildaria smiled faintly and rested her head against his shoulder, murmuring, "I'm already in bed. This is a dream, remember?"

"Yes," he agreed as her eyes drifted closed, and then as he stepped out of the alley and miraculously into the bedroom of her apartment, he added softly, "But next time it won't be."

G.G. didn't know if she'd heard him. It seemed ridiculous to believe that she'd fallen asleep in her dream, but that was how it had seemed. Perhaps exhaustion had just forced the dreaming part of her mind to shut down. Whatever the case, he'd laid her in her bed, then rolled over in his own and woke up.

It had been one hell of a night. One of many they'd had the last week since she'd begun to participate in the dreams they shared. But this one was special. It had left G.G. thinking that maybe they really could risk sex while they were awake. That was obviously why Ildaria had led him to the alley where she'd been attacked. Either to test herself, or to show him that she thought it would be safe and she wouldn't freak out.

He wasn't saying he wouldn't still be a little nervous their first time. But he was willing to give it a go. It was just a shame there weren't Kevlar condoms out there.

Smiling faintly at the thought, G.G. opened his eyes and turned his head to peer at the bedside clock. Shock rolled through him when he saw that it was nine in the morning. He'd slept for twelve hours straight! That was something he hadn't done since he was a teenager.

Oh God, and he'd stuck Ildaria with H.D. She'd obviously slept, or he couldn't have had the shared dreams with her, but he wondered how long she'd waited for him to come get his dog. Sunrise was around a quarter to six in the morning at this time of year, and he usually finished cleanup and stopped in at her place by six thirty or six forty-five. Ildaria had probably dozed off waiting for him to show up. Damn. He was a bad daddy and employer.

Sitting up abruptly, he tossed the sheet and comforter aside and launched out of bed to hurry into the bathroom. Ten minutes later he came out, showered, shaved, teeth brushed, and Mohawk standing straight up and proud. A quick rummage through the closet and he was also dressed. G.G. didn't even stop for coffee, he simply hurried out to snatch his keys off the island and then hustled out of the apartment and across the hall.

Knowing Ildaria would still be sleeping, he didn't knock, but unlocked the door and crept quietly in, expecting to find Ildaria and H.D. curled up on the sofa where she'd no doubt dozed off. But the couch was empty, as was the rest of the apartment until he reached the bedroom. He never would have opened the door had it been closed, but it was wide open, revealing Ildaria curled up in bed, with H.D. snuggled up to her back.

The little fur ball knew better. G.G. never let H.D. in bed. The woman was ruining his dog, he thought with a small smile as his gaze slid over her sleeping face. It was the first time he'd seen her asleep. She looked different. Her face softer without the sharpness that usually cloaked her features when awake. It made him realize that she was usually tense and on the alert for threat or trouble. Hyperaware was what he thought they called it. Without that, she looked like the angel he'd taken to calling her. Sweet and lovely and innocent. Seeing her like this, he could imagine her at fourteen, and simply couldn't understand how anyone would want to harm her. His immediate instinct was to protect her.

Movement drew his gaze to H.D. The fur ball's eyes were open and his head turned toward the door. G.G. made a soft shushing sound so the dog wouldn't bark, and then patted his leg. He needn't have bothered; H.D. was already on his feet and scampering to the foot of the bed. His tags jingled on his collar as he leapt to the floor, and G.G. glanced to Ildaria, relieved that the small sound hadn't woken her.

He bent to pet his dog in greeting, and then urged him out of the doorway so he could close it. G.G. had decided to make Ildaria breakfast, which meant the clang of pots and pans, running water, etc. and he didn't want the noise to drag her from sleep prematurely. The woman might have ruined his dog, but otherwise she was perfect . . . for him. But then she would be, she was his life mate.

Damn, I have a life mate, G.G. thought, and smiled as he led H.D. up the hall. He started to head into the kitchen, but a bark from H.D. made him stop and turn back. The dog hadn't followed him, but had headed to the door instead.

"Right. You need to go out, huh?" G.G. realized and gave his head a shake as he changed direction. That was why he'd gone to fetch him rather than just leaving him with Ildaria until she woke. He hadn't wanted H.D. to wake her up early with a need to go outside.

"Okay, buddy. Let's go," he said as he opened the door. The little mutt rushed out, and then came to an abrupt halt and crouched, barking viciously, which really just sounded like his usual yip, but G.G. knew he was trying to sound mean. Glancing past him, he stopped as well, his eyebrows rising as he took note of the man and woman seated on the floor at the end of the hall, playing cards.

"Mirabeau. Tiny," he greeted, relaxing and pulling Ildaria's apartment door closed when he recognized the pair. Eyebrows rising in question, he asked, "To what do we owe this visit? Is it a visit?" he added wryly, not sure what to make of their presence in his hall.

"Lucian called us at about 5:30 in the morning and asked us to come and guard Ildaria," Mirabeau answered.

"Guard Ildaria?" G.G. echoed, alarm coursing through him. "From what? What's happened?"

"A couple of South American Enforcers tried to grab her when she took H.D. out to relieve himself after work," Tiny said in his deep rumble.

"What?" G.G. barked. "Why the hell didn't she tell me?"

"Maybe she wasn't awake enough to think of it," Mirabeau suggested. "Was she sleeping when you went in?"

"Yes. And I didn't wake her up, but I meant in our dreams last night. She didn't mention it then either."

"Ah." Tiny smiled and nodded.

"Yeah. We heard you two were life mates. Congratulations," Mirabeau said, and then tilted her head. "But if you two are life mates, why are you sleeping apart? The shared dreams usually stop once you mate. You get more sleep that way."

"I wouldn't say more," Tiny disagreed with amusement.

"Well, it's more restful sleep, at least," Mirabeau argued.

"Were you two out here when I left my apartment?" G.G. asked as her earlier words suddenly occurred to him. Lucian had called at 5:30 and sent them over?

"Yeah." Mirabeau grinned. "You didn't even look our way, just came out, crossed the hall, and went into Ildaria's. Good thing we weren't the South American Enforcers, we'd have taken you out and gone in and grabbed her."

"Hmm." Tiny nodded in agreement.

G.G. closed his eyes briefly at the thought. Christ, he'd had no awareness that someone was even in the hall with him. He hadn't looked around at all.

"No reason for you to. It's your hall, and you had no idea there was a problem," Mirabeau pointed out.

"You also haven't lived your entire life having to watch for trouble," Tiny pointed out. "Immortals know better than to mess with you. No one wants Robert Guiscard on their ass."

"And most mortals probably steer clear of you too, because of your size and the Mohawk."

"Ildaria would have noticed you right away though. Probably before she even opened the door," G.G. said with a frown, just now realizing how obliviously he'd lived his life. He'd wandered through it, never afraid, never the least anxious that he wasn't safe and secure. Meanwhile, she'd lived it constantly hunted, constantly on the alert for trouble and threat.

G.G. had hoped she was safe now that she was out of South America, but that bastard Villaverde found out she was here and sent men after her. He could understand his being pissed about her biting off his cock and maybe wanting a little revenge at the time, but hunting her for two hundred years seemed a bit over the top. The guy needed to get over it and move on. As an immortal, he would have grown it back. Maybe. G.G. wasn't sure. Did immortals grow back their bits if someone took them off?

"Uh, yeah. They do," Mirabeau said, obviously picking up his thoughts. Wincing then, she asked, "So that's his beef, huh?"

"He attacked her and she defended herself," G.G. muttered, hoping Ildaria wouldn't be upset that others were learning about the incident. He hadn't said anything. The knowledge had been plucked from his head. Still, it was private, and he didn't want her uncomfortable or embarrassed because of his wandering thoughts.

"Well, I won't say anything," Mirabeau assured him.

G.G. grunted a thank-you, and then glanced to H.D. who was unusually quiet. The dog had sat down and was watching Tiny with interest. But he wasn't barking at Mirabeau or trying to bite her ankles, which was something new. The dog always went after strange women.

"Tiny's good with dogs," Mirabeau commented, shifting her gaze to the dog. "They love him."

As if to prove it, Tiny snapped his thumb and finger and whistled and H.D. stood and moved cautiously forward, head lowering to sniff as he got closer. Much to G.G.'s amazement, his dog walked right up to the big man and even let him pet him, then sat down next to him and turned to look at G.G.

"Traitor," G.G. said with amusement. "I thought you had to go outside?"

That had H.D. standing up at once and moving around Tiny to the door.

Nodding, G.G. moved around the couple to get to the door and said, "We shouldn't be long. Do you two want coffee or something when I get back?"

"Nah. We're good," Tiny said when Mirabeau shook her head. "Thanks though."

"Sure," G.G. murmured and then opened the door to the stairwell and followed H.D. through. His mind was on Ildaria as he followed the fur ball down the stairs. Someone had tried to snatch her last night while he lay sleeping. He'd nearly lost her and hadn't known a damned thing about it.

That bastard Villaverde wasn't going to leave her alone. G.G. had no idea how the man had discovered she was in Canada, but it meant she wasn't safe here anymore. Maybe he should take her to England. Once there, his father would definitely get involved. He hadn't told his parents yet that he was Ildaria's life mate. His mother would be ecstatic when she learned, so would his father. But Robert wielded a bit of power. Tiny wasn't kidding when he said most immortals left him alone because they didn't want to tangle with his dad. Robert Guiscard was a renowned warrior, and on the European Council. He was also known to be fierce and protective of those he cared for. He'd take Ildaria under his protection. Hell, the man would start a war to keep her safe once he knew she and G.G. were life mates. Robert would be disappointed, though, that he still wasn't agreeing to the turn. Which was why G.G. hadn't said anything to his mother when he'd spoken to her a couple days ago. He knew she was hoping he'd meet an immortal and wouldn't be able to resist turning. But he was resisting, and that would disappoint the hell out of her too. It might even crush her. He understood. She didn't want to have to watch him die, but he just—

H.D. started barking, and G.G. glanced around sharply, surprised to see that they were outside. H.D. was only barking at a squirrel that had dared to come near his patch of grass, but it made G.G. realize that he really did walk around oblivious. He'd been so lost in thought, he'd followed the dog downstairs and outside without paying any attention to anything around him. He could have passed half a dozen Enforcers in the stairwell and out here without noticing. He needed to start paying attention to his surroundings. Ildaria's life may depend on it.

Eleven

Ildaria stretched happily and yawned as she woke up, her body arching and twisting under the covers. She'd slept well, and the dreams she'd shared with G.G. had left her feeling lovely, as if all was right with the world. She'd had other dreams afterward, but not shared dreams and not one had included sex. Still, they'd been nice dreams, most of them featuring her abuela telling her she loved and was proud of her. Ildaria had no idea what the psychology behind that was. Perhaps in her subconscious she was forgiving herself for never seeing her abuela again after the day she'd fled Señorita Ana's home. That was something that had always bothered her. She'd tried several times over the two years after that fateful day to approach her, but always there had been at least one Enforcer watching her abuela's home, and following her everywhere she went.

The last time Ildaria had tried, she'd arrived to see

Juan outside, talking to several of the neighbors. She hadn't been able to hear what they were saying, but she'd spotted a friend of her abuela's standing, weeping, amongst the gathering and had read her mind. The woman had been visiting when Ildaria's abuela had suddenly clutched her chest and collapsed to the floor. She'd run for help, but by the time she returned with the local healer, there was nothing he could do. Ildaria's abuela was dead. Juan was now telling them that he would take care of her burial and everything else.

Ildaria had stumbled away, heart both broken and guilt laden. Her abuela had died alone. The logical side of her brain had assured her that it wasn't her fault, but the emotional side had berated her for failing her abuela, the woman who had championed and raised her. Ildaria had wanted to attend the funeral, but Juan was there with Señorita Ana and her fiancé who had surely been her husband by then. There had also been about a dozen Enforcers in attendance. She'd had to watch the proceedings from a distance, unable to see her abuela one last time to say goodbye. She'd simply watched hollow-eyed as a beautiful and surely expensive wood coffin had been lowered into the ground.

Ildaria had stayed until long after most of the others had left, but while the guests, and even the Enforcers had left, Juan had remained behind alone, watching silently as they filled her grave with dirt. Most of the time he'd stood unmoving, but every once in a while he'd glanced around as if expecting someone. Her, she'd supposed, but sure it was a trap, she hadn't dared approach. The man had been furious to the point of hatred that night in the alley, and that had been before she'd maimed him. And he'd hunted her for two years at that point, his men seeming everywhere all the time. A man did not expend that kind of energy and manpower without very deep feelings. She was sure he wasn't doing it because he wished to welcome her to the immortal fold, and was terrified of what retribution he'd demand if he caught her.

Ildaria's largest fear was that he'd have her executed. Señorita Ana had made it very clear that each immortal could turn only one, and saved it to turn a life mate should they be mortal. While Juan hadn't intentionally turned her, his blood was what had brought on the turn. Did that mean he couldn't turn a life mate should he meet one? Unless he killed her?

Or perhaps he'd already turned his one and she was one too many. He had been mated and had children, but his life mate was apparently dead, although Ildaria didn't know the story behind it. She did know that Señorita Ana had said should an immortal turn a second mortal, the immortal that had turned them would be executed. But she was quite sure as head of the Council, Juan could dictate that she be executed instead. He hadn't turned her deliberately after all.

Survival had seemed a perfectly good excuse to put off trying to see her abuela until another time while the woman had still lived, but once her abuela was dead Ildaria had berated herself for not trying harder. She should have risked death and walked straight up to her and told her everything, or as much as she could before she was dragged away and set on fire.

She should have . . . done something. Or so she'd berated herself for decades afterward. The mental self-
flagellation had ended eventually, but the guilt had
remained, clinging to her like cobwebs.

Now though, Ildaria felt she was willing to let go of
the burden of that guilt. She had been very young, and
had done the best she could. Her abuela must know
and understand that.

It left her feeling lighter somehow. Forgiven.

A peaceful smile curving her lips, she glanced at the
clock. It was a little after two in the afternoon. She'd
slept about seven hours. Good enough, she decided
and slid from bed to go to the closet to survey her
clothes. She'd normally wear jeans and a T-shirt or a
pretty summer dress during the afternoon depending
on what she and G.G. had planned for the day. But today she grabbed her leather pants and bustier. If there
were South American Enforcers out there waiting to
try to grab her, she wanted to be prepared for battle.

The thought disrupted some of the serenity she'd
woken feeling, and Ildaria sighed as she felt it slip
away. She might have forgiven herself for the past,
but Juan Villaverde obviously hadn't . . . And he'd
found her. Which meant she had to talk to G.G. and
decide what to do about it. Moving on and hiding
would be her normal action, but she had a life mate
to consider now, Ildaria thought as she closed the
closet door and took her chosen clothes into the bathroom with her.

She'd brushed her teeth, showered, and was dressing when she recalled H.D. G.G. had never come to

collect the pup. An hour after he normally collected the dog, she'd assumed he was still sleeping and had finally taken H.D. into the bedroom. She'd crawled into bed, settling him next to her, and fallen asleep. But the little fur ball hadn't been there when she'd woken up, she realized.

Concerned, she stepped out of the bathroom and took a quick look around the room. She didn't see him right away and would have done a more thorough search, but the fact that the door was closed when she knew she'd left it open last night made her head that way instead. She suspected G.G. had come to get him, but wasn't positive, so opened the door cautiously and peered out before leaving the room.

The hall was empty, but it was also full of delicious smells. Sniffing the air, she stepped out of the room and started up the hall at a more relaxed pace. She was pretty sure neither dog-nappers nor Enforcers from the south who were out to kidnap her would cook bacon before going about their business.

A smile claimed her lips when she stepped out into the living room and spotted G.G.'s wide back at her stove. Her smile grew when H.D. came hurrying around the island and pranced toward her, tail high and tongue hanging out.

G.G. knew the minute his dog jumped up and scampered from the kitchen that Ildaria must be up. Turning from the bacon he was frying, he glanced into the living room and nearly swallowed his tongue. Bloody hell, the woman looked like a walking wet dream.

Ildaria was encased in leather from head to toe . . . well, mostly just from her breasts to her toes, he acknowledged. While she had high-heeled, knee-high leather boots, and tight, body-hugging leather pants on that completely covered her from the waist down, the upper half of her body was trussed up in some kind of bustier/corset-looking thing that was just as tight as the pants, and followed the upper curve of her breasts, ending in a low V between them. It had inch wide straps that ran over the shoulders to help keep it up, but still left a hell of a lot of her beautiful tawny flesh on display. It was sexy as hell. If these were the leathers she'd mentioned wearing when she went vigilante, the bag guys she'd gone after probably hadn't had a chance. They'd have been too distracted by her figure to fight back.

Much to his relief, Ildaria squatted then and leaned forward, her damp hair dropping around her like a curtain as she petted H.D. and G.G. was able to drag his attention away from her. It dropped automatically to his dog, and he immediately rolled his eyes with disgust. The fur ball was on his back, rolling back and forth and twisting his head ecstatically as she petted his belly.

"Come on, H.D., you're embarrassing us both," G.G. said with exasperation. "You could at least pretend to have a little dignity."

Predictably, the dog ignored him. But Ildaria chuckled. He just wasn't sure if it was at his words or the dog's antics, though, since she followed it up with, "Hey baby. How's my furry little sleep buddy?"

"Gloating all over the place that he got to sleep with you first," G.G. said with amusement. When his teasing drew her gaze to him, he smiled and said, "Morning, Angel, you look ready to take on the world."

Ildaria glanced down at her outfit, grimaced, and then scooped up H.D. "I thought I'd better be ready for anything. We had a little trouble last night."

"I heard," he said grimly as she carried H.D. to the island and settled on one of the chairs. "Mirabeau and Tiny are out in the hall keeping an eye out for trouble."

Ildaria nodded. "Tybo and Valerian were out in the hall when I went to sleep last night, but mentioned they'd probably be replaced before I woke up. I assume this Mirabeau and Tiny are the Enforcers sent to replace them?"

"It seems so," he answered, and then told her what he knew of the pair from gossip and comments made in the Night Club. "Mirabeau used to be a full-time Enforcer and Tiny was a private detective for the Morrisey agency. Now they split their time between the two jobs. Today they're enforcing and guarding you."

"An immortal detective," Ildaria said with a faint smile. "He would have been exceptionally good at it if his clients were all mortal."

"He was mortal when he worked as a detective only. Mirabeau turned him. They're life mates."

"Oh," she said, drawing out the word.

Noting the concern drawing her eyebrows together, and knowing what was causing it, he quickly assured her, "But they're past the passed-out-from-sex-all-the-time stage, so should be good."

When Ildaria relaxed at this news, G.G. announced, "I'm making breakfast," and turned back to the stove.

"What can I do to help?" Ildaria asked at once, and he glanced around to see her sliding off the chair and bending to set H.D. on the ground.

"Nothing," he said as H.D. returned to his side and curled up on the floor next to him. The little beggar would stay close until he stopped cooking in the hopes that pieces of bacon would magically fall to the floor for him to gobble up.

"I could make toast," Ildaria suggested.

"It's already made and staying warm in the oven, next to a bowl of fried potatoes," he told her. "The bacon is the last of it, except for eggs, and those can't be made until the bacon is done." And then, to prevent her arguing further, he added, "The kettle should still be hot. Make yourself a tea and keep me company." He'd set the tea to boil three times since returning about an hour ago.

Knowing Ildaria wouldn't be up for a while, he'd gone to his own apartment after taking H.D. out to relieve himself. He'd had coffee and a couple Pop-Tarts there, made phone calls and then puttered around until a little after one when he'd judged it was late enough that she would wake up within the next hour or so. Then G.G. had gathered bacon, eggs, potatoes, and his large grill pan and led H.D. back here to start breakfast.

"Did you want tea too?" Ildaria asked.

"No. I'm rocking the coffee this morning," he responded. "Thank you, though."

She murmured something he didn't really catch over

the clink of a spoon in a cup, and then said, "So, I'm guessing this Mirabeau and Tiny told you about what happened last night?"

"Yes," he acknowledged. G.G. had made them describe exactly what they'd been told about what had happened when he'd returned upstairs with H.D. He should have made them do that before he went downstairs with H.D. It would have made spotting the blood on the grass out back much less alarming had he known it was all from her attackers and not Ildaria's. Seeing the dried blood staining the blades of grass had given him a shock. He'd known she must be okay. She'd been well enough to have shared dreams with him, but she could have been injured and healed. Immortals healed quickly.

Learning she was uninjured and had kicked ass all on her own, had filled him with relief, pride, and concern. He was relieved she wasn't hurt, proud she'd kicked ass like that, but concerned for her well-being now. He was also pissed. She shouldn't have to fight for her life like this, but he suspected she'd had to do that frequently in her two hundred plus years. He doubted she'd been lucky enough that this was the first time her pursuers had caught up with her in two centuries.

"Did they tell you what's been done with Juan's Enforcers?" Ildaria asked, distracting him from his thoughts.

"Last they'd heard, Lucian had called in Rachel to remove your shoes—She's a doctor who's married to Etienne Argeneau, one of Lucian's nephews," G.G. interrupted himself to explain. "But apparently she had some trouble getting your shoe out of the one guy's face. I guess it was hooked on the bone and she had to operate," he explained and heard her grunt behind him in acknowledgment. "The other guy wouldn't even let her near him until they knocked him out. He didn't want the shoe removed. He didn't want the healing to start."

"Si, healing from that would be a bitch," Ildaria said with satisfaction.

G.G. nodded. The shoe had apparently gone through his testicle. The kick that had inserted the shoe would have been swift and excruciating, but that would be nothing next to the healing. That would be much slower, the pain extended over hours as the nanos repaired the damage. The thought wasn't a pleasant one, but it was no less than the man deserved for trying to take his woman, G.G. thought grimly.

Speaking of which, he thought, and said, "After I heard the news about the attack, I thought perhaps we should leave Canada to avoid any further attacks."

G.G. was aware of the sudden stillness behind him, and added, "But as my father said, they may know that we're life mates. If they don't, it wouldn't be hard to find out, and then they'd just follow us to England."

"England?" she echoed, but he couldn't tell how she was feeling. She didn't sound surprised, more curious.

"Yes. At first, I was thinking we could go there, but my father thinks we should handle it here if we can. That way we would have the support of the North American as well as the UK Council because I'm a Brit in Canada. He doesn't think Lucian would be allowed to interfere in England since you're from the

Dominican Republic which is guided by the South American Council," he explained.

"Si, if Juan complained and a summit of Council leaders was called, they might decide Lucian has no business in this if I am not still living in Canada," Ildaria murmured, sounding a little distracted. He understood why when she said, "Your father pointed this out? He knows about me?"

G.G. nodded. "I called my parents after I finished talking to Mirabeau and Tiny. I thought I should tell them about us, and let them know that we might be flying over soon. It seemed better than just showing up and giving my mother fits." He paused briefly, but then quickly added, "I say might be flying over, because I would have checked with you before booking the flights or anything. I wasn't going all caveman on you."

He heard her sigh behind him and then she whispered, "I wish I could hug you right now."

"I do too," he admitted, his voice husky, but then shook his head. "Unfortunately, we have talking to do right now and if you hugged me . . ."

"That talking wouldn't get done," she said, sounding resigned.

He heard her cross the room and the scrape of a chair being pulled out. G.G. wasn't surprised to see her settling at the island again when he glanced around.

"So, we will talk," she said resolutely, clearing her throat. "You told your parents about us?"

There was no mistaking the anxiety in her voice and G.G. turned back to the stove to hide the smile that started to curve his lips. It was the anxiety of the

partner threatened with the dreaded in-laws, something he wouldn't have to worry about since Ildaria's
abuela was long dead and she had no other family.
That thought drove his smile away, and he assured
her, "They were very pleased."

"Si. Of course," she muttered, sounding distracted.
"They have been hoping for this for a long time."

"Yes. So there's nothing to worry about. You could
be a troll and they'd still love you, and you're no troll.
They will adore you. Hell, my mother will probably
drop to her knees and kiss your feet the minute she
gets in the door."

"What? Wait!" she said with alarm. "In what door?
You said we were not going to England."

"We aren't," he agreed. "But my parents are flying
here. Robert wants to help resolve this and Mother—"

G.G. stopped and turned sharply at a choking sound
from Ildaria. His eyes widened incredulously when he
saw her expression. His beautiful brave woman who
had taken on two Enforcers and kicked their asses last
night, looked terrified at the idea of meeting his parents.
She was pale, her eyes golden-brown saucers, her mouth
shaped into a rictus of horror, and she was clutching her
throat as if she were indeed choking. Then she started
to babble away in Spanish, her hands suddenly leaving
her throat to fly about in a way he'd never seen from her
before as she began what sounded like either a rant, or
possibly a plea. He couldn't tell. He couldn't understand
a single word she was saying. But Spanish sure was a
pretty language, he thought. And her hands looked like
little birds as she waved them around. Beautiful.

Stopping abruptly, she frowned and said, "Why are you looking at me like that?"

"I've just never seen you get excited about anything before," he said with a slow smile, and then added, "Well, outside of sex."

Ildaria flushed bright pink and moaned, "They will hate me."

"No, they won't," he assured her. "They'll love you to bits. My mother has been waiting for you for nearly twenty years."

"She has been waiting for an immortal who would make you want to turn. I am not that. I failed her," Ildaria wailed, dropping her head onto the island surface.

G.G. shifted uncomfortably and frowned. "You haven't failed anything. My not turning has nothing to do with you."

"Of course it does," she said, sitting up with irritation. She scowled at him briefly and then closed her eyes and groaned. "She will come here and she will—" Ildaria shook her head and then launched into another spate of Spanish.

It made G.G. wish he understood the language. Or, maybe he was better off not knowing. Her suggestion that she wasn't enough to make him want to turn had been guilt-inducing. He'd never imagined she would take it that way, and it was ridiculous. Because if anyone could have convinced him to turn, he was one hundred percent positive it would have been Ildaria. He'd even considered it, if only briefly before his more sensible side had reminded him he was perfectly happy being mortal and living a mortal life.

"When are they coming?"

The sudden English caught his attention, and G.G. blinked and shifted his thoughts to answer her. "Well—"

"This would not be considered an emergency by the Council there, so surely they could not arrange a flight before tomorrow, could they?" she asked hopefully.

"Er . . . well, Robert is on the Council," he admitted reluctantly. "And he called me after talking to Scotty— he's the head of the UK Council," G.G. explained, and then continued. "Scotty has agreed to accompany him and my mother here to handle the situation with Villaverde."

Much to his surprise that seemed to ease her concerns somewhat. "Oh, good, good. As the head of the Council I am sure this Scotty cannot just drop everything and fly out right away. It could be days before they leave. Si?"

"Er . . ." G.G. shifted on his feet uncomfortably, but finally said, "It won't be days, Ildaria. Scotty is a good friend of my parents and he knows how worried they have been about my finding a life mate, or being a life mate to someone or whatever," he muttered, and shook his head. "He won't make them wait days. In fact, they're probably—"

A knock on the door interrupted him.

"I'll get it," Ildaria said, suddenly solemn and grim.

Nodding, G.G. turned back to his bacon. It was done, so he began lifting it out piece by piece onto the paper towel covered plate he'd prepared ahead of time. He was getting the eggs out of the refrigerator when Ildaria led Lucian into the kitchen. G.G. eyed the man briefly and then shifted his gaze to H.D., expecting the usual barking and hullabaloo, but the dog was sitting still and tense where he'd been lying just a moment ago. He was also eyeing Lucian Argeneau with wariness, not looking the least interested in drawing the man's attention his way by barking.

That was a new reaction from the dog, G.G. thought, and turned back to the refrigerator to grab the second pack of bacon he'd brought over with him. He'd brought it along thinking to offer some to Mirabeau and Tiny, but they'd once again said they were good when he'd stopped to mention it to them on the way across the hall, so he'd only cooked the one package. Lucian, however, never turned down food. The man was always hungry. G.G. was sure that if he didn't fry the second package, he and Ildaria would be lucky to get a piece of bacon each. Lucian Argeneau would eat every last slice of what he'd just finished cooking.

"Lucian," he said in greeting as he carried the eggs and bacon over to set them on the counter next to the stove.

"Joshua," Lucian greeted him in response. The man wasn't one for nicknames unless it was one he had given the person. G.G. was always Joshua to him.

He noted Ildaria's startled expression at the use of his name and then Lucian said, "Call him Joshua then, Angelina. At least, in those moments."

When G.G. glanced between the pair in question at

the odd comment Ildaria scowled and explained, "He was very rudely reading my mind again, and"—her scowl eased—"I was thinking that I like your name and am uncomfortable calling you G.G. when we are . . . being intimate," she said, flushing, and then rushed on. "It is a nickname and feels disrespectful, or impersonal in such special moments."

"And I suggested she use your real name," Lucian finished when she fell silent.

Much to G.G.'s amusement, Ildaria rolled her eyes now. She obviously wasn't the least cowed by the man's power and position. At least, if she was, she had no intention of showing it. He suspected she'd had to put a brave face on a lot over the centuries.

Ignoring Lucian, G.G. met her gaze and said, "I understand. Why do you think I've taken to calling you Angel in our shared dreams and out?"

"Because it is her name," Lucian said dryly.

Now it was G.G.'s turn to roll his eyes. But either Lucian didn't notice, or he chose to ignore it in favor of telling Ildaria, "You should use the name you were given. It is who you are. Who your family wanted you to be."

G.G. noted the way Ildaria's jaw tightened at Lucian's lecture and decided a change of subject was needed. Turning to the package of bacon he'd just retrieved from the fridge, he asked, "Are you hungry, Lucian?"

"I could eat," Lucian said mildly, settling himself on a chair at the island.

"I thought you wanted to talk about the South American Enforcers," Ildaria said laconically.

"I can do that while we wait for Joshua to finish the bacon and make the eggs," Lucian said easily.

G.G. opened the bacon package and started laying out strips on the long griddle he'd placed over two of the burners on the stove. Once the last piece was on, he put the first batch of bacon in the oven to stay warm with the potatoes and toast.

"Coffee or tea?" Ildaria asked, her voice a bit snappy.

"Tea," Lucian said, and when Ildaria simply stared at him, he added, "Please," as an afterthought.

G.G. suspected Lucian was not a man used to saying *please* or *thank you*. Actually, he was pretty sure he wasn't. The man didn't even bother with *hello* and *goodbye* during phone conversations. G.G. didn't think Lucian was intentionally rude, he was just a very abrupt man, used to giving orders. Orders did not usually include *please* or *thank you* unless you were in a restaurant.

"So," Lucian said finally when Ildaria set a cup of tea in front of him and stepped back to eye him expectantly. "The South Americans were not trying to kidnap you."

"What?" Ildaria asked with disbelief. Crossing her arms with a harrumph, she shook her head. "They are lying."

"They cannot lie to me," Lucian said simply. "I read their minds. They approached you to invite you back to South America on the behalf of the head of their Council, Juan Villaverde."

Ildaria's mouth tightened at that name, and she

growled, "I don't care if you've read their minds. They may have been told to simply ask me back, but when I refused, they would have been ordered to take me."

Lucian shook his head. "As I said, I read their minds. They were ordered just to invite you personally. When Juan called a week ago and asked me to send you back to South America, I felt sure it had to do with your time on the pirate ship, so I refused. But, apparently Villaverde has been looking for you for quite a while, and it has nothing to do with the mortals you attacked on Vasco's boat."

"No, it has to do with Juan attacking me a little over two hundred years ago," Ildaria snapped.

Lucian's eyebrows rose and then lowered again and his eyes concentrated on her.

Reading her mind, G.G. thought, and was surprised when Ildaria merely lifted her chin, and apparently let him. Except that he supposed it was a much faster and less stressful way for the man to get the full story. At least, this way she didn't have to relive it again in the telling, he thought as he turned back to the bacon and left them to it. A startled sound from Lucian a few moments later had him glancing over his shoulder in time to see the pained look on the man's face before it cleared.

Guessing he'd got to the biting part, and knowing that there was still more for him to read, G.G. turned back to his cooking.

"I see," Lucian said quietly several moments later. "I was not aware of any of this."

"I'm surprised you didn't read it from my mind when the men first brought me here from Montana," Ildaria commented.

G.G. looked around to see Lucian shrug. "I was looking only for information on the mortals you attacked on the ship, and the reason for it. I was not interested in a recounting of your entire two centuries of life."

Ildaria nodded and walked around the island to drop into the chair farthest from Lucian's before asking, "And now that you know?"

Lucian was silent for several minutes and then sighed and agreed with what she'd said earlier. "I suspect they would have been ordered to take you if you had refused. Villaverde has been hunting you too long to just accept a no thank you."

Ildaria relaxed a little at that, and turned her attention to her own tea.

"How do you want your eggs, Lucian?" G.G. asked when silence followed. "Scrambled, over easy, or sunny side up?"

"Sunny side up," Lucian answered, and then recalled the, "Please," on his own, if a second later.

G.G. grabbed the eggs. He already knew Ildaria preferred hers over easy. This wasn't the first time he'd made her breakfast this week, although she'd made it for him more.

A heavy sigh caught his ear, and then Lucian said, "I do not understand this. The man I saw in your memories is not the Juan Villaverde I know."

G.G. glanced around to see Ildaria staring at Lucian with incomprehension. "What do you mean? You know him?"

"Of course. He is the head of the South American Council," Lucian said as if that should make it obvious that he would of course know him, and then he added, "Aside from that, I have known him for at least a thousand years. We used to be great friends, and the man I knew was always honorable."

"Does an honorable man raise the price of blood to force his people to give up land he wants?" Ildaria asked sharply.

Lucian scowled at the question. "Vasco mentioned that to me, and I could hardly credit it."

"Well, credit it. It is true," Ildaria assured him. "I lived and worked at the shore for decades and saw it happen."

"You had property on the shore?" G.G. asked with interest and wondered if she still owned it. A beach house in Punta Cana might be nice, he thought and then recalled that Ildaria wouldn't be safe there.

"No." Ildaria shook her head. "I never had enough money to buy property of my own. But I knew an immortal who had an old hut on the edge of their property that they let me use when I was between jobs," she said and then explained, "For a long time I took positions with mortal plantation owners, either as a house servant or laborer. Most of those jobs came with a bed in the barracks with the other single women working there. But I could only work so long in one place before one of the Enforcers would come sniffing around and I would have to leave. Even if that did not happen, my not aging made me leave eventually. Then I would return to the hut by the sea, and live off of what money I'd managed to save until I found another position where I thought I would be safe for a while. More recently though, I switched to jobs on the fishing boats."

"Hmmm." Lucian looked dissatisfied. "Vasco said Juan's raising of the price of blood for immortals only started about ten years ago?"

Ildaria shrugged. "That is when Vasco noticed and started the feeding tours. I am not sure how long it has gone on. I could not use the blood banks. There were always a couple of Juan's Enforcers at the blood banks keeping an eye out for me."

Lucian's expression was grim. "Then how did you feed? Biting mortals is against the law in the areas governed by South American Council as well."

"It has only been banned there for the last thirty years," Ildaria said, appearing amused. "And that is when I switched from plantation work to jobs on the fishing boats."

"You were feeding on the crew once the boats reached international waters," Lucian said, sounding impressed, and then he asked, "Is that where Vasco got the idea for his tours?"

"Maybe," Ildaria muttered. When Lucian's gaze grew concentrated as he obviously tried to read the truth from her, she heaved a sigh of exasperation. "Oh, get out of my head, I will tell you. Si, he got the idea from me," she conceded, and explained, "The immortal that was allowing me to use their hut was on the verge of losing his property. He had taken a mortgage out on it for renovations just before Juan started jacking up the price of blood. He could no longer afford the bank payments and the cost of blood too. He had gone to a canteen, considering risking biting a mortal rather than buy blood, so that he could pay his mortgage and not lose his property. I suspected as much and followed to stop him. I was trying to convince him to take the occasional job on one of the fishing boats with me to get the blood he needed without putting himself at such risk. I was so concerned, I did not check to be sure there were no immortals there, but Vasco and Cristo were and heard me pointing out that the Council could not execute him if he fed in international waters."

She shrugged. "They approached me as we left. Vasco liked what I had said and had an old pirate ship. He wanted to fix it up and start tours taking tourists out into international seas where the poorer immortals and those under threat of losing their homes could feed. But he didn't know many of the poorer immortals. And he didn't think they would trust him if he approached the ones he did know of. He was Juan's son, after all," she pointed out. "So he asked me to take Cristo around to convince those who needed it most to join his 'crew.'"

G.G. smiled faintly to himself. He hadn't known this, but leave it to Ildaria to be the clever one behind such an endeavor. It wasn't just her fighting skill that had helped her stay alive and out of Villaverde's clutches all these years. Her wits too had kept her safe and alive. It was probably the main reason for it. Thank

God she'd been born with a sharp mind, he thought as he began to transfer eggs from the pan to the plates.

"Enough talk," he said as he carried the first two plates to the island and set them in front of Lucian and Ildaria. "Time to eat."

He didn't wait for a response, but grabbed a dish towel, opened the oven and grabbed the bowl of fried potatoes and the plate that held the toast. Carrying them to the island, he set them on the cutting board he'd set out earlier to hold the hot plates.

Realizing that Ildaria was no longer in her seat, he glanced around to see that she'd gone to retrieve silverware for all of them. Grateful for the help now that the cooking was over, he grabbed the plate of bacon from the oven next and quickly transferred the newly cooked bacon onto the pile already there, then grabbed the plate holding his own eggs and carried both to the island.

"Eat up," he said as he settled in the chair between Lucian and Ildaria. Paws on his leg drew his attention down to H.D. then, and he scowled firmly. "We are eating. In your basket."

H.D. hesitated, but then dropped back to all fours and moved morosely out into the living room to find his basket. Grunting with satisfaction, G.G. turned to his food. As he expected, the conversation died then as the three of them concentrated on eating.

Twelve

"That was good," Lucian said as he pushed his plate away. "Thank you."

G.G. smiled faintly, impressed that the man had remembered the "thank you" without prompting.

Standing up, Lucian glanced at Ildaria and announced, "I will return to the Enforcer house and inform the two men you injured that you have refused the invitation to return to the Dominican, Angelina. Then I will call Juan and try to persuade him to leave you alone."

Ildaria nodded, but looked dubious. She obviously didn't think a phone call was going to do it. Even one from Lucian.

G.G. opened his mouth, closed it, and then sat hesitating briefly. He knew his father had wanted to talk to Lucian himself, but finally he said, "My parents are on the way here. They are bringing the head of the

UK Council with them. They want to end the situation once and for all, and want to work with you to do it."

Lucian nodded, not looking the least surprised. G.G. supposed he'd already read that from his mind and just hadn't commented on it. Until now. "That is good. But I will still call. It might give me an idea of what Juan might try next now that his men have failed to convince her to return with them."

He left then. Without saying goodbye. The man just walked out of Ildaria's apartment, leaving them staring after him. Definitely not a people person, G.G. thought with amusement and then glanced at Ildaria. She had that sharp look about her again, the hunted, preparing and always watching for trouble. It had been there since she'd woken up. But now it was multiplied by ten. Her jaw was so tense he was surprised it wasn't snapping under the pressure. He couldn't imagine living like that for a day, let alone two hundred years.

There was only one thing likely to distract her from these worries and fears that had hounded her for so long, and she would be helpless against it according to all the lore and tales he'd heard. At least, that was the excuse he gave himself for finally instigating the life mate sex.

Not sure what to expect, G.G. reached out and ran one finger, just one, lightly down her arm. It was only her arm. But bloody hell, it was all that was needed.

Ildaria's mouth slipped open on a small gasp, a visible shiver ran through her body and seemed to course into his as a shaft of pleasure zinged through him, and then her head swung around, her eyes targeting him like a heat-seeking missile.

G.G. stared into the growing gold among the brown of her eyes, and then touched her again, this time allowing his finger to coast along the top of her bustier, riding the curve of her breast before dipping to the spot between them. He'd intended to continue on over the second breast, but never got that far. This time it was a shudder they shared rather than a shiver as they both experienced the touch, and then they were kissing.

In their shared dreams their kisses had usually started out slow, a testing and tasting before it deepened into passion. This kiss was an explosion between them, mouths meshing and mashing, tongues searching, hands reaching, bodies straining as wave after wave of mounting passion thundered through them both. It was out of control, scary as hell and fucking sublime, G.G. thought a little dazedly as he dragged Ildaria off her chair and into his lap.

Shared dreams were a limp biscuit next to this gastronomical feast. Every time and everywhere their bodies met or touched, G.G. felt it to his core. Her pleasure was his, and his was hers and then his again. It was bouncing between them like a tennis ball on a court, beating at his mind, directing his actions, urging him on. He wanted her naked, but with the thundering pleasure pounding at his brain, stunning him, he couldn't seem to manage the task, at least not quickly enough to satisfy the need hammering at him.

In the end, rather than remove her bustier, G.G. ended up just folding the cups down, freeing her breasts to his greedy attention. And dear God, he felt every lick, nip, and suckle at her nipples as if she were doing it to him, and it drove him wild, made him suck harder, pulling almost her entire breast into his mouth.

Meanwhile, his hands had moved on to her leather pants, searching for the expected zipper and opening in the front but finding none. Frustrated by his inability to figure out how they undid, he moaned around her breast, and then groaned at the sensation that sent through both of them. Bloody hell, it was madness.

It didn't help that Ildaria was touching him too, her hands roaming what she could reach of his body and ratcheting up the sensation to even higher heights. When her hand found and squeezed the bulge in his jeans, G.G. froze under the sizzling onslaught of sensation that shot through him. When it then bounced around inside him, like a pinball, making his nerve ends all reverberate to the point that the pleasure was almost painful, he just lost it. His mouth never leaving her breast, he stood, easing her to stand as well. G.G. then gripped the back waistband of her pants in one hand, and the front in the other, and pulled. He hummed with triumph around her breast when he heard the satisfying ripping sound of success as he tore the seams wide open.

G.G. was so far gone that he didn't even notice at first that Ildaria was helping to tear the leather away. When he did, he merely grunted and worked harder to unwrap her from the material keeping her skin from him. In the end, she had to finish the job. The pants disappeared into her high boots, and she had to yank the cloth out and rip it away herself. Leaving her to it,

G.G. turned his hands to his jeans. His zipper and button were still in the front, yet the task of undoing them was harder than it should have been. His hands were shaking and uncoordinated, and he thought the delay was going to kill him, but he finally got the job done.

The minute he finished unzipping, Ildaria's hands were there, pushing his aside and reaching in to find him. G.G. finally let her breast slip from his mouth and straightened abruptly, his breath hissing between his teeth as her fingers touched him, and then he looked at her and could have wept. She hadn't just removed the shredded pants, the bustier was now gone too. She stood before him with only her long hair and high-heeled boots for covering, and the sight was enough to make a grown man weep.

Grasping her by the waist, he lifted her to sit on the island, stepped between her open legs and buried his face briefly between her breasts, nuzzling the skin there as his hands ran over her exposed flesh. They slid from her waist, down her hips and then her outer legs, before riding back up those same curves and farther to claim her breasts.

She was smooth as silk and warm to the touch, her skin as hot as if she'd been lying out in the sun. He wanted that heat wrapped around him like a blanket. Now. But his mind was telling him that a good lover gave his woman foreplay and Ildaria deserved a good lover. This was their first time, at least in real life. That made him hesitate.

G.G. stood frozen, his whole body trembling with his need, his hands clutching her now as he struggled desperately against the urge to sink himself into her. He wanted to please her, knew he should. But the seeming hours of foreplay from the shared dreams was an impossibility when faced with this onslaught of sensation and overwhelming need.

Ildaria suddenly grasped his face with both hands and lifted his head. Eyes on fire with glowing gold, she gasped, "I need you inside me," and G.G. lost the battle with himself. Claiming her mouth with his, he took himself in hand, and they both sucked in a breath as he touched his own sensitive skin, then he stroked her once with the tip of his erection, found her entrance and released himself to grasp her hips as he thrust in.

G.G. felt her pain mix with their pleasure, and froze briefly, but when she clutched his behind and dug her nails in in demand, he began to move. It was nothing like the shared dreams. That had been pedestrian mortal sex, feeling only his own pleasure. Now he was experiencing it all, his, hers, theirs, waves of it pounding at his body and mind as that first burst of pain faded away. Neither of them could take it long. There would be no holding off on taking his own pleasure until she found hers. That was impossible.

G.G. didn't count the strokes, but it couldn't have been more than a handful before his release hit. It was a freight train off the rails, smashing through barriers, crushing brain cells, and blocking out the light. He thought he heard Ildaria cry out with him, her higher voice a counterpoint to his, and then he was falling into the darkness dropping over him.

Ildaria woke up lying on top of G.G. on the kitchen floor. Her mind was slow to understand why she was there, and then her memories flew back to her. They'd had sex. Right. And her first time . . . at least in real life. Which was something of a surprise. She'd been told she was molested as a child and had assumed that had meant . . . Well, apparently it hadn't included intercourse.

Ildaria let those thoughts go in favor of recalling what had just happened. While this might have been her first real sex, she'd had lots of sex in their shared dreams. But it had not prepared her for the reality of life mate sex. That was another matter altogether. There had been no sweet sighs, no building need. It had been brutal, and explosive and exciting as hell.

Just recalling it was making her nipples hard and causing a warm heat between her legs . . . where she and G.G. were still connected, she realized when he hardened inside her in response to what she was experiencing. The man wasn't even conscious, but they were still connected both physically and mentally. The return of excitement to her was translating to his body. She marveled over that as he expanded inside her, filling her and bringing on more excitement.

G.G. groaned and she lifted her head to watch his eyes flutter open. He appeared as confused by their position at first as she had been, and a confused G.G. was an adorable one, she thought with a faint smile, her gaze traveling over his face and hair. His Mohawk hadn't survived their activity. It had fallen and now lay slightly to the side, covering part of the shaved section on one side of his head so that it looked like he had hair there. He would look good with hair, she decided. Although, she liked him with it shaved and just the Mohawk too. But he could never hide with the green Mohawk. It made him easily spotted and recognized in any crowd. Ildaria's life had always been about hiding. At least, it had been since she was fourteen, and if things did not change, she would have to hide again. Which meant that if G.G. wished to join her, he would have to lose the Mohawk.

That thought troubled her. Ildaria didn't want him to have to change to be with her. She didn't want him to have to hide either. He had family and friends and both Night Clubs . . . She couldn't ask him to give all that up for her. This was none of his fault.

"What are you thinking?"

Ildaria gave a start of surprise at G.G.'s question as she was drawn back to the present. She opened her mouth to answer, but then closed it again. She didn't want to talk about her fears for the future. She didn't even want to think about it.

"Angel," he said quietly. "We're life mates. Partners. Your burdens and worries are mine too now, and mine are yours. Tell me what is troubling you."

Much to Ildaria's amazement, she felt tears sting her eyes and threaten to fall. She had been on her own for so long, with no one to care let alone help or share . . .

"Please," he entreated gently.

That was her undoing. The words came out like champagne from an uncorked bottle, flowing so quickly she didn't even realize she'd reverted to Spanish in her upset until G.G. interrupted gently with, "English, please, love. I promise I will learn Spanish eventually, but right now I haven't got a clue what you're telling me and I think it's something I need to know."

He called me love, Ildaria thought, her mind a little dazed. They were life mates, had been having shared sex dreams for three weeks, and dating for one. She knew love would come. It always did between life mates, but she was sure it couldn't come this quickly. He was just using the word as an endearment. She was sure he didn't mean he loved her. But she wished he did. She was already half in love with him, if not wholly. G.G. was the calm in the storm that was her life. He was steady as a rock, compassionate and yet strong. He cared, and not just about her. He cared for his employees and customers too. He listened to all of them patiently and with concern. She'd witnessed that several times the past three weeks. His employees took their problems to him, but so did the customers, all of them knowing he would listen and offer sage advice. It had made her proud each time she'd witnessed it. He was a good man.

He was also a good boyfriend. He was sweet and considerate with her, and while he was the only lover she'd ever had, Ildaria was quite sure she couldn't have asked for a better one. In the shared dreams he had been tender, giving and passionate, always ensuring she found her pleasure first.

Of course, life mate sex had been a little different. There he had been demanding and almost rough, but then so had she. As life mates it was impossible not to be. They became rutting animals, fighting together toward the blessed release awaiting them. In comparison to the shared dreams, life mate sex was also incredibly fast; a hurricane sweeping the surface of their minds, as opposed to the building waves of shared sex creeping up the shore.

"Angel?" G.G. said, drawing her back to him in the here and now. "What were you worrying about?"

"If Lucian and your father cannot make Juan leave me alone, I will have to run and hide again," she said finally.

"If that happens, *we* will run and hide," he said firmly.

"But you would have to give up your family and the Night Clubs, and you would have to shave off the Mohawk and grow normal hair so that you did not stand out," she pointed out miserably. "I could not ask that of you, G.G. I could not subject you to the kind of life I have had to live for so long. It isn't right. I—" Her words broke off in surprise when he suddenly clasped her face in his hands.

"We are life mates now, Ildaria," G.G. said firmly, his tone brooking no argument. "Your problems are mine and mine are yours. If you have to run, I will run with you. Wherever you go, I will follow, and I'd leave everything behind to do it. Do you understand?"

Ildaria stared at him for a long moment as his words ran around and around her head and then melted and dropped down into her heart. They made her feel . . . cared for. She was no longer alone. She felt loved, a feeling she hadn't enjoyed for a very long time.

"Do you understand?" G.G. asked again when she

was silent for so long. "You are mine. Wherever you go, I go."

"Si, wherever I go, you go," she said finally, and then vowed, "And wherever you go, I go too." Ildaria watched the solemnity in his face give way to a smile and then she shifted on him, pushing herself up to a sitting position. The movement made them both catch their breath as she unintentionally shifted on his shaft and squeezed it, sending a wave of pleasure through their bodies.

"Damn," G.G. growled, his hands reaching for her breasts and cupping them as if he couldn't resist, even as he asked, "Are you all right, Angel?"

Ildaria knew he was asking if she felt better about the possibility they might need to run, but between his hands caressing her breasts and his growing erection inside her, her body was feeling pretty damned good too and she moaned, "Si," through the pleasure mounting inside her and covered his hands, urging him on. She then tilted her head back and closed her eyes, her hips shifting against him again, and then again, making them both groan. She'd never done this before, and had no idea of rhythm or technique, she just moved in the way that gave her the most pleasure, giving them both pleasure she knew as G.G. continued to grow inside her. God, he was so big . . . everywhere. At least, it seemed to her that he was as she stretched around him. Then G.G. shifted his hands to grasp her hips and began to help, leaving her to clasp her own breasts as she rode him.

The pleasure overwhelmed them even more quickly this time. It seemed to Ildaria that she was just getting the hang of what she was doing when a bomb went off inside her head. She didn't even have time to cry out this time before she was sucked under the darkness that dropped over her mind. Although she thought she might have whimpered as she collapsed into it.

It was H.D.'s tiny little tongue licking her cheek that woke Ildaria up. Nose wrinkling at the wet kisses, she blinked her eyes open and stared into his furry chest, slowly becoming aware that she was lying on something lumpy. Lifting her head, she turned to look down and saw that she was lying on G.G.'s hairy chest.

Ildaria had just recalled how she'd got there when H.D. started in licking again. This time he went for her ear, and she grimaced and then groaned, "Stop, H.D.," as she turned her head back and let it rest on G.G.'s chest again. She simply didn't have the energy to move yet. H.D. would have to give her a moment, she thought and then glimpsed movement beyond the dog, and tilted her head on G.G.'s chest to see what was behind him. She blinked when she spotted part of a man's very large, black, dress shoe.

Blinking, she lifted her gaze to the dark gray dress pants above it, and then further to the white shirt and suit jacket, before ending on the handsome face of a stranger with dark hair.

Ildaria had never seen the man before, and had certainly not invited him in. Since G.G. was lying unconscious under her, she knew he hadn't either. Yet the man had somehow got past her guards and was standing there in her apartment, staring down at her where she lay naked on top of G.G.

Embarrassingly enough it took a moment for all of that to coalesce in Ildaria's mind in a way that made sense. Once it did, the word that kept repeating through her mind was naked. NAKED. *NAKED!*

Shrieking like an idiot, Ildaria scrambled to her feet, unintentionally kneeing G.G. in the process, which—while unfortunate—had the positive effect of waking him up. Her big man woke with a shout of pain, and immediately rolled to his side, clutching himself. His feet caught hers at the ankle with the movement and would have knocked her down if the stranger hadn't caught her arm and helped her stay upright.

Ildaria was about to thank him for the kindness with a blow to the balls, followed by one to the head when the man said, "You must be Ildaria. G.G.'s told us all about you." He then turned his head and shouted, "I have found them, my love. They are fine." Turning back then, he smiled faintly and told her, "She tends to worry."

Ildaria lowered the knee she'd been about to plant in his groin, pretty sure the man wasn't a threat. The problem was, she had no idea who he was. Some friend of G.G.'s? Then she heard footsteps hurrying up the hall from the bedrooms and glanced that way with curiosity.

"You may want to cover up, dear," G.G.'s friend said kindly.

Suddenly recalled to her nudity, Ildaria gasped and then scrambled around the island with a squeal of alarm, looking for something to cover herself with. There was nothing. Her pants were a shredded mess on the floor, and she couldn't immediately spot her bustier, so she grabbed the nearest thing to hand, a tea towel, and held it over her body.

It was a small tea towel. It almost covered her breasts, leaving the outer curve of each boob visible on either side of the towel, but she wasn't at all confident it reached down to cover her groin. Ildaria was feeling the bottom, trying to see if it did, when three people rushed into the kitchen.

Two women and a man hurried around the island and then stopped abruptly as they took in the scene. Ildaria shifted uncomfortably under their gaping gazes, her own moving over them in return. One woman was a very pretty blonde with blue eyes that matched the summery sky-blue dress she wore. The other had black hair with bright fuchsia tips and was dressed in black jeans and a black T-shirt. She also bristled with weapons. They were all over her; a knife was strapped to her outer thigh, another knife rested in a holder attached to a belt around her waist, while a gun holster dangled from the same belt on the other side. She was also wearing a chest holster with two guns in it. The man was similarly decked out with weapons. He had dark hair, rugged features, and was of a similar size to G.G. except that he was a couple inches shorter, or perhaps it was just that G.G.'s Mohawk made him seem taller, she acknowledged.

"I love the boots," the woman with black and fuchsia hair said finally, breaking the silence.

Ildaria closed her eyes on a sigh, her humiliation complete, and then the blonde woman said, "Joshua, get up off the floor. What are you doing down there?" and Ildaria blinked her eyes open again in time to see G.G. finally drag himself to his feet on the other side of the island with a muttered, "Just writhing in agony. Nothing to worry about."

Ildaria felt a moment's guilt as she recalled that she'd accidentally kneed him, but then scowled when she noticed that he was, of course, fully clothed. G.G. had merely undone his jeans earlier, not removed them, and now his T-shirt was hanging down, hiding his groin area. She couldn't tell if he was still hanging out of his pants or not, but to anyone looking he appeared fully dressed . . . the bastard, she thought resentfully.

"Writhing in agony?" the woman was asking, sounding concerned as she pulled him into a hug. Leaning back, she then peered into his face and patted his chest as if looking for injuries as she asked, "Why? Oh, I knew there was something wrong when we didn't get an answer to our knock. What happened? Are you all right?"

Ildaria's eyes narrowed. The woman was touching and petting G.G. with a proprietary air, as if she had a right to, and she didn't find that pleasing at all. If she didn't stop it, Ildaria was going to make her stop.

"Nothing," G.G. said soothingly. "I'm fine. Ildaria just—" He paused to glance around then, looking for her, she realized when he turned and spotted her on the other side of the island. His eyes widened incredulously as he caught sight of her in her boots and tea towel, and then he pulled from the blonde's hold and hurried around the island.

Ildaria backed up instinctively when he neared, a squeak of alarm slipping from her when he reached out as if to hug her. G.G. froze at once, realization streaking across his face. Touching would not be good. Not with her naked and him sporting the erection now tenting his T-shirt. It had popped up the moment he spotted her, telling her that no, he hadn't tucked himself away.

Cursing, he pulled his hands back, hesitated, and then with his back to the group, tugged his T-shirt off over his head and immediately dropped it over hers. It was huge on her, falling to her knees, she noted with relief as she released the tea towel to slip her arms through the short sleeves.

While she did that, G.G. set to work tucking himself away and doing up his jeans. It appeared to be something of an effort with the erection he was now waving around, but he managed it with a pained grimace or two. She noticed he was very careful about the zipping part though, and really, the bulge once he was done was as obvious as the tent had been.

Sighing, G.G. shared a grimace with her and then stepped to her side and turned to face the four people watching them from across the room. Shoulders straightening, he said proudly, "Mother, Father, this is Angelina Ildaria Sophia Lupita Garcia Pimienta, my life mate."

Ildaria's mouth dropped at those words, and she wheeled on G.G in dismay.

Thirteen

G.G. stared at Ildaria with a somewhat bemused expression as she ranted at him in Spanish, although ranting wasn't quite the right word for what she was doing. She appeared to be having an emotional meltdown; dismay, despair, and accusation were alternating on her expression as she spat words in rapid-fire Spanish, her hands all over the place. She was definitely upset about something. In fact, his brave little warrior looked like she was on the verge of tears . . . or choking him. He wasn't sure which.

He really needed to learn the language, G.G. decided. He was catching a word here and there he thought he understood, like *madre* and *padre*. He knew that was *mother* and *father*. He was quite sure he'd caught *hacienda* in the avalanche of words pouring from her lips too, which meant *house* or *home* or something like that. But she'd also spat out *puta* at one point, which he knew translated to *whore*, and he couldn't figure out where that could work into the conversation.

"Oh myyyy. She speaks Spanish," his mother breathed with awe when Ildaria ran out of steam and just glared at G.G., probably waiting for him to say something. "It sure is a pretty language," she added, and then asked, "What did she say? Does she speak English, dear?"

"Yes, of course she speaks English," G.G. muttered.

It was Mirabeau who told them what she'd said. Lips twitching with amusement, the woman explained, "Ildaria is upset at being caught so . . . unprepared. She apparently didn't expect you to arrive so soon. G.G. had told her you wouldn't arrive for a couple of days."

"Joshua!" his mother said with dismay. "Why would you tell her that? You knew we were flying out right away."

"I didn't tell her that," G.G. assured his mother. When Ildaria made a snorting sound, he turned back and reminded her, "You were the one who suggested they most likely wouldn't arrive for a couple days. I was about to correct you and say their plane was probably halfway here already when Lucian showed up and you went to let him in."

Ildaria stared at him silently for a moment and then her head bowed, her shoulders drooped, and she simply turned and left the room.

G.G. watched with a small frown, his gaze dropping to her bare legs, and H.D. abandoned him to follow her as she took a wide route around the group across the kitchen. The little fur ball caught up to her as she passed through the living room, and pranced along at her side as she headed up the hall toward the bedrooms, his little head turned up, watching her with concern the whole way.

There was a day the dog wouldn't have left his side for anything. Obviously, those days were over. Ildaria had somehow usurped his position as H.D.'s favorite person. He didn't blame the mutt. She was his favorite person too, and frankly, he'd rather be trailing her to the bedroom himself right now. In fact he should be. She was upset and needed soothing. He couldn't blame her. This wasn't how he'd planned her first meeting with his parents to go either.

"She's beautiful, son."

G.G. turned his head at his mother's words and nodded wearily. "Yes. She is. Inside and out."

"Well, of course she is," she said with a nod. "You're lovely inside . . . and would be outside too if you didn't try so hard not to be," she added, scowling as her gaze traveled to the Mohawk on his head and then dropped to the tattoos winding over his now naked shoulders and down his arms.

G.G. grinned. His mother hated his Mohawk and tattoos, considering them mutilations of her beautiful boy. Much to his amusement, she never missed an opportunity to let him know that either. It didn't upset him, but did remind him that he was now standing there shirtless in just his jeans.

Frowning, he shifted on his feet, and then said, "Ildaria seemed upset. I should go talk to her and get my shirt back."

"No!" The four people facing him said the word at the same time. A brief silence followed as they all glanced at each other a bit wryly, and then his mother turned back to him and said, "Of course, she's upset, the poor dear. This isn't how any girl wants to meet her in-laws. No doubt our walking in on the two of you like this was terribly embarrassing for her. But you can't talk to her."

"Of course I can. She's my life mate, I—"

"Your very new life mate," his mother interrupted. "And we all know how that would go. You'd mean to talk and reassure her, but it would end up in shag city."

"Shag city?" he echoed with disbelief.

"You know I'm right," she said firmly.

"Yeah, I just can't believe you'd call it that," he rumbled.

"You have tattoos, I have a potty mouth," she said with a shrug and then headed out of the kitchen. "I will go talk to her."

G.G. started to protest with alarm, but his mother had burst into immortal speed and was already disappearing up the hall.

"Oh hell," he said with dismay.

"It will be fine," Robert said, moving to his side to pat him on the back. "Your mother is just going to reassure her that there's nothing to be embarrassed about and welcome her to the family."

"Right," G.G. breathed, but didn't feel reassured himself. His mother could be . . . mother.

"His parents! The Enforcers would have been bad enough, but his parents," Ildaria told H.D. with disgust. The dog sat patiently next to her in front of the closet, head tilted to the side, seeming to listen intently, as Ildaria pulled clothes out of the closet and ranted to him.

"Oh my God! His father saw my bare bottom," Ildaria realized, stopping to press the top she'd just pulled out to her cheeks as she felt them heat at the memory. Her eyes then widened and she added, "And everything else when I jumped up ready to fight him. Oh *Madre de Dios*. Thank God I did not knee him in the groin." Glancing down to H.D., she explained, "I nearly did. I was about to when he said G.G. had told him about me."

H.D. didn't respond. He merely tilted his head to the other side now as if thinking.

"If he hadn't said that when he did . . . ay yi yi." Ildaria shook her head and pulled out a black skirt next. A glance at the clock as she'd entered the bedroom had told her that it was nearly eight o'clock. She and G.G. usually started work around eight. It gave him an hour to prepare for opening. That meant that Ildaria started at eight as well because one of her jobs was looking after H.D. She usually took the little fur ball down to the office and worked until four A.M., sometimes five if she was in the middle of something, and then she took him up to her apartment until G.G. came to get him.

Ildaria suspected G.G. wouldn't be working tonight now that his parents were here, but she had every intention of working. It would allow her to avoid facing them again.

God, the humiliation. She'd wanted to make a good impression on them. Not that she'd ever even considered meeting them until today. There had been so many other things on her plate of late; she just hadn't got that far in the scenario. But once he'd mentioned his parents coming over, she'd started to fret about it in the back of her mind as they'd talked with Lucian and had breakfast.

Finding her naked and unconscious on top of their baby boy had not been part of her plan.

"Yes, well, you know what they say about best laid plans."

Ildaria swung around sharply at those sympathetic words and found G.G.'s mother standing in the open door of her bedroom. She'd left it open again. She usually did. She lived alone here, after all; there was usually no need for closed doors.

"What do they say about best laid plans?" Ildaria asked finally as H.D. apparently decided she didn't need him to listen to her anymore and walked over to jump up on the bed.

Mary Guiscard opened her mouth, and then closed it again and smiled wryly. "I don't really know. It's just what they always say when things go sideways . . . and they often go sideways," she added gently.

"Si," Ildaria sighed and carried the clothes she'd chosen to the bed to lay them out. "Always for me they go sideways."

"Surely not always?" G.G.'s mother said, taking a

couple of tentative steps into the room as if half expecting Ildaria to throw her out. She wouldn't do that of course, no matter how much she might want to. The woman was G.G.'s mother.

"Si. Always," she assured her, walking to her dresser to retrieve a bra and panties. White cotton as usual.

"Well, I think your luck has changed then. You've met your life mate," Mary Guiscard pointed out, sounding extremely pleased.

Ildaria tossed the underwear on the bed and then turned to survey the woman's happy face. G.G.'s mother was positively beaming. You'd think she was the one who had just met her life mate. But Ildaria knew the truth was she thought her son was safe now, that he would turn and she would never need fear losing him to age or the frailties of mortals.

"Even that has gone sideways," Ildaria confessed unhappily. "I know you are happy thinking G.G. is safe now. I know you hoped he would meet the woman he was a life mate to and agree to the turn, but I am not that woman. He still refuses to turn. I have failed you."

Coward that she was, Ildaria didn't stick around to watch the woman fall apart at that news. She never cried and had never been good with women who did. She suspected Mary Guiscard would be a weeper, so she turned and walked into the bathroom, hoping G.G.'s mother would have her little cry and then perhaps go back out to the others now that she knew what a dud she had gained in her son's life mate.

The moment Ildaria had reached her bedroom after leaving the kitchen, she'd come into the bathroom, taken off her boots and then turned on the water in the shower to allow it to warm up while she searched for clothes. A quick check showed it was warm now, so she tugged G.G.'s T-shirt up over her head, dropped it on the floor next to her discarded boots and stepped into the glass enclosure, then closed the door.

The water was hot and soothing on her body, washing away the evidence of her first time making love, but not the memory. Ildaria stood still and enjoyed it for a moment, and then quickly washed and conditioned her hair, before grabbing the bar of soap. She built up a lather and washed the rest of her body, surprised to find herself sore in some places. It seemed G.G. had been a little overenthusiastic with her breasts. They were tender now as she washed and rinsed them. That surprised her. The tenderness between her legs surprised her too. The pain she'd experienced the first time had been minimal really, sudden, sharp and then quickly gone. She was tender there now, though, and frowned at the knowledge, thinking that the nanos should have healed her already. She and G.G. must have been unconscious on the floor for—

Oh, right, Ildaria thought suddenly. She hadn't fed yet today. She should have grabbed a bag or two the moment she woke up, but she'd been distracted by G.G.'s presence in her kitchen, and then Lucian had arrived, which had been followed by she and G.G. doing the Mimi.

Good Lord, G.G. was lucky she hadn't bit him, Ildaria thought and actually stopped soaping herself up to wonder why she hadn't, or hadn't at least been tempted. In the end, she decided she'd simply been too distracted by other needs to recognize that one among them. And then their coupling had been incredibly swift. Both times.

Ildaria had heard the expression "Wham, bam, thank you ma'am," but with them it had been "Wham, boom" followed by long periods of unconsciousness. She'd guess in the four hours since Lucian had left, they'd spent about three hours and fifty-four minutes unconscious, and perhaps six minutes actually having sex. Three minutes each time. Or perhaps five minutes the first time because they'd had trouble getting her pants off.

Speaking of which, those were a ruin, Ildaria thought as she finished washing and rinsing herself. That was a shame; she had really liked those pants.

Shaking her head, she opened the door and reached out to grab the towel she'd hung up to use earlier. It wasn't there, but suddenly appeared in front of her. Turning her head, Ildaria found Mary Guiscard holding out the towel.

"You aren't a failure," G.G.'s mother told her softly when she didn't immediately take the towel. "I am. I failed Joshua terribly by allowing him to witness the turn. Which ultimately means I failed you too, and I am terribly sorry for that."

Mary Guiscard then released the towel and turned to leave the room.

Ildaria caught the towel as it fell, quickly dried her hair and body, then wrapped it around herself and tucked the end into the top before following the woman out of the bathroom. She found G.G.'s mother seated on the bed next to where H.D. had curled up and gone to sleep.

"I was told you had left G.—Joshua with a neighbor and the neighbor brought him home too soon," Ildaria said as she walked to the bed. Picking up the panties, she stepped into them and pulled them up under the towel as she added, "That is not your fault."

"Yes, it was. Obviously I was not clear about how long I needed her to watch Joshua. Unfortunately, I had no idea myself. Robert had said sometimes it took a night, sometimes two or three days, so I was vague with her. That was my second mistake," she added gravely as Ildaria dropped the towel to don the bra.

Ildaria had hesitated, briefly debating turning her back to don it, but then she'd decided she was acting like a silly virgin and had decided she would brazen it out. It was just a shame she didn't feel brazen. She wasn't used to dressing or undressing in front of anyone. Her grandmother had always been very conservative and given her privacy for dressing once she could manage it on her own. But she'd started this, so she tried to act like it didn't bother her as she slid her arms into the bra, tugged it into place and then reached behind her back to do it up. She was just finishing doing it up when G.G.'s mother said that about it being the second mistake.

Turning to her with surprise, she asked, "What was the first?"

"Robert wanted to take me to his country estate to turn me. But I didn't want to be that far from Joshua." Sighing, she confessed, "I was a hovering type mother, always afraid of losing him to some accident like his father. If Robert hadn't come along when he did, I'm sure Joshua would have ended up a neurotic boy."

That idea seemed absurd to Ildaria. She couldn't imagine G.G. as neurotic. Wouldn't have happened, she decided.

"But the point is," Mary continued, "if I had allowed Robert to take me to the country, Millie, the neighbor, couldn't have brought Joshua home. He never would have witnessed my turn, and wouldn't now be refusing to turn." She shrugged unhappily. "So you see, it is my fault. Not yours. Joshua would already be turned and safe if it were not for my mistakes."

Unsure what to say to that, Ildaria concentrated on doing up the buttons of her blouse. It was true that performing the turn at Robert's country estate would have prevented G.G. from witnessing and being traumatized by it. But she suspected the woman had been flagellating herself for that every day since G.G.'s eighteenth birthday when he'd refused to turn. Ildaria wasn't one to kick someone when they were down. Besides, her abuela had always said that mistakes were part of living, and the important thing was to learn from the mistakes you made so you didn't make them twice, and to forgive yourself for those mistakes, as well as others for the mistakes they made. She said not forgiving led to bitterness, and a bitter heart was good for nothing.

"But I promise you—" Mary caught her hand as she finished with her blouse, capturing her attention along with it. "I promise I will fix this. I will convince Joshua to turn. I couldn't before, but I can now, and it is only possible because you are his life mate," she added, a brilliant smile blooming on her face.

Ildaria stared at her with confusion. "I do not understand. He knows he is my life mate and still refuses. You can't use that to convince him to agree."

"Yes, I can," she assured her, and then grinned and said, "Because I know something about him very few people do."

"What is that?" Ildaria asked with curiosity.

"As a child, Joshua hated to share his toys," she announced, her eyes dancing with glee, and then, her tone turning triumphant, she added, "And he is no better at it as an adult."

Ildaria still didn't see how this was going to help them with the matter, but before she could say as much, the woman with black and fuchsia hair appeared in the bedroom door.

"Hello, Mirabeau, dear," Mrs. Guiscard greeted her, still smiling widely. "Are the men getting restless?"

"No," Mirabeau said, and then grimaced and said, "Well, yes, but that's not why I came to fetch you." Taking a breath, she shifted her gaze to Ildaria and said, "Lucian just called. He wants us to bring you to the Enforcer house."

"Me?" Ildaria asked with surprise, wondering what she'd done wrong now.

"Is Villaverde there?" Mrs. Guiscard asked, her hand tightening around Ildaria's.

Ildaria turned on her sharply, noting the sudden steel in the woman's expression.

"Yes," Mirabeau said grim-faced. "Apparently, his

plane landed shortly after yours. Lucian and Scotty have talked to him and now they want Ildaria there."

"Why?" G.G.'s mother asked sharply.

Mirabeau shook her head. "We don't know. He just called Tiny and told him that we were to bring her there. When Tiny got off the phone and told us what Lucian had said, Mr. Guiscard, Robert," she specified since both Robert and G.G. were Mr. Guiscard, "He called Lucian back, but all he could get out of him was that he and Scotty had spoken to Villaverde, but now they need Ildaria there."

"Juan's convinced them to execute me," Ildaria said, sure that was the only reason they'd want her there.

"Of course, he hasn't," Mrs. Guiscard said at once. "An immortal cannot be executed for biting off another immortal's bits. Especially when defending themselves against rape. If anything, *he* should be punished for his behavior."

Ildaria turned on her with dismay. "You know about that?"

Mary patted her hand, sympathetically. "Joshua had to tell Robert everything so that he could convince Scotty to help him help you, and of course he told me."

"Oh. Si," she muttered and wondered that the woman still welcomed her as G.G.'s life mate.

"What happened was not your fault," Mary said firmly, pulling her into a hug. "I am proud to have such a brave girl as my daughter-in-law."

Ildaria blinked at those words. She and G.G. had not talked about marrying.

"Perhaps not, but he is definitely planning on it, as

he should be," Mary said with a small smile as she pulled back to meet her gaze. "And I will not let anyone execute my future daughter. Besides, there is nothing to execute you for. Villaverde was the one at fault for what happened."

"But he is the head of the South American Council," Ildaria reminded her. "A powerful man. While I am just a peasant. They will not punish him," she predicted bitterly.

"You are not a peasant," Mary exclaimed with outrage. "And as the head of the Council, Villaverde should be above reproach. In fact, I do not know how someone like that could have gained the position of head of the Council. The other Council members would not put up with a leader who rapes children and forces their poorer people out of their homes."

"And yet he does, and they do not protest," Ildaria assured her.

"Yes, well, not for long if Lucian and Scotty have any say in it, I assure you. They'll call a summit of Council leaders to have him removed if necessary. And if they don't, Robert will," Mrs. Guiscard said firmly. She held Ildaria's gaze for a minute, and then frowned. "You don't believe me, but it's true."

"I believe you believe that," Ildaria said solemnly.

"I guess that will have to do for now," Mary said with a faint smile, and then sighed and shook her head. "I suppose we might as well go and see what the men want, get this business over with so you can relax and know you're safe."

Releasing her hands, Mrs. Guiscard started toward

Mirabeau, leaving her to follow, but Ildaria hesitated. She didn't want to go. She had no desire to be anywhere near Juan Villaverde. However, one look at Mirabeau's face told her that the woman would drag her there if necessary. She would carry out Lucian's orders.

Sighing in resignation, Ildaria followed G.G.'s mother to the door, very aware of the way Mirabeau took up position at her side as they walked down the hall.

G.G., Robert, and Tiny were all waiting in the living room when they came out. Ildaria paused just inside the doorway when she saw that G.G. was wearing his T-shirt again. The T-shirt she'd stripped off and left lying on the bathroom floor. "How did you—?"

"I brought it out to him while you were showering," G.G.'s mother explained, apparently reading her thoughts.

"Oh." Ildaria smiled at her faintly and then glanced around with surprise when someone took her arm. It was G.G. He'd crossed the room to her and his hand was warm through her blouse, causing a slight tingle, but not the crazy passion that it had earlier when he'd touched her, she noted with confusion.

"Touching through clothing mutes the effects of the nanos," Mirabeau said helpfully. "But try to avoid bare skin to skin contact. At least, until you're alone. And that includes hand holding unless one of you is wearing gloves."

"Good to know. Thanks," G.G. said, but his gaze was on Ildaria and full of concern. She wasn't at all surprised when he asked, "Are you okay about this?

We can tell them to go to hell if you want and refuse to go."

"Josh," Robert said in a warning tone.

Ildaria blinked in surprise at the name. It just sounded so odd to hear G.G. called that. Between Lucian, G.G.'s mother, and her own thoughts, she was used to Joshua, but this was the first time she'd heard him called Josh out loud.

"Angel?" G.G. asked, ignoring his father.

"I don't think we have much choice," Ildaria said finally.

G.G. didn't look pleased, but he nodded grimly and promised, "I won't leave your side."

"Neither will I," Robert assured her, some of the tension leaving him now that he knew they wouldn't refuse to go. "I will be right there with you both. I will not let anything happen to you. Anything at all," he stressed firmly, and then added, "But this is why we are here, to deal with the matter, and I trust Lucian and Scotty. If they think you need to be there, there is a reason for it."

Ildaria didn't know this Scotty person, but she did know Lucian. He had been nothing but fair with her about the incidents at the university here in Toronto, and more than fair about her vigilante activities in Montana. He could have had her executed twice now and hadn't. She would just have to hope that fairness continued in this instance.

Straightening her shoulders, she nodded. "Let's get it over with then."

Fourteen

They were halfway to the Enforcer house before Ildaria noticed that she wasn't wearing any shoes. She
also hadn't put on stockings or even brushed her hair,
she realized. She supposed the hair was forgivable;
she was stressed out and anxious about meeting the
man who had hunted and haunted her for two hundred
years. But she had to wonder how she could have left
her apartment, walked out to the car and got in without stockings or shoes on.

"I'm sorry," Mirabeau said suddenly from the front
passenger seat. "I was so busy watching to be sure Villaverde hadn't sent his men to snatch you in transit,
that I didn't notice what you were or weren't wearing."

Ildaria glanced at her with surprise at the comment.
The woman had obviously read her mind again, but
had no need to apologize for not noticing her barefoot
state. She herself couldn't have said what Mirabeau

was wearing on her feet right now. She just didn't look at people's feet very often and doubted if many people did. Besides, this situation was a tense one. She, G.G., and his parents were all very worried about the coming meeting, and the Enforcers were all concerned about watching for possible attacks. Ildaria wasn't surprised that none of them had noticed she was shoeless.

"No bare skin to bare skin," Mirabeau said suddenly and Ildaria followed the Enforcer's gaze to where G.G.'s hand now hovered over hers. Obviously, he'd been about to hold her hand to offer her comfort and been stopped just before clasping it. Now he rubbed her arm there through her blouse instead. Ildaria smiled at him in gratitude, but it really didn't have as much impact as his holding her hand would have had.

"Here."

She and G.G. shifted their attention to Mirabeau to see her holding out a pair of gloves. They were bright blue and made up of some kind of thin material, either rubber or silicone, it looked to her. Obviously meant for the Enforcers to use when cleaning up blood or any other wet work they encountered.

G.G. accepted the gloves and managed, with some effort, to pull one on over his large left hand. He then reached out and clasped her ungloved hand, his fingers threading with hers.

"Sam will have shoes at the house you can borrow," Mirabeau said now.

"Shoes?" G.G. peered down at her feet, and then back up to her face with amazement. "We forgot your shoes."

Ildaria smiled at the "we," as if it was his responsibility to see she had shod feet. "It's fine," she assured him, and then asked Mirabeau, "You don't happen to have a brush, do you?" Glancing to G.G. she added, "I forgot to brush my hair too."

"Your hair looks beautiful," G.G. assured her.

Ildaria doubted that, but didn't say as much and simply looked back to Mirabeau hopefully.

"No," the woman said apologetically. "I don't fuss much with my hair when on the job."

"Like you, Beau's a natural beauty and doesn't need to fuss," Tiny said, meeting her gaze in the rearview mirror, and then added, "You look good. You have that sexy tousled look going on."

Ildaria smiled at him for the kind words.

"Crap," G.G. said suddenly and pulled out his cell phone.

"What is it?" Ildaria asked with concern.

"I forgot about H.D.," he muttered, thumbing through his contacts. "I should have let him out to relieve himself before we left. I'll just call Sofia and ask her to do it now and to keep an eye on him while we're gone."

"She doesn't have keys to my place," Ildaria told him with a frown.

"Damn," G.G. breathed, pausing with his thumb hovering over the phone face as he considered the problem, and then he nodded. "I'll have her grab my spare keys out of my office. There's a master key on it that opens every door. She can use that. If that's okay with you?" he added, giving her the opportunity to say no.

"Of course," Ildaria said at once. "We can't just leave the little guy there alone and hungry." Clucking her tongue with irritation, she added, "I can't believe we forgot about him."

G.G. smiled faintly at her using "we" too, and then finished placing the call and raised the phone to his ear.

Ildaria listened absently as he spoke to Sofia, but her attention was on the road. They were close to the Enforcer house now. In just minutes she would be facing Juan. Ildaria would rather face a hundred Enforcers out for her blood than this man. She liked to think she was brave and strong, but when it came to Juan Villaverde, she was still that confused and terrified fourteen-year-old girl trembling and weeping on her knees, and he was the boogeyman.

Disgusted with herself, Ildaria sat up straight and lifted her chin. Screw him. She wasn't that child anymore, and he wasn't the boogeyman, and if the bastard tried anything, she'd bite his dick off again, and maybe cut his head off too . . . if she could get her hands on a weapon. And if Lucian or someone else didn't stop her.

Ildaria rolled her eyes at her own thoughts and told herself to focus on tomorrow. By tomorrow at this time, this ordeal, whatever it was, would be over and she would either be dead or back at her apartment, cuddled on the couch with G.G. and H.D., watching a movie, or passed out on the floor after making love, or in the office at work, or entertaining his parents.

That thought made her wonder when his parents were leaving, and then she turned in her seat to peer out the back window to make sure the second SUV that Mary and Robert were traveling in was behind them. Lucian had sent Tybo and Valerian to collect G.G.'s parents and bring them too.

Ildaria had just spotted the second vehicle when her body swayed to the side as the SUV Tiny was driving turned. She immediately swung back around to see that they were pulling into the driveway to the Enforcer house.

Grinding her teeth, Ildaria felt herself separating somewhat from her emotions in preparation for what was coming. It was an automatic reaction to stressful situations, and one she only became aware of a few decades ago. It was like she had an emotional disconnect button. It allowed her to stick her steel heel through a man's face or groin without hesitation or guilt, and do whatever else was necessary to survive.

"Here we are."

Ildaria didn't respond to Mirabeau's comment as Tiny brought the SUV to a halt in front of the Enforcer house a few moments later. She was looking out the back window, watching the Enforcers that guarded the gate run a mirror on a stick under the SUV G.G.'s parents were in as it sat idling between the inner and outer gate. It was the same search they had endured on arriving. She knew they would be through and parking next to them momentarily, but had no intention of getting out until they did. She wanted all of them with her when she entered to face the lion.

Tiny and Mirabeau got out of the front seat, and moved to stand by her door, but didn't open it. She supposed they'd read her mind and were willing to wait for the others to join them.

"Tiny left the keys in the ignition. We could still make a run for it."

Ildaria shifted her gaze to G.G. at that comment, a small smile breaking the tension that had been pulling at the muscles of her face as warmth swam up through her. "I love you."

The words just slid out, wholly unexpected, even by Ildaria. They stared at each other in surprise, but then G.G.'s surprise faded under certainty and he said in his deep rumble, "I love you too, Angel."

They swayed toward each other, but before their lips could meet, Ildaria's door was yanked open, and she was caught under the arms and dragged out of the car.

"No bare skin to skin," Mirabeau reminded her with amusement as she set her on her feet.

"We were just going to kiss," Ildaria protested with exasperation.

"Lips are bare skin," Mirabeau pointed out as G.G. followed her out of the SUV, looking perturbed. "You would not believe the number of passed-out half or wholly naked immortals Marguerite had littering her house and grounds the last time she had a New Year's Eve party, and all because of the tradition of a kiss to ring in the new year. For new life mates, kissing invariably ends in sex."

"Fine, no kissing." Ildaria sighed the words with resignation as she checked that her abrupt removal from the vehicle hadn't left her blouse rumpled or her skirt twisted. Everything seemed in order, though, so she turned to the second SUV that was pulling to a stop next to them.

"Angelina, dear. Where are your shoes? Did you leave them in the SUV?" Mary asked as she stepped out of the vehicle and moved to join them.

"We forgot them at home," G.G. answered for her.

"Oh dear, I was so worried about this meeting I didn't even notice. I should have checked you over before we left," Mary said with a frown and Ildaria found another smile lifting the corners of her mouth that everyone seemed to want to take responsibility for dressing her now.

"Well, of course we do," Mary said, obviously reading her thoughts. G.G.'s mother gave her a quick hug, and added, "You're family now, dear. And family take care of each other."

Family. Ildaria swallowed a sudden lump in her throat. She hadn't had family in a very long time and now she had them everywhere.

"Are you ready?" Robert asked as he joined them. His expression was as concerned and compassionate as G.G.'s when he met her gaze. They may not be related by blood, but he had obviously influenced his stepson. They shared a lot in the way of personality and mannerisms.

Straightening her shoulders, Ildaria nodded and then found herself surrounded by people and escorted up the short walkway to the door of the Enforcer house.

The door was opened by Mortimer's wife, Sam, before they even reached it. The woman offered a tense smile of greeting, her concerned gaze sliding from Ildaria to G.G. as she stepped back for them to enter. That smile and look, worried Ildaria.

"Angelina left her shoes at home," Mary said as Sam started to close the door. "You don't happen to have any here that she could borrow, do you?"

"She does not need shoes to talk," Lucian announced, appearing in the doorway of the living room just ahead and to their left. "Come, Angelina. The rest of you can wait in the kitchen with Sam."

Ildaria's heart stopped at the thought of meeting Juan alone without her new family to support her. But she raised her chin and acted like the idea didn't bother her. She'd be damned if anyone was going to see how afraid she was in that moment.

It was G.G. who protested, "Not gonna happen, Lucian. I'm coming with her."

"As am I," Robert added, and then when Mary elbowed him, quickly changed it to, "I mean we. We are coming too. Angelina is part of our family now. We will be there to support her."

Lucian scowled at the Guiscards, but then relented. "Fine. You can be in the room, but no talking. You're to sit where I say and listen. This is between Angelina and Juan."

She felt G.G. stiffen beside her at those words. Apparently Lucian noticed it as well, because his gaze turned stern on the man. "This is immortal business, Joshua. You are not immortal. I'm allowing you to be there only because you are a possible life mate to Angelina. I will not have you interfering. If you do, I shall remove you myself. Understood?"

G.G. grunted in the affirmative, and then Lucian took Ildaria's arm and walked her into the living room across from the kitchen. After one quick glance over her shoulder to be sure the others were following, Ildaria turned her gaze forward and scanned the room for her nemesis.

The first man she spotted was not Juan. Standing in the center of the room, the man had long hair that was a combination of deep red and chestnut. It was pulled back into a ponytail. He was tall, and built like a construction worker or a medieval warrior of old with broad shoulders and strong upper arms bulging under the black T-shirt he wore. He looked like he would have been comfortable wielding a heavy broadsword.

Scotty, the head of the UK Council, she thought before continuing her search of the room for Juan Villaverde. Ildaria didn't see him though, and was about to turn a questioning gaze to Lucian when Scotty suddenly moved to the side, drawing her gaze to the man he had been blocking from her view. Juan Villaverde had been seated on the couch, but now stood up, his eyes hot and hungry as they roved from her bare feet to her untamed hair.

Ildaria stumbled under the weight of that look, the old confusion and uncertainty returning to her as if she were fourteen again and seeing him for the first time. She would have stopped walking altogether if Lucian hadn't tugged her gently forward by the grip he had on her arm. With no other choice, she allowed herself to be pulled along, and made herself examine the man who had made her life such a hell.

Juan Villaverde was a beautiful man. With full black hair, golden-brown eyes, and a face only the angels could have chiseled, he could make any woman's heart race. And the suit he wore couldn't hide the fact that he also had the body of Adonis, she acknowledged, and wondered that she'd never noticed these things two hundred years ago. But she supposed she'd been too anxious and nervous around him to notice much more than that he made her feel incredibly uncomfortable. It was that hungry look he was eyeing her with even now. As a child, it had scared her silly. Now . . . well, actually it still made her uncomfortable and a bit confused. It held none of the rage that had contorted his face that last time in the alley.

"There," Lucian said abruptly, and Ildaria glanced at him and then followed his gesture to another sofa at the end of the room, as far from the one Juan was standing in front of as you could get. He was directing G.G. and his parents to sit there, she realized when Robert urged Mary to the sofa.

G.G. didn't follow them right away. His gaze shifting between her and Juan, he hesitated until she gave a slight nod. She'd rather he was closer, right at her side would be good, but she wouldn't risk Lucian making him leave if they didn't obey him. Ildaria tried to convey that in her expression. She wasn't sure if he understood, but he did follow his parents to the couch. None of them looked relaxed, however. They were all perched on the very edge of the sofa, looking stiff and grim and as if they were ready to jump up and intercede if Juan did anything not to their liking.

Ildaria heard Lucian sigh next to her and then he urged her around in front of the sofa facing the one

Juan now stood in front of. A coffee table was all that separated them, she saw unhappily. When she didn't sit at once, Lucian pressed down on her shoulder, making her sit.

"Now," Lucian said once she'd dropped onto the couch. "Tell her what you told us."

Juan finally dragged his gaze from Ildaria. First he shifted it to Lucian, and then to the Guiscards and he scowled. "Who are these people, and why are they here? Why are any of you here? You said I could see her alone."

Ildaria stiffened at those words until Lucian countered with, "I said you could see her, I did not say it would be alone."

"I want to see her alone," Juan insisted.

"That's not going to happen, Juan," Lucian said sounding almost regretful, and Ildaria glanced at him quickly, wondering whose side he was on here.

Juan cursed with frustration. "I have waited two hundred years, Luc. I deserve to—"

"You messed up two hundred years ago, Juan. You attacked her. Now she does not feel safe with you. And I will not make her face you alone and afraid."

Ildaria scowled and sat up straight at that, annoyed with Lucian for revealing the anxiety she was presently feeling.

"I never meant for that to happen, I told you it was the—"

"Now tell her," Lucian interrupted. "You can either do it in front of everyone, or give her up and leave."

Give her up? Ildaria peered at Lucian, but he ignored

her and simply stared at Juan, waiting for him to decide what he was going to do. Giving up on getting an answer to her silent question, Ildaria tore her gaze from Lucian's stern face and turned her eyes down to her hands as she acknowledged to herself that there was a bright side to all of this, whatever this was. It was looking less and less like she had been brought here to be executed.

Ildaria actually felt the scowl Lucian turned on her. "Of course, you are not going to be executed. You are to hear what Juan has to say. There are things about the past that you do not know, and should."

"You thought you had been summoned for execution?" Juan exclaimed, sounding upset. *"Madre de Dios,"* he muttered and then paused and said with wonder, "And yet you still came. You are brave, *mi amor.*"

Ildaria stiffened at the term of endearment, but it was Lucian who responded.

"I told you she thought you had been hunting her all these years to punish her for biting off your—"

"Basta!" Juan interrupted with a wince before Lucian could state exactly what she'd bit off. He then shook his head and dropped to sit on the sofa across from Ildaria. Juan scrubbed his face briefly with frustration, and then raised haunted eyes to her and breathed in Spanish, "I have been searching for you for two hundred years, Angelina. But not to punish you. Never to punish you. I was searching for you because you are my life mate."

Fifteen

"What?" Ildaria gasped, jumping to her feet.

"Let me go!" G.G. snapped, and Ildaria turned dazed eyes his way to see that he was trying to rise from the couch and come to her. But Robert was holding him in his seat, a grim expression on his face that made her think the immortal understood Spanish.

"What did he say? Did he threaten you? Why are you upset?" G.G. asked her, still trying to break loose of his father's iron grip. Strong as G.G. was, he was still a mortal. His immortal father had no problem keeping him in his place.

"He just told her that she is his life mate," Lucian said with exasperation.

"What?" G.G. gasped in the same shocked tone she had used just moments ago, and then rage slid over his face and he began to struggle again. "The hell he is. I—"

"Silence," Lucian growled. "And be still, or you will be removed."

G.G. glowered. "Then make him tell his lies in English."

"I will translate if he does not," Robert assured him, and then added apologetically, "I only hesitated about that first part because I knew what he had said would upset you, son."

G.G. grunted at this and stopped fighting, but his expression was rebellious.

"Angelina."

Ildaria turned reluctantly to stare at Juan, not sure she wanted to hear anything else he had to say. He had to be lying. They weren't life mates. He'd been hunting her to punish her. He just knew Lucian wouldn't have let him punish her and was hoping he could convince them all that she was his life mate, so that he could try to get her to turn from G.G. and go with him. She was positive if she had been that foolish, he would have taken her away and then punished her. That made more sense than the nonsense he was spouting. Life mates?

"I can read his mind, Angelina," Lucian said quietly.

"So can I," Mary murmured, and then added softly, "And he is not lying."

Ildaria turned sharply to look at the woman. An immortal as young as Mary would not be able to read one as old as Juan . . . unless he had met his life mate. The newly mated were often easily read no matter their age. But that usually only lasted a couple of years, and then they mastered control of themselves and their thoughts again. How could he be easily read two hundred years after encountering her and supposedly discovering she was his life mate?

"We regain control of our thoughts once we adjust to the whirlwind of emotion and need that the nanos cause in new life mates," Scotty said, speaking for the first time. "Juan has never been allowed to do that. He was never able to claim you. Seeing you again today has the same impact for him as it did two centuries ago."

He allowed a moment for that to sink in, and then added, "His thoughts and feelings are clear as a bell to any immortal within shouting distance no matter how new they are. Except for you," he added even as she thought it.

She could not hear his thoughts, and she had been immortal nearly two centuries longer than Mary.

Apparently picking up her thoughts, Scotty nodded and said, "And that is another reason why we know he is not lying. It is also why we had to bring you here. You need to know. You have been running from your life mate, not a monster bent on killing you."

Her knees suddenly weak, Ildaria sank back onto the couch and turned to stare at Juan Villaverde. Bewilderment whirled around in her head as she tried to merge the monster of the last two hundred years with the man who claimed to be her life mate. "But you attacked me."

Juan sighed miserably, and ran a hand wearily through his thick hair. "*Lo siento, mi amor.* I'm sorry," he added grimly when Robert translated for G.G., his low voice a distracting murmur from the end of the room. Continuing in English now, he said, "I never meant to. I had planned never to touch you until you were older and ready. But that night—" He shook his head. "Let me start at the beginning."

When he paused, waiting, she gave a slight nod. The beginning was always a good place to start.

"I first saw you in my daughter's kitchen," Juan said quietly. "I had come to visit Ana, but she was still above stairs. Dressing, the maid said. She suggested I wait in the salon and she would let her know I was there. I started into the salon, but the sound of laughter caught my ear. It was like the angels singing. So clear and beautiful, without the artifice other women employ to try to sound enticing. This was a laugh of true delight, so lovely and musical. I could not help but follow the sound down the hall to the kitchen. There I paused in the door and watched you with your abuela. She was teaching you to make *Pasteles en Hoja*. Do you remember that?" he asked eagerly.

"I remember Abuela teaching me to make them, si," she admitted slowly. "But not you being there."

"I never went into the kitchen. I never even spoke," he told her quietly. "I stood there and watched like a child at the window of a sweet shop. You were so beautiful to me. I was enchanted."

Ildaria heard G.G. growl from the end of the room and his mother shush him, but didn't glance that way for fear Lucian would make him leave if she drew attention to him.

"I admit, I wanted you," Juan continued. "And I even decided to have you as my mistress." He shook his head with a chagrined expression. "Even though I had not been interested in taking a lover since the death of my beloved life mate, Xochitl, three hundred years earlier, I did not yet recognize that you were another chance, another life mate. I only knew that I wanted you. But," he said unhappily, "you looked extremely young; little more than a child, and I would never take a child as a mistress."

"No, you just rape them," G.G. snarled from the other end of the room, earning a warning look from Lucian.

Juan's mouth had tightened at G.G.'s words, but otherwise he ignored him and said, "I wished to know just how young you were, so I tried to slip into your mind to find your age, but"—he met her gaze gravely—"I could not read you, *mi amor.*"

Juan paused briefly, but when Ildaria didn't say anything, he continued, "It was only then that I realized you were my life mate, and the knowledge was shocking to me. I was still trying to accept my good fortune when I heard someone on the stairs. I glanced around to see Ana descending. I didn't want to leave you, but I needed to know about you and could not read you, so I left without you or your grandmother ever knowing I was there and went into the salon.

"I did not tell Ana that you were my life mate, and I tried to make my questions sound casual as I asked about you. I wanted to keep the knowledge that I had found a new life mate for myself for a while. You were so precious, I . . . I just wanted to keep you to myself," he repeated helplessly, and then sighed and said,

"I did not find out much from my daughter. Ana did not know much. I learned that from reading her mind. She knew only that you were her cook's granddaughter and that you were thirteen years old."

"Fourteen," she corrected.

"Thirteen," he said firmly. "You did not turn fourteen until three weeks after you disappeared."

Ildaria blinked in surprise and sat back. He was right. Her fourteenth birthday had passed weeks later, unnoticed. She'd been alone, struggling to hide and feed and avoid the hunters and only realized her birthday had passed a month or so after the day. Even then, she hadn't much cared. She was too busy trying to survive.

"I visited with Ana until I heard you leave," Juan continued when she remained silent. "And then I made my excuses and left as well, promising to return for that evening's party. It was to introduce Ana to her life mate's family," he added. "I was expected to attend and really shouldn't have left when I did, but I was desperate to see you again. You were too young to claim, but I could look and torture myself with what I could not yet have."

Meeting her gaze, he said, "You do not know how badly I just wanted to touch you. I wanted to brush my fingers down your cheek and feel if your skin was as soft as it looked. I wanted to tangle my hands in your hair and press it to my nose to see if it was what smelled like flowers, or if that was a scent you wore. I wanted . . . so much," he almost moaned and then shook his head. "But I dared not touch you. You were far too young."

Sighing, he muttered, "I should have sent you to a convent or somewhere else until you were old enough to claim. Failing that, I should have at least stayed away from you. But every time my daughter had a party and you walked home alone I was there to walk with you, trying to engage you in conversation." He grimaced as he added, "You were a very shy child and hardly responded to my questions at all."

Ildaria frowned at the description. "I was quiet because I was uncomfortable with you. I could sense that you wanted something from me, but—" She shook her head.

"You sensed my obsession and need for you and it scared you," he said with a nod, and then, his expression and voice achingly sincere, he said, "I am sorry, *Corazon*. I handled everything in the worst possible way. I should have read your grandmother to learn more about your past. Had I known of the abuse you suffered as a small child, I would have handled things differently. But I did not know, and I longed to be close to you despite it being a torture to me. So, I kept making Ana hold parties for business associates and high-ranking immortals, just so that you would have to walk home alone, and I would have an excuse to accompany you."

He bowed his head briefly, and when he lifted it again, his expression was grim. "And then one such day, you did not come out to make the walk home. I waited an hour, and then I decided that you must have stayed to help your abuela with the cooking, and gave up. By that time, guests were arriving, so I went in to the party. It was only after the meal that I was able to get away to the kitchens. I was hoping just to catch a glimpse of you, but you were not there. Confused, I read your grandmother and learned that you had gone to a birthday party directly from school. I went back to the party, but could not get you from my mind and finally made an excuse to leave early.

"I had gained the address of this party from your abuela, and so I went there. I thought just to check on you, perhaps watch from a distance to be sure you got home all right. But it was over when I got there. So I went to the home you shared with your abuela, but there were no lights on. You were not home."

"We had gone to the cantina where Emilita's brother worked," Ildaria whispered.

"Si," he said sadly. "I learned that when I returned to your friend's house. The parents thought you had all gone to Emilita's cousin's house so that she could play her guitar for you while the parents stayed at her house. But her little sister knew the secret and I eventually read it from her. Of course, then I hurried to the cantina. I intended to drag you out and give you hell for behaving so badly when your grandmother had trusted you. And for taking such risks when the Haitian soldiers were everywhere, raping our women and—" He paused abruptly when she flinched and then ducked his head, his hands clenching. But after a moment he continued.

"I heard you cry out, begging someone to stop as I approached the cantina. I followed the sound around to the alley in back. And when I saw those two men attacking you . . ." He shook his head, his expression tightening with remembered fury. "I have never been so enraged in my life . . . or so frightened. You could have been raped. You could have been killed. I could have lost you," he said with horror.

Swallowing, he closed his eyes briefly and then continued. "I dragged the first one away from you, the one pinning your arms to the ground, and tossed him aside like the trash he was. I then grabbed the one who was actually on top of you. He had your skirt pulled up, but was distracted trying to get his pants undone. He hadn't even noticed his friend's absence. Him, I bit," he acknowledged grimly. "But I did not just feed from him, I tore his throat open on the spot for daring to touch you. It should have soothed me to have punished them so. My temper should have eased then. Instead, heat poured through me and my rage increased, becoming almost unbearable. I wanted to soothe you, but instead I attacked and berated you. And si, I threatened you with shameful violence."

He looked away, shame on his face, and then said, "I wish I could say with certainty that I would not have used you that way, but I fear I would have. Fortunately, the rage in me was twisting me up so much that I stopped to grab you by the shoulders and shake you."

Juan faced her again, his expression bleak. "The change in you was instantaneous. The weeping and pleading stopped at once. Rage suffused your face and you suddenly clamped down on me like a dog with a bone. It was a shock. The sudden change in you as well as the fact that there was anything out for you to bite. I hadn't even realized I had been dislodged from my pants, I remember the pain, and trying to push you away without doing you damage, and then out of desperation I hit you and that ended it, though not the way I had been hoping for," he said with a small, wry smile.

"You ran off then, leaving me rolling on the ground in agony. A few minutes later, Miguel, one of my men who patrolled the streets, found me. He helped me to my feet and started to help me out of the alley when we heard a moan. The man who had been pinning your arms, the one I had pulled from you first, he still lived. I told Miguel to bring him to me, that I would feed from him. He started toward him with me, but paused after a couple of steps and shook his head. He said he was no good for me. He was messed up from opium, mescal, and coca leaves."

Ildaria stiffened, recalling an immortal warning her about that not long after she'd first turned. She'd stopped her from biting a soldier Ildaria had lured behind a building. She'd seen her lead the man there and had followed to stop and warn her. She'd said that the soldier's blood was no good. It was soaked with opium and mescal, and even cocaine from coca leaves. Most of the soldiers seemed to like the combination, but it was not a good mix for immortals. They had been known to go mad from it. Besides, it would not help her. Her body would expend more blood removing the tainted blood and she would simply be in more need.

Ildaria had been very careful after that, always reading prospective donors before feeding from them, to make sure they had none of those substances in them.

When she sighed and met Juan's gaze, he nodded soberly. "That was the source of my uncontrollable rage. And, ultimately, yours."

"Mine?" she asked with surprise, and then protested, "I was mortal then, and I'd consumed no blood."

"Think back," he said patiently. "When did your anger start? The anger that made you want to bite me?"

Ildaria frowned, recalling it well. As she'd told G.G., one minute she'd been weeping with confusion and fear and then Juan had started to shake her and she'd suddenly been suffused with rage. "When you were shaking me."

"When I touched your bare shoulders with my bare hands," Juan pointed out gently. "We are life mates, mi amor. My passions transferred to you in that moment. My need and my rage. The same uncontrollable rage that struck me when I consumed the blood of the bastard who had been attacking you. Before that I was angry, si, but at them, not everything and everyone. And not like I was after I bit him. Then I was just . . ." He shook his head. "It was uncontainable, and confusing. I needed to hurt someone, and you were the only one there after I'd dealt with the men."

Ildaria frowned and then glanced to Lucian. He nodded silently.

"I have regretted that night for the last two hundred years, mi amor," Juan continued. "I have searched for you. I have had my men search for you. Even your abuela tried to help."

Ildaria's head shot back around, her eyes finding his. "What?"

He hesitated and then said, "The moment I healed and recovered from my injury, I started looking for you. With no luck. You were not at your abuela's and neither was she."

"She stayed with me at the plantation for the first few weeks," Ildaria murmured.

"Si." He nodded. "I learned that from a message Ana sent me. It was waiting for me at home when I returned from searching for you one night, but I was tired and did not bother with it until morning. I could not believe it when I read that she had the daughter of her cook, with her. That the girl had been turned, but had no memory of how or by whom despite weeks of healing, and she felt the Council needed to intercede."

He grinned. "I thought God had answered my prayers. Not only were you found, but you did not remember those terrible minutes in the alley; neither the attack by the soldiers, nor by me. It seemed a blessing. I rushed over at once, making plans along the way. You were still too young to claim, but at least I need not worry about your coming to harm before I could claim you. I would see to it that you and your abuela were well taken care of until you were ready to be my life mate. I would see you just this once to assure myself you were well, and then would send you away with your abuela so that I would not be tempted to try to see you until you were at least eighteen. In the meantime, I would keep myself distracted by building you the most beautiful home, and filling it with everything you might like. And I would plan the wedding too.

"I greeted Ana joyfully when I got there, and told her to take me to you. But you were gone when we got to your room. Ana sent servants looking for you. A maid came back several minutes later saying one of the men said you had left. He thought you had gone for a walk. But I feared you may have seen me, and that it had brought your memories back to you. I feared you had fled when you remembered and realized Ana was my daughter."

"Si," was all Ildaria said. It was all she needed to say.

He sighed unhappily, but continued. "And so I started the very long search for you. First I went to your abuela, hoping you might have returned to her, but you had not. I stayed a while to see if you would come. Your abuela served me tea, and I told her that you were my life mate. She was very pleased at the news. She was happy that you would be settled and with a man she considered to be honorable and strong and able to protect you down through the ages." His voice turned bitter at the end, but then he cleared his throat and continued. "I felt like a fraud under her benign eye, and I told her what had happened."

Pausing, he grimaced and said, "I did not intend to, but your abuela . . ." Expression sincere, he said, "She was a very special woman. There was nothing but kindness in her heart and soul. She was most understanding, and assured me all would be well. I would find you and all would be as it should." He sighed. "I enjoyed my visits with her. I went to see her two or three times a week, and we talked of little but you and her hopes for you. Neither of us had any idea you would hide so well or for so long."

"You had tea with her two or three times a week?" Ildaria asked with disbelief.

"Si. I enjoyed her company. It was soothing. And I missed her terribly when she passed. I grieved. I do not often grieve for mortals. I am sorry you missed her death and funeral."

"I was there," she told him, recalling watching him at the graveside. "I had to stay at a distance, but I saw."

"Why?" he asked with bewilderment. "Why did you not simply come and join us?"

"Because your men were everywhere, hunting me."

"They would not have harmed you. They had orders not to harm you," he assured her.

"Well, I didn't know that. I thought you—" Ildaria stopped abruptly and scowled at him. She still couldn't believe that he hadn't wanted to hurt her for what she had done to him. Or that he wasn't the monster in her story. Mouth twisting, she asked, "What of your jacking up the price of blood to force immortals along the shore off their property so you could have it?"

"It is not what you think," he said, and explained, "Three times in the last twenty years my men almost caught you near the shoreline."

"Si, and each time I managed to escape," she snapped triumphantly.

"Si," he agreed, sounding a bit snappish himself for the first time. "But only because they were under

strict orders not to harm you. My men took grievous wounds trying not to harm you while trying to
capture you."

Ildaria straightened, offended at the suggestion that
her escaping had been purely because he'd refused
to allow his men to hurt her. She was a good fighter,
dammit.

"But were you good enough to take on three or four
trained Enforcers and escape?" Lucian asked, apparently in her thoughts.

Ildaria frowned at the question, not wanting to ac-
knowledge that she'd been more than a little lucky
a time or two. She'd always escaped unscathed. Her
hunters had not always been so lucky. She had caused
more than a few grievous wounds. Not wanting to
think about that, she said, "You still haven't explained
the price of blood and taking people's land."

"I had concluded that you had someplace on the
shore where you lived. But a check of the land reg-
istry did not turn up your name, or anything close to
it. Either you had used a different name, or someone there must be hiding you. My only hope was to
force you out of hiding there. To do that, I needed
to force the other immortals out. Perhaps then—"
He paused abruptly, his lips compressing, and then
said, "I was becoming desperate, Angelina. I have
been searching for two hundred years. It was the
only thing I could think to do."

"So you ruined all those immortals."

"No one was ruined," he assured her quietly. "I

know the rumors say I got the land cheap from desperate immortals, but I spread those rumors on purpose. The truth is, I paid more than fair market prices for the properties, and then moved them to properties I own by the shore down by La Romana. Properties I *gave them for free*. All they had to do was show up to sign the contracts, where I could read them to see if they knew of you, or had even unknowingly seen you. After that, I made them agree never to tell anyone, and never to return to Punta Cana. Every one of them was happy to agree. They got the new land plus payment for their old property. And it is nicer there, less developed." His mouth tightened. "I had no desire to ruin poorer immortals, I was just trying to flush you out by taking away your hiding place."

"But Vasco . . ."

"Vasco has no idea what I have been doing. None of my children do. They all believe the rumors and stories they hear. I have not spoken personally to any of them but Ana since the night you were attacked. And I only saw Ana once or twice afterward. Fortunately, she was newly mated as well, easily read and either unable or too distracted to bother reading me."

Ildaria frowned. Vasco had said his father had been distant the last two centuries, but he'd never said he hadn't seen him at all. "Why wouldn't you see your own children?"

"Because I am ashamed," he confessed unhappily. "I attacked you like an animal. Drugs be damned, I should have been stronger than those blasted drugs. I should have resisted the rage. I should have protected you from myself. I will not have my children know I am such a weak, disgusting animal." Closing his eyes, he ran a weary hand through his hair. "I needed to find you first and make it right with you before I could face them."

Opening his eyes, he managed a smile. "But now I can. I have finally found you. I can claim you now and finally make things right. Say you will be my life mate, Angelina."

"The hell she will. She's my life mate!" G.G. roared before she could respond. She wasn't the least surprised by his outburst, or the way he suddenly leapt up and rushed across the room. She *was* surprised when he suddenly stopped dead. His face went blank and he backed up to the couch and sat down.

Ildaria turned back to Juan and demanded, "Let him go."

"I will release him when you give me your answer," he said simply.

When she started to shake her head, he said quickly, "Lucian told me this mortal was a possible life mate too. But he also told me he has refused to turn for you, Angelina. He cannot possibly love you as I do, or he would not hesitate to turn."

Ildaria frowned. He was hitting her where her insecurities lay. G.G.'s refusal to turn and be with her longer than the thirty or so years he had left as a mortal did bother her despite knowing the reason for it. She'd hoped that time and life mate sex would convince him. That he would come to love him and change his mind. But while they'd admitted their love to each

other in the SUV, he hadn't said anything about turning, and she was beginning to fear he never would.
That she wasn't enough to make him want to. Her only
hope was whatever trick his mother had up her sleeve
and she didn't even know what that was.

Ultimately, it didn't matter though. She did love G.G.
But even if she hadn't loved him, Juan had been the
boogeyman to her for two hundred years. And while
she believed it was possible he was telling the truth—

"He is telling the truth," Lucian said mildly, and
Ildaria whirled on him furiously.

"Will you get out of my head and let me think?" she
demanded.

"I am just trying to be helpful. I am telling you that
everything Juan has said is true. He has been desperately searching for you for two hundred years, and became so desperate, he came up with that ridiculous
plan to try to force you out into the open by removing any immortals in the area where you were spotted
most often."

"Thank you, Lucian," Juan said dryly, obviously
taking umbrage at his plan being called ridiculous.

"None of it matters," Ildaria said firmly, scowling
from one man to the other. "The fact is I love Joshua,
mortal or not."

"How can you love him?" Juan burst out, really
looking as if he couldn't understand it. "My men said
they call him G.G. for Green Giant here for heaven's
sake, and look at his ridiculous hair and clothing."

Ildaria did look. Her eyes traveling over G.G.'s
bright green Mohawk, and the jeans and T-shirt he'd

donned that day. The jeans were a faded blue with several rips and frayed holes, and there was a chain dangling between one of the belt loops and his pocket. His keys were on that chain, she knew. As for the T-shirt, it was pale gray with three small boxes on it, one under the other. The top box was empty and had the word SINGLE beside it; the next one down was also empty and had TAKEN beside it. The bottom box, though, had a check mark inside it and the words next to it were *Waiting for a blonde with three dragons*.

Ildaria smiled now as she had the first time she'd seen it. It was a reference to a television show called *Game of Thrones*. G.G. had purchased the entire series from Apple and had insisted they had to watch it when he'd found out she'd never seen the show. They'd only gone through half the first season so far, but she was enjoying it.

"He is a mortal child," Juan said with disgust. "He could never love you as I do."

Ildaria turned back to Juan, taking in his face, more traditional hair, and the designer suit he wore. He was a handsome man, she had to admit . . . but so was G.G., just in a different way. And G.G. had been nothing but kind and loving and passionate with her, while Juan . . .

"I have loved you for two hundred years," Juan said now.

"You've wanted me for two hundred years," she corrected him sharply. "You hardly know me at all."

"I know you," he assured her. "You are all your abuela and I talked about. She told me everything there is to know about you, Angelina. Your favorite foods, that you dislike the color yellow, that you love to dance and sing, that you were in choir and have the voice of an angel, that you love dogs, and cats and every kind of animal. That you would rather cut off your own hand than hurt another living being. That you—"

"Then you know me as a child," Ildaria interrupted. "I'm not that girl anymore, Juan. Just look at what I did to the last Enforcers you sent after me. I have changed. And I do love G.G., big child or not."

He stared at her with bewilderment. "But you are my life mate."

Ildaria sighed, and said more gently, "I'm sorry. But I do love G.G. and I have hated and been afraid of you for two hundred years. You could not imagine that would change in a matter of minutes? Perhaps in time, if there was no G.G., I could have adjusted my thinking. But he is here, and I love him, and my feelings for you are conflicted at best."

She shook her head firmly. "I cannot be your life mate. I already have one."

Juan sat very still for a moment, and Ildaria waited, half expecting him to explode in a fury. Much to her surprise, he didn't though. Instead, he said quietly, "Then I will just have to wait."

"For what?" she asked uncertainly.

"For you," he said simply and then stood and said, "I have waited two hundred years for you, Angelina. I can wait thirty years or so more. It will give your mind the chance to adjust the image you have of me, and clear the way for us to be together." Juan then bowed as if to royalty and said, "Be happy, *mi amor*. I will find and comfort you when the time comes."

He then straightened and left the room. They were all still sitting there in silence when the sound of the front door opening and closing reached them. Juan was gone and she was free, Ildaria realized with something like wonder.

Sixteen

"I'm so glad everything turned out so well for Angelina."

"She prefers Ildaria, Mom," G.G. murmured, eyeing the red light that was holding them up and delaying his return to Ildaria. She had opted to wait at the apartment with H.D. so that Sofia could open the Night Club while G.G. took his parents to check out of the hotel they'd apparently checked into before coming to find him and Ildaria in her apartment, naked on her kitchen floor.

G.G. had learned about the hotel on the drive back from the Enforcer house. He'd been surprised to hear they'd already checked into a hotel, and had seen no need for it when he had a guest bedroom for them in his apartment. And his parents had been more than happy to check out and stay with him instead when he made the offer.

G.G. might have thought twice about making that

offer if he'd realized just how long it would take to drive to the hotel, collect their luggage, check them out, and drive back. City traffic was a grind at this time of day, and then it had taken forever to get his parents' things together and out to the car. After that, they'd spent a good half hour trying to get them checked out. The woman manning the registration desk hadn't understood why they wanted to leave when they'd only arrived that day. Was the room not up to par? The bed uncomfortable? Etc.

G.G. had kept wondering why his father didn't stop answering the questions, and simply take control of the woman and make her get on with it. But since he hadn't, G.G. had been forced to patiently answer her questions, assuring her that everything was fine, they just wanted to spend more time with their son.

"Not really," his mother said now, pulling him back to the conversation. "In fact, before we left she was thinking she might revert to Angelina now that she didn't have to hide anymore."

"Really?" he asked with interest. It was the prettier name to him, and suited her. She was his angel.

"Yes. She's very relieved to be done with all that hiding and running business," Mary said with a faint smile. "And I'm happy for her."

G.G. mumbled agreement, but the subject reminded him of the meeting with Juan Villaverde, and his claims that Ildaria was his life mate too. Bastard, he thought with irritation.

"Tough luck for Juan though," Robert commented from the back seat. "It seems to run in the family."

"What do you mean it seems to run in the family?" G.G.'s mother asked, turning in the front passenger seat to peer back at her husband.

"Scotty mentioned that Juan's son, Vasco, had been one of two possible life mates for a girl named Jess," Robert explained. "The other man was a Notte. Raffaele I think he said his name was."

G.G. glanced at his stepfather in the rearview mirror, curious to hear this. Jess was the name of the friend Ildaria had lived with in Montana. Her life mate's name was Raffaele, but Ildaria hadn't mentioned anything about Vasco being a possible life mate for Jess too.

"What happened?" Mary asked with interest.

"Apparently, Vasco lost out to Raffaele, just like Juan lost out to our boy," Robert said with a shrug. "Bad luck in love seems to run in that family."

"Poor Juan," Mary sighed, and settled back in her seat with a shake of the head. "First his son, and now him. I do feel sorry for him."

G.G. scowled at the words, his hands tightening briefly on the steering wheel as he thought, *poor Juan my ass*. The man was an arrogant arsehole, and he'd taken control of him and made him sit down. That had really pissed him off. G.G. hated being controlled. On top of that, the man had been insulting as hell about him, calling him a childish mortal. And all because he dressed casually and wore his hair in an unconventional style. He owned a nightclub, for heaven's sake. He wasn't a Wall Street drone who had to prance around in designer suits and really awesome gold watches. He could buy that watch if he wanted to. He had money, two businesses, and property. He wasn't some ne'er-do-well flunkie.

"Imagine searching for your life mate for *two hundred years*," his mother said now. "Knowing who she is and that she's out there, but searching year after year, decade after decade, and then finally, when you do find her, it's too late. She's claimed another as her life mate. Poor Juan."

"Yes, poor Juan," G.G. muttered, bringing a sharp look from his mother.

"You don't sound very sympathetic, son," Mary said, her tone disapproving. "Try to imagine if your roles were reversed."

"If our roles had been reversed I wouldn't have been a jackass and attacked Ildaria," he assured her, and then said unsympathetically, "He did it to himself."

"You're right, of course," she agreed sadly. "If he hadn't attacked her all those years ago, she wouldn't have run, and he probably would have claimed her at eighteen as he'd planned. You never even would have met her."

G.G. blinked at that and then frowned. He couldn't imagine never having met Ildaria. The woman had become such a big part of his life in this last month that he didn't know what he'd do without her. Hell, he didn't want to know what he'd have to do without her.

"Of course, that wasn't really his fault," his mother added judiciously. "Attacking her I mean. He was spaced out on that opium, matzas, and cocoa."

"Opium, mescal, and coca leaves," G.G. corrected absently, still thinking about what his life would be like without Ildaria in it.

"Right. That," his mother said and fell silent for a minute, but then shrugged and added, "But I'm glad he's decided to roll with the punches. Although, I suppose that must be easier when he knows it will all work out for him in the end. He just has to be patient for twenty or thirty years more and then he can have her."

G.G. stiffened at the suggestion. "What do you mean he can have her in twenty or thirty years?"

"Well, being mortal, you won't live much longer than that," she pointed out. "And once you die, he can come claim her as his life mate."

"Over my dead body," G.G. muttered.

"Exactly," she said, sounding chirpy.

G.G. eyed her sharply.

"Well, it's true," she said, shrugging helplessly.

"Yeah, well maybe I'll live fifty years just to spite the bastard," he muttered.

"Not the way you eat, dear. You like your fried foods too much," she responded at once.

G.G. glowered at her. Not that his mother seemed to notice. She was shaking her head now, her mind on poor Juan.

"Yes, I imagine twenty or thirty years is the best we can expect, and then we'll lose you to a heart attack or stroke or something."

G.G. thought his left eye might be twitching and looked in the rearview mirror to see if it was visible.

"On the bright side," Mary went on, "at least, we

won't have to worry about little Angelina after you pass. She won't get all mopey and weepy and depressed like most immortals do when their life mates die." Turning toward him in her seat, she exclaimed, "Do you know, I've heard some even go rogue when that happens. But our little Angelina won't. No sir, not with Juan waiting in the wings."

"Great," G.G. growled, his hands tightening on the steering wheel again.

"Don't worry though, we'll make sure she makes it to your funeral."

"What?" he asked with disbelief. "Why the hell wouldn't she make it to the funeral? She isn't going to take up with Juan the minute I'm dead."

"Well, no of course she won't mean to. She obviously loves you. I mean she must. She did pick you over that handsome, sexy Juan Villaverde. And she would want to be respectful when you die."

G.G. nodded with a grunt, but was thinking he could have done without his mother calling Juan handsome and sexy. Did Ildaria think he was handsome and sexy too?

"But you know how new life mates are, Joshua," his mother added now. "Why, you're a new life mate yourself, so I know you understand."

"Understand what?" he snapped.

"About Angelina and Juan," she said as if that should be obvious. "You know the minute he gets word that you're dead he'll shower, shave, put on his best suit, and fly straight to Angelina's side to offer condolences and support. She's his life mate after all."

"She's *my* life mate," G.G. snarled, but in his mind he saw Ildaria opening the door to Juan. The man had flowers and a shit-eating grin.

"And of course, she'll be crying because she loves you so and she's lost you, and he'll take her in his arms to offer comfort, and . . . Well, you know how new life mates are," she repeated.

He did know, and the Juan of the shit-eating grin in his mind was now ravishing Ildaria up against the still open door.

"Bloody hell," G.G. barked furiously, but his mother wasn't done.

"It'll be sex, pass out, sex, pass out, and so on. But we'll be sure to stop by to collect her on the way to the funeral to ensure she isn't passed out and missing it."

That, he realized with dismay, was a very real possibility. Juan could be at Ildaria's side and screwing her the day after he died if he touched her bare skin, even her hand would be enough.

"That's only if you die suddenly of a heart attack or something," Robert commented, his tone thoughtful. When G.G. glanced at him in the rearview mirror, hoping for something encouraging, the man pointed out, "You might end up dying of cancer or some other long drawn out disease."

"Oh, my yes," his mother said with realization and started nodding like a bobblehead. "In that case, Juan would probably be here in Canada, waiting for you to pass."

"Christ," G.G. breathed with dismay.

"I can see it now," Mary went on in a dramatic voice.

"You pale and wasted in your hospital bed, Angelina at your side . . . Juan at hers."

"I will not have that bastard at my deathbed," G.G. snapped. "The vulture can just wait until I die before showing up."

Undeterred, his mother continued, "You'll take your last, gasping breath and then pass peacefully away." She actually made a choking sound, rolled her eyes up in her head, and then let her chin drop to her chest, imitating his death. Him. He was her one and only dear son, and she was making a mockery of his death.

Eyes popping open and head rising again, she continued, "Angelina will start to weep inconsolably, and Juan will take her in his arms to offer comfort and . . . well, you know new life mates," she repeated pragmatically.

Yeah, he knew new life mates, G.G. thought grimly, actually visualizing the scene himself. God in heaven, they'd be screwing on top of his corpse before he was even cold in his deathbed in that scenario.

Mary heaved a sigh and said now, "I suppose I'll just have to think of it like a donor situation."

G.G. blinked away the nightmare of Juan and Ildaria doing it on his emaciated old-man body and asked uncertainly, "A donor situation?"

"Well, they do say the families of organ donors find comfort in the knowledge that the loss of their loved one has given a second chance to the people who have received their organs," she explained. "I'm just thinking I should probably think of it like that too. Your passing may not give organs to others, but it will certainly give Juan a second chance at love and life . . . and Ildaria."

"God in heaven," G.G. muttered.

"It's nice we won't have to worry about Angelina though," Mary added. "Neither emotionally nor financially. Juan apparently has scads of money. And she'll have a title with him too. She'll be a lady. Lady Angelina Villaverde," she informed him, sounding impressed, and then explained, "I gather Juan is a lord by birth."

"Is he?" he asked, grinding his teeth now. Of course his mother was impressed with titles. She was English.

"Oh, yes," she said, sounding enthusiastic. "On the flight here, Scotty told us Juan Villaverde was born in Spain to a lord. He only moved to the Dominican Republic later. He was a lord there, and still is I suppose. Lord Juan Villaverde."

"Don," Robert said.

"What is that, love?" G.G.'s mother asked, craning her head to peer at her husband again.

"The Spanish title for a lord is Don," he explained. "He was Don Juan Villaverde."

There was a moment of stunned silence and then his mother squealed with glee. "Oh my God, Angelina has a real-life Don Juan in her future!"

"The hell she does," G.G. said in a low grating voice.

"She doesn't?" her mother asked with confusion.

"No. Because you're going to turn me."

Ildaria rolled over sleepily and fell out of bed, landing on the hard floor with an "oomph."

Not bed, she realized as she opened her eyes. The couch. She'd fallen asleep on it last night waiting for G.G. and his parents to return.

A yip drew her attention upward to see H.D. standing on the couch, staring down at her with an expression that seemed to suggest he wasn't impressed with her inability to stay on the couch.

Sighing, she rolled over and sat up to give the dog a soothing pet. "Sorry, buddy. Did I wake you?"

H.D. nuzzled her hand, apparently forgiving all.

Smiling faintly, Ildaria yawned and then glanced toward the clock on the wall, her eyes widening when she saw that it was well past two o'clock in the afternoon.

"What the hell?" she muttered, getting quickly to her feet, but then she stood there, briefly frozen by uncertainty. Checking out of a hotel and collecting their luggage couldn't take this long. Maybe G.G. and his parents had returned, found her sleeping, and simply gone to his place rather than wake her. Or had they not returned yet? What if they'd been in an accident?

Cursing, she strode to the door of her apartment, and unlocked and pulled it open. Tybo and Valerian were standing talking by the stairwell door, but paused and turned to her at once. Lucian had decided she should continue to have a guard until Juan flew back to South America. It was just in case the man was tempted to grab and drag her back with him to try to convince her to change her mind and be his life mate.

Ildaria had no idea when Juan was expected to fly back home, but until he did, she had babysitters. Which was actually kind of handy right now, she thought, and opened her mouth to ask them if G.G. and his parents had returned, only to curse instead and scramble after H.D. when he bounded past her into the hall to run barking toward the two Enforcers.

"No, no, no," she said sternly, scooping him up just before he sank his teeth into Tybo's boot. "Bad doggy."

H.D. stopped barking and resorted to growling under his breath at the amused Enforcers as she cuddled him to her chest. With the beast no longer a threat, she offered an apologetic smile to the two men and asked, "Did G.G. and his parents stay at his place last night?"

When Tybo raised his eyebrows at the question, she grimaced and confessed, "I fell asleep on the couch waiting for them and just woke up."

"Ah." Tybo nodded. "Yes. He stayed with his parents."

She frowned unhappily at that news. "I wish he had woken me up when he got back. I baked a cake and . . ." She shook her head. "I guess we can have it today when they wake up. Or maybe I should make them break-fast," she muttered, turning to head back toward her door. Pausing there she turned back to ask, "What time did they get back? I don't want to start breakfast too early and have it go cold waiting for them to get up."

The two men exchanged a glance and then Tybo said, "Yeah, I'd hold off on that then. They might not be up for a while yet. It sounded like they were up pretty late last night."

"Oh." Ildaria swung back to her door, and then re-membered H.D. and peered down at him with resig-nation. "Right. You probably have to go outside."

"I'll take him," Valerian said at once, moving toward her.

"Oh, no, it's okay," Ildaria began, but Valerian was already taking the dog from her. He was careful to keep his hands away from H.D.'s mouth, she noticed.

"It is either me or all three of us since we are to guard you," he pointed out. "And I can use the fresh air."

When she didn't protest further, Valerian headed up the hall, H.D. tucked under his arm like a football. The fur ball had stopped barking, but she wouldn't put it past him to pee all down Valerian's side on the way downstairs. He could be a little bugger when he wanted.

Shaking her head, she glanced at Tybo. "Coffee? Tea? Cake?"

"Tea would go nicely with that cake you mentioned," Tybo said with a grin. "I love cake."

Ildaria smiled, pleased that at least someone would try her tres leches. She'd made it intending to feed it to G.G. and his parents when they returned last night. But they'd never returned. Someone should eat it.

"I'll bring a slice and some tea for Valerian too," she promised and slipped back into her apartment. She didn't bother to close the door. She'd need both hands to carry the tea and cake back, and Tybo was guarding the door. Back in her kitchen, Ildaria set about making tea, but her mind was on G.G. Obviously, he'd found her sleeping and gone to stay at his place with his parents. From Tybo's comment about it sounding like they'd been up late, she supposed he and Valerian had heard their muffled talking and laughter through the door to his apartment.

That was nice, she supposed. She knew G.G. and his parents were close, and they hadn't seen each other for a while what with G.G. being here in Canada setting up the Night Club. So it had probably been nice for them to get to visit alone, and she didn't begrudge them that. If Ildaria had been awake, she might even have suggested it. But she would have sent her cake with them too.

Her gaze slid to the refrigerator where her beautiful cake was waiting. She'd wanted to celebrate the end of her troubles, but she'd also wanted to make a new and better impression on his parents than the first one they'd had of her. She had been sure that returning to find her fully dressed with an apron on, and cake in hand was a better second first impression than her naked on their bambino on the floor.

Ah well, Ildaria thought, she had years to work at removing that image from their minds. Hopefully. If G.G. wasn't in an accident, or didn't have a sudden stroke or heart attack. Pushing that troubling thought determinedly from her mind, Ildaria sliced the cake, made a pot of tea, poured two cups and fixed them the way Tybo and Valerian had requested them last night, and then set everything on a tray and carried it out to the hall.

Valerian returned with H.D. just as Tybo was taking the tray from her, so Ildaria wished them *buenos dias* and carried H.D. back into her apartment. She took a moment to get his food out, set his bowl on the floor in the kitchen and then left him to eat as she headed for her bedroom and the bathroom beyond. She was still wearing her black skirt and white blouse from yesterday and was starting to feel grungy in them. A quick shower and change of clothes were in order.

Ten minutes later she was wrapped in a towel and headed into her room to find clothes, but stopped dead when she saw the man entering from the hall. He was tall, and well built, wearing a beautiful charcoal suit, dress shoes, and she saw the sparkle of a gold watch on his wrist. For one second Ildaria thought it was Juan, but then her gaze lifted to his bald head, and she changed her mind; one of his minions then.

Lucian had been right to be cautious, she thought, and felt a moment's concern for what might have happened to Tybo and Valerian, but was already kicking into defensive mode. With no other weapon at hand, Ildaria grabbed the top of her towel, gave it a tug to unravel it and then swung it out as she rushed forward. She flung it over his head and around his face, jumping upward as she did. Ildaria landed on his back, driving him to the ground as she caught the other end of the towel and pulled back. It plastered the cloth to his face and around his neck, blinding and hopefully choking him at once.

"Joshua? Did you find her?"

Ildaria froze and twisted on the man's back to stare toward the door to the hall as Mary Guiscard entered and came to a startled halt. "Oh. Angelina dear. Uh . . ." Her gaze slid from a naked Ildaria to the man she was perched on, and then a smile began to curl her lips and she said with amusement, "I see my son found you."

"Your son?" Ildaria echoed with confusion, peering down at the man she was presently trying to choke the life out of. Not that this move would kill an immortal, but she could knock him out this way and then truss him up. Or—Oh God, if this was G.G., she could kill him with this choke hold, she thought suddenly, and started to ease her grip, but then shook her head and glanced to Mary to say, "But this man is bald."

"Yes. Well, his hair will grow back, dear," Mary assured her, and then added in a gentle voice, "If you don't take his head off with that towel."

Ildaria released the towel at once and scrambled off the man's back. But it wasn't until he rolled over and pulled the towel off his head that she saw that it was indeed G.G.

"Oh, my God," she breathed as she took in his flushed face and completely hairless head. "G.G.?"

"He isn't G.G. anymore. The Green Giant is dead, long live Joshua," his mother pointed out happily and Ildaria shook her head with dismay.

"I can see that," she said faintly and then asked G.G. entreatingly, "*Madre de Dios*, what have you done? Where is your beautiful hair?"

G.G. turned to scowl at his mother at that, but she just smiled brightly, and said, "Well, I'll leave you two to it. Your father and I will be next door at your place, Joshua. Come see us when you—after you—later," she said finally, and turned to hurry from the room.

Ildaria watched her leave and then shifted her attention back to G.G. as he got up off the floor. Her gaze traveled over him in the fine new suit and shoes and then up to his head again.

"It will grow back," he rumbled, looking uncomfortable under her stare.

"Si," she agreed.

"I was going to leave an inch or so of hair where the Mohawk used to be, but it just looked silly so I shaved it all off, but—" He paused, frowning at her expression, and ran a hand self-consciously over his bald head. "You don't like it?"

"Do you?" she asked cautiously.

He shrugged uncomfortably. "I thought it was time I stopped looking like a mortal child, and more like an immortal man."

Ildaria scowled as she recognized Juan's description of him as a mortal child, but then the last of his words sank in and her eyes shot to his. The blue eyes he had inherited from his mother were now shot through with silver.

"G.G.?" she breathed, moving closer. "You are . . . ?"

"Immortal," he finished for her when she didn't say the word.

"How? When?" she said, reaching out to touch his face and urge him to lower it so she could better see his eyes. She watched the silver shimmer and swim through the blue and thought she had never seen anything so beautiful.

"Mother turned me last night at the Enforcer house. I wanted to surprise you," he explained. "It was apparently pretty quick as turns go. I woke up a couple hours ago, and then I shaved and showered and we went to buy this suit and shoes, and—I bought you flowers too. They're in the kitchen. I wanted to . . . impress you."

"I am impressed," she assured him solemnly.

"So . . ." He tilted his head. "You like me better this way?"

Ildaria frowned, and then said honestly, "I think you look beautiful, but you were beautiful the other way too." She paused to bite her lip, and then admitted, "But I miss your hair. And your laugh lines."

He smiled wryly. "I can grow the hair back, but there's nothing I can do about the laugh lines. They're gone I'm afraid. Actually, it was kind of weird waking up, looking in the mirror and finding a much younger version of myself looking back."

Ildaria grinned, but then alarm covered her face. "Your tattoos!"

G.G. shook his head. "All gone."

"Si," she sighed. Ildaria had known that would happen if he ever turned. The nanos removed piercings, tattoos, and anything that didn't match up with the blueprint of a mortal body at peak condition. Tattoos and piercings hadn't been on that blueprint. It wasn't unexpected, it just made her sad. She had loved his tattoos.

Lifting her head, she raised her eyebrows and said, "You vowed you would not turn. You loathed the very idea. What made you change your mind?"

"I found there was something else I loathed more," he confessed with a wry twist to his lips.

Ildaria's eyes narrowed as she recalled Mary saying G.G. did not like to share his toys. Finally, she asked, "What?"

"The idea of you with Juan after I died," he said, his voice grim. "I'd go through hell and back to make sure that didn't happen."

Ildaria's eyebrows rose and she pulled back when he reached for her. Perching her fists on her hips, she glowered at him and said, "So, you would not turn to be with me, but you will turn to make sure no one else is?"

G.G. pursed his lips briefly, and then grimaced. "Well, when you put it like that, it sounds kind of fucked up, doesn't it?"

"Si," Ildaria said coldly. *"Loco."*

Sighing, he slid his arms around her and tugged her stiff body close. "But now that I've been turned, you're kind of stuck with me. Forever."

"Hmm," Ildaria said, unimpressed.

"And while I may be *loco*, I love you," he pointed out, bending his head to press a kiss to her neck.

Ildaria fought the shiver that wanted to slide down her neck, trying to remain unresponsive but it was next to impossible when he touched her and that new life mate magic kicked in.

"I love your body too," he added, his hands sliding up to cup her breasts. "You should always greet me naked."

Ildaria's eyes were just closing as she gave herself up to the mounting pleasure growing inside her, when his words sank in. In the next moment, she'd pushed away from him with horror. "Oh, no!"

"What?" he asked with concern.

"Your mother," she said unhappily, shaking her head and covering her face. "I wanted to make a good first impression. I baked a cake last night, and I was going to be dressed and wear a pretty apron, and be holding the cake like Betty Crocker. But instead, how does she meet me? Naked on top of her bambino again."

G.G. blinked several times as he processed what she was saying, and then he cleared his throat and said, "Uh, honey, this wouldn't have been a first impression. She'd already met you," he pointed out.

"But I wanted to make a new first impression," she wailed and could have sworn she heard a short huff of laughter before he pulled her back into his arms.

"Angel, love," he murmured, pressing a kiss to the top of her head. "You don't have to worry about making an impression on my parents. They both love you. My mother, especially. They'd take you naked, dressed, on or off me." Pulling back, he urged her face up and added, "But more importantly, I love you."

"I love you too," she breathed, leaning into him as his hands began to slide over her body again. "But you should take off your pretty new suit before we ruin it."

G.G. released her reluctantly, and began to shrug out of his jacket, but teased, "You just want to see my new and improved body."

"Si," she agreed, backing up to the bed as she watched him undo the buttons of the shirt. "You do look fine in a suit, but I like you in jeans and a T-shirt too."

"Yeah?" He tugged the shirt out of his slacks and shrugged out of that too, and Ildaria almost changed her mind. The man was beautiful no matter what he did or didn't wear, she thought as she climbed blindly onto the bed, her gaze locked on the play of muscles in his back as he undid and removed the dress slacks. When he then bent to slide them off and step out of them her gaze slid over his strong shoulders and she thought that she missed the tattoos, but he was still beautiful.

"Well?" he asked, turning to her after folding the slacks over and setting them on her dresser. "How do you like the new vehicle? Want to take it for a ride?"

She chuckled at his teasing, but nodded. "Si, I will ride you hard, señor."

"All the way to shag city?" he asked as he prowled toward the bed.

Ildaria tilted her head with confusion. "Where is shag city? Is it in Canada? Or England?"

"No, it's—" G.G. began, and then knelt on the bed and crawled toward her, promising, "I'll show you."

Epilogue

"You may not have had them long, but at times like this I really miss your bodyguards, Angelina. It would be handy to have them here to carry the shopping bags."

Ildaria glanced to G.G.'s mother with surprise. "Are the bags too heavy for you? I can take some if they are."

"Of course, they aren't, dear girl," Mary Guiscard said, amused at the very suggestion. "But they are large, and awkward, and I think I may have ruined my manicure swinging them around to avoid hitting passersby. I don't think that girl at the salon kept my fingers under that light of hers long enough to set them properly."

"Not a problem, Mary," Marguerite said before Ildaria could respond. "We can fix them up before the party. I have a lovely manicure set for just such occasions."

"Oh, good. I-Is that the boys?" Mary interrupted herself to ask, and then her eyes widened incredulously. "What on earth are they wearing?"

"Leather," Ildaria said as she spotted the men ahead, moving in their direction. "A lot of leather."

All three women were silent as they watched their mates approach. G.G. and his father, Robert, were all decked out in leather. G.G. was wearing very tight black leather pants, black combat boots, and a long black leather coat open over a bare chest now looking tanned and tattooed when it hadn't been that morning. But then neither had he had the high, dark green Mohawk he was now sporting, his real Mohawk had only grown an inch since he'd shaved his head. She was guessing the look was the result of spray tan, temporary tattoos, and some kind of wig. And she thought he looked incredibly hot. His father, Robert, was also wearing the pants and boots, but he had gone for a shorter leather jacket, a black T-shirt, and a red Mohawk. Like son like father, she supposed.

As for Julius, he was the more conservative of the three, wearing a suit made of black leather, with a blue silk shirt under it. He was also wearing some kind of white face paint, delicately applied to make him look pale, and he had his real fangs out. Going for the vampire look, she supposed, noting that some kind of red paint or polish had been applied to his fangs and then dabbed on his cheek to look like a drop of blood.

"My goodness, don't they look fine," Mary said, sounding a little breathy.

Ildaria glanced at the woman with surprise. "But Robert is wearing a Mohawk."

"Yes, dear. I can see that, and it makes him even foxier than usual," she said, her eyes starting to glow.

Ildaria blinked in disbelief at those words. "I thought you hated G.G.'s Mohawk?"

"No. Actually, I think it's adorable on my son. It's hot, though, on Robert," she added.

"But you were always telling G.G. he would be handsome if he only did not have the Mohawk and—"

"Oh, that was just so he'd feel he was being rebellious," Mary said, waving away her comments. "Boys need to rebel. It's in their coding or something. So, I complained about his hair, and he didn't have to go out and do more drastic things to feel like he was being adventurous and naughty."

Ildaria stared at the woman blankly for a moment with amazement. She made G.G. sound like a teenager. "You know he is nearing forty now, si?"

"Forty," Mary breathed with horrified wonder. "And he hasn't produced a single grandchild for me yet." Turning on her, she asked, "When are you two going to get busy on that? I expected to be a grandmother by this age."

"What?" Ildaria gasped with horror as Marguerite burst out laughing. "We are not even married yet."

"You're right," Mary said judiciously. "So when is that going to happen?"

"I don't know, maybe when your son asks me," Ildaria suggested with exasperation. It was the end of October. They had only been together for three months and had been busy during that time working at the Night Club, helping his parents find and move into a house here in Canada, and Ildaria with her new courses at the university. Whatever spare time they had was usually spent either making love, or passed out after making love. They hadn't had time to talk about the future. But she suspected now that his mother had brought up the subject, she would be harassing them nonstop until they got married and produced a grandchild. Ildaria shook her head at the thought. She loved Mary dearly, she was like a mother to her, but she also drove her crazy.

"Well," Mary said on a dramatic sigh. "I guess I can't blame you for that then, can I? I'll have a talk with my son," she promised. "But right now, I'm going to go kiss that foxy hunk of burning love with the red Mohawk . . . and give him the shopping bags to carry," she added, and hurried off to meet the men.

"So, how are things?" Marguerite asked as they followed more slowly.

"Good," Ildaria assured her. "Very good."

"You do seem much happier. You glow with it," Marguerite said with satisfaction.

"Oh." Ildaria felt herself blush at the compliment, but said, "You have a pretty good glow going too, Marguerite. Pregnancy agrees with you."

Marguerite smiled at the words, one hand shifting to smooth over her round stomach. The woman was six months pregnant now and really was glowing with it, but instead of responding to the comment, she asked, "Any word about Juan?"

Ildaria shook her head. "He returned home and there has not been a peep out of him. And none of his men have headed north again. I really think he'll leave me alone now."

"I do too," Marguerite agreed. "But I am keeping my eye out for another possible mate for him anyway to make sure he leaves you alone."

Ildaria glanced at her with surprise, and then stopped to hug the woman. A difficult endeavor with them both weighed down with shopping bags full of decorations for the Halloween party at the Night Club that night. Marguerite and Mary were helping her with the decorations and the menu, and Ildaria appreciated it more than she could express. She'd never arranged a party before, but a Halloween party had sounded fun, and Mary had been so excited at the prospect when G.G. had mentioned it, Ildaria had just got caught up in that excitement and agreed.

"Thank you," she said now to Marguerite, and then releasing her, she added, "For everything."

"My pleasure," Marguerite assured her. "Now let's go tell our men how good they look."

"Yes." Ildaria nodded and turned to continue toward her man and her future.

Turn the page for a
sneak peek of the next
Argeneau novel,
coming to you
this Fall!

Prologue

Mac had just finished setting up his centrifuge when he caught a whiff of what smelled like smoke. He lifted his head and inhaled deeply; there were the astringent cleaner he'd used on the counter surfaces, various chemical and other scents he couldn't readily identify that were coming from the boxes he had yet to unpack, and—yes—smoke.

A frisson of alarm immediately ran up the back of Mac's neck. Where there was smoke there was fire, and fire was bad for his kind. It was bad for mortals too, of course, but was even worse for immortals, who were incredibly flammable.

Straightening abruptly, Mac stepped over one unopened box and then another, weaving his way out of the maze of unpacking he still had to do and to the stairs leading out of the basement. He took them two at a time, rushing up the steps to the special door he'd had installed several days ago. It blocked sound, germs, and everything else from entering the lab he was turning his basement into. He'd also had the walls sealed and covered with a germ-resistant skin. Apparently, his efforts had been successful. Even at the top of the stairs, he was only able to catch the slightest hint of smoke in the air, yet when he opened the door he found himself standing at the mouth of hell. The kitchen on the other side of the door was engulfed in flames that seemed almost alive and leapt excitedly his way with a roar.

A startled shout of alarm slipped from his lips as heat rushed over him, and Mac slammed the door closed at once. He nearly took a header down the stairs in his rush to get as far away from it as he could and crashed into a box as he stumbled off the last step. Pausing then, he stopped to turn in a circle, a mouse in a blazing maze, searching for a way out.

His gaze slid over the small half windows that ran along the top of the basement wall on the back of the house, skating over the flames waving at him from the burning bushes outside, and then he turned toward the rooms along the front of the house and hurried to the door to the first one. It was a bathroom, its window even smaller than the others in the main room. It was also covered with some kind of glaze that blocked the view. Even so, he could see light from the fire on the other side of it.

Rushing to the next door, he thrust it open. This was an empty room about ten feet deep and fourteen wide, with two half windows that ran along the back of the house. Mac stared with despair at the flames dancing on the other side of the glass. He was trapped, with no way out . . . and no way even to call for help, he realized suddenly. There was no landline in the basement, and he'd left his cell phone upstairs on the kitchen counter to avoid interruptions while he set up down here.

I'm done for, Mac thought with despair, and then glimpsed a flash of red light beyond the flames framing and filling the nearer window. Moving cautiously forward, Mac tried to see what was out there, and felt a bit of hope when he spotted the fire truck parked at the top of the driveway and the men rushing around it, pulling out equipment. If he could get their attention, and let them know where he was . . .

Turning, Mac rushed back into the main room, wading through the sea of boxes until he found the one he wanted. He ripped it open and dug through the bubble-wrapped contents until he dug out his microscope. It was old and heavy, and Mac pulled it out with relief and then tore the bubble wrap off it as he moved back to the empty storage room. He didn't even hesitate but crossed half the room in a couple of swift strides and simply threw the microscope through the nearest of the two little windows. Glass shattered and Mac jumped back as the flames exploded inward as if eager to get in. They were followed by rolling smoke that quickly surrounded him, making him choke as he yelled for help.

He was shouting for the third time when dark figures appeared on the other side of the fire now crowding the window. He thought he could make out two men in bulky gear, what he supposed was the firemen's protective wear, and then someone shouted, "Hello? Is there someone there?"

"Yes!" Mac responded with relief. "I am in the basement."

"We'll get you out! Just hang on, buddy! We'll get you out!"

"Get somewhere where there's less smoke," someone else shouted to him.

"Okay!" Mac yelled, backing out of the room, his fascinated gaze watching the fire fan out from the window as the drywall around it caught flame. It would spread quickly now that he'd given the fire a way in, he knew. The smoke was already filling this room and pouring out into the main room, but he could deal with that. Smoke couldn't kill him. Fire would.

Cursing, he turned abruptly and returned to the bathroom next door. There was no fire or smoke in the small room yet, but would be soon enough he knew. Moving to the cast-iron claw-foot tub he'd had refinished before moving in, Mac plugged in the stopper and prayed silently as he turned on the taps. Relief slid through him when water began to pour out. The fire hadn't stopped the water from working yet, and the taps and faucet were old enough not to have an aerator to reduce the speed at which the water jetted out. It gushed from the tap at high pressure, filling the tub quickly, or at least more quickly than his tub back in New York would have filled. There it would have taken ten or fifteen minutes to fill the tub; here it took probably half that, but they were the longest minutes of his life and fire was beginning to eat through the wall between the bathroom and the storage room before it was quite finished.

Mac didn't wait for it to finish filling, but stepped into the quickly heating water in his pajama bottoms and T-shirt when it was three-quarters full, and submerged himself up to his nose. Smoke was coming into the room now, pouring through the air vents, making breathing hard, and the water was hotter than hell, the fire heating it in the pipes on its way to this room and the tub. But it was only going to get hotter. The one wall of the room was now a mass of flames, and the fire was eating its way into the two connecting walls as well. The tile on the floor was catching flame and curling inward toward the tub. The water he was in would be boiling soon by his guess. He now knew how lobsters felt when dropped in boiling water. It was one hell of a gruesome way to die. . . . But it wouldn't kill him. As long as he didn't catch fire, he would survive, but Mac suspected he'd wish he was dead before this was over.